"Bond's memorable and heartwarming romance is funny, irreverent, and thoroughly enjoyable."

— *Booklist*

"Ruefully riotous."

— *Woman's Own*

"Treat yourself to an evening of memorable characters."
— Susan Andersen, author of *Baby, Don't Go*

"A rollicking first novel that's got everything—humor, romance, suspense, and not one but THREE memorable heroines! Great Fun!"

—Jane Heller

"The new queen of romantic comedy is Stephanie Bond. *Our Husband* is a great, rollicking treat—fun, frothy, and romantic and filled with sassy good humor. *Our Husband* is a tall, cool drink of lemonade, sweet but tart. Great romantic comedy with just the right twist of surprise. You'll root for Raymond's wives!"

—Deborah Smith, author of
*On Bear Mountain* and *The Stone Flower Garden*

"A delightful romantic comedy, complete with murder and suspense . . . A rising star in the world of women's fiction."
— *Beachlife*

"Many poignant moments . . . Humor wins out, though, and you'll find yourself rooting for the unlikely three."
— *Old Book Barn Gazette*

"An entertaining contemporary tale . . . well-written . . . an enjoyable novel that successfully combines elements from romance, suspense, and mystery."
— *The Midwest Book Review*

# I Think I Love You

 STEPHANIE BOND

St. Martin's Paperbacks

I THINK I LOVE YOU

ISBN: 0-312-98333-6

Printed in the United States of America

St. Martin's Paperbacks edition / July 2002

St. Martin's Paperbacks are published by St. Martin's Press, 175 Fifth Avenue, New York, NY 10010.

10 9 8 7 6 5 4 3 2 1

# ACKNOWLEDGMENTS

*Many thanks to the people in my circle of friends who provide plausible answers to my questions, no matter how outlandish or obscure. For this book, that group consists of my editor, Jennifer Enderlin; my father, Willis Bond; my husband, Chris Hauck; plus friends Bill Parker and Tim Logsdon. Also, thanks to friends whose support seems to multiply exponentially as deadlines approach: my agent, Kimberly Whalen; writing critique partners, Rita Herron and Carmen Green; and meals-on-wheels gal pal, Jacki Jaynes.*

# I Think I Love You

# PROLOGUE

Regina Metcalf's older sister wagged her finger so close to Regina's nose, she thought she might go cross-eyed—not a good look for someone who already had to contend with the nickname Four Eyes.

"If either of you two brats tell Mom and Dad what I'm about to show you, I'll put bats in your beds, got that?"

Fourteen-year-old Regina nodded, because Justine had a mean redhead streak that she didn't mind un-leashing on her younger sisters at her discretion. Next to Regina, twelve-year-old Mica nodded mutely, then waited until Justine turned away before giving her the bird.

Regina slapped at Mica's hand, although she doubted if her sister knew what the gesture meant. Mica made a face, then followed Justine toward a thicket, twisting her bikini-clad hips in a preteen priss that made Regina roll her eyes. Her dark-haired baby sister was already a head taller, with a lithe figure and knockout looks. Regina pushed her own wet blond bangs out of her eyes, used her finger to wipe the lenses of her wire-rimmed glasses, then squinted to get her bearings.

As near as she could tell, the hill they'd climbed rose above Armadillo Creek where they'd just taken an afternoon dip in the Dilly swimming hole to escape the sauna that was Monroeville, North Carolina, in mid-July. They'd been walking home, swatting at sweat bees and maneuvering gravel roads on bare feet, when Justine had announced in that haughty seventeen-year-old tone she'd mastered that she had a seeeee-cret, although she wasn't about to tell *them*. Predictably, Mica had launched into a whine session that escalated into a full tantrum until Justine had magnanimously agreed to show them—peasants—the secret place she'd stumbled onto.

Regina sighed and watched her sisters disappear into the bushes where they'd tossed their dry clothes on the ground. They wore her out with their constant bickering. Now she wasn't in the mood to do anything except get home to see if Mr. Calvin had delivered his weekly box of books scavenged from flea markets and garage sales. She still needed numbers ten, twenty-one, and forty-four of the Nancy Drew mystery series to complete her set, and sometimes Mr. Calvin's box held treasures. She simply had to sort through the box before her parents unwittingly shelved something important in the recesses of their antiques store and the volume was lost forever or—heaven forbid—sold.

Justine's head appeared through the brambles, and she beckoned, her face screwed up in annoyance. Regina stifled a groan. Knowing Justine, her "secret" was probably a rock covered with dirty-word graffiti or something equally dull. But ever the pleaser, Regina jogged to the opening in the bushes, dropped her dry clothes in the hot grass, and joined her sisters in the underbrush where they lay on their stomachs in what looked like snake paradise. She crawled forward on her elbows, staving off the heebie-jeebies by telling herself that Nancy Drew wouldn't let a little snakebite stand in the way of a mysterious mission. Their intrusion into the knee-high weeds stirred up a swarm of gnats and loosened the scent of moist dirt. She knuckled her nose to ward off a sneeze. "So what's the big secret?"

"Shhh!" Justine elbowed her so hard, her glasses were thrown askew. "Look, you dolt."

Regina righted her glasses, then stared down. Immediately her stomach vaulted—next to snakes, heights were a runner-up phobia not shared by her sisters, who seemed undaunted by the fact that they were lying on a rocky outcropping about thirty feet off the ground. Below them in a sparsely wooded area carpeted with flattened grass sat a yellow Volkswagen Rabbit with the windows rolled down.

"It's Pete Shadowen's car," Justine whispered. "And I'll bet that's Tobi Evans in there with him, the tramp."

Pete Shadowen was a baseball star at their high school—Regina calculated that he would be a junior this fall, one year behind Justine. Tobi Evans, with that name, had no choice but to be a cheerleader. Tobi would be a junior, too, and Justine hated her for no good reason. "What are they doing way out here?" Regina whispered.

Justine looked at her as if she were a tree. "What do you *think* they're doing way out here?"

"Hunting?" Mica guessed.

Justine scoffed. "Don't you two know *any*thing? That's Lovers' Lane down there. They're making out, you idgets."

Mica's eyes bugged, and Regina suspected that her own face looked the same. She'd heard whispers and giggles of the place, but she hadn't known it actually existed. The implication hit her full force, and she swallowed. "You mean they're having sex?"

"Yeah, probably."

The trio fell silent, straining for glimpses and sounds that Regina didn't know if she'd even recognize. But she did know one thing—if their parents found out they were spying at Lovers' Lane, they'd be grounded for the rest of their sorry lives and into the hereafter. Still . . . lately she'd developed a burning curiosity about this sex thing that superseded even the desire to become a teenage sleuth.

Through the trees, she made out two figures in the car who appeared to be grappling for leverage in the backseat, but she couldn't tell who was on top or which body parts were in use. Male grunts and moans floated up to them, so Pete was obviously getting the better end of the deal. Suddenly the driver's seat shot forward and the horn blasted. Regina jerked and Mica screamed, which sent them all scurrying back from the edge. Justine flogged Mica, hissing at her to be quiet. All grunts and moans subsided, and the next noise was the sound of the car engine starting. It took Pete a few seconds to find a gear, then he peeled out of there as fast as his little car would take him. The girls crept back to the edge in time to see his "Monroeville Mudcats" bumper sticker disappear.

Justine rolled onto her back and laughed. She had big boobs. Regina used fruit to monitor her sisters' Cross Your Heart bras that went through the laundry. Justine was now up to a large navel orange, and Mica, a lemon. She herself was looking at a lifetime of bing cherries.

"I would've liked to see the look on Tobi's face," Justine said. "I'll bet she was going down on him."

Regina laughed, too. "What do you mean?"

Justine sighed. "You should read something besides those silly little-girl books."

Regina bit into her lip—it was true that the age difference between her and Justine seemed vaster than three years. Justine was a fully developed woman, who wore high-heeled sandals and required her own bathroom for grooming, while Regina favored Converse sneakers and had not yet broken the seal on the box of Tampax her mother had given her two years ago. Justine was a whiz with makeup and had a suitcase full of mysterious pots and tools. Once she'd talked Regina into wearing mascara, but when Regina's eyes had swollen shut from an allergic reaction, Justine had declared her to be a hopeless "before" and turned her attention to Mica.

"I *do* read . . . other things," Regina mumbled. Although those svelte creatures in *'Teen* magazine might as well be on another planet. Still, she devoured the how-to articles, hoping to mine one nugget of life-altering truth from the profusion of perplexing DOs and DON'Ts lists: DO consider a permanent wave if your hair is thin. (Hers was.) DON'T wear the same pair of shoes every day. (She did.) DO learn to flirt with your eyes. (*Huh?*) To date, she hadn't uncovered the key to an expedient and successful transition into womanhood, but there was always next month, and more DOs and DON'Ts.

Justine picked a wide blade of grass. "Take a look under Cissy and John's mattress if you want a real education."

"You're not supposed to call them by their first names."

"Oh, yeah, they can shack up for twenty years, but we're supposed to follow the rules." Justine held the blade between her thumbs and blew hard through the minuscule opening yet was unable to produce a whistle.

"Don't talk like that," Regina said. She'd heard enough snide comments about their parents from other people, from other kids. *Immoral. Indecent. Illegitimate.* "They're married under common law."

"Common-law marriages aren't recognized in North Carolina," Justine said, blowing again, to no avail.

"They're bohemian," Regina retorted. She'd been so happy to find a word to describe her hippie parents that didn't sound kooky.

Her sisters weren't listening.

"What's under their mattress?" Mica asked, giving Justine's shoulder enough of a shove to dislodge the blade of grass.

"Hey!"

"Tell us, Miss Know-It-All." Mica picked her own blade of grass, mimicked the gesture, and produced not just a whistle but a tune.

Regina shook her head—her two sisters lived to outdo each other.

"You're too young to know," Justine purred.

And Regina didn't *want* to know what her parents kept under their mattress, so she cast about for a diversion. "How did you find this place?"

Justine took the bait. "By accident. I was walking home one day and heard a woman wailing like a banshee. I thought someone was being murdered or something." She laughed. "That lady was yelling for God, all right, but believe me, she was *not* in trouble."

"Who was she?" Mica asked, wide-eyed.

Justine grinned. "Mrs. Woods, the fat checker at the Grab 'N Go."

"Ewww!" Regina and Mica chorused.

"They were in a beat-up Oldsmobile, and was that rattletrap ever rockin'." Then she sat up, her eyes alight. "And get this—I couldn't see who they were, but there were *two* men with her."

Regina squinted. "Huh? Why?" No matter how she sorted the images in her head, the tabs didn't fit into the slots.

"One man was driving," Mica offered.

"Yeah, right," Justine said with a dry laugh.

Regina frowned. "We'd better get home—Mother is expecting us to watch the store this afternoon."

Justine dismissed her with a wave. "It's Monday—no one ever comes by on Monday except that smelly old Mr. Calvin with his smelly old books."

Regina stood and jammed her hands on what she hoped would someday become hips. "If you don't come right now, I'll tell Mom and Dad that you left the jewelry case open and all those things were stolen." Her current case-in-progress—the Mystery of the Missing Stuff.

Her older sister scoffed. "A few pieces of junk, so what?"

"That gold watch wasn't junk, and neither was that letter opener. Mom and Dad are going to be plenty steamed when they find out you were too busy watching Dean Haviland wash his car to keep an eye on the customers." Their parents' new dark-eyed deliveryman was nothing but trouble; Regina just knew it. (In the amateur-sleuth world, this feeling was known as a "hunch.") Flirtatious Dean Haviland was Suspect Number One in her investigation.

Justine bristled. "I was just making sure Dean didn't use too much water from the spigot. Besides, you were supposed to be helping me watch the store instead of holing up with one of your stupid books."

Regina pushed up her glasses. Did no one in her family understand the burning need to read the last few pages of a great mystery? "Mica was supposed to be helping, too."

Mica stuck out her tongue. "Justine, *you* probably took those things. You steal things when you think no one is watching."

"That's a lie!"

"No, it's not!"

"You're a liar!"

"You're a thief!"

Predictably, a shoving match ensued, and soon they were rolling around on the ground. Regina hadn't seen Justine take items from the store, but considering her older sister's contempt for the family business, she could believe it—Suspect Number Two.

"Stop it." She stepped between them and got yanked down with them for her trouble. Her glasses went flying. "Stop it!"

"Shhh!" Justine said, freezing. "I hear a car."

They shushed and disentangled. After Regina reclaimed her glasses, she joined her sisters on the ledge, where they'd parted the grass with their hands. A classic black Cadillac with a white ragtop lurched over the uneven ground; then the engine quieted. At the sight of the familiar car, Regina's mouth went dry. "Is that who I think it is?"

"Well, what do you know," Justine murmured. "Good old Aunt Lyla—and company. This is *great*."

Justine hated Aunt Lyla, too. Granted, Justine hated a lot of people these days, but their mother's sister-in-law ranked high on the loathing list. Their beloved uncle was the mayor of Monroeville, but his wife, Lyla, was the evil queen. Even their mother, who released caught flies outside the kitchen screen door, developed a pucker when Her Highness put in an appearance at the shop to broker antiques she had acquired during her "travels" to Raleigh and Atlanta. "Whoop-de-do," Regina's mom would mutter while opening the cash register drawer. Even though Lyla had a knack for stumbling onto good deals, Regina suspected that Cissy only tolerated the woman because she'd married Cissy's only brother, Lawrence Gilbert.

"Why would Aunt Lyla and Uncle Lawrence come out here to have sex?" Mica asked.

Justine sighed. "She's probably not with Uncle Lawrence, you imbecile."

A combination of the altitude and the suggestion that their aunt would keep naked company with another man tied Regina's intestines into a double-naught knot. Still, she couldn't drag her gaze away from the car.

The Caddy's white ragtop opened up like the mouth of a giant beast, then receded and dropped into folds along the backseat. Through the trees, only glimpses of the occupants were visible, but it was Lyla in the driver's seat all right—the plunging neckline of her yellow dress and acres of white cleavage were a dead giveaway. Their mother told them not to stare there when their aunt dropped by the shop, but Regina couldn't help it with Lyla's huge boobs being at eye level and all. They were magnificent. And store-bought, according to a conversation she'd overheard one morning when she passed her parents' open bed-room door. She wanted to see *that* catalog.

"Who's with her?" Mica whispered.

"I can't tell," Justine whispered back, craning. The man's generic pale shirt gave no hint to his identity, but whoever he was, he had to be roasting in those long sleeves. A local businessman? Regina thought she saw the flash of glasses, but sometimes her own spec-tacles reflected a glare.

Lyla leaned forward; then twangy country music floated up to them. Lots of fumbling, then the front seats reclined. Regina's heart thudded in her ears. "I think we'd better go."

Justine snorted. "No way, it's just getting good."

"Yeah," Mica said. "Shut up, spoilsport."

Regina swallowed hard and stayed put. Aunt Lyla's hyena laugh rang out; then the man sprawled on top of Lyla, obscuring the yellow dress. He started flailing, and Lyla started wailing. The big Caddy bucked like a stallion.

"Are they doing it?" Mica asked, mesmerized.

"Sure sounds that way," Justine said.

Even though she couldn't see anything specific, Regina's stomach felt heavy and tingly. She wanted to bolt upright and run home. Instead she lay there, listening as Dwight Yoakum's honky-tonk voice blended with the song of Lyla's cries rolling up and down, up and down. *"Yes . . . yes . . . yes."*

"Yes, what?" Mica whispered.

"Shut up," Justine muttered.

The man was thrashing away. Regina winced—was sex always this fierce?

*"Yes . . . yes . . . no—NO!"* An inhuman scream rent the air, raising the hair on the back of Regina's neck.

The car stopped moving, and Lyla's partner seemed to be scrambling, groping for the car door handle. Justine's head jutted forward. "Something's wrong." At the unfamiliar concern leadening her voice, Regina's heart bottomed out.

"What?" Mica asked, then grunted when Justine whomped her one.

Aunt Lyla lay still, but the man was a noisy commotion, flinging the passenger door open into the trunk of a small tree so hard the leaves shook. He tried to wedge his body through the opening, then heaved himself over the side of the car. He must have nudged the radio volume in the process, because Dwight Yoakum's yodeling exploded into the clearing and echoed off the wall of rock supporting them. The noise spooked them and the man, who twisted sideways, fell, then got up and ran haphazardly away from them, tearing through the underbrush.

"Why did he run away?" Mica whispered, unfazed

by the previous whomping. "And why isn't Aunt Lyla moving?"

Justine's pale-faced silence transferred pure terror to Regina. The blaring music gave way to a raucous commercial for a car lot. *"Come on down to Alcatraz preowned cars in Monroeville! Our prices are so low, it's a crime!"*

"Let's get the hell out of here," Justine murmured, and clambered to her feet.

Regina stood and grabbed Justine's arm. "Wait— Aunt Lyla might be having a heart attack or something. We can't just leave her here."

"How are we supposed to get down there?" Justine gestured wildly. "The road is at least a mile away, even if we cut through the creek. I say we scram."

"Maybe we should flag down a car," Mica said, chewing on a strand of dark hair.

"And say what?" Justine snapped. "That we spied while our aunt boffed a stranger? She probably just fell asleep, for God's sake!" But the tremor in her voice belied her flip attitude.

"Aunt LY-LA!" Mica yelled through cupped hands directed toward the car. But her echoing voice was drowned out by the blaring radio jingle for Campbell's Soup—*"M'm! M'm! Good!"* Their aunt didn't move.

Regina nudged her glasses and looked around for a spark of inspiration—what would Nancy Drew do? Probably tie her becoming black pedal pushers, neat blouse, and white cotton socks into a rope and have her friends Bess and George lower her, clad only in sensible underwear and loafers, over the rock wall. But Regina didn't trust the thread count of her cutoffs and T-shirt, nor the arm muscles of her girlie-girl sisters. Instead, she zeroed in on a sturdy maple tree that had grown from the floor of the clearing to a few feet past the rock ledge. About the diameter of a telephone pole and studded with enough limbs to likely support a clinging teenager. She walked over, grabbed a limb, and gave it a tentative shake.

"Are you crazy?" Justine said. "You'll fall and break your fool neck. Then Mom will kill *me* for letting you."

All roads led back to Justine. Regina retrieved her clothes and yanked them on over her damp suit, then jammed her feet into her tennis shoes. "Stand back."

She'd waited her entire life to say those words. With a burst of courage, she jumped into the tree branches and hugged the trunk with arms and legs. Behind her, Justine and Mica shouted protests, but she couldn't make out the words over the sound of her heart pounding in her ears. The lanky tree swayed under her weight and vertigo took hold as the air whistled through her hair. She squeezed her eyes shut to end the ebb and flow of the ground below. When the swaying slowed, she opened one eye and began to inch her way down the sandpapery trunk, feeling for a foothold with the toe of her tennis shoe before relinquishing her grip above.

After several long minutes of humping the tree, Regina dropped from the lowest branch and landed with a thud on her back. Her lungs stalled out for a few seconds, then sputtered and expanded with a great wheeze. Her sisters apparently saw the dismount.

"Are you okay?"

"Make a noise or something."

She pushed herself to her feet, righted her glasses, and gave them a shaky thumbs-up. Brushing off the seat of her shorts, she glanced toward the Caddy. George Jones was belting out a cheatin' song, almost deafening as she picked her way closer, through scrub brush and weeds. She covered her ears and tried to swallow past the lump in her throat.

"Aunt Lyla?" she called. At this distance she

couldn't see the reclining woman. She uncovered her ears to listen for her aunt's response, but the earsplitting music overwhelmed any potential sound. Despite the sweltering temperature, gooseflesh covered Regina's forearms. She was filled with dread, half-terrified that she'd find her aunt with her eyes rolled back in the throes of some kind of seizure, half-terrified that a lounging Lyla would grab her and beat her within an inch of her life for spying.

Regina wet her lips and stepped closer to the gleaming convertible, incongruous next to the briers and trees and dried mud. Her shoulder ached from the awkward fall. The song melted into one she didn't recognize, but at these decibels, everything grated. The tufted black leather of the backseat came into view, and her nerve almost left her. She looked back and up. Her sisters were huddled together on the ledge, silhouetted in the slanting sun. She took a good look all around Lovers' Lane, down the rutted path that carloads of horny country folk had turned into a road. There were no signs of life. Regina immediately regretted her thoughts and turned back to the car.

Slowly she put one foot in front of the other until she could touch the front left fender with her hand. The metal was hot beneath the pads of her fingers, vibrating with the boom of the radio bass. She swallowed hard as Lyla's peroxide white hair came into view against the dark upholstery. Her head lay at an odd angle. At the sight of her aunt's kohl-lined eyes staring wide, Regina froze. But her aunt didn't see her—or see anything, for that matter. Lyla was good and dead, all right.

Regina's first thought was that the woman had indeed suffered heart failure while her dress was rucked up to her waist and her lacy panties sagged around one ankle—such physical activity could induce an attack, couldn't it? But her second thought was that more likely Lyla had died of the gaping wound under the curled white hand clutching her chest. The image of brilliant blood against pale skin stamped into the long-term-memory region of Regina's brain. She gagged on a scream and covered her mouth with her hand. Her eyeballs felt big in her head. Her knees buckled and slammed into the car door.

The pain knocked her back, the pain and the most horrific sight of all: the silver letter opener missing from a showcase in her parents' store, now blood-stained and lying on the passenger seat. Her shoe caught on a root, but the jar of the ground meeting her tail loosened the scream trapped in her throat. With apologies to Nancy Drew, she howled like an animal, one long bawl that ended in a throaty gurgle. She scrambled to her feet and ran back to the tree as if the hounds of hell were on her heels.

She didn't remember climbing the tree—one minute she was launching herself toward a lower branch, and the next minute she was being hauled onto the rocky ledge by her two sisters, both wide-eyed and talking over each other.

"What happened?"

"You're all scratched up."

"What did you see?"

"Is she dead?"

Regina nodded, her teeth chattering. "Sh-she's d-d-dead . . . stabbed w-with the letter opener st-stolen from our st-store."

Her sisters stared, agog. "No way," Regina breathed. "You're sure it's the same one?"

She nodded again. "S-silver and gold, and g-green leaves on the handle. It's lying on the seat beside her, with blood all over it." She was crying now.

Mica teared up. "Omigod, omigod, omigod."

Justine seemed dazed, looking past Regina's shoulder to the scene below. "Are you sure she's dead?"

Regina nodded, wincing at the memory of the abiding stillness of the body. "We have to get the police."

Mica started caterwauling outright.

"Be quiet, both of you!" Justine stood and abruptly turned away. She paced in a nervous circle, then stopped and pulled them to their feet. Justine could be a brute. "We weren't here."

Regina sniffed. "What?"

"We weren't here," Justine said. "We didn't see a thing."

"Yes, we did," Mica said tearfully.

Justine shook them each by a shoulder. "Listen to me, and listen good. We didn't see anything, not really. We didn't see the man she was with. We didn't see what happened. We didn't even know she was dead, for God's sake."

Regina gaped at her sister. "We can't just go home like nothing happened."

"Someone will find her soon," Justine said, her voice now soothing. "Especially with that music blaring. Regina, you were very brave to go down there, but there's nothing we can do to help her now."

Regina blinked—Justine thought she was brave?

"And if we went to the police," her sister continued quietly, "the killer might think we could identify him. Then he might come after *us*."

Mica resumed her boo-hooing.

"Shhh," Justine said with unaccustomed gentleness. "It's going to be all right. He doesn't know we were here—no one does."

"Just us," Mica said with a hiccup.

"Right," Justine said. "Just us. And we're not going to tell anyone, are we?"

"Uh-uh," Mica said.

Regina hesitated.

Justine's eyes went narrow and her wagging finger reemerged. "You know, Regina, if the police find out we were here and that the murder weapon once belonged to us, they might think we had something to do with it."

Fear seized her. Would they?

"You didn't touch anything down there, did you?"

Her mind rewound, then replayed painfully. "Just . . . the car."

Justine looked stricken and leaned forward. "Your fingerprints are on the car? Jeez Louise, all the more reason not to tell anyone! You're a real drag most of the time, Regina, but I don't want to see you thrown in jail."

Regina swallowed hard and bit into her lower lip. If only their father were an attorney, like Carson Drew, instead of an antiques dealer, she could depend on him to defend her. As is, however, she had only her sisters. Yikes.

Mica pulled a hank of hair from her mouth long enough to say, "I won't tell, Justine."

Justine gave her a wobbly smile. "Good girl. But we each have to swear that we will never, ever, *ever* tell anyone about what happened here today." She put her left hand over her heart and raised her right hand. "I swear on our sisterhood that I will never tell."

Mica rushed to follow suit. "I swear on our sisterhood that I will never tell."

Regina trembled from the images in her head and from the pressure of their gaze. Justine and Mica stood arm in arm, faces shiny with dried tears, waiting, challenging. She spent most of her time negotiating peace between the two of them, yet afterward, more often than not, they would gang up and turn on *her*. Her sisters were a formidable force when they pooled their attitude.

"Regina?"

"Come on, Regina—swear."

Not telling didn't seem right, but Regina didn't want them to get into trouble for spying—or worse. And she certainly didn't want the killer to come looking for her and her sisters. She couldn't bear it if something happened to either one of them.

Blinking back tears, she pushed her hair out of her eyes, then situated her shaking hands. "I s-swear . . . on our s-sisterhood . . . that I will never t-tell."

## one

*Twenty years later*

"Oh, come on, Regina, you can tell *me*."

"Nope." Regina Metcalf smiled over her coffee at her assistant editor, Jill Lance. "I don't kiss and tell."

"But you and Alan Garvo haven't dated for over six months!"

In truth, Regina hadn't dated anyone for over six months, but she assumed a royal expression. "There's no statute of limitations on my honor."

"You're so full of crap."

Regina lifted an eyebrow.

Jill looked contrite. "You're so full of crap, *Boss*."

"That's better. What's on the agenda today?" She sipped her coffee and winced. Prompted by an article in a magazine at her dentist's office, she had calculated that skipping the cream would spare her an hour on the treadmill every week. Two days in, however, she wasn't convinced it was worth the trade-off.

Jill skimmed a calendar on her lap. "Cover consultation with art and marketing on the April and May releases at ten, and a meeting with legal over the slander suit filed by Dr. Union at three."

Regina pushed up her glasses, more from habit than need. "Do we have the notarized letter from the author stating his comments about Dr. Union's study on sexuality are accurate?"

"Yes, as well as the author's notes from her conversations with two other colleagues of Dr. Union and the editor of the medical research newsletter who refused to print the study. Quote: 'The man's a pervert,' unquote."

"Maybe Dr. Perv will write a book for us. Anything else?"

"Here's the foreword from Dr. Enya English for the June parenting book."

"Any good?"

"Despite her name, grammar is not her strong suit."

"Leave it."

"And the editor of *Vigor* agreed to excerpt the man-eating book."

"Come again?"

"The book about finding a mate by matching his diet to yours—the sales reps call it the man-eating book."

"Where were they when we were brainstorming a title?"

"Probably in Fiji or somewhere. I'm telling you, one of these days I'm going to defect and join the sales department."

"You'd have to buy a car."

"Worse—I'd have to learn to *drive* a car."

"So there you go; you're stranded in editorial. What else?"

Jill shifted in her seat.

Regina looked up from the list she was making. "What?"

"Well . . . you know how excited I am about the manuscript that Laura Thomas turned in."

"The hairstylist? Sure, what about it?"

More fidgeting.

"Spit it out, Jill; we each have a thousand things in our in-box."

"I was wondering . . . that is, since your sister is a hair model . . . and so popular . . ." Jill splayed her hand. "I wondered if she'd be available to give us a quote."

Regina brought her cup to her mouth for another bitter drink, which seemed appropriate considering the state of the Metcalf sisterhood. Still, she managed a smile in Jill's direction. "I don't hear much from Mica these days—she rarely leaves LA unless it's for a photo shoot, and if she travels east, she's more likely to go to Manhattan than to come to Boston."

Occasionally her baby sister sent her incoherent E-mail messages with a time stamp of the wee hours of the morning—presumably after dragging in from heavy partying. The most significant contact she maintained with Mica came from watching the glitzy TV commercials Mica starred in, swirling, twirling, and un-furling that glorious three-foot fall of blue-black hair. Her mane was reported to be insured for a million dollars, and Regina rather believed it.

She fingered a glittery promotional ink pen that read: "Polish Your Inner Glow in 30 Days"—last season's surprise best-seller after being endorsed by a trendy talk show host. "My sisters and I aren't as close as when we were younger." A diplomatic understatement.

"I didn't mean to put you on the spot."

"You didn't. In fact"—she scribbled another item on her growing list—"I can't make any promises, but I'll give Mica a call and see if we can work out something."

Her assistant beamed. "How can I thank you?"

One corner of her mouth slid back. "By getting out

so I can tackle my daily quota of paper cuts."

Jill saluted and vamoosed like the efficient genius she was, closing the frosted glass door as she backed out.

To soothe the roiling unease that the thought of her sisters always induced, Regina straightened the already-straight collection of letter openers on her desk while her unending mental to-do list revolved to reassure her she was a world away from the ghosts of Monroeville, North Carolina: line edits, revision letters, rejection letters, meetings, conferences, book fairs. Authors who delivered late, authors who changed agents as often as shoes, authors who misunderstood the complexities involved in marketing self-help books. Some brilliant books went unnoticed, some mediocre books became stars, and some terrible books . . . well, despite her staff's best efforts, a few duds had managed to slip through during her eight-year tenure.

Still, she loved every aspect of her job, every minute of the process of turning an idea into a tangible product that could, even if only for a few hours, convince readers they could be slender, healthy, popular, happy, secure, rich, successful, creative, loved, climactic, and fulfilled. The books that she brought to market gave people hope.

And the books gave *her* hope.

Hope that despite questionable parenting and a splintered family, she, too, could be slender, healthy, popular, happy, secure, rich, successful, creative, loved, climactic, and fulfilled. Someday.

She swiveled in her chair to face her bookcase—a veritable wall of unread manuscripts bound by enough rubber bands to hold a car together, collectively emanating a slightly pungent odor. Anticipation swelled in her chest.

The founder of Green Label Publishing Group was

of the old school, so they were one of the few non-fiction houses that accepted unsolicited, unagented submissions. The big, glomy slush piles were the consternation of most of her staff, but Regina was downright possessive of her personal mountain. Because every once in a great while she unearthed an extraordinary manuscript from a small-town doctor, a school principal, an inner-city minister, a mother of six— unique people with rich life experiences and true inspirational stories to tell, plus a human interest angle strong enough to give marketing a departmental orgasm. It piqued her that a gem could be hidden in the pile at this very moment, waiting to be discovered. That thrill of discovery was what kept her rolling out of bed six days a week to catch the Massachusetts Bay Transit Authority train for the forty-minute ride to her office on the fifth floor of a retrofitted seventies office building overlooking the Charles River.

She reached back to retrieve her coffee cup, inscribed with "How to Sleep Alone" (the company's best hope for a fall blockbuster), and her glance fell on her to-do list. "Call Mica" niggled at her. It was only five-thirty in LA, but it might be a good time to catch her coming home or before leaving for an early shoot. Or maybe she could leave Mica a voice message to call back when she had time. Then when Mica didn't call back, Regina could in good faith tell Jill that her sister hadn't responded. Yes, now there was a plan. As added incentive to call, she promised herself that afterward she would select three manuscripts from her slush pile to review before the ten o'clock meeting.

She swallowed two more mouthfuls of the cooling coffee before pouring the rest into the pot of an ill-looking African violet that she'd inherited with the office and had yet to produce the first bloom. Jill suggested that she ditch the plant and start over, but

Regina stubbornly refused. As a late bloomer herself, she had faith—and patience. Old Mr. Calvin had once told her that coffee was good for plants, and she believed him, if simply because he'd been the only adult who had fostered her love for reading. She wondered if he knew that she now made her living surrounded by books, or if he remembered her, or if he was even still alive. She made a mental note to ask her mother the next time they spoke on the phone.

After consulting her electronic address book, she punched in Mica's number, breathing deeply to calm her nerves. It wasn't as if she didn't want to talk to her sister; it was just that they had so little to say to each other. Mica had moved to LA the same time that Regina had graduated college and moved to Boston to work as a reader for a textbook publisher. Mica's departure had caused so much strain in the family, Regina wasn't surprised when she didn't hear from her for over a year. Hurt, but not surprised.

Over the last twelve years, she'd seen her baby sister in person only once. She'd flown to LA for a book-sellers' conference and practically shown up on Mica's doorstep (after she'd tracked down the doorstep). That was before Mica's lucrative contract with the world's largest hair care line, and the visit had been a bona fide disaster. Mica was a wreck, strung out and living in a dump with her boyfriend, an exponentially bigger wreck. Regina had sprung for lunch at the safest-looking restaurant in the neighborhood. Mica had eaten like a man and spent the hour extolling the virtues of the city and a new talent agent she'd signed with. She'd seemed content enough, but with Mica, who knew? When Regina dropped her off, Mica had turned and leaned into the open window.

"Have you heard from Justine?"

"We talk on the phone occasionally."

"How is she?"

"Fine. You should call her sometime."

"I wouldn't know what to say."

"I suspect the words would come."

But to her knowledge, the call had never been made—she was sure Justine would have mentioned it. After all these years, Regina was still suspended between her sisters' personalities, knowing that despite their history, they yearned for each other. She was simply a placeholder.

After the sixth ring, Regina expected the machine to kick on. Instead, the receiver was lifted from its cradle, wallowed a good bit, then a deep-throated bleary, "Yeah?" came over the line.

She closed her eyes. *Dean Haviland.* Only the last person on earth she wanted to talk to.

"Who the hell's calling?" he slurred.

"Dean, it's Regina. Metcalf. I was hoping to speak to Mica."

"Hm? Regina? Well, well, long time, no see."

She bit the tip of her tongue. "Is Mica available to come to the phone?"

He grunted. "Can't spare a word for your old friend Dean?"

"The word that comes to mind isn't fit for the airwaves."

His laughter rolled out, sultry and confident, even now. No—*especially* now. Now that Mica was a wealthy personality, one of those rare commercial actors who resonated with viewers to the point that they became more recognizable than the product they represented. Dean Haviland, high school dropout and loser extraordinaire, had hit the mother lode.

"Regina, Regina, Regina. I always knew you were more of a fireball than your sisters if you'd only let your hair down."

She set her jaw, a movement that pulled at the smooth hairline created by her French twist. The man was revolting in his conceit. What her sisters ever saw in him—good God, what *she* ever saw in him—was a mystery even beyond the grasp of Nancy Drew.

"Mica—is she there?"

"She's not in bed, but she could be passed out in the john."

Regina struggled to keep the alarm out of her voice. "Don't you think you should check on her?"

"Not especially."

Clenching the phone, she willed herself not to be sucked in by the man's melodrama. "When you see her, would you please ask her to call me at my office?"

"Sure thang, Blue Eyes."

She slammed down the phone, then picked it up and banged it down again. "Ooooooh!"

A discreet knock sounded at her door.

"Yes?" she called curtly.

The door opened six inches, revealing Jill's pensive face. "Everything okay?"

Regina removed her glasses and massaged the bridge of her nose. "Fine. Would you please hold my calls? I'm going to try to get some reading done before the ten o'clock meeting."

"Absolutely." Jill hesitated a split second, then closed the door.

Regina sighed and jammed her dark frames back onto her face. She was a respected senior editor known for her level head, yet smarmy Dean Haviland could set her off with a few casual words from three thousand miles away. How many times had she wished he'd never entered their lives? If she'd known the havoc the dark-eyed teenager would unleash on her family when he walked into M&G Antiquities twenty years ago and asked for a job, she'd have found some way to convince her parents to send him on his loose-hipped way.

But she couldn't turn back time, no matter how many circumstances she longed to change.

In an effort to shake her black mood, she slipped off her gray suit jacket and draped it across the back of her chair, then faced her bookcase and the massive slush pile. Removing three manuscripts from this heap would be like removing a bucket of water from the river that ran past her building, but today could be the day she struck gold. She slowly scanned the bundles of paper, many with protruding pages or curled edges, and randomly selected three manuscripts of varying bulk.

After settling into her chair, she removed the clips and rubber bands, then skimmed the first cover letter. A local taxi driver had written a collection of short stories about his experiences and customers' conversations. Actually, the writing wasn't half-bad, but she had to pull the "sorry, we don't publish fiction" form letter from a file and fasten it on top. She did take a few seconds, however, to scrawl "Try Anne Frankel at Thornton House" on the bottom of the otherwise-impersonal letter.

Next, a Vietnam veteran from Ohio had turned his war experience and his passion for outdoor sports into a survival guide. The man's credits were impressive (if frightening), and the manuscript was meaty, though poorly organized. Still, with the popularity of reality television shows, they might be able to parlay the material into a series of guides for outdoorsmen. She turned to her computer and typed a quick memo of her ideas to the editor on their staff who specialized in sports-related books, then dropped the entire kit-and-kaboodle into an intercompany mailer.

The last manuscript looked less promising—the cover letter was printed on bright pink paper, and when she removed the clasp a handful of star and heart cutout confetti showered her desk. She swore under her breath and spent the next few minutes tossing the colorful bits into the trash, and very nearly chucked the manuscript, too. But she prided herself on reading at least a few pages of every submission, so she sighed and scanned the pink cover letter:

> *My name is Libby Janes. I live just north of Atlanta, Georgia, and I carpool every day to my downtown technical writing job with three other women—Belinda, Carole, and Rosemary. Two of us are single, and between the four of us we've been married nine times (yes, nine times). As you can imagine, our carpooling conversation usually turns to men—why we thought we were in love, what we've learned, the advice we want to pass on to our daughters. Out of boredom, I began to write down bits of our group advice on falling in and out of love, and I believe other women would like to hear what we have to say. I'm enclosing the finished product for your publishing consideration.*

Regina pursed her mouth and turned to the cover sheet.

### I THINK I LOVE YOU
(Relationship DOs and DON'Ts for Grown Women)

Crossing her legs, Regina dangled a leather pump from her toe and turned the page.

# two

**DO assess the risk level of a relationship before you proceed.**

Justine Metcalf found it hard to concentrate on the words she was imparting to her staff of twelve women with the feel of Randall Crane's hands still on her breasts.

"As most of you know, I directed the addition of noncosmetic items to the Cocoon product line last year that moved us from number six in the cosmetic industry to number four." She coughed to mask her growling stomach. If she kept meeting him so often for lunch rendezvous, she was going to have to start brown-bagging an afternoon snack.

"By adding silk scarves and evening bags to the fall lineup, we can expect to see a sales increase of three to three and a half million dollars for the first two quarters of next year." When she stood to pass out folders imprinted with the company's signature caterpillar, the rush of cool air past her thighs reminded her that Randall had kept her panties, the naughty boy.

Justine reclaimed her seat and crossed her legs to stem the draft, wincing inwardly at the twinge of her thigh muscles. Randall's lovemaking had been particularly intense today. Bruising . . . almost like Dean's.

She registered the sharp pain of a bad memory, then mentally shook herself. "Now then—"

"May I say something?"

She looked down the table, fighting a frown of disapproval for the intrusion, especially when her gaze landed on Barbie Donetti, a perky little regional director who, Justine had heard through the grapevine, had her sights set on Justine's executive VP position. *Fat chance, Barbie Doll.*

"Yes, you may," Justine said, but checked her watch to indicate the girl had better hurry the hell up.

Barbie assumed a smug smile and leaned her elbows on the table. "Well, it seems to me that we're drifting too far away from our core product line." She spoke with the nasal thickness of the locals here in the headquarters' town of Shively, Pennsylvania. A homegrown girl whose mother worked on the Cocoon assembly line, Little Barbie seemed to have gotten above her raising. "Instead of putting the Cocoon name on all this *stuff,* why don't we expand our skin care line?"

All eyes cut to Justine, and she saw agreement in their stupid expressions. Clenching her fist in her lap, she bestowed a tolerant smile in Barbie's direction. "I'll take your comment under advisement." She put pen to paper. "Let's see, the fancy marketing term you used was *stuff,* wasn't it, Barbie?"

The offender turned scarlet and sat back in her chair like a good girl. "My name is *Bobbie,* Ms. Metcalf. Bobbie Donetti."

"Oh, my mistake. One of the few mistakes I've made in my career, I might add."

A repentant silence fell, but Justine wasn't satisfied. She pursed her mouth and crossed her arms over her runway-quality laser-red suit—whoever said that redheads shouldn't wear red had never gotten a gander at her. "Before we move on, I'd like to take a moment to remind everyone seated here that Cocoon is a classy firm—if you intend to stay here, you might want to reevaluate your business wardrobes." She glanced around the table, lingering on Barbie-Bobbie, daring anyone to make eye contact. No one did.

"Now then, are there any other questions about the new product line?"

There weren't.

She opened the folder in front of her. "Good. As I was about to say before I was interrupted, the new sales quotas and bonus structures are in your folders—"

The door to her office burst open, and Justine jumped to her feet, her patience spent. "Dammit, what now?" She didn't recognize the slight woman who stood in the doorway, her graying hair disheveled, her eyes glassy.

The woman wet her lips. "Are you Justine Metcalf?"

"Yes. *Who* are you?"

"Lisa Crane."

"I don't—" Justine stopped as realization hit her. Randall's *wife*. She swallowed and forced a note of calm into her voice. "Did you need to speak with me in private, Mrs. Crane?"

"No," the woman said, closing the door behind her and turning the lock on the handle. "I want plenty of witnesses."

Her heart thudded. "Mrs. Crane—"

The woman raised a revolver. "Shut up, slut."

Cold terror gripped Justine, and shrieks rang out.

"Don't anyone move," Mrs. Crane said, sweeping the weapon over their heads, and the group obliged. She smiled at Justine. "I understand you're screwing my husband."

Justine was paralyzed in her crocodile pumps. "I d-don't know what you're talking about."

The woman reached into her purse and tossed a wad

of something on the table that slid down the glossy length and stopped in front of Justine's notebook.

Her panties. A pair of tiny sheer silk undies with a yellow butterfly design. One of the noncosmetic items she'd added to last year's product lineup.

Justine's mouth went dry. "Those . . . aren't . . . mine."

The woman cocked the hammer. "Prove it—lift your skirt."

Panic rolled over her in waves. She leaned against the table, the edge cutting into the fronts of her thighs. "I—"

The woman raised the gun and fired. Everyone screamed except Justine, who simply waited for blood to begin spreading over some portion of her upmarket suit jacket. When it didn't, she realized that the woman had shot high and into the wall behind her. As her knees weakened, her mind raced—at least security would be alerted, although the Keystone Cops milling around Cocoon's lobby had never dealt with anything worse than a malfunctioning fire alarm.

The Crane woman cocked the hammer again. "I missed on purpose. Lift your little skirt, or I'm going to start picking off your friends here."

Her "friends" were weeping, but Justine was dry-eyed with disbelief. This couldn't be happening, not to her. Not when she finally had the world by the balls after years of clawing her way up from the degradation of in-home makeup parties. *For instant cheekbones, apply blush on the apple of your cheek.* Christ, didn't she deserve to enjoy her success for a few lousy years?

"I'm going to count to three," Lisa Crane said, pointing the gun at wide-eyed Terri Birch, vice president of human resources. Terri had three kids and a vacation home in Aspen. "One . . ."

And Justine had shagged Terri's husband, Jim, in

the catering pantry at the company Christmas party.

"Two . . ."

Terri began to sob.

"Okay," Justine said with a tiny chopping motion. "Okay." She smoothed her hands down her thighs and began lifting the hem of her skirt one millimeter at a time. She'd stall the woman as long as possible, hoping that by some miracle, help would arrive before the bullets started flying again. "You've got it all wrong, Mrs. Crane. Randall and I are just friends."

"That's not what he said." The woman laughed. "Right before I shot him."

Her heart pummeled her breastbone. Randall was . . . *dead*? Good God, the woman was mad. "M-Mrs. Crane, why don't you let these people go? They're innocent in this matter."

"Nobody's going anywhere until you expose your ass to the world. Somehow I don't think these folks will mind, because I'll bet they've had to kiss it a few times." She motioned with the gun for Justine to keep lifting, then pressed the barrel to Terri Birch's head. Terri's big hair nearly enveloped the gun.

Justine swallowed and slowly inched her skirt upward. The air touched her skin above the black thigh-high stockings. The woman was riveted, and so were most of Justine's staff. A couple of them had the good grace to look away, and Justine made mental notes for future pay raises. If she lived.

Her hem snagged on a garter belt fastener, then bumped higher. When the bottom of the fabric brushed her pubic hair, Justine set her jaw—she'd lifted her skirt for less compelling reasons than to avoid death. Of course, the woman was likely to shoot her anyway if the cavalry didn't arrive soon. She'd balled enough cops in this town that they'd damn well better save the day before she got her ass shot off. Her only flash of vindication standing skirt-up in the path of the air-conditioning vent was that she had one fine-looking ass.

"Guess those *were* your panties," Mrs. Crane said dryly, but she seemed deflated in the face of truth.

"You've proved your point, Mrs. Crane," Justine said, dropping her skirt. "Now put down the gun. Randall isn't worth all this."

The woman squinted. "No, *you* wouldn't think so, would you? *You* didn't work as a waitress to put him through law school. *You* didn't give him two sons. *You* didn't nurse his mother through Alzheimer's. Randall means nothing to you, but he is *everything* to me!" The woman was crying now, and pressing poor Terri's head to the side with the barrel of the gun.

"Relax, Mrs. Crane," Justine soothed.

"A person can't just go through life destroying relationships and get away with it!"

The faces of the married men Justine had slept with over the years passed before her eyes. "Please put down the gun."

The woman suddenly laughed. "I don't think so." She moved the gun from Terri's temple and aimed for Justine's chest. Justine inhaled and closed her eyes.

When the shot rang out and mayhem erupted, she fell to the ground and waited for the pain to overtake her. She hadn't talked to Regina in weeks, to her parents in months, and to Mica in years. She curled into a ball and wondered if her backstabbing baby sister would have the heart to show up for her funeral.

# three

DO wake up and smell the leftovers.

Mica was trapped in a cabinet of some kind. She inhaled the pungent, mossy scent of walnut wood, and her eyes flew wide in the darkness. She was inside the wardrobe. The antique wardrobe that she, Regina, and Justine had repaired and refinished for Justine and Dean's future household. Beneath her fingers, the wood of the door was smooth and hot from all the sanding—so hot that she cried out in pain.

"Let me out!" She flailed at the door. "Let me out of here!"

The door fell open and she tumbled onto a slick, cold surface. She closed her eyes and welcomed the coolness against her feverish cheek and bare breasts. She was lying on hard water—the word escaped her . . . *ice*. No, not ice . . . tile. The Italian tile in the master bathroom she had fallen in love with. She had been in the linen closet, not the walnut wardrobe. She was safe . . . free from the suffocating memories. For now.

"Ms. Metcalf?"

She opened one eye and tried to focus on the female voice with the British accent emanating from the intense light. "Hm?"

"Ms. Metcalf, what were you doing in the linen pantry? Are you all right?"

"Hm."

"Let me help you up."

Mica acquiesced because she didn't have the strength to do it herself and she needed a drink. "Who . . . the devil . . . are you?"

"I'm Polly, ma'am. The new housekeeper."

Mica groaned as a chunk of memory fell into place. Firing the former housekeeper had been Dean's concession after she walked in on them kissing in the pool house. A weak moment, he'd assured her, and promised to hire someone else, someone less kissable, she'd assumed. But as Polly's angelic face came into focus, Mica knew she'd been had. Another redhead. She laughed, sagging against poor, unsuspecting Polly as the woman dragged her across the floor and settled her into the vanity chair.

Mica blinked back miserable tears as her mind flew in all directions. Maybe if she demanded that Dean marry her once and for all, his flirtations would end. He was generous with his winks and kisses, but he swore that he'd been faithful to their bed all these years and she believed him. Hadn't he forsaken her own sister at the altar to be with her? She sighed noisily. Maybe they could save some money and she could take a sabbatical from modeling next year. They could have a baby. They could buy this house with the bathroom tile she loved.

"Ms. Metcalf . . . your *eye*."

With much effort, Mica peered into the mirror at the purplish bruise. She swallowed and touched the tender skin. Dean had never hit her in the face before.

"I'll fetch you an ice bag, ma'am."

"No! I fell is all. I'll be fine. Leave me."

"Ma'am?"

*"What?"*

"I came to let you know that you have a visitor."

Mica closed her eyes. "Who is it, for Christ's sake?"

"A Mr. Everett Collier."

Her agent. Some part of her brain registered concern that he had come to see her at home, but at the moment she couldn't process all the inputs. She wound her hair and held it off her neck to relieve the pressure from her tingling scalp. One thing she did know: she couldn't allow Everett to see her hungover.

"He said it was urgent, ma'am, or I wouldn't have disturbed you."

Mica ran her tongue over the roof of her mouth to dispel a disgusting taste. "What time is it?"

"Just before the noon hour."

"What *day* is it?"

"Er, Thursday, ma'am."

Oh, crap . . . did she have a booking today? Surely Dean wouldn't have let her miss *another* shoot. "Is Dean—is Mr. Haviland home?"

"Mr. Haviland left around nine o'clock."

And left her passed out in the closet . . . or had he put her there? Panic rose in her chest, her gaze darting to far corners of the room. "Did . . . did he say where he was going or when he'd be back?"

"No, ma'am. He received a phone call and left soon afterward."

Another mysterious phone call. When she would ask who called, he'd mumble something about a wrong number; then later he'd disappear.

"Mr. Haviland instructed me not to disturb you, or I would have helped . . . that is, ma'am, I would have . . . already cleaned your room."

"I'll let you know when to clean our room," Mica snapped, then pressed her hands against her screaming temples. The last thing she needed was this pretty little redhead traipsing in and out of their bedroom dressed in a short uniform. She exhaled, then spoke through clenched teeth. "And find something respectable to wear if you expect to work here."

The woman's gaze flicked over Mica's partial nudity. "Yes, ma'am."

"And stop calling me ma'am!" Christ, it was bad enough that other models had taken to calling her Aunt Mica. She still had plenty of good years left in the industry. Plenty. She pushed her hand against her agitating stomach. "Tell Mr. Collier that I'll call him later, and then bring me a drink. Vodka, straight."

"Make that coffee," a male voice said from the doorway. "And aspirin."

Mica looked up to see Everett Collier standing in the doorway. Medium height, medium build, medium attractive, dressed in an immaculate suit and pristine white collarless shirt. Other than being perhaps a little less quick to smile, the forty-something man was unchanged from when she had signed with his agency nearly five years ago.

"Everett." She tried to stand but failed.

The man nodded to Polly. "I'll take over from here. Please add two pieces of buttered toast to the coffee tray for Ms. Metcalf."

"No butter," Mica corrected.

"*Extra* butter," he told Polly, then jerked his thumb pointedly toward the door.

Polly fled.

He sighed. "Hello, Mica."

Mica turned away and covered her eye. Her bare breasts were a non-issue—Dean had assured her the reserved man was supremely gay. Her vision blurred, then doubled. "I'm sorry, Everett. . . . I don't feel well, and Dean isn't here."

He shrugged out of his jacket and settled it around

her shoulders. "I didn't come to speak to Dean; I came to speak to you. Quite a shiner you have there."

"I fell."

"Really? When Dean called to cancel your shoot this morning, he said you had an eye infection."

She shrugged. "He probably didn't want anyone to know what a klutz I am."

"Or maybe he didn't want anyone to know what an asshole he is."

Her instincts rallied to Dean's defense, but her body betrayed her. She dropped to her knees by the marble tub, slung her head over the side, and threw up. She'd been doing a lot of that lately.

Everett knelt beside her and held her hair—his prime concern—out of harm's way. His jacket that she wore, however, didn't fare so well.

"I'm sorry," she said, wiping her mouth.

"Don't worry about it. Can you sit?"

She nodded and allowed him to help her back into the chair. He lowered himself to the edge of the tub, then leaned his elbows on his knees and clasped his hands. "Mica, you're in trouble here, and I don't think you realize it."

Mica conjured up a strangled laugh. "I just celebrated too much last night."

"Mica, look at yourself—you're a sickly, skinny, hungover mess." He waved toward the piles of clutter on the vanity, the dirty clothes on the floor. "You don't meet your work obligations, you live in squalor, and the man you sleep with hits you."

She flinched. "You don't understand—"

"I understand perfectly. I've seen it dozens of times over in my clients. They come into a little money and success, and allow themselves to be dragged down by alcohol and drugs and people who take advantage of them."

"I'm *not* a druggie."

He pushed to his feet and walked over to the counter. After a bit of rummaging among the chaos, he held up three prescription bottles. "What are these?"

She pulled his jacket tighter around her shoulders. "The painkillers are for my neck. And my doctor said I wouldn't have to take the Prozac for very long."

"You won't, and you know why?" He spiked the bottles of pills into the sink. "Because at this rate you probably won't *live* for very long. You'll either starve yourself to death, accidentally overdose, or your boyfriend will throw you down a flight of stairs."

Tears welled in her eyes. "It's not that bad."

"Yes, it is." He pulled his hand down his face. "Let me give it to you straight, Mica. The marketing director from Tara said if you miss one more shoot, you're history."

She bit down on her tongue to stem her tears.

"And from here out, Dean is banned from the set."

"But . . . but Dean will never agree to that." Besides, she was accustomed to having him nearby, having him handle everything.

Everett splayed his hands. "If you want to keep working, you're going to have to get rid of him, Mica; it's that simple. Get rid of Dean, and get your act together."

She brought her fist to her mouth. *Get rid of Dean?*

"But even more important than saving your career, it might save your life."

But she couldn't . . . she loved him . . . and Dean knew things . . . damaging things about her . . . about her sisters. . . .

Her agent pulled a card from his shirt pocket. "I arranged for you to be off for a few weeks to recuperate. And I made an appointment for you with a reliable doctor to get a complete physical this afternoon." He folded the card into her hand and gave her a look that said this medical business, too, was part of the deal. "I'd be happy to stay and explain the situation to Dean myself, if you're . . . concerned."

She shook her head. "No, I'll talk to him."

"Do you need a place to stay?"

"What?"

"In case he doesn't take the news well, do you need a place to stay?"

"No . . . I'll be fine."

He looked unconvinced. "Do you have protection?"

"Protection?"

"You know, a baseball bat or something in case he comes after you again?"

"I don't think—"

*"Do you?"*

"Well . . . there's a handgun in the bureau, but—"

"Do you know how to use it?"

"I grew up in the country; of course I know how to use it." She touched her forehead. "Everett, you're scaring me."

"Good. Maybe now you'll take this situation with Dean seriously."

Her laugh was dry, unbelieving. "For God's sake, I'm not his punching bag. This was a one-time incident. I'm sure it won't happen again."

He was pacing now. "Maybe you should take a vacation—leave town for a while and let things settle down."

To pacify him, she murmured, "Maybe I'll do that."

He stopped pacing and nodded, clearly relieved. "Call me if you have any problems. I'll come, day or night."

"Thank you, but I'm sure that won't be necessary."

Polly appeared with the tray.

"Make sure Ms. Metcalf eats the toast," he told her. "All of it." He looked back to Mica and pointed his finger. For a split second, she thought of Justine and her wagging finger. "If Dean hits you again, Mica, I'll kill him. Hell, I might take a shot at him anyway for this."

She blinked, then realized that Everett's threat was motivated by his need to protect his income.

"Good-bye, Mica."

She nodded mutely. After he strode out, her knees started bouncing up and down uncontrollably. What now? If Tara dropped her, she'd be relegated to catalog work or something equally demeaning and poor. She simply would not revert to their previous transient lifestyle. Modeling lingerie, dodging landlords, shoplifting clothes for auditions.

She chewed the toast slowly under Polly's watchful eye, trying not to think about the calories sliding down her throat. Dean would fly into a rage when he heard the client's demands—she had to think of a way to break the news to him that would flatter him, but the thinking would have to wait until her mind cleared. She downed the coffee and dismissed Polly, willing the aspirin to kick in. Everett's stained suit jacket went on a hook, her thong underwear on a pile of dirty clothes on the floor.

She gingerly stepped under the cool spray and leaned her head back—she'd learned to forgo hot water because it wasn't good for her hair. In fact, her daily routine pretty much revolved around washing, conditioning, and protecting her "product." In a business where extensions were common, her thigh-length fall of dark wavy hair was the real deal, and in demand. At least it had been yesterday.

She roused herself with a bar of the best soap her modeling money could buy, a silk-infused hand-friendly

wedge made by a cosmetic company called Cocoon.
She inhaled the soothing scent that was somewhere between white chocolate and cherry pie filling, and held
the fragrance in her lungs as if she'd taken a hit from
a joint. Slowly she worked the soap into a lather and
massaged it into her scalp.

It was her only contact with Justine, this decadent
soap produced by the company she worked for. And
wouldn't her sister get a kick if she knew that Mica
used *her* soap to maintain her valuable mane and
poured Tara Hair products down the drain by the case?
It was a tenuous, one-sided connection, Mica conceded,
but using the soap made her feel better about the past—
every day she washed away a little more of the guilt.
One day she'd step out from under the water and be
completely exonerated.

But not today, she observed as she toweled dry. Today she was inexplicably homesick for Justine—which
probably explained her earlier hallucination about being inside the wardrobe. The summer she and her sisters had worked on that cabinet was the last good time,
a symbol of sorts that they'd silently overcome the
trauma of that horrid summer years before. They'd all
been on the verge of escaping into their adult lives, on
the brink of a collective exhale. When she left with
Dean on the morning of his and Justine's wedding day,
she'd shattered the delicate facade of sisterhood that
they had presented to the world, especially to their parents. But after all these years of silence between her
and her oldest sister, she still felt Justine's obstinate
pull. She looked eastward. Especially today.

Her shoulders bowed from the strain as she exited
to the bedroom wrapped in a bath sheet, walking to the
beat of her throbbing hangover. Going clubbing last
night with assorted acquaintances had seemed like a
good idea when Dean had suggested it. They so rarely

went anywhere together anymore, she'd been as eager as when she'd first met him on the sly as a teenager. Back then they had sipped beer in the back of his jacked-up Chevy Nova. Now Dean's idea of a good time required hard liquor and a limo.

The night had started well enough, with an outrageously expensive dinner at a new hot spot in the Hills—Dean had paid with yet another new gold credit card. An E! cameraman had stopped in looking for Penelope Cruz, who, the bartender told them, had used the ladies' room earlier in the evening. Not about to leave empty-handed, the guy had shot film of her, the Tara Hair Girl, as part of a series they were doing on celebrity hairstyles. Ecstatic about the potential coverage, Dean had ordered more drinks; then the group had gone dancing. After that, things were blurry, but she had the vague recollection of an argument here in the bedroom—accusations of her flirting with the cameraman. She had gone to the bathroom to get something, probably a wet cloth for her eye, which would explain why she woke up in the linen closet.

She picked her way across the carpeted floor, through discarded clothing, liquor bottles, and plates of half-eaten food. Mica paused and bit into her lip, thinking how her mother would chide if she could see the mess.

Of course, Mica had made her bed where her family's opinion was concerned years ago. There was too much water under the bridge now for trivial regrets.

Easing down on the foot of the unmade bed, she scanned the high-ceilinged room, the once-stunning white contemporary walls and furniture much compromised by flying objects and general abuse over the past couple of years. The room had seen the best and worst of times. Hours of lovemaking, giving way to hours of arguing, then more lovemaking. Love and hate and sex and sadism. Dean knew how to push every button on her panel. He came to her shoots because she came alive under his scrutiny. Those smiles and winks and flirtatious swings of her hair captured so vividly by the clients' cameras were for Dean sitting slightly offset. He could still stop her heart with one well-placed smile.

God help her for loving him. He was unbearable to live with but impossible to live without. Truthfully, she owed her career to him—without Dean, she'd be just another pretty face in LA, where even the housekeepers were gorgeous. His networking opened doors, and his attention gave her the spark to set herself apart. If she got rid of Dean, she might as well flush her future down the drain. Some love and some success was better than none.

At the thought of breaking Everett's news to Dean, panic licked at her nerve endings. Her freshly powdered underarms grew moist. Her hands shook uncontrollably. The bravado she'd shown her agent crumbled. She'd seen glimpses of what Dean was capable of doing—he'd kill her before he'd step aside. She rescued her antidepressants and downed one, plus a glass of water. Pacing from bathroom to bedroom, she hugged herself, trying desperately not to cry. First things first, she had to convince this doctor of Everett's that she was okay.

She held the ice bag against her puffy eye for fifteen minutes, then put in eyedrops and carefully applied concealer to the bruise. Bronzer all over her face gave her a nice glow. Baggy jeans, padded bra, T-shirt, and a bulky summer sweater plumped up her figure. She gently combed her wet hair and left it to dry naturally. She did take time to pull an alarming amount of hair from the comb and flush it down the toilet.

When she rummaged for her pink-lensed sunglasses,

she remembered the gun in the bureau. Everett's warning hung in her brain. Mica pulled out the cold black pistol, hefting its weight in her hand. Her father had given the semiautomatic to Dean—not surprising considering the men's once-close relationship—and it was one of Dean's prize possessions. The feel of the gun brought back memories of sneaking out with Dean to park at the city landfill. They would sit on the hood of his car and neck and listen to the radio. After Dean had downed a few beers, he'd pick off rats scurrying around the base of the mountain of buried garbage. She'd stuff paper napkins in her ears and occasionally he'd let her hold the gun and pull the trigger. She remembered thinking it was surprisingly easy, and even now she could feel the lingering vibration in her hand and taste the smoky tang that hung in the air afterward.

She removed the cartridge from the grip to find one round inside, then pulled back the slide to make sure the chamber was empty. Mica hesitated, then slipped the gun into her big shoulder bag—she didn't intend to use it, but it wouldn't hurt to know its whereabouts during what promised to be an unpredictable few days.

A check of the time hurried her movements. She trotted to the phone to write a message for Dean in case he came home while she was gone. Her stomach pitched when she lifted a smelly pizza box to uncover a pad of paper. Then she frowned down at the note in Dean's handwriting:

*Call your sister at work.*

No question which sister. Mica pursed her lips.
Or was there?
Regina had never called her from the office before. Meanwhile, Justine had been preying on her mind all morning. The image of her flame-haired sister was so

clear in her mind, she could almost hear Justine's voice calling out to her. Obeying her premonition, she picked up the phone and dialed directory assistance.

"Shively, Pennsylvania, please. Cocoon Cosmetics."

# four

DO be honest, because your past always catches up with you.

The telephone was ringing as Regina unlocked the door to her condo. *Mica?* She swung open the door and dropped keys, mail, briefcase, groceries, and dry cleaning on the sofa, then grabbed the portable phone.

"Hello?"

"Hello, dear," Cissy said, and the tone of her voice sent a quickening to Regina's stomach.

"Mom, is everything okay?"

"Am I that transparent?"

She closed her eyes. "Yes—tell me." Her father? Justine? Mica?

"No one's dead if that's what you're worried about."

Relief bled through her. "What, then?"

Her mother burst into tears. "Your father and I are separating."

Regina sighed and stepped out of her shoes. "Again?" Growing up, she'd lost count of the times her father had moved his clothes and portable television into the apartment over the antiques store, only to pack them back to the house a few days or weeks or months later. In the beginning, she had hoped his return would result in a wedding—a ceremony that would make her and her sisters legitimate in the eyes of the townspeople. It hadn't happened.

Cissy sniffled. "It's different this time. We're selling the business."

Regina blinked. "You're selling the business?"

"And the house."

She sat down hard. "You're selling the house?" A one-hundred-thirty-year-old Victorian with original ceiling murals.

"Actually, we're going to auction off everything. Your father believes we'll make more money if we sell it piece by piece." Her mother's voice wobbled.

Regina touched her temple. "But . . . what happened? Did you and Dad have an argument?"

"Yes, but it's been a long time coming. I decided I've been playing house with your father long enough."

"Playing house?" Regina struggled to keep her voice steady. "Thirty-eight years and three children is more than playing house, don't you think?"

"John is a good father to you girls, but he isn't good husband material."

"But you're not married."

"Exactly. And I wouldn't marry him."

Regina squinted. "Did he ask you?"

"He knows better. Besides, John agrees that splitting up is for the best. Our relationship is over, Regina, that's all. Nothing lasts forever."

Her mind reeled. She hadn't visited often enough. She hadn't been able to mend the breach between her sisters. She hadn't given her parents grandchildren. And now their entire family unit was disintegrating. No possibility of a big, happy reunion, Norman Rockwell—style. No multigenerational family portrait. No matching T-shirts. "Maybe you and Dad should see a marriage counselor."

"We're not married, dear."

"A family counselor, then."

"We're past counseling, Regina. I know you think that everything is fixable, but it isn't."

"Most situations *are* fixable," she insisted. "Unless you give up."

"You sound like one of your books, dear. Life and people are far too complicated to manage with an emotional checklist."

*Your Emotional Checklist.* The author had dedicated the book to her, and she'd sent a copy to her mother thinking Cissy would be proud of her accomplishments. Regina swallowed the stinging barb. "B-but you and Dad have worked through rough times before." She stood and paced. "I'll come home. We'll all talk."

"Actually, I was *hoping* you'd agree to come home for a few days. We're going to need help sorting all the property, and of course I want you to select whatever things you'd like to have for your own home."

Her own home. From this one spot Regina could see her entire living, working, eating, sleeping, and bathing space. She didn't have room for a footstool, much less any of the hugely ornate pieces of period furniture crammed into her parents' gargantuan house. Her heart pounded at the prospect of having her childhood memories ripped out from under her, but she reasoned that if she were home to talk with her parents face-to-face, she could help them over this bump in their relationship. Her father was probably drinking too much, and her mother, who was a high-maintenance creature by design, wasn't the easiest person to live with. When Regina was younger, she'd always been able to concoct little schemes to get them talking again.

"Of course I'll come," she said, mentally fast-forwarding through the workload shift at the office, the travel arrangements, the packing. "I'll be there sometime tomorrow, depending on the flights."

"Thank you, dear. There's just so much to be done."

"Have you talked to Justine or Mica?"

"I left a message for Justine, and your father left one for Mica."

"Were you planning to ask them to come home?"

"Oh, no. They're much too busy."

Regina poked her tongue into her cheek. "Well, I can only be away from my office for a few days."

"Of course. Shall I have your father pick you up at the airport?"

For all her mother's feminist beliefs, she still delegated chauffeuring duties to the male species. "No, I'll get a rental car and drive in. Mom, promise me that you won't make any rash decisions between now and then."

"Sweetheart, some of the happiest moments in life result from rash decisions. You should try it sometime."

She sighed, perpetually mystified by her free-spirited mother. And sisters, for that matter. "I'll see you soon. Give my love to—" But Cissy had already hung up. Regina looked at the phone in her hand and muttered, "Dad." And in the odd way that one's brain works, she remembered she hadn't asked Cissy about old Mr. Calvin.

She sagged into the chair, biting down on her tongue to keep the tears at bay. The afternoon meeting with legal had droned on until after six, then the trains were delayed, and her errands had taken forever. Her feet hurt and her head hurt and now her heart hurt.

The sun was setting on a cloudy summer day, the light further diffused by the half-lowered shades over her four precious windows. The grays and browns and slate blues of her simple decor faded into the shadows, the lines of the furniture exaggerated against the pale walls. It was a widely known but scarcely admitted fact that it is easier to cry in the dark, and she didn't have the strength to carry herself over to the light switch on the wall. The clap-on light from television she'd once deemed ridiculous now seemed like a missed opportunity.

The tears fell down her chin and she ached with helplessness. And loneliness. And regret. So many secrets and falsehoods in the nooks and crannies of her family. She always believed that time would smooth the rough edges of hurtful deeds and unspoken concerns. That they'd all come together someday for a long weekend and she'd look around the table and know that the people she belonged to cared about her and one another.

Regina cried boisterously until her nose ran. When she dragged herself up to get a tissue, she flipped on every light along the way. In her tiny bathroom, she blew her nose and washed her face. She sighed into the towel and peered into the mirror. Laser surgery had corrected her vision to better than perfect, but she'd looked so hollow-eyed without her frames, she'd had the prescription lenses replaced with clear glass and still wore them when she was around others. She leaned into the sink and squeaked out a laugh at her reflection—she was not a pretty crier, not like Justine, who could release big smiling Julia Roberts tears, or Mica, who dribbled perfect Demi Moore tears. Either one of them could turn on the waterworks and bend Cissy and John to her will. She, on the other hand, did not cry willingly, and her face revealed the squinchy, painful effort to unfortunate effect.

She pulled the combs from her hair and worked her fingers through to the ends as she walked back to the bedroom, her mind spinning in all directions. Off went the tailored suit; on went the most consoling jeans she owned and a "How to Sleep Alone" promotional nightshirt. She backtracked to the living room, scooped up her mail, and absently sorted bills while she pondered the trip back to North Carolina.

She tried to get home a couple of times a year to see her folks, although the Monroeville city limits sign never failed to put a stone in her stomach. And disturbing images in her head. She had last been home over New Year's for two days. Justine had breezed in long enough to have brunch on the arm of a smarmy guy named Fin who drank like a fish and didn't bother to hide his wedding ring. No one had mentioned Mica, who hadn't been home since she'd flown the coop with Justine's fiancé all those years ago.

Since Justine was especially close to Cissy, and Mica to John, the girls' enduring rift had put a strain on John and Cissy's relationship over the years. Indeed, Regina had seen unsettling signs in January that repercussions of the incident still hovered just beneath the conversational surface.

"Justine will never grow up until she comes to terms with the past," her father had muttered.

"At least she comes to see us occasionally, unlike our youngest daughter," her mother replied in a voice that told Regina they'd exchanged similar sentiments many times. She had bitten her own tongue to keep from reminding them that they could visit Justine or Mica anytime they chose, but to Cissy and John, roads only led *into* Monroeville.

And even though her parents seemed appreciative of her own visits, she had the distinct feeling that if they could have traded her company for either Justine's or Mica's, they would have. At the moment, however, they seemed resigned to accepting her assistance through this difficult time, whatever that entailed. But the thought that her parents' relationship might also become a casualty of her sisters' discord was almost too much to bear. Especially since the trouble between Justine and Mica had begun to snowball soon after that fateful summer day overlooking Lovers' Lane. . . .

Her appetite had fled, but she recognized that she needed something on her stomach. While a pasta entrée rotated in the microwave, she put away her single bag of groceries and stowed her dry cleaning in her bedroom closet. *Keep busy; don't think.* When the beep sounded, she peeled the layer of clear film back from her dinner and poured herself a glass of skim milk. She'd always defended her parents' decision to remain unmarried—they didn't need a marriage certificate to be committed to each other, she'd parroted over and over. If Cissy and John split up now, all those people who gave the Metcalfs sideways glances would be right.

And she really needed those people to be wrong.

She carried the steaming plastic tray to her desk and sipped the bubbles from the top of the milk. While her computer booted up, she flipped on the evening news and eyed her briefcase. She'd brought home the manuscript from the carpooling women in Atlanta to finish reading, but in light of her last-minute vacation plans, she needed to tackle a progress report and several sets of blurbs that would be due during her absence. She'd have to take the manuscript with her to North Carolina in the event she had some free time on the plane or once she arrived.

The penne marinara wasn't bad once she got past the first couple of gluey bites. After she logged onto the Internet, she checked her personal E-mail account. There was a coupon from an on-line cooking site, which she deleted. The *Flying Solo in the Kitchen* cookbook notwithstanding (three printings to date), she rarely fixed something completely from scratch, and when she did, her palate didn't command gourmet ingredients.

There was a notice of travel deals from the site she typically used to book accommodations, but unfortunately, Monroeville hadn't made the discount list this week. She sighed, clicked over, and paid a ridiculous price for a short-notice round-trip ticket. She seriously hoped someone topped her bid for the antique ivory letter opener on the Internet auction site she frequented, since her "play" money for the month had just been seriously compromised.

While it was on her mind, she clicked onto the Web site and checked the auction, which still had two days to go. She remained the high bidder, but the picture of the carved ivory letter opener cheered her. Worth more than what she'd bid, it would be a nice addition to her collection, even if she couldn't easily afford it at the moment.

Considering the past, it was an absurd collection, even macabre. But satisfying in the sense that it forced her to remember. She'd spent so many years trying to forget about what she'd seen that summer, only to realize that she felt better, less guilty, when she remembered. She and her sisters had never talked about what they'd witnessed that day, not even to voice relief when Aunt Lyla's pool man had been arrested and convicted of her murder. But she suspected they'd wrestled with their own demons after walking away from the crime scene.

Out of curiosity, she clicked on the "see similar items" button. There were new listings for antique executive desk sets, several letter holders, pencil holders, memo pad holders, and two letter openers. She scanned the first description—a common brass letter opener distinctive because it had once belonged to Frank Sinatra. Allegedly. She glanced at the seller's name to estimate the legitimacy of the claim and saw that anteek-lady23112 was rated high for customer service. Still, since Regina wasn't into celebrity memorabilia, she moved to the next listing:

RUSSIAN STERLING-AND-GOLD LETTER OPENER,
GREEN-LEAF ENAMEL INLAID HANDLE.
RUSSIAN HALLMARK AND SILVERSMITH MARKINGS.

Her heart dipped, and she bit her tongue mid-chew. In the ensuing pain, she wiped her mouth and relaxed a bit. There was more than one, of course. Still, her palms were moist as she clicked on the photo link. The grainy picture loaded quickly, innocently, and hurled her back to the scene of Lyla's murder. The silver-and-gold letter opener on a plain white background pulled forgotten details from the recesses of her brain—blood caked in the green enamel inlay, bits of flesh on the blade.

She stood and sent her chair crashing to the floor. Her mind chugged at the bizarre coincidence. Same shape, same design. She hurried to her bedroom closet and fell to her knees. The floor was stacked with storage boxes, some of which she hadn't opened since two moves ago, some not since she'd left home. She dragged out the carton marked: "Misc. Keepsakes" and tore aged tape from the box seams. The odor of dust and old paper rose from the contents. Pictures of school friends she vaguely recalled, a little jar of arrowheads she'd collected at the creek, a rabbit's foot key chain. After rummaging, her fingers closed around a small chalk box in the shape of a treasure chest.

She blew dust off the box and raised the lid to survey various pieces of childhood jewelry—the little self-piercing loops that had produced the crooked holes in her ears, a Cinderella watch that had stopped with both

of her arms pointing backward to nine, a bracelet made
from soldered pennies. She lifted the divided tray and
dumped strands of fake pearls and tarnished rings onto
the floor. Loose beads rolled in all directions. On the
bottom of the tray she'd fastened a little manila envelope with Scotch tape, now yellowed and brittle. She
pulled away the envelope, slid her nail under the tiny
flap, and withdrew a folded index card. Her parents
had maintained a simple inventory system for their antiques business.

On the card in block print was the description of an
item:

> Silver-and-gold letter opener; green enamel leaves, Russian hall-
> mark spread-wing eagle (RH1004 in hallmark registry), silver-
> smith I.J., mid–nineteenth century, bought from H.S., $50

According to the newspaper reports, Lyla's murder
weapon hadn't been found, but the coroner had con-
cluded the wounds had been made with a blunt knife.
The case against the Gilberts' pool man, ex-con Elmore
Bracken, had been made when the police discovered
that Lyla Gilbert had fired him the day before the murder and he owned numerous knives. In fact, Regina
remembered the brawny, balding man coming into the
antiques store to purchase collectible knives. Dressed
in black motorcycle gear, Bracken had always made
her nervous, so she had no trouble believing he'd stolen
the letter opener from the store's display case and used
it to stab her aunt. And she'd spent many sheet-soaked
nights imagining what would've happened if the man
had returned for the murder weapon before she'd made
her escape.

Her parents had never missed the letter opener—not
unusual considering the thousands of items in the store,
plus the fact that she'd swiped the inventory card as

soon as she'd gotten home that awful day. And hidden it in a place that Nancy Drew herself would have been hard-pressed to find.

She carried the index card back to the computer and reread the description on the screen. Was it possible that the letter opener listed on-line was the murder weapon? That someone had found it after Bracken had disposed of it? Or that Bracken had given it to someone for safekeeping? Or that someone else had happened upon the scene and taken the weapon?

Then Regina scoffed at her musings, realizing that she was letting her stress level override her good sense. The most likely story was that the item listed was simply a duplicate or a reproduction. The reserve price was steep—$750. Out of her price range, but she could at least make an inquiry for more details. The seller's nickname, a43987112, meant nothing to her. She clicked on seller history, but there was none, and, strangely, a search for other items offered by the seller produced zero hits.

She clicked on the link to E-mail the seller directly and typed in: "Can you tell me the origin of the Russian sterling letter opener, when it came into your possession, and identify the silversmith markings?"

She sent the note, then bit into her lip when she realized her buyer nickname, ReginaM, would be visible to the seller. A few seconds later she laughed at herself—in the unlikely event that a43987112 *had* stolen the letter opener from the murder scene and was now, twenty years later, trying to unload it on the 'Net, he wasn't apt to connect her indistinct nickname to Monroeville, North Carolina, and even less likely to connect her to Lyla's murder. Her emotional energy would be much better spent preparing to deal with her impending visit home. She shut down her computer.

The penne marinara had set up like red mortar. She

dropped it into the trash and grabbed a Fudgsicle from the fridge. Her briefcase called to her, so she answered with a sigh and dragged out the paperwork she didn't want to do. Her mind wandered idly to Alan Garvo, as it was prone to do during bouts of loneliness. A perfectly decent man with no visible defects. But they seemed to have run out of things to talk about after a few dates. And after they'd seen every movie released, there wasn't much left to do. In truth, most of the time they both preferred a good book to each other's company. When a book wasn't enough, they spent the night together and parted as satisfied friends until the next occasion.

She wished, however, that she missed Alan other than just the lonely times—she wanted a lover who would make her pause when she dressed in the mornings, distract her from business meetings, sidetrack her when she read on the train. But she'd come to the conclusion, at the ripe old age of thirty-four, that a woman couldn't endure that kind of attraction without losing too much of herself. If she needed proof, she had no further to look than her derailed sisters.

A news title on the television caught her attention—"Shooting at Cocoon Cosmetics in Shively, Pennsylvania." She leaned forward and nudged up the volume.

"—the woman, identified as Lisa Crane, is accused of seriously wounding her husband, Randall Crane, with a handgun, then storming the Cocoon headquarters and wounding a female executive whose name has not been released."

A picture of an attractive, smiling woman flashed on the screen. Lisa Crane didn't look like someone who would go on a shooting rampage, but then again, everyone had their breaking point.

"Police are warning residents in the Shively area that the suspect is armed and considered dangerous. If you see Lisa Crane, do not approach her. Contact the state police or the FBI at the numbers on your screen."

How bizarre. If the employee shot was an executive of Cocoon, Justine probably knew her. The sketchy details suggested some kind of a love triangle. . . .

*Justine.* Regina lunged for the phone.

# five

When you're in deep relationship hooey, DO stop digging.

Justine frowned at the emergency room nurse. "Shouldn't you keep me overnight for observation or something?"

The nurse angled her head. "I know you had a scare, Ms. Metcalf, but you're free to go after you talk to the police. Change the Band-Aid every day, and it probably won't even scar."

Justine rubbed her forearm where a chair leg had gouged her. "Okay."

"Your friend is waiting outside."

"Friend?" She didn't have any friends. Even her Secret Santa at the office had left her a gift-wrapped broom.

"A Ms. Birch, I think she said her name was."

*Oh, shit.* "Thanks." She pushed herself up and swung her legs over the side of the hospital bed. She still had no underwear. She retrieved her soiled suit jacket from a sterile-looking credenza and found her shoes. She needed a cigarette but bad.

After slipping into her jacket, she exited the emergency area through a series of ominous-looking doors. To prevent the sweet medicinal odor from turning her empty stomach, she brought her sleeve to her nose. Terri and Jim Birch sat on a bench in the hall just inside the registration desk. Terri looked as if she'd been pulled through a hedge. She saw Justine and stood, clutching Justine's Hartman briefcase and Prada bag. Jim Birch stood, too, but hung back and kept his gaze lowered as Terri stepped forward.

"Are you okay, Justine?"

She nodded. "Just a scratch. How is Bobbie?" Apparently the Barbie Doll had saved the day by tackling Lisa Crane and had been shot in the shoulder for her heroics.

"She's out of surgery. The doctors say she'll have a full recovery."

"That's good news." She'd send huge flowers, of course. And fruit. "I don't suppose you know anything about Randall Crane?"

"We heard on the television that he's still alive, but that's all I know."

That was something anyway. "And the Crane woman?"

Terri fingered her hair where the barrel of the gun had pressed into her head. "According to the news reports, she's still a fugitive."

How hard could it be to find a middle-aged woman waving a gun in Shively, Pennsylvania?

"I thought you'd need these," Terri said, extending the briefcase and purse. "And Jim drove your car over. It's in visitor parking."

Justine squelched a flicker of annoyance that someone had driven her car, even if she had slept with the man. "Thanks. Really." She glanced at her watch. Only three-thirty—unbelievable. "Under the circumstances, Terri, I think I'll take the rest of the day off."

Terri glanced at her husband. "Wait for me outside."

Jim flashed Justine a panicky look, then left. The

man wasn't nearly as good-looking in the daylight when she was stone sober. Terri Birch was a loyal, low-maintenance coworker who didn't deserve to be humiliated behind her back. For the first time in a long time, Justine experienced a stab of remorse for her behavior. *"A person can't just go through life destroying relationships and get away with it."*

"Terri, thank you for—"

"Justine, you're suspended."

She blinked. "What?"

"You're suspended without pay for three weeks. During that time a panel of managers will convene to determine if you will remain at Cocoon in the same capacity, or perhaps in another position."

She smiled in disbelief. "You can't be serious. You're blaming me for that lunatic storming in with a gun?"

Terri sighed. "Justine, you've run roughshod over your coworkers for years—"

"I get results."

"—and your indiscretions are legendary."

"My private life is no one's business."

"It is when you sleep with the husbands of your peers."

Justine balked at the hurt in Terri's eyes. Jimbo had a big guilty conscience, and a mouth to match. "Look, Terri, Jim and I were both drunk—"

"I don't know what you're talking about."

She surveyed the woman's lifted chin, the careful stare, and she understood. Terri couldn't very well contribute to her demotion for personal reasons, so she would deny knowledge of any incident between Justine and her husband.

"But I do know, Justine, that your immoral behavior led to today's episode. It's a miracle someone wasn't killed, or all of us. At the very least, it's bad publicity for Cocoon."

Justine took a deep breath. "I'd like to talk to Deidre about this." She and the CEO had never been friends, but the woman respected Justine's role in improving the company's bottom line.

Terri pressed her lips together. "Deidre wanted you fired. Legal insisted on a review period."

Okay, that hurt.

"It's a gift, Justine. Accept the suspension gracefully and reflect on . . . what you've done."

Like a child being put in time-out. Justine blinked rapidly, tightening her grip on her briefcase until her fingers ached. She refused to cry.

The door opened and two police officers walked in. The taller one she vaguely recognized, although it took a few seconds to remember that she'd had an affair with his partner last year—or maybe it was the year before. She'd met them both in a bar, and this one hadn't approved of his friend's extracurricular activities. At the moment, however, the names of both men escaped her.

The man's stiff demeanor indicated that he remembered her, too. "Ms. Justine Metcalf?"

She nodded.

"We're Officers Lando and Walker."

Ah—Lando. Broad guy, receding hairline. His friend had been a lean, dark-headed looker.

"We need to ask you some questions."

Terri nodded to the men as she left—apparently she'd already chatted with them.

Justine sat on the bench and opened her purse. "Care if I smoke, Officers?"

Lando lifted an eyebrow. "This is a hospital."

"Oh. Right." She closed her purse. "What can I do for you?"

The other guy, Walker, flipped open a notebook. "How well do you know Lisa Crane?"

"I'd never seen her until today."

"But you knew her?"

She watched Lando watch her cross her legs. "I know her husband, Randall, and he'd mentioned her name. By the way, how is Randall? She said she shot him."

Walker made a rueful noise. "Got him in the business area, if you know what I mean."

She winced.

"He's at the university hospital, in stable condition," Walker added. Then he pulled a plastic Baggie from inside his jacket pocket. "Ms. Metcalf, are these yours?"

Lando looked up at the ceiling. Justine smirked. Her panties—were they to be exhibited all over town? "Yes. May I have them back?"

"I'm afraid not," Walker said, and stuffed the evidence back into his pocket. "You were having an affair with Randall Crane?"

"I was."

"He's a partner in the firm Crane and Poplin?"

"Yes."

"Do you know how his wife found out about the affair?"

"No, I don't."

"When and where did you meet Mr. Crane to . . . you know."

"During our lunch hour at the Rosewood Hotel."

"Every time?"

"Yes. Same room, Four-ten."

"How many times did the two of you, um, rendezvous?"

"I didn't count."

"More than ten?"

"Yes."

"More than twenty?"

She sighed. "Two or three times a week, for about three months now. Do the math."

"Did you use your real names when you booked the room?"

"Randall always got the room; I don't know what names he might have used."

"When did you last meet with Mr. Crane?"

"Let's just say I put on those panties this morning."

Walker squirmed, then scribbled something on his pad. "We haven't been able to locate Mrs. Crane."

"That's what I heard."

"Do you have a friend you can stay with tonight?"

"Why? Do you think she'll come after me again?"

"It's a possibility. We have a guard posted at Mr. Crane's hospital room."

She swallowed hard. "I have a state-of-the-art security system." And she had nowhere else to stay, unless she went to a hotel.

"Still, be careful. And you might want to avoid going into your office until we have Mrs. Crane in custody."

"That won't be a problem," she murmured. "I . . . I'm taking some time off."

He nodded. "Keep us posted on your whereabouts. Meanwhile, if you see Mrs. Crane, call nine-one-one."

"Sure thing. Can I go home now?"

Lando cleared his throat. "Would you like for us to drop you off?"

She stood. "No, my car is here. Thanks anyway."

"We'll walk you out—there's quite a press mob outside."

The crush of reporters shouldn't have surprised her. In Shively, where the headlines usually consisted of art festivals and school board meetings, a workplace shooting was big honking news. Toss in a disgruntled housewife of a community pillar and heck, a local reporter might land a twenty-second spot on the network evening broadcast.

Justine held up her purse to cover her face until they were clear of the crowd, then used the panic button on her key chain to locate her custom yellow Mercedes in the parking lot. As she walked, her mind raced in conflict to the pleasant July weather, trying to process the day's events and figure out what might happen next.

"Nice ride," Lando said as she opened the door.

"Thanks." She set her briefcase on the floorboard, her purse on the seat, and nodded toward his partner, who stood on the sidewalk talking on a cell phone. "What happened to your other partner?"

"Milken?" Lando worked his mouth side to side. "He and his wife split up, then got back together and decided to move closer to her family for the sake of the kids."

"Oh. That's nice."

He shuffled his feet. "Listen, it's not every day a person gets shot at. Are you going to be okay?"

"Fine."

"A unit will patrol your street. If the Crane woman shows up, we'll know about it."

"Thanks, Lando." She slid behind the driver's wheel.

"Justine?"

"Yeah?"

Lando scratched his head. "I don't get it. You're a great-looking dame, with a good job, and you're no slouch in the smarts department. Why do you fool around with married men?"

Molten anger hemorrhaged through her at his self-righteous stance. "Don't you *dare* judge me because the men I sleep with don't have the fortitude to be faithful to their wives. They took vows, not me."

Lando stepped back, and she slammed the door. She turned over the V-8 engine and revved it twice before peeling out. Lando looked after her, shaking his head. She offered him her finger in the rearview mirror and pulled out of the parking lot onto a side street. When she stopped at an intersection, she lit a cigarette and flipped on the radio.

"—armed and dangerous. Bobbie L. Donetti, the Cocoon employee who subdued the assailant, is recovering from a gunshot wound to the shoulder. Doctors report her prognosis is good. No official word on the motivation behind the shooting, but unofficial sources say the Crane woman was distraught over an alleged affair between her husband, who was seriously wounded in an earlier incident, and another Cocoon employee. Lisa Crane was last seen wearing a brown sweater—"

She flipped off the radio and gripped the steering wheel. A cold sweat enveloped her, and her arms shook as the gravity of the situation slowly sank in. She could be dead right now. Or maimed like poor Randall. Dead over an affair whose importance to her fell somewhere between having a pleasant meal and finding the perfect shade of red lipstick.

A beeping horn sent her heart into her throat. Spent ash dropped from the tip of her cigarette and scorched a circle of precious pearl leather next to her thigh. Her gaze shot to the rearview mirror, her pulse pounding in anticipation of seeing Lisa Crane at the wheel of the car behind her. Instead it was a minivan mom, with kids hanging out the windows. The woman honked more insistently, and Justine pulled through the empty intersection, tingling with new awareness. She drove slowly, glancing back and forth, expecting to see the madwoman leap out behind every tree to gun her down.

What if Lisa Crane was lying in wait for her in her driveway? In her garage? In her bedroom? Justine had no illusions about the ability of the police to protect her.

At the next light, she snubbed out her cigarette and turned away from the expressway that led to her zip code. Twenty minutes later, the surroundings had deteriorated considerably. After two more turns her car was starting to attract attention.

She scoured the retail frontage until she spotted a faded sign for a pawnshop. Bars covered the store windows, and a dented Ford Pinto sat in the grubby parking lot. She parked carefully, then set her car alarm. A bell sounded as she entered the shop. A skinny redneck-looking guy gave her the once-over and a curt nod, then turned back to a young man looking at cameras. Justine pretended to browse the jewelry cases until the camera purchase was made and the other customer left.

"Can I help you?" the grungy guy asked. He needed dental work. Badly.

"I'm looking for a handgun."

He made a rueful noise in his throat. "Computer is down, and we can't sell handguns without a background check. System should be up and running tomorrow, though." He thumped on the jewelry case. "Meanwhile, we got some great-looking watches."

She pulled up her jacket sleeve and unhooked her own great-looking watch. "Want another? Solid gold."

His eyebrows went up.

"It's yours for a thirty-eight revolver and a box of shells. No paperwork."

He inspected the watch with a magnifying glass, then weighed it. He looked impressed but concerned. "I could lose my license."

"I can keep a secret."

He squinted. "You a cop?"

"Do I look like a damn cop?"

He looked out the window and considered her ride. "Guess not." He regarded her for a few more seconds, then set the watch aside and disappeared into a back room. Several minutes later he emerged with a zippered handgun case and a box of shells. She removed the revolver from the case, then inspected the cylinder and the sights.

"You know how to use that thing?"

"Uh-huh." She opened the ammo box and loaded six rounds in the cylinder, then clicked it home.

The man was starting to squirm. "You ain't gonna shoot me, are you?"

She eyed him. "Not unless this thing jams on me in a pinch."

He held up one hand. "Nah, it's sweet. Just came in yesterday. Not even on the books yet."

Justine returned the gun to the case and zipped it. "Good. Nice doing business with you."

"Hey, lady."

She stopped at the door and looked back.

He held up her watch. "This is a righteous piece. Is it a family heirloom?"

Justine hesitated, then decided what did it matter if one greasy guy in the world knew the truth? "No. I stole it when I was a teenager." She smiled to herself but didn't stick around for his reaction.

After locking herself in her car, she removed the weapon and placed it on the seat within reaching distance. Her jacket came off and provided adequate coverage. Anger had replaced her fear—nutty Lisa Crane wasn't going to take another undefended shot at her. She had a life to live, even if no one else thought much of what she'd done with it so far.

Despite her response to Lando, his observation about

her penchant for married men rankled her. As if to say that she had some deep-seated motivation for pursuing men who were unavailable. She scoffed—married lovers were the best gig going. Romantic getaways, expensive gifts, great sex, and she didn't even have to share her closet. She always knew where she stood with married men, what to expect. It was the women who bought into that " 'til death do us part" crap that were fooling themselves. Men were faithful only until something better—or different—came along.

Take Dean Haviland, for instance.

She smoked three cigarettes on the drive home and avoided the news, until she pulled into her gated neighborhood. Two local television vans flanked her driveway, and a knot of people had gathered in the road in front of her two-story white-brick home. She shoved on sunglasses and parted the group—she recognized one busybody as the head of the neighborhood association—with the nose of her car, then reached up to her visor console to touch the button for her garage door opener . . . except it was gone.

Her gaze flew up to the sunroof that stood open about three inches—fresh air had seemed like a good idea on the way back to the office after meeting Randall. She hadn't imagined that Lisa Crane would see the opening as an invitation to sprawl on top of her car and snatch the garage door opener.

A knock on her window startled her so badly, her hand was halfway to the concealed gun before she realized it was a reporter. She slammed the car into reverse and backed onto the street, scattering onlookers. As she exited the upper-class neighborhood, she called the police department and asked for Lando. After an eternity, the phone clicked.

"Lando here."

"This is Justine Metcalf. I just arrived home and

realized that my garage door opener is missing from my car."

"You think that Lisa Crane took it?"

"Yes. We have gated security to keep out cars, but she could walk into the neighborhood and get into my house with the garage door opener—I don't lock the door leading in from the garage."

"What about that state-of-the-art security system?"

She sighed. "I didn't set it this morning."

"Ah. Walker and I'll come to check out the house. Will you be there?"

"No, I'm going to a hotel. Then I think I'll head to my parents' for a few days."

"Where's that?"

"Monroeville, North Carolina." She gave him her cell phone number and directions to override the garage door opener.

"I'll let you know what we find."

She disconnected the call with shaking hands, then drove away from her neighborhood, east toward the coast. Dusk was falling; tiny bugs collected on her windshield. The decision to visit her folks had been spontaneous, but somehow it felt right. A few do-nothing days to hide out and make her parents happy at the same time—Cissy was always badgering her about coming to visit. Alone. She'd drive down tomorrow and surprise them, like a good daughter. Get some sun. Fresh air. Besides, Lisa Crane would never find her in Monroeville.

The day's events descended on her and she relived the humiliating incident in the staff meeting in excruciating detail. For years they'd be talking around the watercooler about Justine Metcalf, Miss Unshakable, lifting her skirt at gunpoint. She ground her teeth at the thought of people laughing at her behind her back—she simply had to return to Cocoon and redeem herself, redeem her reputation. Helplessness and rage took hold of her—damn Lisa Crane for destroying her life.

As her anger escalated, so did the need for release. Her throat constricted and her mouth watered for the bitter taste for which she'd acquired an affinity. She wiped her stinging eyes and tried to concentrate on the road. First things first—find a grocery store. A few minutes later, she pulled into a parking lot and gathered herself enough to go in.

"May I help you?" a smocked young woman asked.

"Spices?"

"Aisle Seven."

"And tea?"

"Aisle Eight."

She found the tea first and selected bags for a lemon variety. By the time she reached the spice aisle, she was sweating profusely. She scanned the racks and experienced a rush of relief at the plentiful supply of nutmeg—as if sometime since her last purchase, everyone else in the country had discovered her secret. The store carried her favorite brand and, thinking ahead to her trip to North Carolina, she selected two tins.

To cast off any suspicion at the checkout counter, she selected a box of sugar cubes and, while she waited in the express line, a pack of gum. The checker gave her a curious glance, but Justine realized that she probably looked like hell and wondered if there was a chance that her picture was being shown on television by now. She averted her glance, paid with cash, then drove until she came to a hotel that looked safe.

It was nearly eight, and darkness had overcome Shively. The hotel sign announced a vacancy but no valet parking, so she parked the car herself. A light blinked on in the gauge panel—*low fuel*. She smacked the steering wheel. If a damn cow could have four stomachs, why couldn't luxury cars have four gas tanks? She seemed to forever ride on empty.

The triviality was the final straw, bringing tears to her eyes. She gave in to the tears for a full minute, gulping air and making humiliating little noises. Then she dabbed her eyes, blew her nose, and shoved the gun into her purse. At least she'd have enough toiletries and makeup to get by, she thought as she walked around to the trunk to retrieve her gym bag.

The night breeze whipped around her, delivering the sultry city scent of cooling asphalt and restaurant exhaust. She swept a hank of wayward hair behind her ear and the movement sent a pain through her gouged arm. She winced, suddenly beset by the seriousness, the isolation, of her predicament Shively wasn't a big city, but she'd never felt as completely alone as she did at this moment, standing in a half-empty parking lot, listening to the wind whistling through her half-empty life. And she still wasn't wearing underwear.

Just as she aimed the keyless remote at the trunk, a horrific thought hit her. What if Lisa Crane was lying inside the trunk, poised with her gun, just waiting for Justine to open the lid? It was just the kind of thing the woman might do. Justine looked all around the deserted parking lot, then pulled the revolver from her purse. With heart thrashing in her chest, she aimed the remote with her left hand, the revolver with her right, and took a deep breath.

With the press of a button, the trunk sprang open, and just as she feared, its contents came alive. Justine squeezed the trigger. The reverb stole her hearing, but she felt her lungs pinch with her gasp. Two seconds later she realized that she'd put one hell of a hole in her fluttering dry-cleaning bag and the suit underneath.

"Dammit," she muttered. "Two suits ruined in one day."

Too late, she realized she might have put a hole in

her gas tank, too. But closer inspection showed the bullet had embedded in one of the bags of rock salt that she, like many Pennsylvanians, stocked for icy traveling emergencies. What a mess. She shoved the gun into her purse, hid her wounded suit, and yanked out her gym bag just as a side door opened and a security guard came running out.

"What was that?"

"Sorry," she said, slamming the trunk lid. "My car backfired—watery gas does it every time."

He bought the story, even carried her gym bag into the hotel lobby. She asked for a nonsmoking room and paid cash in advance to avoid the risk of name recognition, but the desk clerk was too absorbed in the story of fugitive Lisa Crane playing on the television behind the counter to notice anything going on right in front of her.

The room was unremarkable but smelled clean. She fastened every locking device on the door, then stepped under the showerhead and scrubbed her face and body. From the gym bag she pulled clean underwear—at last—and a T-shirt.

Her cell phone bleeped. The tiny screen revealed that the call had originated from the police department. "Hello?"

"Lando here. We checked out the house and the surrounding area, but we didn't find anything. If you want me to set the alarm, I need your code."

She gave it to him.

"Did you get settled?"

"Yes."

"Listen, I want to apologize for what I said earlier—who you spend time with is none of my business."

"I know."

"Well, good night then. We'll be in touch."

She disconnected the call and stared at the phone

for a few seconds, wondering if she should call Regina. At times like these, she missed her sisters most—too bad that Mica had turned out to be such a traitor, and Regina, such a prude. Oh, Regina meant well, but she took ownership of everything wrong in the lives of people around her and tried to mend them. And right now, a lecture from her little sister didn't rank high on her list. She set down the phone and gave her hair a light combing, then filled a coffee mug with the hottest water the bathroom tap would serve up.

In the bedroom, she lowered lights and mounded pillows. Into the lemon tea went a carefully measured amount of nutmeg according to her mental chart, and a single sugar cube. While she stirred, she estimated that the home-brewed hallucinogen would flood her system within twenty minutes since her stomach was virtually empty.

Students, hippies, and prisoners had been getting high on nutmeg for years because it was cheap and accessible. As a teenager, she'd simply liked the idea of being able to zone out right under her parents' noses on something from the kitchen pantry.

Justine drank the mug of bitter tea without stopping, then reclined on the pillows. She typically used this time to help funnel her impending trip. Tonight, she fell back on a favorite—killing Dean Haviland, if for no reason other than to deny her spoiled little sister something for once in her charmed life. Lisa Crane's words came back to her.

"A person can't just go through life destroying relationships and get away with it."

Unless you were Mica.

# six

DON'T underestimate the extent to which men underestimate women.

Mica flipped through the pages in a beauty magazine and was instantly bored. She knew some of the divas in the ads and no one looked that good in person except Stephanie Seymour.

She tossed the magazine aside, feeling itchy and leaky and miserable after being lubed and poked and prodded in one test after another. The doctor had counted her moles, for God's sake. Mica stood and approached the receptionist. "Dr. Forsythe wanted to see me before I left, but I can't stay much longer."

The woman turned to a nurse, who checked something on the computer. "Your lab results just came in a few minutes ago. Dr. Forsythe should be calling you back soon. Can I get you a snack? A piece of fruit, maybe?"

"I don't think—"

"You really should have something to eat, Ms. Metcalf."

Mica squinted at the nurse's earnest expression. "Okay."

A red apple materialized, and she returned to the chair she'd abandoned feeling bribed. She rubbed the apple on her jeans leg, then took a bite, mostly to stay awake. Being kept waiting was not a good sign. The doctor assured her they were conducting standard tests to get a handle on her general health, but she suspected a lecture awaited her. In truth, though, she was ready to get her strength back and to feel good again.

In addition to the malaise that pulled at her muscles, disappointment wallowed in her stomach at the fact that after all these years, she'd finally gotten up the nerve to call Justine, only to be informed that the Cocoon office had closed early. She'd called directory assistance for Justine's home number, but it was unlisted. She could always get the information from Regina, but she really didn't want to get her involved—or to get Regina's hopes up, for that matter, that a reconciliation was in the works. Poor Regina took everything to heart. Granted, it was sad that she and her sisters hadn't shared the milestones in one another's lives like they'd always assumed they would . . . although admittedly, Justine's marriage milestone hadn't quite turned out as everyone had imagined.

The night before the wedding, Mica had resigned herself to the idea of her sister marrying the man whom she loved. After all, Justine had seen him first, had staked her claim, and Dean publicly acknowledged Justine as his girl. Only Mica knew that Dean had taken her virginity when she was seventeen while Justine worked nights doing cosmetology at Williams's Funeral Home. Only Mica knew that he continued to seek her out whenever Justine was occupied. Only Mica knew that she loved her sister's fiancé to utter distraction. After the wedding rehearsal, she'd happened upon Dean and he'd admitted that he didn't want to spend the rest of his life with Justine in Monroeville. Mica had already made plans to go to LA to break into modeling and, she hoped, acting. He said LA sounded good to him.

They'd left a note and departed before dawn, and Mica did harbor guilt over not breaking the news to Justine face-to-face. But Justine had a fiery temper and neither Mica nor Dean wanted a scene. She justified her actions by telling herself that she'd saved Justine the inevitable heartbreak of discovering years down the road that her husband didn't love her. She had imagined that, like every other time they'd disagreed, Justine would eventually come around and they'd be friends again. Twelve years later, she was beginning to realize it was up to her to extend an olive branch. Maybe she could make Justine understand that she and Dean hadn't meant to hurt her, that they truly loved each other.

Tomorrow, she resolved with a sigh. Tomorrow when she felt better she'd take the first step toward repairing her relationship with Justine, and she'd work things out with Dean—maybe he could watch her shoots from a screening room. Mica smiled, happier than she'd been in a long while. Everett was right: she just needed some downtime, a little vacation.

Back east? She pursed her mouth and tried the idea on for size. Go see her folks first, then her sisters. Maybe she and Regina could meet and visit Justine together. Yes . . . it could work. Soon they'd be laughing like old times.

She laid her head back and cheerfully munched the apple. Her gaze strayed to a chubby baby on the front of a parenting magazine. She smiled and reached for the issue, overcome by curiosity for an alien world. She'd always wanted a baby, but Dean . . .

Mica stopped and put her hand on her stomach.

Could it be? Headaches, nausea, fatigue . . . could she be *pregnant*? Her mind raced as fast as her heart as she tried to think back to her last cycle . . . a swim party at their house . . . two months ago? Yes! She covered her mouth and laughed into her hand. Other patients glanced up from their magazines.

Omigod, she was going to have a *baby*. A little *person*. Wouldn't Dean be surprised? And her mother? And her *sisters*—oh, Justine would melt like ice cream when Mica put her niece or nephew in her arms.

"Ms. Metcalf?"

She looked up to see the nurse standing in the doorway.

"Dr. Forsythe will see you now."

With a burst of energy, Mica sprang up and followed the nurse to the doctor's office. She was grinning when she sat down in front of Dr. Forsythe's desk.

"You look chipper," Dr. Sandra Forsythe observed with a little smile. She nodded for the nurse to close the door as she left.

"That's because I just figured out why I've been feeling so draggy lately."

"Oh? And you're happy about it?"

Mica laughed. "Of course. I can't wait to tell Dean— he's my boyfriend. He'll be so pleased!"

Dr. Forsythe pulled off her glasses and clasped her hands in front of her. "Ms. Metcalf, I believe you're confused."

"Confused? I'm pregnant, aren't I?"

The doctor pressed her lips together. "No, you're not pregnant."

Mica blinked back burgeoning tears. "Are you sure? I haven't had a period, and I've been nauseous, and I go to the bathroom every fifteen minutes."

"And it burns when you urinate?"

Mica shrugged. "Sometimes. But I'm prone to urinary tract infections."

Dr. Forsythe sighed. "May I call you Mica?"

She nodded.

"Mica, for starters, your cycle is intermittent because you're malnourished. I'm putting you on a well-balanced diet."

"A diet?"

"The kind where you eat regularly and take in healthy fluids. You need oils and fats in your diet. Stay away from alcohol, and cut back on your caffeine."

"But I—"

"Mica, if you don't start eating correctly, your health will continue to deteriorate and your hair will continue to fall out."

She averted her gaze. She hadn't mentioned the hair loss; was it that noticeable?

"You're also anemic, and your bone density test shows that your bones are more brittle than is normal for your age."

"What does that mean?"

"The anemia is contributing to your fatigue, and the fact that your bones are brittle means that they will fracture and break more easily than they should." Dr. Forsythe raised an eyebrow. "Which makes living with an abusive boyfriend even more dangerous."

"I fell," Mica choked out. "Dean isn't abusive—he loves me."

The doctor nodded calmly, as if she didn't believe her. "Also, you don't have a urinary tract infection. You have gonorrhea."

She tried to laugh, but no sound came out of her throat. She swallowed. "That's . . . impossible. I've only had one sex partner my entire life."

"And what about your boyfriend's sex partners?"

"He hasn't . . ." Her words trailed off as the implication hit her. Of course he had. Dean had given her the clap. His declaration that he'd always been faithful to their bed . . . a lie. The mysterious phone calls over the last couple of months . . . his unaccounted absences . . . his increased irritability with her. The lying, cheating bastard.

"I'm going to kill him," Mica murmured.

"I know this is a bit of a shock," Dr. Forsythe said in a soothing voice. "But gonorrhea is curable with antibiotics."

Mica listened as the doctor droned on about scripts and dosage and latex condoms while her heart quietly caved in. *I gave up my family, my sisters, for this?* A few minutes ago she was contemplating motherhood and having a child with the man she loved, a child who would help heal her divided family. Now she was contemplating murder. Her hand tightened on the shoulder bag that held the rodent-killing gun.

"Mica?"

She blinked and shot back to the present. "Yes?"

The woman gave her a kind smile. "There's a shelter in Santa Monica. You could go there to recuperate in private. It's a secure location, and you would be guaranteed confidentiality."

"A shelter?" Mica stood. "You mean a clinic, don't you?"

Dr. Forsythe balked. "They do offer round-the-clock medical care."

"No thanks. I have somewhere to go."

"Is it a safe place?"

"Yes."

"And will you have a support group?"

She hesitated. "I hope so."

# seven

DON'T trust a man whose most long-term relationship is with his
dog.

Regina took a deep breath as she rounded the curve
and the little green-and-white sign came into view.
MONROEVILLE, NORTH CAROLINA, POPULATION 5,400.
Someone had pasted a "Monroeville Mudcats" bumper
sticker at the bottom of the sign, and the image of a
yellow Volkswagen Rabbit disappearing from Lovers'
Lane flitted through her mind. The parking teenagers
Pete Shadowen and Tobi Evans never knew how close
they'd come to an encounter with a murderer that day.

Regina and Pete had actually dated for a few months
during her sophomore and his senior year. The previous
summer she had finally sprouted breasts—respectable
little peaches—plus hips, and to her astonishment, Pete
had noticed. He was handsome and popular and knew
how to kiss her without mashing her glasses against
her face. After the Homecoming dance, she had let him
get to second base (a hand up her shirt), but when he
rounded for third (a hand down her skirt), she'd balked.
And when he'd suggested that they park at Lovers'
Lane, she'd refused rather hysterically. By the end of the
semester, Pete had left her for greener fields, but she

hadn't minded so much. In fact, she often wondered if the reason she hadn't been able to conjure up enthusiasm for the great Pete Shadowen was because she indirectly associated him with the events of that traumatic day.

Regina shivered, hoping to shake off some of the gloomy thoughts of her aunt's untimely demise. She adjusted the rearview mirror to survey her appearance. Between the nonsense with the letter opener on the online auction, her concern over Justine, who had yet to return her call, and her parents' alleged breakup, she figured she'd gotten about three hours of sleep last night. And the shadowy crescents under her eyes certainly told the tale. She looked forward to falling asleep on the soft mattress of the four-poster canopy bed in her old room and pushed away the niggling thought that this could be the last time she'd stay in her childhood home.

Monroeville was a small town that behaved largely, situated close enough to Asheville to snag wayward tourists but far enough away from anywhere to maintain its quaint veneer. Drivers lured off Interstate 40 with tantalizing billboards promising antiques, country cookin', and general stores would first see the WMON-EZ Listening Radio Tower, the Burl County Community College Satellite Classroom Building, the Licked Skillet restaurant, and the People's Bank of Monroeville. After that little stretch of prosperity, things went downhill considerably.

Not much had changed over the years except the size of the trees and the names of the businesses. Spindley's Jewelry Repair had transformed into Harper's Jewelry Repair, which had transformed into Logan's Jewelry Repair, which had transformed into the current and more courageous Miller's Jewelry and Clock Repair. The town council had never met a zoning ordinance that couldn't be overridden, so authentic Victorian and Georgian residences rubbed gutters with squatty cinderblock buildings housing hair salons and video arcades.

Regina pulled into the Grab 'N Go to stretch her legs, clear the windshield of ill-fated insects, and buy a bottle of water. She glanced at customers and clerks, looking for a familiar face, or a hint of recognition— classmates, customers of the shop, a friend of the family? Nada. Her two best friends from high school, Mary Stamper and Gina Gonower, lived in North Dakota and Florida, respectively, and she seriously doubted if anyone else in the school would remember her, unless it was in reference to Justine or Mica: *"Regina . . . wasn't she the plain Metcalf sister?"*

She did recognize one face—that of Mrs. Woods, the fat checker whom Justine had told them she'd seen romping at Lovers' Lane . . . with *two* men. Regina understood the whole ménage à trois thing more now than she had twenty years ago, but she still couldn't get her mind around Mrs. Woods, now white-haired and bigger than ever, doing the nasty in a car in the woods.

"Dollar forty-nine," Mrs. Woods said when Regina held up the bottle of water.

Regina counted out the money.

"You're one of the Metcalf girls, aren't you?"

She smiled. "Yes. Regina."

"Home for a visit?"

"Yes. For a few days."

Mrs. Woods frowned. "I've heard all about your sisters, but where did you wind up?"

"Um, Boston."

"Boston?"

"Massachusetts."

"What's in Boston?"

"I edit books."

"Oh. Well, you have a jim-dandy time while you're in town."

Regina started to step away; then a small headline in the weekly newspaper stand caught her eye.

### ON ANNIVERSARY OF GILBERT MURDER, BRACKEN GRANTED HEARING

Her breath caught. "I'll take one of these, too."

Mrs. Wood frowned at the last-minute purchase but took her money. "Catching up on the local news?"

"Uh-huh."

The woman snorted. "Ain't nothing happened around here in twenty years."

Regina manufactured a shaky smile for the round-faced woman, struck by the phenomenon of six degrees of separation that bound strangers to random people and places and incidents. "Thank you."

She shoved the newspaper into her shoulder bag and walked out into the bright sun. The parking lot was busy, full of backslapping friends and tailgaters kicked back drinking pop. The happy summer day made her worries and musings seem downright paranoid. Laughing at herself, she climbed into the car and rolled down the windows to enjoy fresh country air. A few minutes later she stopped at one of the three celebrated stoplights in town and learned, compliments of a huge red, white, and blue banner over the street, that she had arrived in time for Monroeville Heritage Days, a Festival of History and Tradition, exclamation mark, exclamation mark.

Indeed, the sidewalks were more crowded than she'd expected, even for late Friday afternoon. Bake sales abounded and a giant Uncle Sam hobbled around on stilts, waving. The water in the fountain at the entrance to the Lyla A. Gilbert City Park had been dyed a dubious pink for the occasion, and the corkscrew metal slides were festooned with streamers and balloons. Lyla would be proud of the showy tribute Uncle Lawrence had built after her death, despite the fact that her aversion to children had been infamous. Regina and her sisters knew that firsthand.

Lyla and Justine especially grated on each other. Regina remembered an incident when an expensive vase Lyla had brought into the store to sell had wound up on the floor in pieces. Each woman had accused the other of dropping it. Justine, who engaged in constant competition for her father's attention, had been wounded when John had taken Lyla's side. Justine had miserably worked off the price of that vase all summer . . . until Lyla's murder.

Steeped in bittersweet recollections, Regina steered through Main Street, hung left at the tire store, and drove past the gated entrance to the Williams Rock Quarry, which provided the most substantial source of employment to the residents of Monroeville, next to tourism. Over time, Tate Williams had expanded the quarry spin-off products to include grave headstones and yard ornaments. The fact that Tate Williams also owned a funeral home and served as the county coroner made the headstone business a lucrative venture. And there wasn't enough rock dust in all of North Carolina to make enough garden gnomes to meet the regional demand.

She made two more turns and drove a little over a mile to a big red barnlike structure on the right crowned with a half-dozen windmills and a gigantic sign that read: M&G ANTIQUITIES, STOP HERE FOR GOOD DEAL$. Her heart kicked up a flurry of emotion at the sight of the lopsided sign that her mother had always hated and her father had always meant to fix. She pulled into the paved parking lot that could hold up to about fifty vehicles, although she personally had never seen more than twenty-five or so there at a time. It was a few minutes past closing time and the only other vehicle in sight was an unfamiliar blue extended van parked near the rear delivery door, no doubt her father's latest acquisition. Her spirits ratcheted up a notch—she'd hoped to get a chance to talk to him alone before she drove on to the house to face Cissy.

She parked next to the van and stepped out to pull her cotton pants and summer sweater away from her sticky skin. Surveying her surroundings, she was bombarded by so many impressions, she could scarcely process the images. Riding her bike to the shop, planting flowers in the metal boxes out front, getting ice-cold RC Cola out of the pop machine.

The antiques store sat back off the road about fifty feet with a beautifully wooded backdrop. The former tobacco barn had been reinforced and added to over the years as her parents accumulated inventory faster than they could sell it. No one ever accused John and Cissy of operating a tight business, but the couple had managed to generate a good living and raise three children.

The back door was unlocked, so she stepped inside the massive cluttered storeroom to the tune of a loud chime. She blinked against the relative darkness after the bright sunshine. "Dad? Dad, it's me, Regina."

She headed toward the showrooms, inhaling the ever-present scent of old books and furniture wax. The unending assortment of fascinating objects was always different but somehow the same, anchored by one-of-a-kind finds that would likely never leave the premises, such as the eight-foot stuffed giraffe and the six-foot neon sign blazing DANCES FOR 10 CENTS that had leaned against the same wall for as far back as her memory stretched.

She walked through the main showroom to the bottom

of the stairs leading to the apartment. "Dad? Are you up there?"

No answer, but he was probably on the phone or in the bathroom. He was still here somewhere, because at least two radios were tuned to the blues station that he liked. John Lee Hooker was crooning about one bourbon, one scotch, and one beer. She hummed along and meandered over to the display cabinets next to the ancient cash register, tracing her finger over the fine scratches accumulated over decades of leaning and looking. Inside were trays and trays of sparkling rings and watches and necklaces and pins, cuff links and buttons and eyeglasses and thimbles.

She smiled at a pair of retro pink cat-style eyeglasses and thought it would be fun to add them to her accessory drawer. She walked behind the counter, removed her own dark-frame glasses, and set them on the cabinet. Then, using both hands, she tilted the locked latch and gave it a quick jerk to the right. As it had done many times before, the latch popped open. She carefully slid the heavy glass door to the left on its rusty track and reached inside.

A big hand curled around her forearm. "Stop right there."

She gasped and yanked back, but the owner of the hand maintained his hold. Her first thought that her father had snuck up on her was quickly replaced with the two realizations: she didn't know this big, sandy-haired stranger, and someone had let in a barking dog. She screamed and wrenched loose, then grabbed the handiest weapon available—an old baseball bat leaning against the wall. She assumed a swinging position, squaring herself in the space between the man and his barking black dog. "Stay back!"

The man snapped his fingers and the dog fell silent, then padded over to sit at his master's feet. The man scrutinized her stance. "I wouldn't do that if I were you.

DiMaggio used that bat to hit a home run in the '41 All-Star Game."

She narrowed her eyes. "DiMaggio didn't hit a home run in the '41 All-Star game. Who the hell are you and what are you doing here?"

He crossed his arms over a B. B. King Blues Fest T-shirt. "I might ask you the same question."

"Except I asked you first."

"But I didn't just break into a locked jewelry case."

"I *didn't* break in."

His eyebrows shot up.

She swallowed. "I mean . . . I know the trick to get in."

"You seem to know your way around this place."

"This *place* belongs to my parents."

"Oh, you're the daughter from Boston. I wasn't expecting you so soon."

She lowered the bat to her shoulder, still wary. "Do I know you?"

"No. I'm the appraiser. The bank sent me, and over the last couple of days I've become acquainted with your parents." He scratched his temple. "Interesting pair."

His unsolicited observation rankled her. "What bank sent you to do what?"

He angled his head. "You don't know what's going on, do you?"

"Evidently not."

"You should talk to your folks."

Regina closed her eyes and counted to three. "That's precisely why I'm here. Where's my father?"

The man studied her in a way that said he didn't trust her. "Running an errand. He should be back any time now." He stepped forward and extended his hand. "Mitchell Cooke."

She stared at his big fingers until she started to feel silly, then lowered the bat and shook his hand. "Regina Metcalf."

"Metcalf. Not married, huh?"

She dropped his hand, seized by an irrational urge to whack him after all. "No. And with your charm, I assume you aren't, either." She bit her tongue, instantly regretting the childish words.

He seemed amused. "No. Maybe because I've never met a girl who knows her baseball."

Regina jumped when she felt a decided push at her crotch. The dog apparently had taken their touching as a sign that he, too, could offer a greeting. She pursed her mouth. "I take it this is your dog?"

"Yeah. Sam's a real lady-killer."

She nudged the dog's muzzle from between her legs. "I'm more of a cat person myself."

The man lowered his hand and Sam scampered back. "Guess we're both out of luck, old boy."

He was tall, with wide shoulders and long arms, and his jeans hung from lean hips. Mitchell Cooke seemed comfortable with his big self. An ex-athlete? Not a baseball player, she hoped, considering his serious trivia gaffe. Regina stalked back to the cabinet and refastened the latch. "I'm leaving—if my father returns, please tell him I'll see him at home."

"Will do. I guess I'll see you around."

"I don't see why that would be necessary. Good-bye, Mr. Cooke."

She retraced her steps, tingling over the awkward encounter. An appraiser from the bank? Surely her parents hadn't already put things in motion for an auction. She burst out of the back door and struggled to control her emotions as she climbed behind the wheel of her rental car. She needed sleep, she reminded herself. And food. *And a sane, intact family.*

The house she'd grown up in was on the same piece of land as the antiques business, and accessible from the store on foot by a winding path through thick masses of trees, but accessible by car only by driving another half-mile, then turning left to double back into the heart of the property. The sprawling blue Victorian hadn't changed much in her lifetime. Since they were little girls, they had called it the Doll because the gables and gingerbread trim resembled a hat; and the wraparound porch, a ruffled skirt. John and Cissy had meticulously restored and maintained the bones of the house but tended to the acres of exterior painted surfaces only on an as-needed basis. As a result, some section of the three-story gal was always in need of a fresh coat of custom Sherwin-Williams.

Referring to the bramble that encased the house as "landscaping" required a kind countenance—thank goodness the Metcalfs had never had to contend with neighbors who were particular about adjacent lawns. Oak and weeping willow trees sprawled unfettered. The grass in the yard was of indistinguishable lineage, shin-high, and studded with white clumps of clover that bowed from the weight of hungry bees. The ivy that had provided gentle ground cover for the mulch beds when she was a girl had evolved into tough, waxy Jurassic foliage. Blue and purple hydrangeas had managed to stay one step in front of the choking vine, producing mophead blooms as large as basketballs. Everything else had apparently succumbed, including Regina's mother, who appeared to have resorted to adding color to her yard with a menagerie of concrete animals—pink bunnies, green turtles, yellow deer. But Cissy hadn't stopped with animals—Snow White and all the dwarfs lined the sidewalk leading to the stone steps that carried Regina up to the front door. Noah's Ark took over at the porch.

Before Regina could take it all in, the front door swung open and Cissy emerged, dressed in cut-off jean shorts and a T-shirt. No bra. Her gray-streaked red hair was bundled under a blue bandanna scarf, and she was barefoot. "Regina! Oh, I'm so pleased you're home!"

Regina noticed the wineglass in her mother's hand but smiled her best-daughter smile before they embraced. "It's good to see you, Mom."

She stroked Regina's shoulder and squinted. "You look tired, darling."

"I *am* tired."

"You've finally stopped wearing your glasses, I see."

Her hand flew to her temple. "No, I . . . stopped at the store first and I must have left them there." Darn it. That man had truly seen her at her worst.

"Oh. And did you see your father?" Cissy spoke carefully, then drained her glass.

"No. But a man was there—an appraiser?"

Cissy frowned. "That would be Mitchell Cooke. I don't trust him."

"Then why is he at the shop by himself? And why is he here in the first place?"

Cissy puffed out her cheeks. "Let's get out of this heat."

Regina dutifully followed her inside the cool, cavernous house. They had never installed central air, but the hum of fans in every room was comfortably familiar, as were other things—same supremely cluttered interior, same squeaks in the wood floors, same stale scent that set up in a home when activity ceased. How many months, years, since that cushion had been plumped? That book opened? That rug walked upon?

They moved through the entryway and the formal living room, down a hall to the most modern room in the house, the kitchen, which was an eclectic mix of 1870s furniture and 1970s Formica. Regina sank into a padded chair, wondering about the equivalent of the breakfast bar in the Victorian Age. Every serious talk she'd ever had with her mother had occurred in this kitchen, with her mother standing up on the sink side and she seated on the other. Once again they assumed the position.

"Lemonade?" Cissy asked.

"Sounds good." Regina could have gotten it herself, but she knew her mother needed to do something with her hands. At fifty-seven, Cissy was still a striking woman, with smooth, moist skin and acute green eyes. But since their last visit, Cissy's shoulders seemed to have given in to gravity.

When the lemonade was handed over, Regina sipped. "So what's going on?"

Cissy sighed. "Your father and I are deeply in debt."

The lemonade went down hard. "What? How?"

"We made some bad investments, and I suppose we've neglected the business. The bank agreed to give us thirty days to liquidate, and they arranged for Mr. Cooke to appraise everything for auction." Cissy bit into her lip. "The store inventory has to go, of course . . . and everything in this house. And maybe the house itself."

Regina reached for her mother's hand. "Is this why you and Dad are splitting up?"

Cissy shook her head. "No. I didn't even know how bad our finances were until I told your father I wanted to end our relationship. He knew I'd find out, so he had to tell me everything." A dry laugh escaped her. "Believe me, it was a double betrayal to find out that not only will I be starting over, but I'll be starting over with nothing."

"A *double* betrayal?"

Cissy averted her eyes. "Some things you don't need to know, sweetheart. Let's just leave it at that."

But it was clear from Cissy's expression that John had had an affair. Regina's mind violently rejected the idea, unable to reconcile her shy, somewhat befuddled father with infidelity. In fact, Cissy had always been the flamboyant flower and John seemingly grateful that she let him hang around. One of Regina's earliest memories was the knowledge that her parents were devoted to each other . . . to the exclusion of their daughters.

"How can I help?" Regina asked in a choked voice.

Cissy smiled. "There's my girl. I need for you to help Mr. Cooke."

"Huh?"

"You know our filing system, and with your help, the appraisals will go twice as fast."

"But—"

"And that will allow me to tackle this behemoth of a house."

"But—"

"And you can keep an eye on him and let us know if anything seems out of kilter."

"Mom, I met the man, and I didn't particularly care for his company."

Cissy laughed. "You don't have to marry him—just watch him."

Regina searched for a straw to grasp. "But why can't Dad help him?"

Cissy smiled sadly. "Your father is drinking . . . a lot. I'm afraid he's rather undependable these days. To be honest, I'd feel better knowing you were at the shop keeping an eye on him, too."

And how could she possibly argue with that?

Her mother's head pivoted toward the window. "I hear a car. Maybe that's your father now."

Regina was closer, so she pushed herself up to look—and to check that she could still make her limbs move. She didn't think she could take any more shocks today. She parted the curtains and watched as a yellow Mercedes came to a halt next to her pathetic little rental. She inhaled sharply when the realization hit her.

"It's Justine," she murmured. "And she's alone."

Cissy hurried to the window. "What's Justine doing here? Did you tell her about me and your dad?"

"No. In fact, I couldn't reach her on the phone. You didn't tell her?"

"No, I only left a message for her to call me."

"Maybe Mica told her?"

"Even if they were on speaking terms, Mica doesn't know, either—unless you told her."

"No, she's been hard to track down lately, too."

"Well," Cissy said cheerfully, hugging Regina's shoulder. "Maybe Justine had a feeling that we needed her."

Regina nodded, but *she* had a feeling that Justine's sudden appearance was more about needing something for herself.

# eight

**DON'T let bygones be bygones, by golly.**

Regina studied Justine as she and Cissy hugged and Justine gushed that—surprise—she'd just decided to drive down for a few days. Something was wrong, all right. Oh, sure, Justine's immaculate makeup, brilliant red hair, and impeccable clothes were as glamorous as always, but her eyes were beyond bloodshot and her perfect nails were gnawed down to the quicks. Regina suggested that she and Justine retrieve their luggage, and the second the door closed behind them, she said, "Okay, what gives?"

Justine had the nerve to give her an innocent look. "I don't know what you mean."

Regina crossed her arms. "I mean it's quite a coincidence that you show up here, unannounced, the day after a shoot-out at your company's headquarters."

"You know about that?"

"Just enough to think you might be involved. Didn't you get my messages? I called you at home three times last night and this morning. And when I called your office, all I got was your voice mail."

"Sorry—I didn't know you'd called. I spent the night in a hotel."

"What the hell happened?"

Justine sighed. "The wife of some guy I was seeing went off the deep end."

Regina nodded. "Wife? The *wife* of a guy you're seeing?"

"Oh, God, don't start with the lecture—I knew this was how you'd react." Justine walked down the steps, every footfall punctuated with attitude.

Regina took a deep breath and followed her. "Okay, I'm sorry, but I've been worried about you. Was anyone injured?"

"The woman shot her husband earlier, and he's still in pretty bad shape. And a lady I worked with was wounded, but she's going to be fine."

"This man . . . was he someone special to you?"

Justine looked rueful. "No. He reminded me of . . . someone."

Regina knew that look. "Dean?"

Justine scoffed and thumbed away a tear. "Ain't that a kick in the pants? The bastard is still screwing up my life."

Regina had her own ideas of who was screwing up Justine's life, but Justine didn't seem to be in a mood for self-analysis. "I heard on the news that the shooter was a fugitive—did they catch her?"

"No. Which is why I'm here."

"You came to Mom and Dad's to hide out from a killer?"

"She'll never find me here," Justine snapped. "The woman's a lunatic; they probably have her in custody by now." She stopped. "Hey, wait a minute—why are *you* here?"

"Mom and Dad are splitting up."

Justine rolled her eyes. "Again?"

"No, this time it's for real. Mom didn't come out and say it, but I think Dad had an affair."

"No way."

"That's what I said, but she swears that their relationship is over."

"There's no divorce to file, so what's all the fuss?"

Regina frowned. "There's still a matter of property settlement, and apparently, they're broke. Everything at the shop and in the house is going to have to be auctioned off."

Justine blinked. "Dibs on the Tiffany silver candelabra."

"Is that all you can think about?"

"Well, Jesus Christ, if they're splitting up, they're splitting up. Don't look so wounded, Sis—what did you think, that after all these years they were going to get married?"

She hated herself for having a telltale face.

Justine's eyes bugged. "I don't believe it—you actually thought that someday they'd get married?" She laughed. "Don't you get it? Marriage isn't for the Metcalfs. Look at Mom and Dad. Look at me. Look at you." She snorted. "And look at our darling baby sister. Nary a marriage among us."

"But that's better than a bunch of divorces."

"Oh, come on, Sis—if you tell someone you're divorced, they don't even blink, but tell them you've never been married and they wonder what's wrong with you."

It was true, Regina conceded. Divorced people at least exuded the *potential* of being able to make a commitment.

Justine pulled a brand-new suitcase from her trunk. "So, did you come down to counsel the folks with one of your self-help books—*How to Live Happily Ever After* or something stupid like that?"

Regina pulled out her own suitcase and frowned.

"Mom wants me to work with the appraiser to make sure he doesn't rob them blind."

"Ah." Justine turned her head at the sound of another car coming down the winding driveway. "Must be Dad."

But at the sight of a blue extended van, Regina developed a sour taste in her mouth. "No such luck—it's the appraiser."

Mitchell Cooke pulled in on the other side of Regina's car, stopped the engine, and climbed out.

"Yum-yum," Justine muttered.

"Don't get excited," Regina muttered wryly. "He's not married."

He walked toward them, holding up Regina's glasses. "Thought you might need these."

She took them and smiled tightly. "Thanks."

He gestured to the Doll and her surroundings. "Nice place."

"Uh-huh." She had no intention of engaging the man in conversation.

Justine broke the awkward silence. "I'm Justine Metcalf."

He nodded. "Mitchell Cooke. I'm doing some appraisal work for your parents."

"Yes, my sister was just telling me she's going to be working with you to make sure you don't rob them blind."

Regina wanted to kick Justine.

"Was she now?" He seemed highly amused when he looked back to her. "I guess you had a chance to talk to your mother."

Regina squirmed and nodded.

"And our working together is agreeable to you?"

"Whatever it takes to help my parents."

"Good. When can I expect to see you tomorrow?"

"Is nine too early for you?"

He smiled. "Why not make it eight?"

She smiled back. "Why not make it seven?"

"Great. I'll bring doughnuts."

They stood looking at each other until Justine cleared her throat. "Well, I think I'll take my suitcase in now."

"I'm right behind you," Regina said. "Good-bye, Mr. Cooke—"

"Call me Mitchell." He shifted foot to foot and watched Justine walk away, then turned back to Regina. "Listen, I really stopped by to tell you that your dad returned a few minutes ago. I didn't want to say anything in front of your sister in case you wanted to keep things . . . private."

"Has he been drinking?"

He nodded. "I helped him up to the apartment and he was sleeping when I left, but I thought you should know."

She jammed on her glasses and blinked away tears of humiliation. "Thank you . . . thank you."

He shrugged. "Unless you have a brother showing up, I'd be glad to go back later and check in on him."

"No—no brothers. Just two sisters."

"Where's the other one?"

"She's—" Regina broke off at the sound of another car approaching.

"Busy little place," he observed.

"Probably someone lost."

He squinted. "In a limo?"

Regina's vital signs increased as a black stretch limousine nosed its way down the twisting driveway. "Oh . . . no."

"Who is it?"

She swallowed. "You're not going to believe this . . . *I* don't believe this . . . I think that's my other sister."

"Is she someone famous?"

"Sort of."

Her heart hammered as the limo pulled alongside Justine's Mercedes. Justine had made it as far as the porch and was riveted on the arrival. A stone settled in Regina's stomach at the ramifications of the scene unfolding.

"I'll be going," Mitchell said. "I don't want to horn in on your family reunion."

She touched his arm without looking at him. "Um . . . would you stick around for . . . a few minutes?"

"Sure. I always wanted to meet a celebrity."

When the vehicle stopped, the driver hopped out and jogged back to open the door. One long tanned leg appeared, followed by another; then all six feet of Mica emerged, clad in a black miniskirt and a white silky blouse. Her hair flowed around her shoulders like a cape. Regina never stopped being in awe of her little sister's beauty. Next to her, Mitchell exhaled a low whistle. Mica had that effect on men.

The driver set bag after bag on the ground. Mica pushed back her sunglasses, gave him a wad of bills, and waved him off. Then she turned large, luminous eyes in their direction and waved. "I'm home!"

Regina grinned back and started walking, but a noise behind her caused her to turn. Justine had dropped her suitcase and was stalking down the sidewalk toward Mica. "You little backstabbing tramp—how dare you show your face here?"

Before Regina could position herself between the two of them, Justine had launched herself at Mica. They fell to the ground grunting, then rolled into a bed of ivy, legs kicking.

Mitchell Cooke looked thunderstruck.

"Help me," Regina said with a sigh.

# nine

DON'T reveal all the skeletons in your closet at once.

Regina arrived at the shop ten minutes before 7:00 A.M., but Mitchell's van was already there. She sneaked a peek into the visor mirror and conceded she should have taken him up on his offer to meet at eight—she certainly could have used an extra hour of sleep last night. She'd covered the circles as best she could and hoped her glasses camouflaged the rest.

The upside of leaving the house early was that her mother and sisters were still sleeping, so she didn't have to witness a brawl before breakfast.

She closed the car door quietly, and took a moment to appreciate the early-morning stillness of the trees, the citrusy scent of heavy dew, the dawn song of an unidentified bird. Nature went on about its beautiful business, heedless of the screwed-up humans passing through. She sighed. This visit home had all the makings of a catastrophe.

Regina entered the back door quickly to circumvent the chime in case her father was still sleeping in the apartment above. The warm, peppery scent of good coffee rode the air, lifting her mood ridiculously. She followed her nose to the cluttered room between the stockroom and the showrooms that had been originally set aside to serve as an office but had over the years become part kitchen, sitting room, and chaotic catchall. A decrepit refrigerator sat in one corner. Mismatched cabinets and counters lined the perimeter of the room, overflowing with manila file folders and catalogs. To his credit, Mitchell had cleared a path to the massive metal desk in the middle of the room, where he now sat with his long legs propped up, enjoying a mug of that great-smelling coffee. Sam looked at her from his resting place on the floor, with droopy eyes that said he, too, could have used a few more z's.

"Good morning," Mitchell said way too cheerfully.

She wanted to smile, but the image of him peeling apart her sisters was still a little too vivid for comfort. "Good morning."

"Coffee?"

"Absolutely." She walked to the coffeemaker and poured a cup, then rummaged around the counter clutter. "Did you happen to see any creamer?" To heck with her resolution to do without—at the moment she needed all the solace she could get.

"You haven't even tasted it yet."

She looked up. "Hm?"

"My coffee—taste it. It doesn't need dressing up."

She took a dubious sip, then pursed her mouth. "I'm impressed."

He smiled. "I'm glad." He lifted the lid on a box of doughnuts. "Jelly or cream-filled?"

"Jelly."

"Ah, thought so."

She frowned but took the proffered doughnut and leaned against the counter. She chewed, thinking he probably expected an explanation for the scene last night, but considering her father was sleeping off a hangover upstairs, she wasn't inclined to volunteer yet more information about her dysfunctional family.

"Looks like it's going to be a nice day," he said.

She sighed noisily. "All right—if you *must* know, twelve years ago, Mica ran off with Justine's fiancé on the day of their wedding."

He stopped chewing, cheeks full, then swallowed. "Oh."

"You were wondering, weren't you, what would cause two grown women who are blood-related to roll around on the ground and call each other names?"

He shrugged. "I figured there was a man involved."

She set down her coffee. "You *figured* a man was involved. Why?"

Another shrug. "Female nature."

She gaped at his conceit . . . and accuracy.

"Let me guess," he said. "The guy is a loser?"

Reluctantly, she nodded.

"Where is he?"

"Thank goodness he stayed in LA."

"I don't suppose he ever married your younger sister?"

"No."

"Typical. Women can't get enough of that kind of guy."

She glared. "That's a sexist thing to say."

He splayed a hand. "But it's true. Women want the bad boy, but once they get him, they want him to settle down, and he won't. Vicious cycle. Take it from a former bad boy."

"A *former* bad boy?"

"Yeah, now I just have bad knees." He rubbed his shin through his faded jeans. "By the way, your sisters kick like mules."

She winced. "I apologize for dragging you into the middle of it."

He dismissed her concern with a wave. "Glad to

help—I'm a full-service appraiser-slash-bouncer."

She indicated his laptop on the desk. "I'm still not clear on what I'm supposed to be helping you with."

"Other than making sure I don't rob your parents blind?"

Her cheeks warmed. "Justine spoke out of turn."

"Well, no offense, but your parents would be an easy target if I were the unsavory sort. This place is a wreck."

"I know. John and Cissy love antiques and they're good with customers, but they're not much when it comes to the nuts and bolts of running a business."

"I see a lot of that in my line of work."

"What exactly *is* your line of work?"

"Appraisals, mostly. Managing estate sales, consulting for insurance companies, that kind of thing. The bank officer handling your parents' business loan contacted me about this job. I'm going to put a reserve price on everything here so the bank will have a ballpark idea of what the auction will gross. I could use your help with the paperwork, and maybe some other things. Your father told me you have a good eye."

"I only plan to be here through next weekend."

He nodded. "I work fast and I've never had a helper before, so this should go quickly."

"Will the store be open for business while all this is going on?"

"Sure, move what inventory we can. After everything is appraised, it would be best to close for a couple of weeks to get ready for the auction."

She pressed her lips together, wishing the world would slow down until she could adjust.

"Hey, don't be depressed—there's a lot of good stuff here. I plan to get the word out to collector friends. With a little luck, your folks will be able to keep that great house of theirs."

"My parents are splitting up." She covered her mouth with her hand. Oh, God, more proof that her family was a mess.

"I'm sorry to hear that," he said quietly, then removed his legs from the desk. "Ready to get started?"

She nodded gratefully and carried her coffee to join him at the desk. Between doughnuts, he explained his simple inventory and appraisal software, although she didn't absorb much of what he was saying. He was sitting too close, and his bigness got in her way—too much knee-bumping and elbow-brushing. While he watched the screen, she watched him. She guessed the self-proclaimed former bad boy to be approaching forty, even though his T-shirts and tennis shoes gave him a more youthful appearance. His thick dark blond hair lay close to his head, and his face was all mature planes and angles—high, wide cheekbones, a broad nose, strong chin. His short sideburns were dark, like his eyebrows and lashes. From his fit physique and tanned extremities, she surmised he enjoyed outdoor sports. Indeed, he was wearing a faded "Kayaking Rules" T-shirt, and it didn't take a stretch of imagination to visualize him naked from the waist up, battling the current.

"We can start with furniture if you want," he offered, picking up the laptop.

"Where are you from?"

He seemed surprised at her question.

"I . . . can't place your accent."

"I'm from all over the South, really. My folks were wheeler-dealers, always dabbling in antiques in some form—flea markets, auction houses. We moved around."

"Where do you live now?"

"I have a post office box in Charlotte."

A former-bad-boy drifter. She helped him load the

laptop and other supplies onto a rolling cart.

"So, what do you do in Boston?" he asked.

She pushed up her glasses. "I edit books."

"What kind of books?"

"Nonfiction. Reference books, health books, self-help."

"Those Mars—Venus books?"

"Some."

"Sounds dull."

She blinked. "It's not. Are we going to get started or what?" She pushed the cart ahead of him, over the uneven wood flooring into the main showroom. His footsteps sounded behind her, as well as the rhythmic clicking of Sam's toenails.

"All I meant was that I'd rather *do* things than read about them."

She kept walking. "Sorry my job isn't glamorous enough for you. I'm not as comfortable in the spotlight as my sisters are."

He snagged her arm and came around to face her. "Hey, relax. I didn't mean to offend you. And who said anything about your sisters?"

She stared up at him with defiance.

"Do I detect a little sibling rivalry here?" His mouth curved into a teasing smile. "Oh, wait—don't tell me you had a thing for the loser bad boy, too?"

His audacity floored her. She itched to slap him, but she didn't want him to think he could so easily provoke her. Instead she matched his smile. "I keep my distance from bad boys." She pulled her arm away from his grasp. "Including former ones."

"Ouch." He looked down at Sam. "That, my friend, is what's called a brush-off. Luckily, I'm thick-skinned."

"Could we please get started?"

"Yes, ma'am."

Much to her relief, when they got down to business Mitchell was serious and efficient. They quickly worked out a system—she fed him info for the program from the massive file of index cards that her parents still used to maintain inventory records and, when no card could be located, from inspecting the piece of furniture. At first her tongue was rusty, but soon the vocabulary came back to her: Empire, Federal, Art Nouveau, Arts and Crafts, Rococo, Regency, Shaker. Once he had fixed a reserve price, she tagged the piece and they moved on. She did stop occasionally to admire a particularly nice piece.

"I hadn't realized how much I missed this business," she murmured, running her hand over a fine chestnut wood table.

He laughed. "I don't think you can ever truly get away from it. I tried but found my way back. Are you a collector?"

She shrugged. "All my childhood knickknacks are still at Mom and Dad's—junk mostly. Now I like letter openers, but I'm not a serious collector."

"Letter openers? Why letter openers?"

She looked up, then back down. "No reason. What do you collect?"

"Books."

She looked back up. "Books?"

"I can't be good-looking *and* well-read?"

A noise from the stairs saved her from a response. Her dad came into view, favoring an arthritic foot, but all smiles for Regina.

"There's my girl," he said, opening his arms.

"Daddy." She went willingly and buried her face into his neck, inhaling Old Spice—the official Dad smell. "It's good to see you. How's your foot?"

"Fine. Better if I'd get more exercise. Let me look at you." He held her face in his hands and grinned.

"Yeah, still pretty as a picture." Then he gave her a sad smile. "Sorry I wasn't home to see you last night. I . . ." His eyes grew moist.

"It's okay," she soothed, alarmed at the despondent look in his blue eyes—*her* blue eyes. "I know you're going through a tough time, but things are going to be fine." She pecked him on the cheek, then grinned. "And guess what? Justine is home."

He brightened. "Alone?"

"Yes."

"I know your mother is happy about that."

"And guess what else?"

"I can't stand any more good news."

"Then I guess I won't tell you that Mica's home, too."

"All my girls are home?"

"Looks that way."

His hug lifted her off her feet. When he set her down, he looked over her shoulder. "I see you've met Mitchell."

"I'm helping him. Why don't you go home and see the girls? We'll hold down the fort here, and I'll be home for dinner."

"Regina, why don't you go, too?" Mitchell offered. "I know you'd like to be with your family."

To be honest, she wasn't ready to face them again. And as crazy as it sounded, she knew from experience that Justine and Mica argued more when she was around because they counted on her to referee. Cissy and John deserved a few hours of peace and quiet to enjoy the daughters they rarely got to see.

She gave him a pointed look. "I'll stay here and help you."

He looked back to his work. She watched her father leave, thinking of all the good times they should have had—should still have. She had to believe everything was going to work out, but at the moment, things looked pretty bleak.

Behind her, Mitchell cleared his throat. "You could have gone with him—I'm not going to steal anything." He sounded put out.

She wiped her hand over her eyes and turned. "And just maybe this isn't about you. Now, where were we?"

# ten

Justine sat straight up in bed, the image of Lisa Crane's menacing face seared in her brain. The room was bathed in shadows, and she sensed the woman lurked within their cover. Terror clawed at her heart as she leaned over and groped for the gun under her mattress. Her arm was caught on something—the woman was going to kill her in her own bed. Sobs tore at her throat as panic overwhelmed her. When her body reached maximum tension, something broke loose in her mind, and she realized her arm was hung on a bedsheet. She stopped flailing when she noticed her surroundings. The ornamental brass bed she'd slept in as a child. Peach-and-green paisley quilt. Matching curtains.

She was home. Safe.

She dropped back to the pillow in sweaty relief. A few seconds later, she remembered that Mica, too, was home and that their first greeting after twelve years hadn't been the stuff that Hallmark commercials were made of. She rolled over and groaned into her pillow. The nutmeg tea she'd drunk last night left her feeling lethargic this morning. Maybe she'd pretend to be ill and stay in bed all day—no one could very well argue with that. Her eyes had closed on the comforting idea when the bleeping of her cell phone sounded. She hesitated, then realized that Lando could be calling her with good news. She sat up, fumbled for the lamp switch, and yanked the phone off the nightstand. "Hello?"

"Justine?" A male voice.

"Yeah. Who's this?"

"Officer Lando. Did I wake you?"

"Yeah." She felt for her watch, then remembered it now belonged to a guy in Shively with bad teeth. "What time is it?"

"A little after nine. I wanted to give you an update."

"Did you find her?"

"Not yet."

"Not yet? Do you know where she is?"

"That's why I'm calling. Are you in North Carolina?"

"Yeah, at my folks' house."

"I'm going to need that address."

"Why?"

"We think Lisa Crane might have left the state."

She slung back the covers, walked over to one of the two long windows in her room, and raised the shade. The sunlight nearly blinded her. After her eyes adjusted, she looked out over the front yard and long, winding driveway. Her car sat where she'd left it. Regina's car was gone, but she'd had to meet that hunky junk guy at the shop. The sprinkler was running, as if any of that giant green stuff down there needed encouragement. A hammock swung empty in a slight breeze. Cement animals stood at attention. All seemed quiet and well.

"Are you still there?" he asked.

"Yeah. I don't see her lounging in the front yard. What makes you think she left the state?"

"A woman matching her description left a convenience store without paying for a tank of gas at the Pennsylvania–Maryland state line."

She swallowed. "When?"

"Last night about ten. It might not be her, but I wanted to let you know in case she somehow followed you. I'll notify the local sheriff."

She winced. "Is that absolutely necessary?"

"Yes."

"Okay, but do you have to go into detail with the local yokels? They know my parents."

"I'll be discreet," he said, and she heard the unspoken words: *Even though you weren't.*

"Do you have an update on Randall Crane's condition?" she asked, rummaging in her bag for a cigarette.

"Upgraded to 'good.' We're still guarding his room."

She lit the cigarette, sucked it to life, and exhaled. "Good."

"Those things will kill you."

She smirked and took another drag. "They can get in line."

"How are you holding up?"

"Fine. Although considering my whacked-out family, I might should've stayed and taken my chances with Lisa Crane."

"That messed up, huh?"

"Understatement." She told him her parents' address.

"Take care of yourself," he said. "I'll keep you posted from this end."

She disconnected the phone thoughtfully. No one ever told her to take care of herself—everyone just assumed she could.

Justine took another lusty drag from the cigarette.

And she could take care of herself, by God.

Exhaling the smoke in a sigh, she realized she'd have to put in an appearance downstairs after all. And face Mica again. After the "incident," Regina had relegated them both to opposite ends of the house to cool off. Justine and Mica had both offered to go to a motel, but Regina wouldn't hear of it—they were sisters, after all. Justine shook her head—Regina the negotiator. Regina, who thought everything could be fixed with a group hug and a to-do list. Regina, who didn't realize that she was just as screwed up as they were.

She knocked on the door of the bathroom between her room and Mica's. Actually, the bathroom had been all hers until Mica turned thirteen, upon which John had yielded to his darling Mica's demands and added an entrance from her bedroom. After that it seemed that Mica was always in the way . . . and sharing far more of Justine's belongings than Justine had realized.

How long had Dean and Mica been carrying on behind her back? Months? Years? On top of the humiliation of discovering that her groom had left her standing at the altar so he could run off to LA with her little sister, she hadn't had the satisfaction of confronting them, of telling them what she thought of them . . . of looking into their eyes and seeing if they were even a little remorseful for deceiving her.

Until yesterday. Whatever fantasies she'd harbored about Mica coming to her for forgiveness with her heart in her hands had vanished when she'd burst out of that limousine and announced that she was *home!*, home to rub everyone's nose in her gorgeousness and her success. Not home to make amends, but home to make an impression. And all Justine could think about was leaving Mica's impression in the driveway.

Hearing no sound on the other side of the door, she dropped her cigarette into the dregs of the nutmeg tea and entered the bathroom, stepping on and around Mica's model paraphernalia to get to the sink.

She drank water from her cupped hands to rinse the foul taste of nutmeg from her mouth—ugh. Then she lathered up her skin with a plain old bar of hand soap— a big no-no in the makeup industry, but one day wouldn't undo her Botox injections. The soap stung in a few places, and she noticed the red marks on her face had the pattern of claw marks.

That little witch had scratched her face. Okay, she'd blacked Mica's eye, but Mica'd had it coming. The clawing, however, would not go by without comment. Justine tossed the towel into the sink and yanked open the door leading to Mica's bedroom to find an empty rumpled bed. She grunted in frustration, then stopped at the ringing of a cellular phone. Not hers, she realized, but the one peeking out of Mica's obscenely expensive purse. The display screen lit up with the caller's name: DEAN HAVILAND.

Her heart vaulted. She hesitated until the third ring before getting up the nerve to answer in her best Mica impersonation. "Hello?"

"Hey, baby, what's going on?"

Justine closed her eyes—his voice was still chocolaty. "Um, I just woke up."

"Where the hell are you?"

Justine lifted an eyebrow—trouble in paradise? Her mind raced for a noncommittal response. "Can't you guess?"

"Look, this isn't funny. I called this damn cell phone number a hundred times; I checked with all your friends. All your dumb-ass agent will tell me is that you're taking some time off. By the way, I found his jacket hanging in the bathroom—if he's been bagging you, I'll rip off his pecker."

She blinked and said nothing.

"Tell me where you are, and I'll come get you. We'll talk, baby. We'll work everything out."

So they *were* having problems. A sliver of vindication cut through her chest. And if Dean came here, she'd get the opportunity to see him again, to confront him. "I decided to come home for a few days, to see my folks."

"You're in *Monroeville*?"

"Uh-huh."

He cursed loud and long. "This is not a good time for me to be back in that hellhole. I need to be here, working on a deal."

"Are you coming or not?"

More frustrated noises and banging. "Dammit, I guess so."

"When?"

"I don't know. Might take me a couple of days. I have to clear up some things here—one of us has to work, you know."

"I know."

He sighed, a thrill-raising sound. "You're killing me, woman; you know that?"

Justine smiled slowly into the phone. "Yes. I know that."

She disconnected the phone, tingling with anticipation. With the push of a couple of buttons, she disabled the phone's ringer and turned off the power. Then she buried the phone in the bottom of Mica's purse. Her hand brushed several prescription bottles, and a tiny alarm went off in Justine's head.

Was Mica ill? She had felt a little bony when Justine had her down on the ground, but Justine had assumed it was her standard model weight.

Antibiotics, more antibiotics, painkillers, more painkillers, *antidepressants*? From three different physicians, and the antibiotics prescription had been filled only yesterday.

Hm.

# eleven

DON'T expect copulation and conversation at the same time.

Mica sat in the den, tucked into a big comfy plaid chair that had nothing to do with the Victorian Era and everything to do with her dad having a good place to watch TV. She could smell him on the chair—his Old Spice cologne and the cherry almond tobacco he smoked occasionally. Behind the pillow she'd found a fifth of whiskey, half-empty. His sippin' spirits, he used to say. But according to Cissy and Regina, he was doing more than sipping these days. A man with a splintered family.

From the depths of an overloaded bookcase, she had pulled a photo album with brittle acetate-covered pages, purchased and filled before the general public was informed that the adhesive on the pages was permanent and that the pictures would yellow in tandem with the overlays. Black-and-white photos of Justine as a toddler gave way to faded color pictures of Justine and baby Regina. Justine had developed a personality for the lens, while Regina surrendered only shy smiles behind her big glasses. And suddenly another baby appeared in the pictures, this one with loads of dark hair. Justine had toted her around like her personal doll. "My

MICA" had been written across one photo in permanent marker in Justine's careful five-year-old block printing. Mica traced the letters with her pinkie, trying to pick up a vibe of the devotion her sister had felt for her then.

Mica sniffed. This mess was all her fault for falling in love with Dean.

At first she thought that Dean was being nice to her because she was Justine's little sister. She adored Justine, so she was thrilled when they invited her along to movies and ball games. At her sixteenth birthday party, Dean had given her a brotherly kiss, and she remembered feeling overwhelmed and confused. After that kiss, Dean had started seeking her out for conversations, offering to take her to the library, that kind of thing. His brotherly kisses yielded to more adult versions until, one year later, she surrendered her virginity to him. He'd sworn her to secrecy, declaring that neither of them wanted to hurt Justine. He was so mature and so handsome, and their chemistry had been electric. When Dean made love to her, nothing else in the world mattered. She'd fallen head over heels for him but kept her feelings studiously hidden from Justine. Three years later, on the eve of his wedding, when Dean suggested that he accompany her to LA, no one had been more surprised than she.

Except perhaps Justine.

*And what goes around, comes around.* How naive she'd been to think that the man who'd cheated on another woman with her wouldn't do the same thing *to* her. Dr. Forsythe had gone on to explain that in addition to gonorrhea, she also had chlamydia, another nasty little sex bug. She hoped they had caught the infections before either had permanently affected her ability to conceive. *Hoped.*

Her telephone conversation with Dean had been

short—she told him the diagnosis, he denied cheating on her, and she hung up. It was that moment that she'd decided to leave town, because, frankly, she couldn't promise herself that she wouldn't kill him if she stayed. If there was a thin line between love and hate, she'd crossed it with Dean Haviland. And with herself. She'd chosen Dean over her family, and now she had neither.

She continued to flip pages, scanning photographs through misty eyes. She smiled at the one of the three of them at Disney World. She was seven, Regina nine, and Justine twelve. She couldn't remember the ride they'd just gotten off, but it must have been high and fast, because she and Justine were grinning and glowing, and Regina looked a little green around the gills. She and Justine were thrill seekers—they were drawn to the same rides, the same limelight, the same man. Regina, on the other hand, was the good sport. The one who followed their lead and the one who usually took the blame in order to keep the peace.

Another picture caught her eye, this one more sobering. They were mugging for the camera in their new bathing suits the summer that Aunt Lyla would be murdered. She knew because she had been allowed to wear a bikini for the first time. That summer was one of the hottest on record, and they'd spent every spare moment at the Dilly swimming hole. On that one particular day, their timing had been ill-fated. And for the first time, Regina had taken the lead, setting aside her fear of heights to shinny down a tree and gaze upon what must have been a horrific sight for a fourteen-year-old. Mica could still see Regina's face, chalk-white and trembling. Then she and Justine had forced her to agree to a pact of silence. The irony was that it was a harder choice that day for Regina to swear she wouldn't tell— it went against her innate judiciousness. Yet of the three of them, Regina would be the last one to break the pact.

Mica pulled her hand down over her mouth. *She* had broken the pact, and only weeks ago—another irony. After keeping her word for twenty years, she'd decided one warm night when she and Dean were sharing a pillow that she wanted him to open up. To talk about his childhood in a scroungy little borough of Monroeville. She reasoned that if they talked more, maybe they could become more intimate on an emotional level. Dean rarely spoke of his childhood, or any serious topic, for that matter. So she had decided the best way to get him to share something with her that no one else knew would be to share a secret with him first, to break the ice.

"Do you remember," she'd asked, lying on her side, facing him, "when Lyla Gilbert was murdered?"

He'd been half-asleep by that time—good sex did that to him. "Yeah. Wasn't she kin to you?"

"My aunt."

He'd grunted.

"I've never told anyone this, but . . . Justine, Regina, and I saw the whole thing."

One of his eyes had opened. "Huh?"

"We were spying from a rock ledge over Lovers' Lane, and we saw the whole thing."

His other eye had opened. "No shit?"

She'd nodded.

"You saw the murderer?"

"Yeah . . . and no. We didn't get a real good look at the guy."

He had sat up and put a pillow behind his back, now fully awake. "You didn't go to the police?"

"No. We were afraid if the killer thought we could identify him, he'd come after us."

"So could you?"

"What?"

"Could you identify him?"

"Well . . . I don't think . . . *I* could have. Of course I can't speak for Justine and Regina." She shook her head. "Regina even went down there to make sure Lyla was dead."

"Regina?"

"We couldn't believe it, either. I think it nearly scared her to death. She said the murder weapon was all covered with blood."

"Murder weapon? They never found the murder weapon."

It was at that point that Mica realized the conversation wasn't going as she'd planned. "I . . . didn't know."

He'd leaned forward. "Well, what did she see—was it a knife?"

"She . . . didn't say." She'd tugged on his arm to get him to lie back down with her. "It's been so long, I can't remember. Maybe Regina just said there was blood all over. I've blocked out a lot of it, I think."

He resisted her tug. "So you might've seen the murderer's face and blocked it out?"

She frowned. "I don't . . . know. Anyway, it all turned out okay. We were so relieved when they caught that pool guy and locked him up."

Dean had seemed thoughtful, so she'd taken a chance. "Tell me what you were like when you were a little boy."

"Aw, come on, Mica; you know I hate to talk about this crap."

"Please?"

He'd thrown off her arm. "Sad, okay? I was sad. My old man beat my mom constantly, and when she wasn't handy, he knocked me around."

She had tried to touch him, but he'd retreated into

that hard shell of his. "Surely there must have been some good times?"

"One. My twelfth birthday."

She'd smiled. "What did you get?"

"I got big enough to hit him back, and after that he left me alone." He'd climbed out of bed. "Want a drink?"

She'd shaken her head no.

"I think I'll watch some TV—don't wait up."

Mica closed the photo album and hugged it to her chest. She'd told her biggest secret to the person who had betrayed her physically and emotionally. It was a darn good thing that Dean had declared he'd never return to Monroeville.

She'd hate for them to get into trouble after all this time had passed.

# twelve

DO be mysterious—it drives men wild.

"Take a break?" Mitchell asked from the doorway of the stockroom.

Regina looked up warily from a tray of sterling serving pieces. They had barely exchanged a word in two hours. She had waited on customers in her father's absence and still managed to work ahead of Mitchell, sorting and grouping and collecting information from the files to make the data entry more streamlined.

He extended a cold soda. "Peace offering. I shouldn't have been so defensive this morning." Sam appeared and set his black head on her knee—apparently he was sorry, too.

Caught off guard by the apology, she slowly swiveled on the stool she occupied and took the soda. "Let's forget it." She didn't like to be surprised by men. Surveying the sterling pieces she'd tagged, she asked, "How much of this stuff will you bundle for the auction?"

"A good number of the small pieces," he admitted. "Excluding the jewelry and the pottery."

She took a drink from the can and sighed. "It's good—thanks."

"You've been mighty quiet."

Regina tried to smile. "A lot on my mind, I suppose." She stood and walked around the jam-packed stockroom, shaking her head. "I'll bet Cissy and John don't know half of what's in here."

"It's interesting that you call your parents by their first names." He spoke carefully, casually.

She shrugged. "My mother had liberal ideas about raising children. She was a bit of a feminist in her younger days. Still is, when it's convenient."

"How long have your folks been married?"

She conjured up a cheerful smile. "They're not married."

He tried to cover his surprise but didn't quite succeed.

"They're bohemian," she said, nodding as if she made perfect sense.

"Oh."

To smooth over the awkward moment, she poked around the floor-to-ceiling stacks of tables, chests, picture frames, and various junk in the storeroom, most of it in some state of disrepair. "We probably need to send some of this stuff to the dump."

" 'Fraid so," he agreed. "A few poor pieces will reflect on the entire lot. Best to get rid of them altogether."

She stepped between two warped headboards to lift a dusty sheet from a tall object, then gasped.

"Find something?"

"An old wardrobe." The wardrobe she and Mica and Justine had repaired and refinished for Justine and Dean's wedding gift. It had been Mica's idea, but she and Regina couldn't work on it and keep it a secret. When they told Justine, she wanted to work on it with them. The three of them had spent hours stripping, sanding, and waxing the lustrous walnut wood and connecting with one another as they never had before.

Justine had been flush with anticipation at her and Dean's impending wedding, Mica had made plans to take her regional modeling success to the West Coast, and she herself had been looking forward to graduation and the job that awaited her in Boston. They had been swept up in the knowledge that they were about to go separate ways, so they'd forsaken friends to cram in as much sister time as possible. Their one area of agreement: living together simply wasn't good enough—they all wanted to be married to the man of their dreams.

Ha.

"Nice, big piece," Mitchell said, rousing her from her musing. He ran his hand over the dozens of deep gashes in the wood. "Too bad somebody hacked it up. Exquisite firewood, though."

Regina smirked—she imagined that Justine hadn't been contemplating toasty hearth fires when she'd taken an ax to the lovely wardrobe not too long after finding Mica and Dean's getaway note. It was the only entertainment the guests got that day, watching the bride, in an ax-wielding rage, destroy the beribboned wardrobe that sat behind the gift table. A genuine Kodak moment.

He swung open one of the dragging doors and winced to find the inside in similar condition. "Definitely a candidate for the dump."

She nodded, thinking it was for the best, even if she could still hear their giggles and laughter coming from its depths. "I'll tag it."

He pulled open a drawer and withdrew a vase that had been broken and badly glued back together.

Regina's laugh was dry. "This was a vase that my Aunt Lyla and Justine argued over—they both said the other one dropped it. They didn't exactly get along."

Mitchell studied the piece. "Was it of sentimental value?"

She shook her head and pointed to the mark on the bottom. "It's a Lalique—Lyla found it on one of her treasure hunts. I remember Justine had to work off the price of it—a couple of hundred dollars, twenty years ago. Can't imagine what it would be worth now if it were in one piece."

"About twenty bucks," he said.

She frowned. "What?"

"It's not a Lalique—it's a good knockoff. See, the mark is blurred. And the coloring is off. Your aunt was conned."

She winced. "Whatever you do, don't tell Justine— she'll be furious all over again for having to work off the debt."

The door chime sounded, announcing a customer. Regina smoothed a hand over the front of her jeans, then walked into the main showroom to see a tall man in a khaki uniform with his back to her. "May I help you, sir?"

He turned and grinned. "Hi, Regina."

Dark hair, touch of gray, blue eyes, hooked nose, toothpick clenched in his teeth like an accessory. A vague memory chord stirred, but she couldn't come up with a name.

He removed the toothpick and held out his hands. "It's me—Pete."

Her racing mind finally put the pieces together. "Pete Shadowen."

"*Deputy Sheriff* Pete Shadowen now." He thumped an official-looking hat he held in the crook of his arm. "At your service."

She smiled and embraced him. He wanted to hang on a little longer than she did.

"Wow, Regina, you look *swell*."

"Thanks. So do you. Is your dad still sheriff?"

He nodded, then looked over her shoulder. "Hello." The toothpick went back to the space between his eye-teeth.

"Hi," Mitchell Cooke said.

Regina's smile encompassed them both. "Mitchell Cooke, this is Deputy Sheriff Pete Shadowen, an old friend of mine."

"And old *boy*friend," Pete clarified.

Mitchell looked amused. "Yes, I could see right away that you were a boy. Nice hat."

Regina glared at him.

Sam appeared, took one look at Pete, and bared his teeth in a snarl. Mitchell snapped his fingers and Sam retreated. "Sorry—it's the uniform."

Exasperated, Regina turned back to Pete. "Mom and Dad are going to auction off the inventory. Mitchell is an appraiser."

"Ah." Pete gave an open-mouthed nod, then used his toothpick to point back and forth between them. "So you two don't . . . know each other."

"No," she said.

"Yes," Mitchell said at the same time.

"Not really," she added, then served up a smile. "Pete, what brings you up this way?"

He winked. "Well, Mrs. Woods at the Grab 'N Go told me you were back in town, so I was looking for an excuse to come see you."

"What excuse did you come up with?" Mitchell asked with a glib smile.

*Stop,* Regina telegraphed with her eyes.

Pete stared at the other man, then set his hat on his head and straightened his shoulders. He turned back to Regina. "I just left your house. I had to speak with Justine about an official police matter." His gaze flicked back to Mitchell. "Maybe I shouldn't—"

"It's okay," Regina said with a sigh. Mitchell already knew most of their family drama. "Does this have something to do with the shooting at Cocoon?"

Pete nodded. "I got a call from the Shively, Pennsylvania, Police Department, and it's possible the shooter might have left the state."

Mitchell leaned in, clearly confused but riveted.

Regina swallowed. "Could the woman be headed here?"

"It's possible," Pete said in big-eyed seriousness. "But I'm going to be on the lookout." He plucked a piece of paper from his shirt pocket and unfolded a faxed photo that was so dark and indistinguishable, Regina couldn't even tell that it was a woman.

### WANTED: LISA CRANE
### CONSIDERED ARMED AND DANGEROUS

Pete used his tongue to direct the toothpick toward Mitchell. "Where are you staying, Cooke?"

"At the Russell Motel."

"See any woman hanging around who looks like this?"

Mitchell glanced at the photo and wiped away a smile with his hand. "No, thank goodness."

"Well, if you do, contact the sheriff's office at once."

"Will do."

Pete refolded the fax and tucked it into his pocket. "Regina, I suggested to Justine that she stay close to home until this Crane woman is found. Your Uncle Lawrence offered one of his security guards to watch the house at night, but I told him it wasn't necessary—we'll patrol."

She looked at Mitchell. "Cissy's brother, he's a U.S. representative, running for the Senate." She was glad to impart that at least one person in her warped family was accomplished.

"Lawrence Gilbert is your uncle?"

She nodded with pride, then looked back to Pete. "Uncle Lawrence is in town?" He rarely returned to Monroeville—and who could blame him, with all the bad memories? She hadn't seen him in four, maybe five years.

"Yeah, he's back to testify at the Bracken hearing next week."

She remembered the unread newspaper at the bottom of her purse, and unease plucked at her. "What kind of hearing?"

"The scumbag wants a new trial—claims he's innocent and that there was some kind of police conspiracy to convict him."

Her stomach plunged.

"What was the crime?" Mitchell asked.

"M-murder," Regina offered. "The man murdered Uncle Lawrence's wife, my Aunt Lyla. He's served twenty years of a life sentence with no parole."

Mitchell whistled low. "Twenty years? He's either guilty as hell or patient as hell."

Pete scoffed. "He's guilty as hell. My dad conducted that investigation. I hear Bracken has some new hotshot lawyer who's looking for publicity. Just wasting the taxpayers' money, if you ask me."

"Right," Regina said with a nervous laugh.

"Well, guess I'd better be going," Pete said, jerking his thumb toward the door.

"It's nice to see you, Pete," she said, and meant it.

"I'm not married," he blurted.

Mitchell coughed.

"Oh?" she asked.

"Well, me and Tobi Evans, we gave it a stab for a couple of years, but that's over. Tobi lives in Florida now, selling real estate. We didn't have any kids, but I'm not sterile or anything like that."

"Oh. Good."

"Are you married?"

"Nope, never did."

Pete frowned. "Never did, huh?"

She knew that look. "None of us girls are married."

He laughed. "Yeah, I remember Justine wigging out and chopping up that cabinet at her wedding when Dean ran off with Mica." Pete kept laughing.

Mitchell raised one dark eyebrow, Regina ignored him. "Yeah—she wigged out, all right."

"Mica looks hot," Pete said, rambling now.

"Yeah," Regina said, nodding.

"So Mrs. Woods tells me you write books in Boston."

"Well, actually, I edit books."

He smiled. "You always were a smart one."

"Still am," she assured him with a smile.

He laughed at her joke and pointed his toothpick at her. "We need to go out sometime."

She looked at Mitchell. "Don't wait on me if you need to get back to work."

He shook his head. "No. I'm enjoying this . . . break. Take all the time you need."

She looked back to Pete. "Why don't you call me this week?"

He grinned. "I will." Pete said good-bye and lost his hat when he walked through the door.

Regina waited until the door closed before she turned around.

Mitchell was nodding, mouth pursed.

"Don't say a word," she said.

He lifted his hands. "I don't *have* words for what I just witnessed."

She headed back toward the storeroom. "Do you have Internet service on your laptop?"

"Yeah."

"Can I borrow it for a few minutes to look up something?"

"Sure—if you tell me what's going on with your sister and this faceless shooter."

She talked as she walked. Sam trotted alongside. "Long story short, Justine had an affair with a married man. His wife found out and went to Justine's office with a gun. Someone else was wounded instead, and they still haven't found the woman."

He caught up to her at the door of the storeroom. "Wow, you Metcalf girls have bad taste in men."

"What?"

"Well, Mica's guy knocks her around—"

"Whoa—why would you jump to *that* conclusion?"

"I could be wrong, but she does have a black eye."

"Justine gave her that black eye, remember?"

"No, she had that black eye when she arrived."

Regina squinted. "Are you certain?"

He nodded, then gave her a sheepish smile. "I noticed, um, everything."

She smirked, then said, "I'll bet Dean did give her that black eye—that would explain why she showed up out of the blue."

"See? Bad taste in men. And Justine got involved with a married man—bad taste."

She crossed her arms. "I still don't see what that has to do with *my* taste in men."

"What about Dudley Do-Right back there?"

"I was *sixteen*—that was . . . a long time ago."

"And you don't find me irresistible, so that definitely throws your taste into question."

She narrowed her eyes. "You were going to get me onto the Internet."

He sat down in front of his laptop, inserted a phone cord into a small card in a side port, and within a few keystrokes was on-line. "This dial-up is slow, but go for it."

With trembling hands, Regina went to the site for her E-mail provider, then entered her log-on and password to access her E-mail. No response from the seller of the letter opener to her request for more information. Deciding not to read anything into the lack of response, she went onto the auction site.

"I've bought and sold a few things through this site," he said, looking over her shoulder.

The pages were slow to load, but eventually she made her way into the auction for the carved ivory letter opener. Someone had topped her bid by a buck a mere ten minutes before the auction had ended, but she didn't mind. She clicked on the "see similar items" button and scanned the listings, which were pretty much the same as when she'd browsed two nights ago . . . except the listing for the Russian sterling-and-gold letter opener was gone. She performed a few searches using different criteria, but the listing didn't come up.

She breathed into steepled hands—*don't panic.* "How can I find an item that's been pulled?"

"If the auction has ended, this particular site keeps the data out there for sixty days. That's in case the sale falls through and they have to repost the listing. But you'll need the item number to look up an archived listing."

Which she didn't have. "What if the item was pulled early, before an auction could begin, or before the auction was scheduled to end?"

He shrugged. "The buyer has the right to pull the listing at any time before the electronic gavel comes down. But this site doesn't keep historical data on items that aren't sold."

She groaned.

"It must have been something important."

"Maybe. I honestly don't know."

He hummed. "Well, if you remember the name of the seller, you might see if they have another item for sale and contact them that way."

She shook her head. "I checked last week, and the seller was only offering this one item. And there was no history for the seller."

"That's odd."

"I E-mailed the seller, but they didn't respond. In fact, I think my questions might have precipitated the item being pulled."

"Do you have reason to believe the item was stolen?"

She hesitated. "Maybe. Then again, maybe it wasn't what I thought it was."

"But you're thinking that the listing being pulled is pretty coincidental."

"Yes." Not to mention the coincidence that the letter opener was being sold at the same time the man convicted of her aunt's murder was lobbying for a new hearing.

He scratched his temple. "I don't guess you want to tell me what this thing is?"

She shook her head. "I can't."

"You could always let the authorities know. Maybe they could track down the person through their E-mail account."

"I can't do that, either."

He sat back in his chair, clasped his hands behind his head, and studied her so scrupulously, she needn't have bothered getting dressed this morning. "And I was starting to think you were the only one in your family without secrets."

# thirteen

**DO develop a system for keeping your lies straight.**

Justine slung her bag over her shoulder as she walked down the stairs, gratified at the weight of the weapon inside. Lando had called her again this morning while she was in bed—hm, later she might have to analyze his timing—to tell her the female gasoline thief had turned out not to be Lisa Crane, but they hadn't yet found the woman. So she wasn't taking chances, even if she was only taking a walk with Regina. After all, Lando had reminded her to take care of herself.

In truth, she'd never felt so alive. Her anticipation at seeing Dean again after all these years made her alternately giddy and malevolent. Despite their obvious problems, she and Dean had always shared an incredible chemistry. She paused at the mirror in the entry-way to check her appearance—hair, skin, clothes. Casual and sexy. A slow smile curved her mouth—not bad for thirty-seven.

Then she grinned—who was she kidding? She wasn't bad for *twenty*-seven.

She closed the door behind her and skipped down the steps into the sunshine—then stopped dead. In the side yard, beneath the shade of the oak tree, Mica watched her from the hammock, looking lean and fit in shorts and tennis shoes. So far they had managed not to be together alone, and Justine rather wanted to keep it that way.

Justine pursed her mouth. "Have you seen Regina? We're supposed to go for a walk." She'd almost said no for fear of missing Dean in case he arrived early, but Regina had assured her that they'd be back before noon and Mica had plans, so she'd be gone, too. Perfect.

Mica stood and it took that ridiculous hair of hers a minute to catch up. "*I'm* supposed to go for a walk with Regina."

"Good," Regina said from the porch, hefting a backpack. "You're both here. Ready to go?"

The setup hit Justine, and she shook her head. "Oh, no—I'm not going if she's going."

Mica headed toward the house. "Yeah, Regina, this was not a good idea."

Justine worked her mouth back and forth—why was it that she and Mica could always agree when it came to disagreeing with Regina?

"Stop," Regina said. "Both of you. For a couple of hours, you two are going to set aside your differences, because we need to talk about something serious."

Justine crossed her arms. "Cissy is not going to change her mind about leaving John, and I don't blame her. If he cared about her, he wouldn't have cheated."

"Well, I don't care what Mom thinks," Mica said. "Daddy would never cheat on her."

"You always take Dad's side."

"And you always take Mom's."

Justine wondered how Mica would look with her other eye blackened.

"Time-out!" Regina shouted, then walked down to stand between them. "This isn't about Mom and Dad, all right?" she said in a lowered voice. "I begged us off from going to church with Mom because we need to talk about Aunt Lyla's murder."

Okay, now she had their attention.

"So," Regina said, looking back and forth. "Let's take a walk."

They took off in the direction away from the shop, through gentle woods along a footpath that they'd once worn to the dirt but was now overgrown so badly, the path sometimes disappeared. The sky was July blue beautiful, with big lazy white clouds. The temperature hovered near ninety, and Justine's shirt was already sticky, the backs of her knees moist. Their lush surroundings provided a background of ticking, clicking insects and birds that seemed to rise and fall in conducted rhythm. She walked on the right, Regina in the middle, and the traitor on the other side. They were silent for a good ten minutes. Finally she couldn't stand the suspense.

"So what's this all about?"

Regina pushed up her glasses. "Pete Shadowen stopped by the shop to see me yesterday."

"He still has a thing for you," Justine teased.

"So does that Mitchell guy," Mica said.

Regina rolled her eyes, but her cheeks turned a decided pink. She had no idea how lovely she was, Justine realized. Naturally blond, dainty features, unbelievable skin, and great eyes if she would stop hiding behind those spectacles.

A hank of hair had escaped from her low ponytail, and Regina tucked it behind her ear. "Pete mentioned that Uncle Lawrence is in town because the man convicted of Lyla's murder is lobbying for a new trial."

Justine scoffed. "After this long? On what grounds?"

"According to Pete and a report in the newspaper, on the grounds of a conspiracy theory."

"Conspiracy?" Mica asked.

"The newspaper said that Bracken claims he's a scapegoat, that the police were pressured to make an arrest because Uncle Lawrence was mayor at the time. Pete said Bracken has a new gung-ho attorney."

Justine frowned. "So how does this affect us?"

"I think we should go to the police and tell them what we saw that day."

She stopped and clasped Regina's arm. "Are you crazy? We can't say it was or it wasn't Bracken." She'd decided that the impression that the murderer seemed familiar was a manifestation of her replaying the scene in her mind a thousand times over the years. "We'd open a can of worms for nothing."

"But we can offer other corroboration, like the approximate time of death."

Mica grabbed Regina's other arm. "But the man is *guilty*. He killed her because he was pissed off when Aunt Lyla fired him."

"If she fired him, then why was she with him at Lovers' Lane?"

"One last fling," Justine said. "Anger can be a powerful aphrodisiac."

Regina looked down where they held her. "Are you going to pull me in two?"

They released her, and Regina resumed walking. They followed.

"There's something else," she said.

Justine didn't like the sound of Regina's voice. "What?"

"The murder weapon was never found."

"That's impossible," Mica said. "I remember you saying the letter opener was lying on the seat."

"It was," Regina said. "So why wouldn't the police have found it?"

Justine shrugged. "Maybe Bracken came back and removed it."

"Or maybe the person who found her body and reported it to the police took it—wasn't it a hunter?"

"Two squirrel hunters," Justine added.

Regina stopped walking. "I think I saw the letter opener last week listed on an on-line auction house."

After she explained the strange circumstances, Justine waved off her suspicions. "But you don't *know* that it was the same letter opener."

"That's right," Mica said. "If we came forward, we could create enough doubt to get Bracken off—you wouldn't want that, would you?"

"I would if he's innocent."

Justine turned around to face Regina. "Who else could have done it?"

"That's for the police to figure out, isn't it?"

Mica joined her to face Regina. "Don't you think poor Uncle Lawrence has been through enough?"

"I believe Uncle Lawrence would want to know that the right man is in prison." Regina frowned. "And you can't tell me that keeping this secret all these years hasn't weighed on your mind. Wouldn't it be a relief to get it out in the open?"

"No," Justine and Mica chorused. Justine glared at Mica, who glared back.

"Don't forget we have our own lives to think about," Justine added. "I don't want to get dragged down into a scandal."

Regina lifted her eyebrow. "Since when?"

Justine sighed. "All right, I'll be honest. This shooting thing has put me on shaky ground with Cocoon. I simply can't afford to be associated with a murder investigation, too."

"It wouldn't look good to my sponsors, either," Mica said. "I could lose contracts."

"But *we* didn't murder her!" Regina said.

"We could still be brought up on charges," she reminded Regina. "Leaving the scene, not reporting the crime."

"But we were children."

"I was seventeen," Justine said. "They might look at me differently than you and Mica. No—going to the police is not an option. We all have too much to lose and nothing to gain."

Regina clenched her teeth and a little vein popped out in her temple. "What about doing what's right and being able to sleep at night?"

"I sleep fine; don't you, Mica?"

Mica nodded. "Fine."

"It's settled then," Justine said. "Nobody talks to the police. And they have no reason to come to us, since nobody knows we were there that day." She angled her head. "Nobody knows—right?"

"I haven't told a soul," Regina murmured.

Justine surveyed Mica's high color with narrowed eyes. "How about you, Benedict Arnold?"

# fourteen

DON'T make yourself a target for potshots.

Mica swallowed under Justine's stare. A hot, guilty flush crept up her neck, but she covered it with her hand. Her sister already didn't think much of her, so she wasn't about to admit her indiscretion. From Justine's perspective, revealing their secret would be bad enough, but revealing it to *Dean* . . .

"No. I didn't tell anyone." It wasn't a lie really, since Dean was more rodent than human.

Justine looked unconvinced, but Mica didn't waver. Finally Justine nodded, "Good," and turned back to Regina. "We're keeping our mouths shut."

Regina shifted her backpack, her expression reserved. "Twenty years ago I let you talk me into keeping quiet, and I've regretted it ever since. But now, knowing that an innocent man could have spent all this time in prison because we were too cowardly to come forward . . . I can't live with that on my conscience."

Justine wagged her finger in Regina's face. "If you were any kind of sister, your *conscience* wouldn't allow you to drag us through the mud."

Regina's face was a mask of hurt. "If I were any kind of sister? You mean the kind that still follows your orders, regardless of the consequences?"

Justine simply lifted her chin in defiance.

Regina looked her way. "Mica, do you feel the same?"

She was torn between sympathy for Regina and concern about her own livelihood. She'd given the limo driver all her cash except ten dollars and prayed that Cissy and John wouldn't take her up on her offer to stay in a motel. If her money woes weren't enough, imagining the look on Everett Collier's face when she told him she was enmeshed in a murder trial tipped the scale. "I'm sorry, Regina; I have too much to lose. If we knew the man was innocent, it would be one thing, but he's probably guilty."

"But we don't *know* he's guilty."

"Yes, we do—a jury decided twenty years ago based on the evidence."

"They didn't have all the evidence."

"They obviously didn't need it!" Justine practically shouted. "Regina, why can't you ever leave well enough alone?"

Mica recognized the signs—high-pitched voice, bulging eyes—Justine was on the verge of saying something terrible. She put out her hand, but her redheaded sister was like a boulder on an incline—once she got rolling, there was no stopping her.

"Stop living vicariously through your meddling and your stupid books, Regina! Let people live their lives, and get one for yourself!"

Mica averted her gaze, tingling for Regina. She wanted to say something to defend her, but she recognized the value of being on Justine's side of this argument, even if her methods were unkind.

The silence dragged on and on as everyone absorbed the words that still hung in the air and waited for the fallout.

"Well," Regina finally said with a little laugh. "Don't hold back, Justine."

Justine released an exasperated sigh. "Drop this, Regina. Forget about it. We all have enough going on in our lives without you bringing more grief down on our heads."

A loud crack penetrated the air, and a few seconds passed before Mica identified the noise as a gunshot. A second loud report sounded, and bark flew off the tree nearest Justine. Mica screamed and hit the dirt, landing on top of Justine, who lay on top of Regina.

"It's that Crane woman," Justine gasped, groping in her bag. A hairspray bottle went flying. "She's found me."

Regina's eyes flew wide. "What are we going to do?"

Mica was too frightened to offer advice.

"I have a gun!" Justine shouted in the direction of the shot, still rummaging. She tossed out her makeup bag, her wallet. "Do you hear me, Lisa? I'll shoot the next thing that moves!" Cell phone. Sunglasses.

"Justine?" a man shouted. "Justine, don't shoot. It's Pete Shadowen."

Mica went limp with relief and Justine grunted under her deadweight.

"Pete!" Regina shouted. "Someone's shooting at us!"

"No." His voice sounded closer. "It was just a rabbit hunter."

He emerged from the trees, and the sisters began to untangle.

"Are you all okay?"

They were slow to respond but finally stood and brushed off their clothes. Mica's knees knocked, and her bladder felt loose.

"What are you-all doing out here?" he asked.

"We were taking a walk," Justine said, glaring at Regina.

Regina looked at Pete. "What are you doing out here?"

"Got a call from the Hendersons over the hill about a prowler, and I thought it might be our fugitive." Pete had apparently taken ownership of Justine's predator. He pointed. "Damn fool hunter left a shell in a tree down there, too. You-all could've been killed."

"Did you get him?" Regina asked.

Pete shook his head. "When he saw me, he ran. I wanted to make sure you-all were okay."

Justine leaned over and gathered the items scattered from her bag. "You don't have to be so paranoid on my account. The woman crossing the Pennsylvania state line wasn't Lisa Crane."

"But she hasn't been caught."

Justine hesitated. "No."

"So she *could* show up."

"It's a stretch," Justine said. "But yeah."

"Thanks, Pete, for looking out for us," Regina cut in with a smile. "We thought we were goners."

He saluted. "No way I'd let someone hurt you, Regina." He gestured behind him. "I'm going to knock on a few doors and see if I can find the jerk. You-all have a safe walk back." His gaze lingered on Regina before he turned and walked away.

Regina refastened her backpack and from the expression on her face, Mica knew she was thinking about the words Justine had said before the commotion. "You two go ahead. I think I'll sit here for a few minutes and sort things out."

Justine shrugged. "Fine. I'm going back. Mica, are you coming?"

Mica blinked, but her heart leaped childishly at the spontaneous invitation. "Sure, I'll walk back with you."

She gave Regina an apologetic look, then turned to follow Justine. As the minutes passed, her mind raced for a safe subject, but with everything going on in their lives at the moment, she couldn't think of a topic that wasn't a land mine.

"I like your car," she ventured.

"Thanks. It was a gift from the company."

"They must think a lot of you."

"Yes. I have everything I could possibly want."

Mica was happy for her, truly.

Justine reached up to grab a leaf from a limb as they walked by. She twirled it by the stem. "I gather from your commercials that you're doing well, too."

For now. "Oh, we're—I'm comfortable."

"Must be exciting, all the parties, the clothes, the celebrities."

The booze, the debt, the sucking up. "Yeah, it's exciting, all right." Then she sighed. "Look, Justine, I've been waiting for the right time to tell you this, but I left Dean."

Justine tore the leaf in two, then tossed the pieces to the ground. "How am I supposed to feel about that, Mica? Sad? Happy? Indifferent?"

She shrank from the venom in Justine's voice. "I just thought you should know."

Justine's laugh was brittle. "Did you meet someone else?"

Mica was stunned. "No."

"I mean, you hear stories about models and their agents hooking up."

*Everett?* She laughed. "My agent is gay."

Justine frowned. "Are you sure?"

"Yeah. I mean, Everett's never told me, and he isn't effeminate at all, but I have it on good word." Then *she* frowned—Dean knew how much she respected Everett, adored him even. Had Dean told her Everett was gay to circumvent any possible attraction on her part?

"So," Justine said. "Now that your affair with my fiancé has run its course, you expect that you and I can just pick up where we left off?"

Mica chose her words carefully. "I was hoping we could start somewhere."

Justine stopped and turned her back, staring over a rolling field of Queen Anne's lace. Mica took the fact that her sister wasn't swinging as a good sign and tried to think of the next step on the road to forgiveness. Of course! "How about us driving to Asheville to do some shopping? I missed your birthday last month."

"You missed my birthday for the last twelve years."

"So let me make it up to you." She'd write a check for everything and worry about it later. "Come on; it'll be fun."

Justine turned to look behind them, but they were alone on the trail. "Should we invite Regina?"

She loved Regina, but she didn't want the subject returning to Lyla's murder and more questions about keeping their pact. "Let's just me and you go—it'll be like old times."

For the first time since she'd arrived, Justine looked at her without contempt. "Okay. Let's go spend an obscene amount of money."

# fifteen

DO touch, but DON'T look. Too closely.

By the time Regina got past the initial hurt of Justine's words, rehashed the decision at hand—to no good end—and walked home, Justine's car was gone. But another car was there, a black Lincoln with D.C. tags. She smiled—*Uncle Lawrence.*

She jogged up to the house and found her favorite relative sitting on the front porch with his sister, Cissy, drinking lemonade. He stood and clasped Regina in a bear hug. "How's my best girl?"

She grinned, always at ease with Lawrence's happy-go-lucky personality. He was still ramrod-straight, still handsome. "I'm fine. I saw you on *Meet the Press* a few weeks ago. You stole the show."

Uncle Lawrence had such presence, and his life story was so fascinating—impoverished childhood, academic wonder boy, Vietnam war hero, successful entrepreneur, beloved political figure, the total package.

His smile was humble. "Thank you, sweetheart."

"Where are your sisters?" Cissy asked from the rocking chair. Her hair was bound up loosely. She still wore her flowery church dress and jewelry, but she was barefoot.

Regina gave her a kiss on the cheek. "I don't know. We went for a walk, but they came back before I did." She omitted the part about being shot at. Her mother had enough on her mind.

Cissy tsk-tsked. "Lawrence dropped by to see all of you, and you're the only one here."

And she wasn't worth the trip.

Lawrence squeezed her arm to cover Cissy's gaffe. "Don't tell them, Regina," he said in a conspiratorial whisper, "but you were always my favorite anyway. Sit down with us, my dear. Your mother says you've come to save her and John from the poorhouse."

Regina sat on the top step with her back against a white column. "I'm just helping the appraiser from the bank."

"He's probably at the shop right now, robbing us blind," Cissy said.

"Mom, Mitchell Cooke isn't going to rob you blind. Besides, Daddy is at the shop with him." She looked back to her uncle. "I believe Mitchell's connections will help bring more attention to the auction."

"Cooke—is he local?"

"No, he . . . travels around."

"That name's familiar to me." Then he laughed. "But heck, every name is familiar to me."

"She has a crush on him," her mother said with a "pshaw." "Regina, you just wait and see—he's flirting with you so he can take advantage of you."

She winked at her uncle. "Thanks for the warning, Mom."

Lawrence laughed. "How's the book business?"

Dearest Lawrence, he always showed an interest in whatever she was doing in life—high school, college, and now her career. "It's wonderful—I love my job. How's the campaign going?"

"It's looking very good, very good indeed." He

leaned over to scratch his ankle, then ran a finger along the inside of the heel of his stiff wingtip and sighed. "I'm starting to feel as if all these years of wearing bad suits and uncomfortable shoes might have been worth it."

She laughed. "I can't wait to call you Senator Gilbert."

"Fingers crossed." He gave her a coy smile. "You know, my manager has been approached by a couple of publishers for my memoirs if this race pans out. Haplin, I think, and Grass House. Do you think your press would be interested?"

"Are you kidding? Of course we would, but I'm afraid we can't offer the kind of advance that those publishers will put on the table."

He dismissed her concerns with a wave. "Nonsense. I've got all the money I need, but I'll only have one shot at a book, and I want it to be good. I'd want you to be my editor, of course."

Anticipation welled in her chest—Green Label had never released a political best-seller. She couldn't deny it would be a feather in her cap. "I'd be honored, Uncle Lawrence."

He raised his finger. "*If* I win."

"You'll win."

"Lawrence has offered me a job with his campaign," Cissy announced.

"That's great." Regina gave her uncle's hand a grateful pat. The position would transition Cissy back into the working world. Regina had meant to talk to her sisters today about possible financial assistance for their parents, but she'd let their petty words get to her and distract her from what was important. As usual. "How long will you be in town?"

His smile faded a bit. "Just tonight—I'm afraid I

have some unpleasant business to attend to in Charlotte next week."

"That murderer Elmore Bracken wants a new trial," Cissy said. "The nerve of that scum. Disrupting Lawrence's life after all this time, now, when he's about to run the biggest race of his career."

Guilt was a foul-tasting substance. How could she take her shaky story to the authorities and possibly plow a furrow through Uncle Lawrence's life? He'd been through so much, including the humiliation of Lyla's indiscretion and sensational murder. He'd channeled that pain into public service, and Monroeville had profited hugely from his political influence—new roads, a new water plant, new schools.

"There, there," he said, soothing Cissy. "I'm certain the timing is precisely the angle Bracken and his attorney are going for. They think I'll be too busy to attend the hearing, or that the judge will grant a new trial to avoid the appearance of favoritism because my name is connected to the case."

A new wrinkle occurred to Regina. "Do you think your political adversaries could be behind the hearing?"

He made a rueful noise. "You don't get to this level without making a few enemies. A new trial and the commotion around it would be a gift to my opponent."

"I believe the voters would sympathize with you," Cissy declared, already sounding like a good campaign worker.

"Maybe," he conceded. "Or my constituents might be convinced that I'd be so distracted by a new trial that I couldn't fulfill my duties." He shrugged. "And maybe I couldn't."

She digested his insightful words. She hadn't considered all the motivations coming into play, or all the ramifications of a cathartic confession. Maybe Justine and Mica were right . . . for all the wrong reasons, but still . . .

Then her uncle brightened and pushed himself to his feet. "I've just decided to take it one day at a time. I'm afraid I must go—I'm presiding over Cub Scout presentations at your aunt's park." He grinned. "Too bad the tykes can't vote."

Regina laughed and walked him to his car for a last hug. "Uncle Lawrence, I hope that . . . everything turns out the way you want."

"My dear, I learned a long time ago that things don't always turn out the way you want, but things generally turn out for the best." He sobered. "It's good of you to come home and look after your mother."

"Since Justine and Mica are home, they're looking after her." She glanced toward the porch where her mother sat rocking. "They're both closer to Mom."

"Maybe. But everyone in this family knows you're the one to count on in a pinch."

He always knew what to say, how to make the middle daughter feel special. And she loved him for it. Such a shame that he'd never had any children of his own.

Uncle Lawrence climbed into the car and started the engine, then rolled down his window. "Oh, and some advice on your Mr. Cooke." He winked. "Flirt back."

"You're here early," Mitchell said from the office door.

Regina looked up from a ledger, annoyed that she was glad to see him, then reasoned that it was only because he wasn't related to her. "It was the least I could do since I left you on your own yesterday." Plus she'd wanted to get out of the house as soon as possible this morning.

"I only worked half a day," he said. "I tagged a few more pieces for the dump—the truck is coming Wednesday." He held out the requisite box of doughnuts.

Many missed gym visits crossed her mind, but she took one anyway. "What did you do the rest of the day?"

"Filled a cooler with beer; then your dad, Sam, and I went fishing."

She frowned. "I thought Dad was watching the shop."

He shrugged. "Business was slow, and he looked like he could use some male company. No offense."

The idea of her father turning to a stranger for support rankled her. "He did seem better when he stopped by the house last night." He hadn't been hammered.

"Your dad isn't much of a talker—or a fisherman, for that matter—but he does adore you girls."

"He and Mica were especially close. Her absence has been hard on him, and now that she's back—it's almost as if he's afraid to talk to anyone."

"He blames himself for hiring that loser guy to work here."

"Dad couldn't have known how things would turn out with Dean."

He shrugged. "Bottom line, he believes he didn't protect his daughters." Then he held up his hands. "But you didn't hear that from me."

She nodded, dismayed to discover yet another layer of family disharmony. She pointed. "I made coffee, but don't expect miracles."

He poured himself a cup. "So what did you do yesterday?"

"I spent time with Justine and Mica, got shot at, and I helped Mom in the garden."

"Run that middle thing by me again."

She waved her hand. "We took a walk; a hunter mistook us for game; we're fine."

"O-*kay*." He snagged two doughnuts from the box. "How are your sisters getting along?"

"A temporary truce." So they could gang up on her. And go shopping, according to the bags they'd toted in. But at least they were talking, and that was something.

"You look tired."

She shrugged. "Just missing my own bed, I guess."

He tried the coffee, winced, then dropped into one of the desk chairs. "Hm. Don't think I've ever been attached to one particular bed." He flashed her a cocky smile. "Yours must be special."

Over her coffee, she gave him a withering look.

He looked at Sam and shrugged. "Just trying to get her to smile. She's really something when she smiles, isn't she, Sam?"

Sam barked in agreement, forcing her to smile and shake her head at their silliness.

"Ah, there it is. Now, Sam, if we could only figure out why she wears her hair in such a tight little bun."

She smirked.

"Or why she wears glasses that she obviously doesn't need."

She lost her smile. "I like my glasses."

He took out half the doughnut with one bite and chewed thoughtfully. "I think you hide behind them."

"You're ridiculous. And way out of line."

"Out of line, maybe, but I looked at your lenses when you left your frames here. They're clear glass."

She looked back to the ledger. "I've worn glasses my entire life. After I had laser surgery, I couldn't get used to looking at myself without them."

"Take my word for it, you look fine without them."

She lifted her pencil and surveyed the sexy tilt of

his smile. "Don't flirt with me, Mitchell. I'm sure you have a girl in every port, but this girl isn't interested."

"Do you have a boyfriend back in Boston?"

She thought about Alan Garvo and their studiously corporate—and corporeal—affiliation. "No."

"Still carrying a torch for someone?"

*"No."*

"So what's the problem? I'm free, you're free, and there's a definite attraction between us."

She lifted an eyebrow. "Speak for yourself."

The rest of the doughnut disappeared. "All right—I'm attracted to you. I'm a red-blooded American guy who appreciates a nice view. Have dinner with me tonight."

He was appealing, but he knew that, of course. She looked back to figures in the ledger. "I'm having dinner with Pete Shadowen."

"What?" He made a disgusted noise. "You're going on a date with that fathead?"

"It's not a date; it's two old friends catching up."

"So have lunch with me."

"I brown-bagged a sandwich."

"We can have a picnic." He signaled Sam, who immediately came over to nuzzle her knee.

She was starting to get annoyed at the man's doggedness. And his pimp dog. "Knock it off, Mitchell. I publish entire books about guys like you and why women like me should keep their distance."

"Do you always follow your own advice?"

She pushed up her glasses. "Yes."

He sighed noisily, then snapped his fingers. The dog withdrew from her leg and trotted back. "We're wearing her down," he assured Sam.

She gave him a "fat chance" look, but he seemed undaunted.

"Did you make any decisions about the, um, *thing* you were looking for on-line?"

"No." But she'd thought of little else since her walk yesterday with Justine and Mica. And since her visit with Uncle Lawrence. The simplest solution would be to keep her mouth shut.

"Do you want to talk about it?"

"Not with you."

He worked his mouth back and forth. "Fair enough. Can I offer a piece of advice?"

She shrugged, not about to let on she was interested.

"Well, in my experience, the most difficult option is usually the right one."

His words went down like a big, bitter pill. Beneficial, but not what she wanted to eat.

He stood up and clapped his hands. "Okay, I guess I'll get to work."

Better to forget the missing letter opener for now and concentrate on the job at hand. "Want to get started on the pottery? I just need to make a few more entries here."

"Sure. Maybe we'll find a piece of early Rookwood."

She nodded. "Then we could all go home." Literally, since a find of that magnitude might negate the need for an auction. Cissy and John could liquidate, split the money, and go their separate ways. As is, how either of her parents would make a living, she wasn't sure. She'd wrongly assumed they'd prepared for their retirement. She had some savings, but not enough to make a difference. Maybe Justine would pitch in, or Mica, since she was making such great money. Too much to think about, and Mitchell's flirting had put her in a skittish mood.

*"Flirt back."*

From beneath lowered lashes, she watched him

leave the room. His red T-shirt fitted snug across his shoulders, and his Levi's were equally well acquainted with their contents. She slid her glasses down her nose for an unobstructed view. Unbidden, the tip of her tongue curled out to touch her upper lip. She was human, after all. Sam looked back, caught her looking, and barked happily.

Mitchell turned. She stabbed at her glasses and sent them flipping off her face. She juggled them to the tune of his amused chuckle, then jammed them back on her face. "What?"

He smiled wide. "Nothing." Then turned around, kept walking, and gave his behind a little shake.

Regina closed her eyes in perfect mortification, then stuck her tongue out at Sam. Now there would be no living with the man.

He didn't tease her when she joined him in the showroom a few minutes later, but he did maintain an infuriating smile as he sang along under his breath to Muddy Waters' "(I'm Your) Hoochie Coochie Man" playing on the blues station. She ignored him as much as possible, but when she wasn't looking, someone had turned up the sexual thermostat in the room. Suddenly she was fidgety and self-conscious every time their hands brushed or their gazes met. He, meanwhile, maintained a graceful, athletic command over his body. Even though they processed dozens of pieces of pottery and porcelain and glassware, two hours *crept* by as she fought Mother Nature. Her hormones were on a slow, steady drip. Building. Accumulating. Preparing. When she almost dropped a Van Briggle crock, Mitchell's hands went under hers to cradle the valuable piece.

"Easy," he said, but didn't seem to be in a hurry to remove his hands.

"I've got it," she said, noting that he had a workingman's hands—strong and work-hewn.

"You sure?"

"Y-yes." And warm. Very warm.

He rescued the dark piece of earthenware and, much to her chagrin, ran his hands over the smooth surface, feeling for defects. Unerring. Sensitive. Deft. Feeling utterly defeated, she watched unabashed.

"No cracks or chips," he announced. "Needs cleaning, but it's a nice example. Common, but definitely collectible."

She murmured agreement but shifted uncomfortably as he set the crock aside and entered info into his laptop. Her father should be coming downstairs soon and would dispel the intimate atmosphere that had sprung up between them. Meanwhile, she decided that talking would be the best use of her pent-up energy.

"We were joking about Rookwood earlier, but have you ever run across anything truly remarkable that someone didn't know they had?"

He shrugged. "Once I found an ancient prayer rug at a roadside sale. Amazing condition. The old lady was asking ten bucks, and I knew it was worth about a thousand times that much."

"What did you do?"

"I gave her the ten bucks and got her address. When I found a dealer for the rug, I took her the money, less a twenty percent commission."

"That was generous of you."

"It was worth it to see the look on her face. It's the thrill of the find that drives me, not the money."

"You mentioned that your parents were in the business—are they still living?"

"Yeah. They live near Charlotte. My younger brother is there, with his wife and two daughters."

"Is he your only sibling?"

"Uh-huh. He's an attorney, private practice."

"*Oh.*" Too late, she heard the comparison in her

own voice—the same way people reacted when she told them her little sister was the Tara Hair Girl. When he looked up, her cheeks warmed. "I didn't mean to imply . . . anything."

He smiled. "That's okay. It's natural for people to compare siblings. I guess it's a fascination with the different outcomes of the same environment. And it's true—David is an attorney, and I'm a junk man."

For some odd reason, she didn't want to hear him denigrate his profession. "That's not true."

He laughed, a pleasing, sexy rumble. "I'm totally comfortable with my line of work. It might not command the prestige of practicing law, but doing on-the-road appraisals fits my lifestyle right now."

Right now. As in living for the moment. She duplicated his casual smile. "No sibling rivalry in the Cooke family, then?"

"Once upon a time, perhaps, but not now."

Ah, so he *used* to be jealous of his brother. "Are you close to your family?"

He nodded. "I see them often, and I stick around until they start pressuring me about settling down." He laughed again, irresistibly.

Even as she laughed with him, Regina realized that he was giving her what was known in the singles world as "the disclaimer." He wanted to sleep with her and promised it would be a supernatural experience, but he had no intention of becoming involved in any kind of liaison that resembled a relationship. *Sign on the dotted line, please.*

His smile went from carefree to carnal in the blink of an eye. When the impact of his stare hit her, she stepped back and tripped over the base of a wooden cigar-store Indian. She flailed, then took the chief down with her and wound up flat on her back with the wind knocked out of her. This couldn't be happening. She was a respected senior editor for a prestigious publishing house.

The statue was lifted off her and Mitchell stared down. "Are you okay?"

She inhaled and nodded.

He burst out laughing and extended his hand down to pull her to her feet.

Her pride was mortally wounded. "I didn't think that was funny."

"You didn't see it from here. Are you sure nothing's broken?" He gave her a cursory pat-down until she pulled away.

"*Yes,* I'm sure."

"Good. Can I kiss you and get it over with?"

Regina blinked. His eyes danced while he waited for her to say yes or to fall into his arms. A reasonable assumption considering every cell in her body—excluding the few brain cells that were operating—strained toward him. God help all the women over the years who had lost their hearts to this traveling man.

He leaned closer. "Is that a yes?"

"I . . ." The door chime sounded, and she jerked her thumb over her shoulder. "Have to wait on a customer."

She turned toward the door and puffed out her cheeks with relief. But when she rounded the corner to see a salt-and-pepper-haired man pulling a handcart, she broke into a genuine smile. "Mr. Calvin!"

The man's turtle head jutted forward; then a smile split his face. "Regina?"

"You remember me." She clasped his dry, leathery hand between both of hers and inhaled the perpetual scent of mothballs and Listerine that clung to him. "How *are* you?"

"Pretty good for an old man," he said with a chuckle.

"I've thought of you so often over the years, and all the books you used to bring me."

"Did you ever find number twenty-one of your Nancy Drew mystery series?"

"No. And I can't believe you remember."

"I remember," he said. "I've never seen a child read as much as you did."

"And still do—I'm an editor at a publishing house in Boston."

He smiled. "I've been keeping up with you over the years. I knew you'd be the one who would make it."

"That's sweet of you to say, Mr. Calvin, but my sisters are both very successful."

"But you were special, Regina. You remind me of my own daughter."

She angled her head. "I didn't know you had a daughter."

He nodded. "Rebecca. Blond and petite, just like you. She's been gone from here for a long time, though."

She was thinking how sad that the woman never visited her father when Mitchell came around the corner, looking as if he'd recently been in pain. "Mitchell Cooke, I'd like you to meet Mr. Calvin, an old friend."

Mitchell extended his hand. "Hello."

"Are you Regina's boyfriend?"

"No," Regina said quickly. "Mitchell is helping Dad appraise all the items in the store." She glanced at the cardboard box on Mr. Calvin's handcart. "We're closing the business soon—I'm afraid we can't take on more inventory."

"Oh? Sorry to hear that. John's been a good customer over the years."

"What do you have in there?" Mitchell asked.

"Books."

"Care if I take a look?"

She'd forgotten he was a collector.

"No, go ahead."

Regina retrieved a soda for Mr. Calvin, and by the time she returned, the men were poring over two leather-bound volumes.

"I'll take them both," Mitchell said. He peeled off several bills from an impressive stack in his wallet, then loaded the box of books onto the handcart and wheeled it out to Mr. Calvin's truck.

She handed Mr. Calvin the soda and said good-bye. The books that Mitchell had purchased lay on a small table next to the door. She fingered the hand-sewn welts on the spine, then opened the cover of one. *A Collection of Law Essays, 1965–1975.* The other one, *Laws That Shape Everyday Life.* The bindings were exquisite, but it was the subject matter that intrigued her. Law? Mitchell must be more hung up on the rivalry between him and his brother than he let on. But then, no family was without its blemishes.

She closed the books and leaned against the doorjamb to study the puzzling man through the screen door. He hefted the box of books into the flatbed truck as if it weighed nothing, then situated the load according to Mr. Calvin's directions. Mitchell leveraged his big body with such deliberate ease, she could believe that he had never made an unintentional move—physical or otherwise. The man was in enviable control of his personal space and, in an alarmingly short period of time, had extended a persuasive invitation for her to share that space.

Tempting and temporary—Mitchell Cooke was straight from the pages of *Top Ten Types of Men to Avoid* (a national best-seller last winter). Effortlessly male, eminently sexy. Tall and substantial and ripe. Hmmnnn-um. She could do worse for a summer fling.

She sighed. But not this summer.

# sixteen

DO prepare for inevitable setbacks in your relationship, such as sex.

"You look swell," Pete said through the screen door. A toothpick bobbed in the corner of his mouth.

Regina smiled, glad she'd settled on the pink sundress. "Thanks. I'll be right out—let me grab my purse." Inviting him around to the back porch to chat with her family would have been the polite thing to do, but she didn't want to make a big deal out of their "date." Just as she retrieved her purse from the table, Justine appeared at the end of the hallway, cooling her neck with a paper fan on a stick. Since the walk yesterday, they had spoken very little.

"I heard a car—oh. Are you going somewhere?"

"To dinner."

"With the junk man?"

"No, with Pete Shadowen."

Her eyes narrowed. "Why?"

"Because he asked me." And it would be a relief to escape the tension radiating throughout the house.

Justine walked closer. "Let sleeping dogs lie, Regina."

Regina noticed her sister's green eyes looked suspiciously glazed—was she on something? "You don't have anything to worry about, Justine."

The fan resumed its rhythmic movement. "I hope not." She turned and walked away with the mild threat hanging in the humid air.

Regina's eyes stung, and her decision to reveal the truth to Pete was once again turned on end. *"The most difficult option is usually the right one."*

A headache had begun its ascent when she returned to the entrance. "I'm ready."

Pete seemed nervous, scratching and fidgeting as he held open the door for her. He wore what appeared to be his khaki deputy uniform, minus the accoutrements.

"Sorry, I'm on call this evening because of the Heritage Days. But you know how quiet it is around here." He took out the toothpick and laughed. "Having Mica and Justine back is town is the biggest thing that's happened in a while."

Her smile went a little flat.

He blanched and used the toothpick as a pointer. "I didn't mean . . . I mean Mica is such a celebrity, and it isn't often that we're on the lookout for a fugitive."

"Right. Did you find that hunter who was using us for target practice?"

He made a rueful noise and scratched below the waist. "No, but I asked the Hendersons to keep an eye out, and I posted No Hunting signs all over that area."

Her feet faltered a bit at the sight of the police cruiser, but she walked on, thinking her assistant, Jill, simply would not believe this date.

Pete held open the passenger side door. "I'm not used to having someone ride up front with me."

She slid into the seat and stared at the handcuffs dangling from the rearview mirror. She was starting to have a bad feeling about this.

Pete opened the door and climbed in, looking happy

enough for both of them. "Thought we'd go to the Crab Hut, if that works for you."

There were only a handful of local eateries to choose from, and crab was perfectly filling. "Sure. Do you still have your yellow VW Rabbit?"

"No, I sold it a couple of years ago. That was one great car, though." He sucked on the toothpick. "Yeah, that car saw some good times."

She had the feeling they were both thinking of Tobi Evans.

"Is she remarried?" Regina asked him.

"No," he said thoughtfully.

Five minutes in, and she had him fantasizing about another woman. That had to be some kind of record. Granted, though, she hadn't left him many memories to pine over.

They had to cruise town once just to make sure everything was contained before going to dinner. The streets of Monroeville were hopping, filled with gleaming sports cars filled with gleaming teenagers. Trucks were a favored mode of transportation, too, and Pete reported that neon-colored motorcycles, known as crotch rockets, were becoming all the rage. The girls looked impossibly thin and half-dressed; the boys, buff and tattooed. She felt positively retro by the time Pete backed into a parking place at the Crab Hut.

The Crab Hut was also hopping. And a bit pungent. Beach music played over the speakers, with an occasional country song thrown in to keep the locals happy. They decided to sit on the patio and split a bucket of crab legs. She ordered a beer; he ordered iced tea since he was on call. His screeching radio went on the table between them.

"Man, it's hot," he said, wiping at his forehead with his paper napkin.

"I forget about the heat," she said. "It always surprises me when I come home."

"You look good in a sweat," he observed, taking in her cleavage.

"Um, thank you." She shifted on the metal chair and decided to do it before she lost her nerve—tell him off the record that she alone had witnessed Lyla's murder and get his advice on how to proceed. It was the only way she could assuage her conscience and still protect her sisters. "Listen, Pete, I'd like to talk to you about something that goes way back."

"Okay, shoot." He got a goofy grin on his face, as if he expected her to say she regretted not letting him go to third base when they were dating in high school and she was back to make it up to him. She stared at the toothpick and had second thoughts. Maybe she wasn't ready to report the incident . . . yet. Maybe she simply needed to run it by an objective party to see if she sounded certifiable.

She glanced around them at the crowded tables, looking for . . . she didn't know what. The answer? A revelation? All she saw were couples and families sucking crab legs . . .

And Mitchell Cooke approaching, wearing a *Jeopardy* game show T-shirt and a thousand-watt smile. Her blood pressure skyrocketed.

He sidled up to their table. "Hi there."

"Hello," she murmured, and not pleasantly.

"It's Peter, isn't it?" Mitchell said to the other man.

"Pete, actually."

Mitchell clapped him on the shoulder. "I'm Mitchell."

"I remember." Pete looked befuddled.

"I just came out to get some dinner and a beer," Mitchell said. "But it sucks eating by yourself."

Regina poked her tongue into her cheek. "I would ask you to join us, but—"

"Are you sure you don't mind?" He pulled up a chair between them, forcing Pete to scoot farther around the table. "Wow, lucky I saw you guys sitting here."

"Yeah," Pete said. "Lucky. We already placed our order."

"I'll just add mine when the waitress comes back." He tipped up his beer bottle for a swig. "Were you two waxing nostalgic about proms and first kisses?" He laughed at his own wit.

She wanted to crack something of his with her crab leg tool.

Pete's radio belched static; then a woman's voice said his name. "I need to check in on the car radio," he said, talking to Regina but looking at Mitchell. "I'll be right back."

She waited until he was out of sight before turning on Mitchell. "You followed us!"

He was the picture of calm innocence. "That's not true. There aren't that many places in town to eat, and I had a hankering for legs." He tilted his head and scrutinized hers. "Nice dress."

"Is your MO to exasperate a woman into your bed?"

"Is it working?"

"Not even."

"Look, we were getting somewhere today before Mr. Calvin arrived and your dad put in an appearance. I think we owe it to ourselves to play it out. Pete will understand."

"Drink your beer, then get lost."

He sighed his acquiescence.

She noticed an absence at her crotch that seemed unusual when Mitchell was around. "Where's your dog?"

"I left him in the hotel room with the air-conditioning and a big pillow." He wagged his eyebrows.

She ignored him and swallowed a mouthful of beer. To her relief, Pete returned, but as soon as she looked at his face, she knew their date was over.

"Tractor trailer carrying paint turned over on the connector. I'm sorry, but I'll have to take you home."

"No injuries, I hope?"

"No, apparently just orange paint as far as the eye can see."

"I'll take Regina home," Mitchell told him.

"That won't be necessary," Pete said.

"But she hasn't even had dinner."

"We'll get it to go."

"Guys? I'm sitting right here."

They looked at her.

"What do you want to do?" Pete asked.

She drank from her beer. Well, she didn't want to have dinner with Mitchell, but compared to going home to spend the evening with her sisters, he was the lesser of two evils. "I'll stay, Pete. We'll do this again sometime."

He nodded morosely and left.

Mitchell gave her a wry smile. "It would've been much simpler if you'd just said yes when I first asked you to dinner. But I'm not complaining." He rubbed his hands together. "So, what am I having to eat?"

"We're splitting a bucket of crab legs."

"Sounds great."

She pointed to his shirt. "You're a fan of *Jeopardy*?"

"No. But I was a contestant ages ago."

She was slightly impressed. "Did you win?"

"Sure."

Of course. "I take it the Final *Jeopardy* question wasn't about Joe DiMaggio?"

He angled his beer bottle at her. "I was testing you with that All-Star Game remark. If you hadn't passed, I wouldn't be here."

She smirked. "I don't peg you as being quite that discriminating."

"Oh, but I am."

Despite her resolve to resist him, Regina had to admit the man was pulling her chain. His handsome face would be easy enough to dismiss if he were dim-witted or mean-spirited or lascivious. But dammit, his mind was sharp, his interaction with her dad and Mr. Calvin was gentle, and his sexy bantering left her stomach tingling low with promise. Thank goodness their bucket o' crab legs arrived, so she could stop thinking about the magnetism of Mitchell Cooke, former bad boy.

The waitress looked back and forth between them. "Wasn't there another guy sitting here before?"

"He was just holding my place," Mitchell assured her.

They both ordered another beer and started cracking handfuls of bright coral-colored legs—her with the tool, him with his bare hands. Of course.

"So you grew up here?" he asked, dredging a strip of white meat through drawn butter.

She nodded. "I was born here."

"Your parents?"

"Cissy grew up here. John grew up in Virginia."

"How did they meet?"

"Dad went to college with Cissy's brother."

"That would be Lawrence Gilbert?"

"Right."

"What's he like, your uncle?"

"Incredible. He and Cissy were orphaned, and he managed to raise her and himself. Then he won an academic scholarship to the University of Virginia, went into the military, and distinguished himself in Vietnam. Came back to Monroeville and made money in all sorts of little businesses and the stock market, then got involved in local politics."

"He was mayor when his wife was murdered?"

She nodded.

"What's the story there?"

She cracked more legs. "She was stabbed by their pool man after she fired him."

"Bracken?"

"Yes."

"In her house?"

"No."

He looked up.

Regina shifted on her chair. "Lyla was found stabbed in her car at a place the locals call Lovers' Lane."

"A make-out spot?"

"Yeah."

"She was doing the pool guy and he stabbed her?"

"That was the general theory, I believe."

"Were there any witnesses?"

*Act naturally.* "It happened in the woods, in a remote location."

"Who found her body?"

"A couple of hunters, I believe."

"Did Bracken confess?"

"No. But he was an ex-con, and he collected knives. He bought several from our shop even though it violated his parole. There was . . . fluid at the scene."

"Semen?"

She nodded. "It matched Bracken's blood type. Plus he had motive, and means."

"So he stabbed her with a knife?"

She squirmed. "The murder weapon wasn't found."

He chewed thoughtfully.

She busied herself meticulously picking out a ribbon of white meat.

"How old were you when it happened?"

She pretended to think. "About fourteen, I suppose."

"Where is this Lovers' Lane place?"

"Near Armadillo Creek."

"Near your house?"

She shrugged. "I guess so."

A teasing smile came over his face. "Ever been there?"

Regina pointed her cracking tool. "That's none of your business."

He smiled but turned thoughtful again so soon, she grew uneasy. After a drawn-out silence, he leaned forward until their faces were mere inches away. "I enjoy puzzles."

She remained silent, but she had a bad feeling about the direction of the conversation.

"I enjoy linking little disjointed bits of information and putting it all together." He took another drink from his beer. "Let me give you a scenario."

"I don't see what this has to do—"

"Humor me."

She knew the danger of overreacting, so she simply averted her eyes and kept her hands busy.

"The scenario goes like this: A woman is surfing an on-line auction and notices an item that looks like the weapon used in her aunt's murder. She thinks it's a coincidence, so she E-mails the seller, and the item is immediately pulled from the auction. Very suspicious, especially when she realizes it coincides with the convicted man lobbying for a new trial."

The bite of crab went down hard. "Interesting story."

"Uh-huh. Especially when you take into account that the murder weapon wasn't found. So in order for this woman to know what it looked like, she would have had to either witness the murder itself or come upon the scene shortly thereafter."

Heat suffused her face, but she tried to sound casual. "You have an active imagination."

"So my mother always said." He popped another bite into his mouth and took his sweet time chewing it. "But the really confusing part is that knowing the girl, I would've bet that she'd gone straight to her parents, or to the police. So I can only conclude that she was with someone she shouldn't have been with, or doing something she shouldn't have been doing, and didn't want to get into trouble herself." He smiled. "How am I doing?"

"I'm entertained." Not to mention on edge.

"I figure this girl thought she was off the hook because the bad guy was locked up. Only now she's starting to have doubts. Maybe the small-town investigation took a few shortcuts to bag the most obvious guy and left a killer walking the streets—"

"That's enough," she cut in, then wiped her mouth and tried to smile. "I mean, murder isn't exactly dinner conversation, is it? I almost prefer you when you're hitting on me." She drained her beer.

He studied her for a few seconds, then smiled to break the tension. "And that was my plan all along."

She pushed away her plate. "Whew, I'm stuffed."

"You barely ate."

"Excuse me; I'm going to the ladies' room." She pushed to her feet too abruptly for the alcohol she'd consumed, but he saved her chair and even stood up when she left the table, damn him. She hurried to the rest room and claimed a stall for pacing. So that's why he'd tracked her down tonight—he'd chained together all the pieces behind her secret. How stupid of her to borrow his laptop and ask questions about the auction site. She'd known him for three lousy days, yet he'd managed to inject himself into the most vulnerable area of her life and psyche.

The man was dangerous, on more than one level.

She washed her hands and dabbed cool water on her neck, then tried to repair her French twist. Her reflection revealed the extent to which Mitchell and the beer had compromised her barriers—pink cheeks, bright eyes, glistening skin. She looked as if she'd already been tumbled. She inhaled and exhaled a few times, telling herself she didn't have to own up to anything the man had said—it was purely conjecture on his part.

At the same time, she acknowledged a smidgen of relief to have heard the words come out of someone else's mouth instead of her own. And even if she didn't acknowledge the truth of his words, the conversation itself had relieved a good amount of tension that she hadn't even realized had built up over the past twenty years.

She returned to the table, feeling much refreshed.

"Better?" he asked.

"I'm ready to go."

He looked surprised but relented. He tossed a few bills on the table and walked—much to her annoyance—with his hand at her waist until they were at his big van. Night had fallen and the hot summer sky was filled with sparkling stars. Strains of the restaurant beach music carried on the air. In the distance, the top of a lighted Ferris wheel could be seen from the carnival set up in what she guessed was the high school parking lot. Because of her dress, he helped her climb into the passenger seat. It put them on eye level, and she saw that he wanted to kiss her. She wet her lips and waited, her heart pounding like a teenager's. Ten seconds, fifteen. Then he stepped back and closed the door.

*"Some of the happiest moments in life result from*

*rash decisions. You should try it sometime."*

*"Let people live their lives, and get one for your-self."*

While he circled the front of the van, she calmly took off her glasses. He climbed in and closed his door, then did a double take. And before she could analyze the good sense of it, she leaned toward him and kissed him soundly. His initial surprise quickly faded into hungry compliance, and he gathered her closer. His mouth was warm and fragrant and flavorful. His touch was just gentle enough to show restraint, just firm enough to show enthusiasm. His hands slid down her back and pulled her onto his lap. She was a goner.

A knock on the window startled them both. "Hey!" A man was at the next car with his big-eyed family. "Get a room, why don't you?"

They looked at each other and laughed. "Okay by you?" he asked so carefully that she couldn't even pretend to resist. She nodded, and they were at the Russell Motel, Room Number 8, in record time. "It's not fancy," he said, turning on the light. "But it's clean and the bed is king-sized."

She blushed down to her knees. Sam was thrilled to see them and gave her his standard greeting.

"In the bathroom with you, pal," Mitchell said, and led him across the room. "I'm not sharing."

When Mitchell returned, he extinguished all but the minimum of lights and looked her up and down with serious brown eyes. "Regina Metcalf, you are one great-looking woman."

She didn't know what to do with her hands. The synopsis of every sexual how-to manual she'd ever edited flashed before her eyes. DO this. DON'T do that. DO this twice—but only if he does *that* first.

Her mind spun with an impossible array of tips and techniques and tactics to guarantee an unforgettable sexual encounter. Caress. Lave. Linger. Tuck, clench, moan—or was it clench, moan, tuck? Too late, she realized it didn't matter—the *Top Ten Types of Men to Avoid* only wanted big breasts anyway. She folded her useless hands over her chest. In the face of impending inadequacy, she felt compelled to offer her own disclaimer. "M-Mitchell, I just want you to know, this isn't the kind of thing I normally do."

"I know." He lifted his T-shirt over his head.

Gaping was not sexy, but she couldn't help it. The man was . . . wow. Broad shoulders, smooth skin, indented muscle, smattering of dark hair that whorled into the waistband of his jeans. He extended his hand, and she went, acting on pure instinct. To hell with the how-to manuals.

They kissed past the point of her patience, so she started losing clothes. He followed suit but never took his eyes from her. When they were both nude, he caught her by her hands and pulled her down on the bed with him. She was overwhelmed by his blatant want of her, and by her own urgency.

But he slowed their frantic pace with a thorough exploration of her neck, breasts, and navel, then returned to her breasts unapologetically. She arched into his mouth, skimmed her hands over his shoulders, and drew his male scent into her lungs. The hardness against the inside of her thigh triggered a hum low in her stomach, a timeless calling that he answered by sliding his body higher. She unfolded beneath him, shamelessly female in that moment, and their bodies met to the tune of relieved murmurs. They clasped hands overhead, found a rhythm, and rocked with a fluid intensity that tested the limits of the bed. For the span of several long breaths they filled each other again and again. He kissed her feverishly and whispered in her ear, coaxing her to an explosive end of bright lights and involuntary shudders. Then his body was wracked with the spasms of his own release.

She closed her eyes and absorbed the sensation of his relaxed body entwined with hers, reveling in the immediate security of afterglow before the inevitable after*math* set in. As long as neither one of them moved, they could fake it a while longer. But they must have been more vocal than either one of them realized, because Sam's insistent barking from the bathroom invaded their world.

Mitchell laughed and lifted his head. "Sam, that's enough." The dog fell silent. "He thinks you're hurting me," he murmured against her neck, then carefully rolled onto his back. "Although I can't be sure I didn't strain something."

She laughed, relieved at his ease. And why not—it was just sex, after all, a summer fling. Hormones and high temperatures.

He found her hand on the bed between them. "Stay the night."

She closed her eyes in the semidarkness—his offer was soooooo tempting. "No, I should get back so no one will think . . . I mean, so no one will worry."

He rolled onto his side and picked up a strand of her hair. "I guess I wouldn't want Deputy Pete to get the credit for putting color in your cheeks."

She smiled. "Well, no one said I had to go right away."

His laugh was low and throaty. "I'm not as young as I used to be. Give me about ten minutes." He sighed and pulled her hand onto his stomach. "You were going to tell your story to Pete tonight, weren't you?"

She hesitated, but the cloak of darkness and the touch of his big hand made her feel safe. "Something like that."

"I wondered if you were with him when you saw whatever you saw, but then I remembered when he told you about the hearing. He was completely unaware of your reaction." He squeezed her hand. "You were with your sisters, weren't you?"

She swallowed audibly. "Why would you think that?"

"Because you protect them."

How could a man who made his living in the junk business be so insightful? "Even though my family is in shambles, they mean everything to me."

"I'd just hate to see you compromise your principles for your sisters' sake."

She tried to find shapes in the shadows on the ceiling. "You don't know what it's like to love your siblings so much that you'd give up just about anything for their happiness."

"I have some idea."

He used his thumb to make circles on her palm—why did that strike her as intimate?

"By the way, if you decide you need an attorney, let me know."

She'd forgotten his brother lived near Charlotte. She didn't think the situation would get to that point, but she didn't want to drag out the subject. "Thank you."

"You're welcome." He pulled her over to face him. "And your ten minutes are up."

# seventeen

**DON'T** trust a man farther than you can blow—er, throw him.

Regina had forgotten what good sex could do for a person's disposition—she winced slightly as she descended the stairs—and for a person's muscle tone. She'd slept in and decided to have breakfast with her sisters before going off to face Mitchell in morning-after mode. She'd waited for regret to settle in for her lapse last night, but truly, the only thing she regretted was that she only had a few more days off work to . . . exercise.

From her purse she retrieved her cellular phone and sat on the bottom step to phone her office. Jill answered on the second ring.

"Miss me?" Regina asked.

"Boy, oh boy—it's been dull around here without you. I hope you're having a good time down there."

Regina smiled. "Things are fine."

"Any old flames flickering around?"

She laughed. "No."

"How about new ones?"

Regina twirled a hank of hair at her ear, feeling like a co-ed. "I'll have to get back to you on that one."

"No way—you met someone? What does he look like?"

"Think Brad Pitt meets Harrison Ford."

"I'm going to kill myself. What does he do for a living?"

"He appraises antiques."

Pause. "Oh. That's . . . different. Maybe he can write a book for us."

"How's my African violet?"

"I've been giving it coffee, just like you said."

"And?"

"And it's not dead. Will you be back in the office Monday?"

"Actually, something has come up that might delay my return by a few days."

"Does this have anything to do with the junk man?"

Only indirectly. She was going to talk to Mitchell today about consulting with his brother regarding the best way for her to divulge the information she had on the Bracken case. She'd say that she alone had witnessed the murder and seen the murder weapon—partial perjury was better than not telling at all, she'd decided. Then she'd explain about the letter opener on the Internet auction site, and she would have done her civic duty.

"Are you there?"

"Yeah. Um, no, it doesn't have anything to do with . . . him. It's family business."

"Okay, I'll let Gene know. By the way, have you had a chance to talk to your sister about a quote for the Laura Thomas book?"

She winced. "I completely forgot. Actually, Mica is here—a surprise visit. I'll ask her today."

"Great. The Betteringly manuscript came in, and the Jarvis proposal for the next parenting book."

"Good. By the way, I am getting *some* work done—

I brought a manuscript from the slush pile with me that might turn out to be something."

"We like to hear that."

"And I need for you to give Gene a heads-up in the staff meeting today. My uncle Lawrence Gilbert is in town—"

"The politician? He's your uncle?"

"Yes. If he wins the North Carolina Senate race this fall, he said he'd consider bypassing offers from other houses to do his memoirs with us if I work on the project." Who knew—the Bracken hearing might turn out to be an interesting footnote.

"Gene will wet his pants."

"And on that note, I'll let you go. I'll check in with you again later in the week, when I know more about my schedule."

Regina disconnected the call and sighed, feeling better just knowing she'd made a decision. She considered talking to her Uncle Lawrence first but held out hope that the leads she provided would turn out to be nothing. If the judge determined that her testimony wouldn't influence the hearing arguments either way, the entire incident could be moot. But at least she could sleep at nights.

She heard laughter from the kitchen, and the sound buoyed her spirits. If there was a silver lining to the black cloud that hovered over the Metcalf family, it was the burgeoning reconciliation of her sisters. She pushed herself up, dusted off her jeans, and walked into the middle of a story Justine was telling.

"—and then Mica said, 'Senior prank, sir.'" Justine doubled over laughing, and Mica and Cissy slapped the table in their mirth.

Regina smiled at their silliness and dropped a crumpet into the toaster. "Good morning."

"Good morning," Cissy said.

"You were out late," Mica accused, as if she weren't allowed to have fun.

Justine handed her a glass of juice. "And I could have sworn that a blue van dropped you off in the wee hours instead of a deputy cruiser."

Regina maintained a placid smile. "Mitchell ran into us at the crab place, then Pete had to leave on a call, so Mitchell"—she waved vaguely—"brought me home."

Justine nodded. "Uh-huh. And exactly how many times did he 'bring you home'?"

They all laughed, and Regina decided she rather liked being the center of their girl talk. Justine and Mica had always been so much more outgoing, the family table conversations typically revolved around their social lives.

"Where are your glasses?"

On Mitchell's nightstand. "It's so hot, I decided not to wear them today."

No one believed her.

Cissy shook her finger. "Somebody who looks that good isn't about to stick around."

Apparently her mother thought she couldn't handle the ramifications of the "do something rash" advice. Regina buttered her crumpet and took a bite. "I don't expect him to."

"Men are snakes," Cissy declared, then teared up.

Guilt sliced through her over engaging in a summer fling while her mother and father were headed for Splitsville. "When was the last time you and Daddy talked?"

Cissy blew her nose. "Nothing left to talk about. I just want things to be settled quickly." She shook her finger again, and Regina realized why Justine had developed that finger-wagging habit. "Don't distract that young man from his work—after he appraises everything at the shop, he still has to come here and go through the house. I need him more than you do."

"Okay, Mother, I won't distract him." She checked her watch—ten-thirty. She was looking forward to seeing him—was that a bad sign?

The doorbell rang and her first thought was that he'd come after her. When that fantasy fizzled, she decided it was probably her father. Justine, however—dressed to kill in a tight new outfit—made a beeline for the door.

"Guess she's not worried about the Crane woman anymore," Regina muttered into her juice. "Any news on that front?" she asked Mica.

"Status quo."

She sat down next to Mica. "Sis, I know this is asking a lot, but would you be willing to lend a cover quote to a book by a hairstylist author of ours?"

Mica averted her gaze and stammered excuses until Regina touched her arm.

"You're busy—maybe another time." While Mica looked relieved, Regina looked for another topic of conversation, quelling hurt feelings—Mica didn't owe her anything. "Have you talked to Dean?"

"No." Mica's hand strayed to the bruise around her eye that was fading.

Regina set her jaw. She could kill Dean for what he'd done to her family—no wonder her father felt so remorseful about allowing the man in the vicinity of his daughters. She wanted to reach out to Mica, but her sister was so standoffish. "Mica—"

"Regina, Mica," Justine said from the hallway. There was a note of alarm in her voice.

They looked at each other and walked to the door, with their mother trailing. On the other side of the secured screen door stood a tall, slender man in a suit, mopping his forehead. Justine was as white as his handkerchief.

"What's wrong?"

"Are you Regina and Mica Metcalf?" the man asked.

"Yes, I'm Regina. Who are you?"

"My name is Byron Kendall. I'm an attorney with the firm representing Elmore Bracken."

Her knees weakened. "What does this have to do with us?"

"With all three of you actually. Our office received a tip early this morning that the three of you witnessed the murder of Lyla Gilbert twenty years ago and might be able to provide testimony that could help our client."

"What?" Cissy shrieked. "That's insane—get off our property."

"This is a law enforcement matter, ma'am."

"Mother," Regina said. "Let me handle this."

"You little do-gooder," Justine murmured behind Regina's ear. "I knew you couldn't keep quiet."

She sent a silencing glare to her big-mouth sister. "Mr.—I'm sorry, what did you say your name is?"

"Kendall."

"Mr. Kendall, tell me more about this 'tip' you received."

"It was an anonymous phone call to our office, and the details were credible enough to warrant an investigation."

She ignored Justine's huff. "What exactly do you want from us?"

"Just to answer a few questions."

"And if we decline?"

He pointed over his shoulder. "Then I get the sheriff involved."

She looked past him to where Pete Shadowen stood at the top of the steps. He gave her a stone-faced nod—

no doubt a little sore over her staying to have dinner with Mitchell last night.

Her heart thudded in her ears, and she grabbed onto the doorknob for support. "Can we do this here?"

"Fine with me."

"Do we need to have our own attorney present?"

"That's at your discretion."

"But we don't have an attorney," Mica said.

Regina bit down on the inside of her cheek—not one but *two* helpful sisters.

"This is just a preliminary interview," the man said. "If you tell me anything that I think will be of value, I'll ask you to sign an affidavit. You'll have time to consult with an attorney before that time."

Regina sighed. "Then I guess you'd better come in, Mr. Kendall."

♥

She watched with trepidation as Byron Kendall flipped back through the pages of notes he'd taken over the past couple of hours. She was completely drained from dealing with Cissy's tearful outbursts as the story unfolded and from arbitrating Mica and Justine's squabbling about details. Pete had joined them to take down information about the letter opener she'd seen on the Internet auction site. She provided a copy of the unanswered E-mail message, and from her purse she pulled the old inventory card she'd swiped from her parents' files.

" 'Bought from H.S.,' " Mr. Kendall read, then looked at Cissy. "Do you remember who that was?"

"Hank Shadowen."

Incredulity crossed Mr. Kendall's face. "The sheriff?"

Her mother nodded. "Hank traded with us on occasion."

Surprised at this new wrinkle, Regina glanced at Pete. "Did you ever see the letter opener?"

Pete clawed at his neck. "No, sorry."

Mr. Kendall pursed his thin mouth to hold back a smile. "Guess I'll have to talk to the sheriff again to let him know the murder weapon once belonged to him."

Another brick for building their theory of a police conspiracy, she realized with a sinking heart.

Pete kept scratching.

Mr. Kendall looked back to the three of them. "Are you certain that this letter opener was stolen and not sold?"

Regina nodded. "It disappeared from the display case along with some other items on a day we were supposed to be watching the store. We didn't want our folks to know it was gone."

"What other things were stolen?" Pete asked, taking notes.

She looked at her sisters. "I remember a gold watch, but that's all."

"A lipstick holder," Mica said. "It had rhinestones on it, I think."

Justine had nothing to add.

"They were all in the same display case," Regina explained.

"A locked display case?" Mr. Kendall asked.

She wet her lips. "Yes, but—" She gave her mother an apologetic look. "There was a way to get in, if you knew the trick."

"And how many people knew the trick?" he asked.

"We girls knew." She looked at her sisters and sighed. "And we occasionally used it to open the case in front of customers if we couldn't find the key." Actually, she never did that, but she didn't want to rat out Justine and Mica.

"So anyone who frequented the store might have known how to get in?"

"Yes," she said, then angled her head. "Including Elmore Bracken."

He acknowledged the hit, then stood and flipped his notebook closed. "I guess that'll do it."

She stood, too. "Mr. Kendall, about this phone tip you received—was it a man or a woman?"

"A man, from a number traced to a Monroeville pay phone."

Her mind raced. It wasn't possible that Mitchell . . . no. What earthly reason could he have to call in a tip?

"Here's my business card with my contact information," Mr. Kendall said. "If you think of anything you'd like to add to your story, even if it's a detail that seems unimportant, call me immediately."

"What happens next?" she asked.

"I'll review the information with my colleagues, and we'll decide if there's anything here that would help our argument for a new hearing. If so, we'll be asking for affidavits." He gave them a flat smile. "I'll be in touch within a couple of days. Meanwhile, don't leave town without letting our office know how to reach you."

They followed him to the front door, and Regina scanned his card idly. LAW OFFICES OF ROSE, KENDALL, AND . . . *Cooke*? Her lungs squeezed painfully. "Mr. Kendall?"

He turned back.

"Your partner, would his name happen to be *David* Cooke?"

"That's right, David Cooke—do you know him?"

Cissy, Mica, and Justine turned accusing eyes her way. She pinched the back of her stupid hand to stem the stupid tears that threatened to gather. "N-no, but I know his brother."

She shoved past them and out the door, then down the steps. She headed toward the footpath through the trees that would take her to the antiques shop. As she pumped her arms and legs, she wiped hot tears. Stupid, stupid, stupid to have trusted the man. As a result of her loose lips and his duplicity, now her sisters were going to be dragged into the fracas with her. She'd wanted to protect them, and now this.

She trudged through the weeds and pushed past low branches, ignoring the scratches and scrapes. A few minutes later, she broke into the clearing around the shop and ran the rest of the way. She burst into the back door and triggered the chime. Sam appeared from the direction of the showroom and loped toward her.

"Not now, Sam."

She marched into the showroom, grateful that no customers were around to hear what she had to say. Mitchell straightened from a tray of jewelry he was examining with a magnifying glass and smiled wide, the cad.

"There you are. I wondered if you'd—"

She punched him in the mouth.

"Aw!" He covered his jaw with his hand. "What was that for?"

She punched him in the mouth again.

"Aw!" He backed up and held out his hand. "Whoa. If this is about last night, I was under the impression that things went rather well."

"You smooth-talking sack of shit." She shook her throbbing hand.

"Give me another chance, I'll—"

"An attorney from your brother's law office has been at our house for the past two hours. He said they received an anonymous tip from a man on a local pay phone that my sisters and I witnessed Lyla Gilbert's murder twenty years ago."

He squinted. "My brother's law office?"

She tossed the business card on the counter. "Your brother's firm is representing Elmore Bracken at his new-trial hearing. But you already knew that."

He picked up the card. "No, I didn't."

"I can't believe you have the nerve to lie to my face. Not after—" No, she wasn't going to bring sex into it. "I trusted you. I even listened to your advice—I was going to Charlotte tomorrow to tell my story, but I wasn't going to implicate my sisters. Thanks to you—"

"Stop," he said. "I didn't know that David's firm was involved with this case, and I certainly didn't make a phone call to reveal something we discussed in bed."

She crossed her arms. "I don't believe you."

He sighed and massaged the bridge of his nose. "Who came to see you?"

"Byron Kendall."

"Did you talk to him?"

"We had to!"

*"Without an attorney?"*

"We didn't have one handy."

"I told you to call me if you needed an attorney."

"Oh, so you were going to call your brother to represent our interests in this case, too?"

"No." He pulled his hand down over his face. "I'm an attorney."

She blinked. "What?"

*"I'm* an attorney. I was going to offer my services if you needed someone to sit in with you."

Of course—the law books, the sibling rivalry with his brother. "Why didn't you tell me?"

He rubbed his jaw. "It's a part of my life that I don't talk about."

Her mind raced. "How much trouble are we all in?"

"I don't know. Give me a chance to talk to Kendall and see what's going to happen."

She eyed him warily.

"Regina, I didn't betray your confidence. I swear."

He looked so sincere, she wanted to believe him. "But you're the only person I've discussed this with in twenty years."

"Then one of your sisters must have told someone."

"They said they didn't."

"Are your sisters completely trustworthy?"

She looked at him. "Are you?"

His expression was immobile, but he splayed his hands. "I guess those are questions you'll have to decide for yourself. Meanwhile, I'll call David and try to head off his partner." He gave her a wry smile. "Unless you want to hit me again?"

"Don't tempt me."

He walked a wide berth around her and retreated to the office. She lowered herself onto an 1890s settee and lay her miserable self down. She should never have come to Monroeville. *"Let people live their lives, and get one for yourself."* She closed her eyes, conceding that Justine was right. She had arrived with lofty ideas of mending her parents' relationship; then everything had snowballed out of control. Mitchell and his doughnuts. Justine and her fugitive. Mica and her black eye. Justine and Mica rolling on the ground. Justine and Mica turning on her. Deputy Pete and his toothpick. Mitchell and his . . . squiggle maneuver.

And now this Bracken hearing looming over her and her beloved uncle and sisters. All her fault. In fact, as a result of her arrival in Monroeville, pretty much everyone's life was more screwed up than before, especially hers. The one bright spot had been sleeping with Mitchell, and look where that had gotten her . . .

Despite his serious brown eyes, she didn't trust him ... not completely. ...

She must have dozed, because she was roused by the feeling of his lips on hers, warm and firm and practiced. She murmured beneath the pressure and inhaled his scent into her lungs ... wrong scent. And he was barking. No, Sam was barking. Her eyes flew open and wider still when she realized it wasn't Mitchell kissing her. The black-haired man pulled back and she sprang up in disbelief. *"Dean?"*

Dean Haviland was as dark as Satan and twice as handsome. "Hey, Blue Eyes." He flashed a killer grin. "Thanks for the welcome home."

Regina shoved at Dean's chest. "Get off of me!" She stood and backed away from him, marveling at his appearance.

Sam was still barking, then stopped suddenly and trotted over to stand next to Mitchell, who had materialized. "Is there a problem, Regina?" He stood close enough to pose a threat but hung back far enough to leave discreetly if need be.

"No problem here, man," Dean said, sauntering forward. "Regina, who's this guy?"

He didn't wait for her to introduce him. "My name is Mitchell Cooke. I'm doing some work for Mr. Metcalf."

"That's how I started out," Dean said, all borrowed suave and sophistication.

"Oh? And who are you?"

"Dean Haviland's the name."

Mitchell's slow and derisive scrutiny said he recognized the man by reputation. "Well, Dean, if you touch Regina again without her permission, I'll break your goddamn arm." Then he smiled.

Dean snorted at Regina. "Does this guy mean something to you?"

She narrowed her eyes. "Why are you here, Dean?"

He held open his hands innocently. "I'm on my way to your folks' house. Mica asked me to come."

She inhaled deeply, then exhaled. So Mica had lied about not talking to him. What could she have been thinking to invite this man back into her life? And with Justine visiting—oh, God, *Justine.*

"Regina," Mitchell said quietly, then nodded toward the office. "I have some information about . . . what we discussed."

Dean was already backing toward the door. He winked. "See you soon, Blue Eyes." The front door banged shut.

Mitchell wore a bemused expression. "So that's the guy who tore you and your sisters apart?"

Regina looked in the direction Dean had gone. "No. He's the guy who recognized we were already torn apart."

# eighteen

DO rehearse your "I'm over you" reunion scene.

Justine sat on the side porch smoking her third cigarette since the attorney had left. Dammit, dammit, dammit—everything that had ever gone wrong in her life she could trace back to one sister or another. It was obvious that Regina had blabbed the story to her fling thing and he'd promptly reported it to his brother. The man had probably come to town under the guise of appraising just to sniff around for local gossip that might help the case. If she got bogged down in a resurrected murder trial, she'd be fired for sure. And what kind of a recommendation letter was she going to get after she'd slept with the husband of the vice president of human resources?

She took a deep drag on the cigarette. She should've gone to Florida or to the Bahamas for a few days and found a tall beach bum to help her forget her troubles. She still wasn't sure what she'd been hoping for when she came back to Monroeville—maybe the warm fuzzies of having her parents all to herself like the three precious years before Regina came along. Just her luck and timing that Cissy and John would decide to split up this very week. And as for her father, well, she truly had believed him to be above the debauchery of most men. Tears welled in her eyes at the thought of lost father—daughter moments—those, too, seemingly stolen by Mica, John's little darling. Because when she'd absconded with Dean for LA, instead of offering Justine a shoulder to cry on, John had grieved for Mica.

She blew a stream of smoke into the air and scoffed at her genuine—albeit sappy—reason for returning home: the hope that she'd rediscover the basically good-hearted, loving girl she'd once been. Here was where she'd left that girl, the moment she discovered Dean and Mica's betrayal.

No one knew what she'd gone through those first few months. Regina had escaped to Boston to her new job. Cissy and John, as usual, were so wrapped up in each other that they hadn't paid her much attention. In their defense, they had never been demonstrative parents and didn't know how to help her through a traumatic experience that one of their other children had created. Meanwhile, all her own friends had gone off to college and exciting careers, which she had forsaken to be near Dean. Suddenly she was a jilted twenty-five-year-old with no prospects, and the only real talent she had was helping Tate Williams pretty up the corpses in his funeral home when his cosmetologist wife, Sarah, went to visit her mother in Atlanta.

"You have a real knack," Tate had told her. "These people didn't look this good when they were alive."

But since she hadn't wanted to work on stiffs the rest of her life, she'd answered an ad for a Cocoon makeup representative. Her life became a blur of home makeup parties, which she'd hosted in a much-laundered yellow suit. She'd zoomed to the top of the sales charts in no time. A couple of years later, she visited the Cocoon headquarters in Shively during a sales conference and realized that the real money was being made by the women in the offices on the penthouse level. She set her sights on one of those offices and, without the aid of a college degree, worked her way up the ladder by sheer grit. She was making more money than she ever dreamed of . . . and it still wasn't enough. It would never be enough until Dean Haviland could see her success and acknowledge that he'd made a mistake. That Mica's glamorous lifestyle couldn't compare with the authentic intimacy they'd once shared. That if he'd stayed with her, he could've had money *and* love.

After the jilting, she knew people had laughed at her, had pitied her. It was true—she hadn't seen it coming, because her connection with Dean had felt so powerful and deep. Nearly every night he would climb the trellis leading to her bedroom window and slide into her bed. Sometimes they would make fervent love while everyone in the house slept, but most nights they would simply lie awake talking about whatever came into their heads. Dean, she discovered, mostly wanted to talk about his meager childhood. She didn't mind, though, because he'd always end by saying their children would have a different life, a good life. They had plans. . . .

She stood and walked over to the porch railing. After one more drag, she stubbed out her cigarette and tossed the butt over the side into the jungle of shrubbery below. She leaned into the rail and stretched her back, arms, and legs. She felt itchy for a man. That was one thing about the South she had missed—the constant sensual bombardment from the environment. Heavily perfumed flora, humid, sticky temperatures, juicy, fleshy foods—relentless cues to make a woman ultra-aware of her body and its urges.

In the distance, a car engine revved, coming up the long driveway that set the Doll off the beaten path. Her pulse picked up, like every other time a vehicle had approached. She craned, waiting for the first glimpse, and soon the hood of a silver sports car came into view. A Jaguar——Dean's dream car. Her muscles felt weak, and her hands shook in anticipation of seeing him again. She'd taken pains with her own appearance, striking a perfect balance between casual and sexy with a white halter dress and red sandals. Her hair was down, the way he liked it; her perfume, his favorite. Mica had gone into town with Cissy to buy groceries—— the timing couldn't be better.

He pulled into the driveway and she was struck by the familiarity of his profile. She forced herself to breathe evenly as she made her way to the front porch and positioned herself to good advantage against a column. He climbed out and slammed the door, then glanced all around the property. Dressed in white pants, red shirt, and dark sunglasses, he was just as she remembered him——lean and beautiful, sexy as hell.

His gaze landed on her and stopped. Slowly he pushed back his sunglasses, and even at the distance, she could feel the impact of his black eyes. Her breasts hardened, and her thighs hummed, Pavlov-style. Dean walked closer, still staring, and she fixed her expression into aloof amusement.

At the bottom of the steps he stopped, wide-legged. "Hiya, Justine."

"Hiya, Dean."

"Long time, no see."

"Uh-huh."

"You look good."

"I know."

He laughed, flashing strong, white teeth. "Same spunk, I see."

She hadn't expected to be so affected by his smile. "What brings you back?"

He scratched his temple. "I lost something."

She angled her body to expose the high side slit of her dress. "And you think you'll find what you're looking for here?"

"Maybe." He perused the length of her leg. "Are you home alone?"

"Yes."

He wet his lips carefully, and she was shot through with sweet vindication that he still found her attractive, that they could still turn each other on with a few veiled words.

But the mood was broken by the appearance of Cissy's station wagon. Justine bit back a curse as Mica stared out the passenger-side window. She was out of the car practically before it stopped moving, charging toward Dean.

He smiled at her. "Hey, baby."

"What are you doing here?"

He looked confused. "You asked me to come here, remember? I couldn't get a flight, so I put two thousand miles on this car in two days flat."

Mica shook her head. "I don't know what you're talking about."

"I called you on your cell phone—you told me where you were and said to come get you."

"No, I didn't."

His frown gave way to an ingratiating smile. "You said you had just woken up—you just don't remember. A little too much painkiller, maybe?" He slipped his hand into her hair at the nape of her neck. "Has your neck been bothering you?"

She removed his hand. "I didn't invite you here."

"Okaaaay." He slipped his arms on either side of her waist. "Since I'm here, can't we at least talk?"

Justine's heart shivered—it was the first time she'd seen them touch intimately. Over the years, she'd imagined them together in so many configurations, but some part of her couldn't get past the idea of her sister being twelve years old when Dean came into their lives. All the pictures of them she had in her head were innocent—Dean blowing up balloons for Mica's birthday parties, teaching her how to bowl, the three of them going to high school basketball games together. Seeing his hands on Mica gave her more torturous images to ponder.

Mica twisted out of his grip. "I don't want you here. Leave. *Now.*"

*Don't leave.* Justine had to bite her tongue not to cry out. *I want you here.*

"I'm not going anywhere until you talk to me," he said with equal parts charm and firmness. "Everett told me about Tara's stupid demands. But you and I need to stick together on this. The only reason they want me off the set is because I demand high quality. Without me, they'll take advantage of you."

"That's only part of the problem," Mica said. "Not only do I want you off the set, but I want you out of my life. It's over, Dean. I'm moving out of the condo."

He scoffed. "With what? You don't have any money."

Justine blinked. By her estimation, Mica had written over three thousand dollars' worth of checks when they'd gone shopping.

"And without me," Mica said, "neither do you. Now leave."

"You can't cut me out of the business," Dean said. "I won't let you."

Then from out of nowhere, Regina and her bed buddy appeared, along with John, probably from the path through the woods. Now that the entire fam damily was here, she thought wryly, the fireworks could begin.

"Hey, Mr. Metcalf. How's it going?" Dean seemed genuinely happy to see John, but John stared at him stonily. Of course, John was probably stoned.

Mitchell Cooke was a good head taller than Dean and, from his body language, was spoiling for a fight. "I distinctly heard the lady tell you to leave."

"Hey—this is none of your business, pal. If you know what's good for you, you'll stay out of it." Dean grabbed Mica by the wrist. "We're going for a ride."

But the big guy was agile. He yanked Dean's arm up behind him and walked him to the Jaguar. When Mitchell released him, Dean twisted away, his face dark. "I'll be back."

"No!" her father shouted, and everyone froze.

John never raised his voice. Ever.

"I treated you like a son," he told Dean in a shaking voice, his eyes wide. "And you split this family in pieces. Stay away, or you'll be sorry."

Justine's chest swelled with sympathy for her father. John had been fond of Dean and had assumed that he and Justine would take over the business. She herself had always hated the musty old shop but tolerated it because of Dean. He had betrayed them all in one fell swoop.

Dean seemed as surprised by John's outburst as everyone else, and Justine thought for a moment that he might even apologize. Instead, he swept his arm to indicate John's perpetually disheveled appearance. "I split this family in pieces? Let me tell you something, old man—this family was in bad shape *before* I landed on the scene. But I guess that was hard for you to see through the bottom of a Jack Daniel's bottle."

John lunged for Dean, but Mitchell held John back, for his own sake, of course.

Justine pressed her lips together. Dean wasn't perfect, but he'd spoken the truth that no one else had the guts to say. He smirked at John, then climbed into his car and peeled out with a flourish.

She watched his car disappear and leaned into the column, feeling cheated. Twelve years of daydreams about a reunion, and this was the memory she had to take away. Frustration boiled in her stomach. If only everyone hadn't arrived. Once again, her family had ruined everything. She and Dean should have left Monroeville long before they'd planned, should have eloped, but Dean had shown a stubborn regard for the antiques shop that had baffled her at the time. She blinked furiously. On hindsight, perhaps he couldn't bear to leave Mica.

Regina climbed the steps and touched her arm, breaking into her thoughts. "Come inside. Mitchell has some news for us about the information we gave to Mr. Kendall."

Justine crossed her arms and glared at them both. "*Mitchell* is the one who spilled the beans—how can he possibly help?"

"I didn't make that phone call," Mitchell said.

She looked at Regina. "But you don't deny telling him?"

"Don't blame Regina. I figured it out on my own."

"Oh? And are you some kind of psychic?"

"No, I'm an attorney."

She lifted her eyebrows. "So you're not an appraiser?"

"I am an appraiser, but I'm also an attorney."

"And he's going to help us," Regina said, holding open the door.

The entire world had gone mad, it seemed. They all trekked inside and sat around the perimeter of the TV room, where Mitchell carefully explained that he hadn't known his brother David in Charlotte was working on the Bracken case and hadn't known about any connection of the case to the Metcalfs until the day Pete Shadowen mentioned the hearing to Regina.

"I haven't practiced criminal law in years," he said. "But I feel responsible by association to ensure you don't open yourselves to prosecution. Can you tell me what you told Mr. Kendall?"

They dutifully repeated their story in bits and pieces. Their father, who was hearing it for the first time, was visibly shaken. Cissy wept exuberantly and refused John's comforting hand.

Mitchell's expression became more and more dire. "Why didn't you come forward when it happened?"

Regina sighed. "We were afraid that if the killer thought we could identify him, he might come after us."

John stood and paced. "Why didn't you girls tell *me*? I would have protected you."

Justine had never seen him so agitated. His face was redder than usual, and he seemed a little disoriented. She moved toward him, but Mica intercepted. "It's okay, Daddy."

Knowing he'd rather have her sister's reassurance, Justine looked back to Mitchell. "What can we be charged with?"

"Leaving the scene and failing to report a crime. Maybe obstruction of justice, although that's a stretch. And the fact that you were minors at the time will mitigate the charges." He looked serious. "Except possibly for you, since you were older. But hopefully, it won't get to that point."

"Could this lead to Elmore Bracken getting off?" John asked, wringing his hands.

Mitchell hesitated before he responded. "It could postpone the new-trial hearing. And they might use this testimony to support their conspiracy theory in the context that the police didn't conduct a thorough investigation. Or they could imply that the police knew about the testimony and disregarded it."

"But that last part simply isn't true," Justine said.

"I'm afraid sometimes it's the perception that matters."

Her patience snapped. "Well, my perception is that I don't trust you."

"Justine," Regina chided. "Mitchell is trying to help."

"Yeah? Well, I want my own damn lawyer. One that doesn't share a last name with the opposing side, not to mention a *bed* with the person whose testimony could have me brought up on charges."

"Justine—"

"No, she's right," Mitchell said. "If this goes much further, each of you should consider having your own attorney."

"It doesn't have to be like that," Regina insisted. "We should be sticking together right now rather than letting this drive an even bigger wedge between us."

Justine emitted a muffled scream of frustration. "There you *go* again, trying to fix everything, trying to pretend that we're one big happy family that just doesn't get the chance to be together as often as we'd like. Well, I have a news flash." She waved her finger across the room. "Given the choice, I wouldn't want to be related to any one of you."

She didn't stop to absorb their hurt expressions— screw them all. They weren't there when she needed them, and now she didn't want them. She didn't need anyone.

She climbed the creaky stairs and walked down the hallway to her bedroom, locking the door behind her. God deliver her from her sisters. She'd leave tomorrow and drive down the coast to a friendlier town with air-conditioning. If the attorneys in Charlotte needed to talk to her, they could damn well pay AT&T.

She sagged against the cool wood and leaned her head back. She was exhausted and the late-afternoon breeze coming in through the half-open window did little to revive her. Across the room, the six-panel whitewashed closet door spoke to her, lured her. She knew what lay behind it could very well send her into a spiral, yet she was drawn like an insect to a zapper.

The inside of the closet smelled like old pressed flowers and the bayberry candles that Cissy stored on a shelf. Over the years, it had become a catchall for holiday decorations—a ceramic jack-o'-lantern, red, white, and blue garlands, cornucopia place mats. She pushed aside a plastic snowman and blindly reached into the depths of the closet until her fingers encountered the nubby cotton of a garment bag hanging from the utilitarian pole. After a few gentle tugs, she withdrew the long, bulky bag made of unbleached muslin, with twelve years of downy dust attached to the bottom.

She hung the bag on the back of the bedroom door. A series of muslin ties secured the outer bag. She loosened them gently one by one, then pushed the fabric aside. The ties on the inner muslin bag were closer together, so she spent several minutes unfastening them. A strange numbness had overtaken her, perhaps in preparation for the onslaught of emotion. She inhaled deeply and peeled back the inner bag to reveal her glistening white wedding gown, just as beautiful as the day she'd worn it.

With trembling hands, she removed the dress from the padded hanger and held it against herself. She'd made her veil and glued sequins on her shoes herself to be able to afford this dress. Paper-thin white satin, sleeveless, V-neck, empire waistline, gently flowing skirt and train. Perfection.

She peeked at her reflection in the standing mirror, and the years melted away. The day had dawned the happiest of her life. Cloudless sky, birds singing, the whole nine yards. No one had even realized anything was amiss until the guests were seated. Her father had arrived without Mica and the best man had arrived without Dean. Both were missing in action, and still no one connected the incidents. She had sat in her underwear putting the finishing touches on her makeup, telling herself that everything would be fine and trying to ignore the pinch between Regina's eyebrows. Regina, she reasoned, was simply being sensitive because she had asked Mica to be her maid of honor.

Mica, with her flair for drama, had pinned the note to the wedding gown itself—probably reasoning that Justine would find it before she put on the dress. Except Mica had placed the note high on the bodice, and Justine hadn't noticed it until Regina had zipped her up and they were both staring into the mirror.

"What's that?" Regina had asked.

"That Dean," she'd said, removing the folded note. "He's always leaving me notes where I'll find them."

"Maybe he's letting you know he'll be late," Regina had said wryly.

But the note was in Mica's handwriting, not Dean's. Simple, to the point. Her vision had blurred; then she'd fallen to her knees. Regina had caught her, then delivered a solemn "pull yourself up by the bootstraps" pep talk, when all Justine had wanted was to be held.

She ran her fingers over the pinholes in the tender fabric where the note had been attached. Unnoticeable to anyone else, but blatant to her eyes. She looked into the mirror and used one hand to pile her hair on her head. She had been beautiful that day, and so anxious for Dean to see her walk down the aisle.

She angled her body—would the dress still fit? She cast off her sandals and cotton dress, then slipped into the gown, reveling in the cool slide of the fabric over her heated skin. The zipper was tricky, but she managed, and was pleased with her reflection. For the briefest second, she caught a glimpse of the optimistic, happy woman she'd once been.

On impulse she dragged a chair over to the closet, then climbed up and steadied herself. The vent in the closet ceiling could be loosened with a little tug. One end came down, revealing a thin gold cord. She pulled the cord and a brown velvet bag emerged.

A roused layer of dust fell into her hair. She climbed down, coughing and waving to clear the air.

The bag was about the size of a sheet of paper, with a drawstring closure. She'd found it in the stockroom of the shop when she was a teenager after she'd stolen something and needed a way to transport it home. After that, the bag had held many finds from the shop and other mementos.

She eased down on the bed and emptied its contents onto the comforter. A silver baby spoon, a deck of sex-position playing cards that she'd found under her parents' mattress, a small kaleidoscope, a filigree compact she'd lifted from Mica's purse, one topaz earring, a rhinestone-studded lipstick holder. A green velvet ring box lay on its side. She opened it carefully and fingered the trio of rings inside—her modest engagement ring and the gold bands she and Dean were to have exchanged. She slipped on the rings meant for her finger, still a perfect fit. Wearing a wedding ring was such a public gesture of commitment—was that why she found them so irresistibly challenging on the men she dated? To prove that they were no more committed than Dean had been? Or was it the only way she was going to get a man with a ring?

She returned all the items to the bag except for the note that lay innocently on the comforter, only slightly yellowed on the edges. She unfolded it, although the words written in red ink had been emblazoned on her brain.

*Dean is going with me to LA. We're sorry.*

*M.*

She laughed softly. *"We're sorry."* Like they'd stepped on her foot or forgotten to water her plants.

Justine's eyes flooded with tears as the hurt slammed into her again. Her own sister. She ripped the note in two, then again and again until it was in tiny bits at her feet. It wasn't fair—she'd loved them both. She lay back on the bed and curled into a miserable ball. It wasn't fair. . . .

She dozed on and off. At some point when daylight began to fade, someone knocked on her door, but she mumbled for them to go away. She wallowed on the warm covers, achy and itchy. The tears came and went, then came again. She slept and dreamed of Dean, smiling and laughing . . . with Mica.

Around ten, she sat up, swung her legs over the side of the bed, and turned on the lamp. Her cheeks were raw and her head felt heavy. The silky skirt of her wedding gown shimmered in the low light. She wiped her eyes with the back of her hand and sighed. What a day . . . what a week . . . what a life.

A noise outside caught her attention—familiar but unidentifiable. At first.

Adrenaline swamped her limbs and she was at the

window in two steps, opening it fully. The sloping roof leading to her bedroom window ended about five feet out. Dean heaved himself over the edge, looked up, and smiled.

She thought she was still dreaming until he stuck his feet through the window and sat on the sill, facing her. He had changed into black jeans and black T-shirt. He looked dangerously sexy. His eyes were serious and sad as he looked her up and down. "Is that what I think it is?"

She nodded, paralyzed with warring emotions.

"You're beautiful."

"I was beautiful on our wedding day, too."

"I'm sure you were. I'll never forgive myself for running out on you like that."

His words were like balm to her injured heart, but she wasn't going to let him off the hook so easily. "That makes two of us. If you were in love with Mica, you could have told me and saved me the humiliation of being stood up at the altar."

He looked down at his hands and fidgeted. "I wasn't in love with Mica. I was scared."

"Scared of what?"

He shrugged. "Of waking up someday an old married man working a junk store in Nowhere, North Carolina."

"I thought you wanted to be here. We could've moved." She choked. "You know I would have gone anywhere with you."

He stood and reached for her slowly. She didn't relax, but she didn't resist. "We never got to dance," he whispered, clasping her hand and waist, and moving into a slow waltz.

She closed her eyes and reveled in the details that she'd forgotten over the years—the way their bodies meshed, the salty scent of his skin, the quiet strength in his arms and fingers.

"You kept the rings," he murmured, thumbing her third finger in his clasp.

"They were in the closet—I just slipped them on."

"I've missed you." He lowered his mouth to her hair—he always said he loved her red hair. He kissed her temple, and her resolve crumbled. She lifted her mouth and they kissed with the intensity of a decade lost. When he lifted his head, his eyes searched hers. "Let's make love."

She was shameless in her want for him, only because she believed that if she could have him one more time, if she could prove to herself that she hadn't imagined their powerful connection, she might be less tormented. It would be the wedding night she'd always dreamed of. He undressed her carefully, leaving only her white bra, and draped the wedding gown over the footboard with uncharacteristic care.

He started to unfasten his pants, then pulled something out of his pocket. "Look what I have." He shook a pill bottle. "Something to make it . . . better."

Dean had introduced her to nutmeg, so she wasn't surprised that he still used mood enhancers, but she didn't want anything to cloud her memory tonight. "Not this time."

"Oh, come on," he said, unscrewing the lid. "It's just a muscle relaxer." He pressed three pills into her hand.

She pulled her hand back and the pills fell to the floor. "I don't want it, Dean."

Frustration flashed across his handsome face; then he was all charm again. He removed three more pills from the bottle. "Come on, baby, you're all tense. Let's get happy. It'll be like old times."

Justine bit into her lip, wavering.

# nineteen

**If he's a fink, DO warn other women.**

Mica walked into the bathroom in search of a glass of water to take a painkiller. Her neck ached, and the stress of seeing Dean had brought on a headache, too, so she felt her way by the soft glow of the night-light.

As far as her sisters went, she couldn't seem to do anything right. She'd hurt Regina's feelings when she turned down her request to give a quote for one of her authors, but how could she explain that she was on the verge of being fired? Better to say no to the only favor Regina had ever asked of her than to risk embarrassing her later.

And guilt plucked at her for telling Dean about their secret.

Her ears perked, because she could have sworn she heard his laugh. She looked over.

From Justine's room.

She pressed the water glass against the door leading from the bathroom into Justine's bedroom. Her worst fears were confirmed when she heard the murmur of Dean's voice. She closed her eyes against the thrust of pain to her chest. He had climbed the trellis to Justine's bedroom window, just as he used to do when they all lived at home. They thought no one had been the wiser, but Mica had heard them once through the bathroom door, making love, and figured it out.

Hurt washed over her in waves as she sagged against the door. Deep down, hadn't she known that Dean had never gotten over Justine? His gaze lingered on every redhead that crossed their path, and despite his steadfast support in Mica's career, he'd never really committed to her emotionally. In truth, he'd never even told her that he loved her. She would ask him occasionally, and he'd say, "You know I do, baby."

Tears ran freely down her cheeks. How stupid she'd been, allowing herself to believe that she had a future with Dean, that they might even have a family. He couldn't be faithful to one woman—

She inhaled sharply. Dean was, at this moment, preparing to give her sister a double shot of VD. Maybe she hadn't always done right by Justine, but she couldn't in good faith stand by and allow him to start a family-wide epidemic.

Taking a deep breath for courage, she composed herself, then knocked loudly on the door and walked in. "Don't do it, Justine!" She flipped on the light switch.

Dean turned, squinted, and had the grace to look chagrined as he zipped his pants. "Mica—I can explain."

Justine sprang up from the bed. "What are you *doing* in here? Get out!" She grabbed the white dress at the foot of the bed to cover herself.

Mica blinked—Justine's *wedding* gown? This was worse than she thought. She glared at Dean. "Have you no morals whatsoever?"

"We were just talking," he declared in a familiar naughty-boy voice. *"That kiss didn't mean anything. I was only flirting. She came on to me."*

"Mica," Justine said through gritted teeth. "Get out."

"He has VD."

That got her attention. "What?"

"That's a lie," he said.

"Then why am I taking antibiotics?"

He shrugged. "Maybe you've been screwing that agent of yours."

She raised her hand to slap him, but he grabbed her arm and leaned into her face. "Careful, I just might black your other eye."

Justine gasped. "He blacked your eye? I thought *I* blacked your eye."

Mica shook her head, wrenched her arm loose, and rubbed her wrist. She moved around him to stand next to Justine, who hurriedly stepped into the dress to cover her nudity. Mica gave her a quick zip; then Justine turned on Dean.

"You hit my sister and gave her VD, and you were about to sleep with me? You pig!" She was screaming now, eyes bulging, arms waving. *"I could kill you!"*

Mica was frightened to death, but Dean was unfazed. In fact, he laughed. "Listen, girls, since you're both here . . ." He gestured toward the bed.

Her gasp of horror was masked by a loud knock at the door.

"Justine?" It was Regina, sounding concerned. "Justine, are you all right?"

Mica turned back in time to see Justine pull something from under the mattress. *A gun?* Pure instinct drove her forward. "Justine—no!" She grabbed for Justine's hands as she pointed the gun at Dean. They struggled and Dean dived for the floor. The gun fired and the discharge vibrated her arms to the shoulders. Plaster rained down on them.

*"Justine?"*

The doorknob rattled frantically. Mica saw rather

than heard it, because her eardrums had surely been ruptured. She covered her clanging ears with her hands, relieved that the blast seemed to have dazed Justine enough to loosen her hold on the gun.

The door burst open and Mitchell Cooke charged in, followed by Regina. "What's going on?" Regina demanded.

"She tried to kill me," Dean said, scrambling to his feet.

Mitchell approached Justine cautiously, then took the gun from her shaking hands. She was crying.

"What did you do to her?" Regina asked Dean.

"Nothing," Dean said, holding up his hands. "She wanted me here. Look at her—she was waiting for me, for God's sake."

Justine choked on a sob and turned her back. She tugged on the rings, but they were stuck, frustrating her further. Mica's heart went out to her.

"I'll show Mr. Haviland out," Mitchell said, then shoved Dean toward the door. He held the gun by the trigger guard but gave the impression that he'd use it if he had to.

John limped down the hall toward them, followed by Cissy. "We heard a shot."

"Everyone's fine," Mitchell said. "Justine's gun misfired."

A kind half-truth.

John fisted his hands in the front of Dean's black T-shirt. "I told you to never come back here."

"You're pissed off at the wrong person," Dean said with an insolent smile. "It's your daughters who can't get enough of what I got." He looked back to where they stood in the bedroom. "All three of them, right, Blue Eyes?"

John popped him in the jaw, and although Mitchell

restrained Dean, Dean didn't attempt to retaliate; he only laughed.

Blue Eyes? Mica squinted—Regina was the only one with blue eyes. The implication of his words hit her and she gasped.

She and Justine turned to look at Regina and, to Mica's dismay, found her wearing a guilty flush.

# twenty

If the relationship isn't working, DO kill it quickly.

Regina emerged from the footpath into the clearing around the antiques shop, both perplexed and relieved to find no cars in the parking lot. After leaving their house last night, her father had probably gone to a bar to get blitzed. No doubt he was parked on the side of the road somewhere sleeping it off. Mitchell either hadn't yet arrived or didn't plan to after witnessing another chapter in the *Metcalf Family Guidebook to Broken Families*.

She could write that book, all right, but who would want to read it?

She sighed, quelling tears that had hovered just below the surface since last night's nightmare of an incident. Justine in her jilted-bride garb with a smoking gun, Mica screaming about the communicable diseases that Dean had given her, Dean bragging that he had all three sisters wrapped around his finger.

An overstatement of gigantic proportions, at least where she was concerned, even though his words had stirred the guilt that she'd carried around for years. She'd known Dean was a cheating cad before the wedding. She was a sophomore in college, home on Christmas break, when he'd cornered her under a spray of mistletoe hanging in the shop. Over the years she'd become accustomed to Dean's flirting and teasing, but this time his hands had gone beyond platonic patting, and his mouth, beyond a brotherly buss.

"I've been dying to kiss you for years," he'd murmured. "Really kiss you."

She'd made a bad split-second decision, based on remnants of the hormonal crush of a fourteen-year-old and the ridiculous justification that they were, after all, standing under mistletoe. So she'd kissed him back, and liked it. He had crushed her against him to let her know where his intentions lay. And she hated to think what might have happened if her father hadn't suddenly appeared.

Regina closed her eyes—she would never forget the look on John's face. The accusation, the shame, that she would betray her own sister. But his disappointment in her had been nothing compared to her disappointment in herself. For the remainder of the holiday break, her father had avoided her, and she had avoided Justine. When Dean had sought her out again, she had threatened to tell Justine if he didn't stop.

"You won't tell," he'd said with infuriating confidence. "Because you wouldn't dare cause trouble, Regina."

She'd hated him for being right—she wouldn't burst Justine's bubble of happiness. So she'd believed Dean's excuse that he'd slipped because he was feeling pressured to set a date for the wedding, and she'd returned to school. And, from that point on, had endeavored not to be alone with Dean.

And because she'd kept her cowardly mouth shut, look at how their lives had unfolded.

*Even if you'd told her, Justine wouldn't have believed you,* her mind whispered.

Maybe not, but at least when Justine read that thoughtless note pinned to her wedding gown, she would've had some forewarning; she wouldn't have looked as if she'd been hit by a truck.

God, what a horrific day that had been—Regina had awakened with a heavy heart, fearing that Justine was making a big mistake by marrying Dean but feeling powerless to stop it. She had offered to go with Justine early to the church to get ready—Mica wanted to sleep in and come later with their parents. When John and Cissy had shown up alone, Regina had the first niggling that something was wrong. And when Dean's best man had shown up alone, her suspicions compounded. She'd seen the looks Mica had cast in Dean's direction when she thought no one was looking—Regina recognized those looks from her own misplaced fantasies about Dean, the man they'd grown up idolizing. Still, she had naively worried that Dean and Mica had spent the night drinking and had overslept. Even in her worst nightmare, she hadn't imagined that they'd skipped town together. When Justine had collapsed in her arms, she'd been so angry at herself, she could barely face her sister and, in hindsight, hadn't been nearly as supportive as she could've been.

A car drove by on the road in front of the antiques shop, breaking into her troubled thoughts. She shook herself, reminded of her wide-eyed resolve during the night to focus on the things she could control, such as finishing the appraisal work with Mitchell.

And Mitchell . . . she groaned. What a mess that had turned out to be. As he himself had pointed out, she had terrible taste in men.

The items designated for the dump were sitting on the ground by the back door—decrepit pieces of furniture, industrial-sized bags of trash, rolls of ruined carpet. A brown squirrel poked its twitching head out of one of the bags, and she smiled for what felt like the first time in days. They would all get through this— the alternative was unthinkable.

She unlocked the back door and entered, flipping on lights. The place was starting to look a little forlorn in its orderliness, everything stacked together and lined up, instead of the usual welcoming sprawl. They had made remarkable progress in a short time. She looked around and sighed—in a few weeks, M&G Antiquities would be gone, and so would M&G, Metcalf and Gilbert. Her parents, as a result of the story about the girls' witnessing Lyla's murder, and the disturbance over Dean, had grown even farther apart. The few times they were together, they exchanged furtive whispers and hateful glares, as if they blamed each other for what was happening. Regina hadn't had time to think of a way to get them together, to get them talking and remembering how much they needed each other.

Regina picked up a handful of what, in her estimation, were the saddest of all antiques—vintage photographs, most of them portraits of one type or another. Sepia-toned shots of stiff, unsmiling people who were undoubtedly related to one another. She laughed wryly—they looked so unhappy, they *had* to be related to one another. It was sad, this mishmash of pictures, because the families had apparently died out, the photographs sold in estate sales for—she looked on the back of a portrait of three somber-faced girls, circa 1900— twenty-five cents. Destined to become souvenirs for conversation pieces, or craft supplies for decoupaging end tables.

She looked into the bright eyes of the three chubby-cheeked girls. Matching dresses and mountains of banana curls. More than likely, they were all deceased now. "What did you do with your lives?" she murmured. "Did you grow up to do terrible things to each other?"

"Talking to yourself is not a good sign," Mitchell said.

She turned to see him spanning the doorway and blushed. "I wasn't talking to myself—I was talking to . . . them." She held up the picture.

"Oh, well, in that case," he said. "Pardon the interruption."

Sam scampered over and registered his hello. Mitchell followed, looking tentative. "I wasn't sure you'd want to work today."

She gave a little laugh. "What else am I supposed to do? Spend the day with my loving sisters?"

"Maybe you should."

"Maybe I should, since no blood has been spilled yet."

He pursed his mouth. "How was it after I left?"

"Not good. Justine now thinks that I, too, was having an affair with Dean behind her back."

One of his dark brows rose. "And you weren't?"

*"No."* She rubbed the back of her neck, and her shoulders fell. "But he did make a pass at me, and I should've told her."

He whistled low. "That Dean guy seems like a real piece of work."

"That's an understatement. I could kill him for what he's done to my family."

"From what I saw last night, you'd have to stand in line."

She sighed. "I hope we've seen the *last* of Dean Haviland." She started to return the photo of the little girls to the shoe box, then turned to Mitchell and held it up. "First sale of the day."

"I'll take care of you right over here, ma'am." He

walked behind the counter and she reached into her purse for change.

He squinted at the photo. "Cute. Anyone you know?"

"Not personally, but they're sisters, so we have something in common."

He handed back her change. "Every family has its story."

She pretended to rummage in her purse. "And what's yours?"

"Nothing too dramatic." He lifted his shoulders in a slow shrug. "I studied law, and so did my younger brother. We wound up opposing each other on a case and let it affect our relationship. Stupid, really. I got out."

"You could have moved."

"Yes, I could have, but then, that wasn't the point, was it?"

"And what *was* the point?"

He looked uncomfortable philosophizing about his own situation. "I didn't want to be part of something that I would choose over my own family."

She frowned. "That's being a little hard on yourself, don't you think?"

Another shrug, averted gaze.

"Who won?"

He looked up. "What?"

"The case between you and your brother—who won?"

"He did."

"Oh."

"Oh, what?"

"Just 'oh.' I'm doubly sorry now to have dragged you into this Bracken hearing. I'd hate to be the cause of more trouble between you and your brother."

He walked out from behind the glass counter and

picked up her hand. "You have enough on your mind without worrying about me."

She swallowed against the desire pulling at her, then pulled back her hand. "Yes, you're right." She needed to keep a level head, which seemed more difficult when he was in her proximity.

"Regina, I'd like to help you through this."

She frowned. "Why?"

"Why? Does there have to be an ulterior motive?"

"In my experience, yes."

"Well, you haven't *experienced* me."

She crossed her arms. "*Funny,* but I think I have. Twice."

He straightened. "*Funny,* I don't remember you complaining at the time."

A loud horn sounded outside.

"That'll be the truck from the dump," he said.

She set down her purse and moved toward the back door. "I'll take care of it."

"You'll need my help."

"I *don't* need your help," she said over her shoulder, but he followed her anyway, muttering under his breath. She got it now—he was like some kind of TV superhero who moved around the country under the guise of appraising junk to patch up people's pathetic lives. Hadn't he realized that her family was like an old dike? When one hole was filled, another leak developed elsewhere. She was running out of fingers and toes, but she didn't need his help. She couldn't, because he would be moving on in a few days.

Outside, the big ugly truck was already backed up to the heap of rubbish. Two men, one hefty guy and the other a runt, were surveying the goods.

"All this go?" the big guy said.

"Yes," she and Mitchell said at the same time.

"Gonna cost extra 'cause it's such a big load. Cash on the barrelhead."

"That's fine," they said in unison.

She glared at Mitchell, then signaled the men to begin loading.

Sam ran into the trash and started barking. He'd undoubtedly found that squirrel to torment.

"Big pieces first," the hefty guy said, lowering the enormous tailgate.

While the men loaded the relic of a refrigerator, she tried to distract Sam from his make-believe hunt, but he wouldn't let up. A couple of broken beds went in next. By the time they approached the hacked-up wardrobe, Mitchell had lost his patience with the dog. "That's enough, Sam!"

The dog quieted but whined miserably and got underfoot as they leveraged the big piece between the three of them.

"Christ," the little guy said on the initial lift. "What's in this thing?"

"It's supposed to be empty," Mitchell said.

The little guy stumbled, and the wardrobe rocked forward, toward Regina. She backed up, and Mitchell and the hefty guy saved it from falling, but the doors swung open, snapping the rubber strap meant to hold it closed.

And out rolled Dean Haviland. Shot through his cheating heart.

# twenty-one

DON'T ever relax.

"Relax," Mitchell said from a bench with the stenciled message PROPERTY OF BURL COUNTY SHERIFF'S DEPARTMENT.

Regina stopped pacing and looked down at the end of the hallway where Mica and Justine sat opposite each other, rigid and not speaking. Cissy'd had to be sedated and left at home. John was missing in action. She looked back to Mitchell. "Relax? A dead man rolled out onto my shoes, my entire family is implicated, and you tell me to relax."

"I'm just saying it's not going to help matters if you have a stroke."

She covered her mouth to choke back a sob. "What's going to happen now?"

"I don't know. They must want to ask more questions, or they would have let us go."

She chewed on a nail. "What did you tell them about last night?"

He frowned. "The truth."

She winced. "I was afraid you'd say that."

A door opened and a dour-faced Sheriff Hank Shadowen emerged. "Y'all come on in here now."

Mica and Justine, both red-eyed and stoic, made their way down the hall in slow motion. They all filed into a meeting room with a rectangular table and comfortable-looking chairs. Out of habit, Mica and Justine situated themselves across from each other. Regina sat next to Mica, across from Mitchell. She wasn't sure what she expected, but there wasn't a spotlight or two-way mirror in sight. Just a television, magazine rack, and vending machines.

Sheriff Shadowen, a big man whose thick head of hair had turned white since she'd last seen him, gestured toward one of the machines. "Can I get y'all something to drink?"

They declined. He retrieved a can of Dr Pepper for himself and cracked it open as he sat at the end of the table in front of an open file folder. He reviewed the forms with much sighing and grunting, then looked up. "Got a real mess on my hands." His expression was mournful, as if culling their sympathy. "Got a man shot through the chest with a thirty-eight slug. Got another man who threatened the dead man, missing. Got a thirty-eight automatic, given to the deceased by the missing man, in the possession of the missing man's daughter, who's been living with the deceased. Got a report of the missing man's other daughter firing at the deceased last night with a thirty-eight revolver. And I got a missing thirty-eight revolver." He sighed and took another drink from the can. "Hell of a mess."

No one spoke. Mica looked drawn and vacant, her glorious hair pulled back into a long braid. Justine was equally pale and toyed frantically with a cigarette. They'd taken the news of Dean's death badly.

The sheriff leaned forward to rest his elbows on the table. "According to your statements, you girls were at your parents' house from last night until this morning."

They all nodded.

"Do any of you girls know where your daddy is?"

"No," they chorused.

"When was the last time anyone saw him?"

Mitchell cleared his throat. "I walked with Mr. Metcalf from the house back to the antiques shop last night after the incident at the house. When I drove off, he was going in the back door."

The sheriff looked at him. "Cooke, isn't it?"

Mitchell nodded.

"What were you doing at the Metcalf house?"

"I was at the antiques store with Regina when Haviland stopped by. He said he was on his way to the Metcalf home. Regina was afraid of a confrontation, so she asked me to go with her. John arrived when we were on our way out, so he went with us."

The sheriff glanced at her. "Why were you expecting a confrontation?"

Her heart rate picked up, and she stole a glance at her sisters before answering. "Because Justine hadn't seen Dean since . . . he broke their engagement. I thought they might have words."

"Sounds to me as if you were gathering reinforcements; you were expecting more than just a shouting match."

"I . . . was afraid Dean might become violent." Or her sisters.

"Did you have reason to believe he was a violent man?"

She flicked her gaze to Mica, then back. "No proof, just suspicions."

He followed her movement. "Mica, was Dean a violent man?"

She hesitated. "Not normally, but he did hit me once."

"When?"

"Last week, before I left LA. He was drunk and we argued."

"Is that why you left, because he hit you?"

She shook her head. "I . . . discovered that Dean had been unfaithful."

"Is that when you took his gun?"

"No, I had already removed it from the bureau. I had to break some bad news to Dean, and I was afraid . . . that is, my agent encouraged me to protect myself. I didn't intend to use the gun, but I wanted to keep it out of Dean's hands."

"What was the bad news?"

"My biggest client threatened to cancel my contract unless Dean stayed off the set."

"And you didn't think he would take the news well?"

"No." From the tremor in Mica's voice, it was apparent she suspected Dean would do her bodily harm.

"What did he say when you told him?"

"I didn't tell him; I just left town."

"So when you left, you took the gun with you?"

She nodded. "I checked it in my luggage and left it in my suitcase after I arrived. It was still there when I gave it to your deputy."

He verified her statement against a report, then nodded. "So Haviland followed you here?"

"Yes."

"How did he know you were in Monroeville?"

"He said he called me on my cell phone and I told him where I was, but I don't remember doing that."

"Could someone else have answered your phone?"

She started to shake her head, then looked across the table at Justine. *"You.* You answered my phone and pretended to be me, didn't you?"

Justine broke the cigarette in two. "So?"

Regina set her jaw—she thought that Justine had

insisted on staying close to the house because she was afraid of the Crane woman stalking her.

Mica leaned forward. "You *witch*. And to think I was worried about you last night when I realized Dean was in your room."

Justine scoffed. "You burst in because you were jealous."

"Girls," Regina said. "Let the sheriff finish."

The sheriff took another drink. "Justine, you were at home alone when Haviland arrived at about three in the afternoon."

She nodded. "But everyone else arrived within a few minutes."

"What happened?"

"Mica and Dean had words. Apparently, he'd talked to her agent and found out that he'd been banned from the set. He was trying to talk Mica into siding with him. She told him that she was cutting him out of the business and leaving him."

"And what was his response?"

"He said he wouldn't let her cut him out."

Mica glared.

Regina's heart shattered to see the accusation in their expressions.

"Justine, when your father got there, did he and Dean exchange words?"

Justine hesitated. "Yes. Daddy accused Dean of splitting up the family, and Dean called him a drunk."

"Did your father threaten Dean?"

Another hesitation.

"Did your father tell Dean that"—he looked back to the paper—"he'd be sorry if he didn't stay away?"

"Yes."

"Then Dean left?"

"Right."

"But he came back?"

She sighed. "Right."

"What time?"

"Around ten."

"He climbed the trellis to the roof and came in through your bedroom window."

"Yes."

"Did you have intercourse with him?"

"No."

"Were you taking drugs?"

"No."

"The officers found some tablets on the floor of your bedroom—what were they?"

"I don't know—Dean wanted me to take them, but I refused."

"What did he tell you they were?"

She pushed her cheek out with her tongue. "Muscle relaxers."

"Was Dean into drugs?"

"Ask Mica—she's the one with a purse full of pill bottles."

Mica gaped. "What about the tins of nutmeg in your dresser drawer?"

Justine gave her a lethal look. "Shut up or I'll tell everyone how broke you are and how desperate you might have been to get rid of Dean."

Regina stood and leaned her hands on the table. "Stop it, both of you. Act your age until we can get through this."

The sheriff studied them all as he polished off his Dr Pepper. "Mica, was Dean into drugs?"

"Uppers, occasionally, and a little pot. It's everywhere out there."

"And *your* pills?"

"Prescriptions. Painkillers for my neck and back and antibiotics for . . . an infection."

"VD," Justine clarified sweetly. "And don't forget about the antidepressants."

"At least I don't self-medicate, Miss Spice Rack."

Regina gritted her teeth—airing their differences privately was simply too boring for her sisters. "What are you talking about, Mica?"

"Justine takes nutmeg to get high."

Regina frowned. "Is that possible?"

"Old hippie trick," Mitchell said. "Cheap, legal, and it doesn't show up in corporate random drug testing."

"You make me sound like a freaking addict," Justine said to Mica. "And what I do to relax recreationally has nothing to do with any of this."

"I'll be the judge of that," the sheriff said. "You were saying, Justine, that you refused the pills that Dean offered you."

Justine exhaled. "And then Mica came in."

"And told you that Haviland had VD?"

"Yes."

"Then you withdrew a thirty-eight revolver from under the mattress and shot at him. That's attempted murder."

Justine scoffed. "I wasn't going to kill him—just scare him. That's why I shot into the ceiling."

He flipped to another report and skimmed it with his finger. "According to Mica, you told Dean, 'I could kill you,' then produced the gun. She said you were aiming for Dean when she tried to wrestle the gun away from you."

Justine glared at Mica. "She grabbed for the gun, but like I said, I wasn't trying to kill him."

"What happened to the gun afterward?"

"I took it," Mitchell said. "It was unloaded. I left it on the downstairs hall table."

"And were you still at the house *appraising,* Mr. Cooke?"

"No. After Haviland left, I talked to the family about the ramifications of testifying at the Bracken hearing."

The sheriff grunted. "Oh, that's right—you're a non-practicing attorney and your brother represents that scumbag Bracken, who's accusing my department of a goddamn conspiracy. It's a small effing world, ain't it?"

Mitchell frowned. "As I was saying, I talked to the Metcalfs over dinner—"

"All of them?"

"No. Justine went upstairs around four-thirty, and I didn't see her again until the shot sounded."

"You didn't realize that Haviland was in the house?"

"No."

"Did anyone?"

Regina shook her head and looked at Mica.

"Not until I heard his voice through the door of the bathroom that separates my room from Justine's."

"So Mr. Cooke left the gun on the hall table and no one has seen it since?"

Everyone shook their heads.

"Where did you get the gun, Justine?"

"At a pawnshop in Shively. Last week."

"Why?"

"For protection. I had reason to believe I was in danger."

"Oh, yeah, the scorned wife. I took the call from Officer Lando in Shively when he was concerned the Crane woman might be on her way here. Whew-wee, you Metcalf girls are single-handedly causing overtime for my department." He gave them all a flat smile. "And we haven't even gotten to the Bracken situation yet."

Regina closed her eyes.

"But first things first. Justine, aside from your gun being missing, there were two shells missing from the box of ammo we found in your bedroom. We dug one out of the plaster in the ceiling—which, by the way, we'll compare to the one we dug out of Haviland's chest—and Mr. Cooke just said the gun was unloaded when he left it on the table." He steepled his fingers. "So where's the other bullet?"

Justine reddened. "I accidentally shot into the trunk of my car, into a bag of rock salt."

He scribbled something on the form. "So that's where we'll find it."

"No. The trunk was a mess, so I stopped on the drive down to clean it out and throw away the bag."

"Any witnesses?"

"No."

"Figures." He scribbled something else. "Dean stood you up at the altar a few years ago, didn't he, Justine?"

She nodded.

"And tell me again about this wardrobe where the body was found."

She sat back in her chair. "It was a wardrobe that my sisters and I refinished as a wedding gift for me and Dean."

"And you—let's see here—'hacked it up with an ax' on your wedding day."

"Those aren't my words."

"No, they're my boy Pete's—he was at the wedding."

Justine shrugged. "I was angry with Mica and Dean at the time, and I didn't exactly need a wedding gift, now did I?"

He scratched his temple. "Quite a coincidence that the body was found in the same wardrobe, eh?"

Justine fidgeted. "I don't know anything about that."

He studied her dubiously. "Well, I'm going to need for all you girls to take a polygraph exam. And a ballistics test for gunpowder residue."

Regina shuddered.

The sheriff turned his attention to Mitchell. "So you're working for John and Cissy?"

"Yes. Doing appraisals of the business inventory and some pieces in their home to be auctioned."

Sheriff Shadowen made a rueful noise. "Cissy said they were going through some rough financial times. And that she and John were splitting up. That kind of news could make a man depressed, maybe even a little crazy."

Regina blinked back tears—no matter how bad the evidence looked, she still couldn't picture her father pulling the trigger.

"Had you girls noticed anything strange about John's behavior since you arrived?"

Since she was the only one who'd seen him enough lately to know the difference, she answered. "He was quiet, but he's always been quiet. He's been drinking quite a bit."

Shadowen looked at Mitchell. "Did John say anything out of the ordinary when the two of you walked back to the shop last night?"

"No, he barely said anything."

"Did you see Haviland actually leave the property earlier?"

"Yes, on foot. He headed toward the path leading to the antiques store—I assumed he'd left his car parked there so no one would hear him."

"How long after he left did you and John leave?"

"Maybe a half hour."

"But Haviland's car wasn't at the shop when you got there?"

"No. Sheriff, Dean Haviland was from around here, wasn't he?"

"Yeah, he was homegrown."

"Is it possible that he had unfinished business with a buddy or a relative?"

The sheriff's eyes narrowed. "I ask the questions around here, boy. You lawyers make a living trying to twist things all around, but in my experience, the most obvious explanation is usually the right one. John Metcalf shot Haviland for messing with his daughters, then took off. Obvious." A muscle ticked in the man's jaw. "Just like Elmore Bracken murdered Lyla Gilbert."

Mitchell looked like he wanted to respond, but Regina threw him a warning look.

The door opened and Deputy Pete stuck his head inside. "Sheriff, we found Haviland's car about a mile away from the shop, just off the road in the woods. Keys were on the seat and the whole thing was wiped clean of fingerprints."

The sheriff hummed. "John Metcalf probably dumped it, then walked back to the shop to leave in his own car. Any word on that APB?"

"Not yet."

"Well, come in. Now's as good a time as any to talk about the Bracken case."

And just like that, the day got worse.

Pete took a seat next to his father. He gave Regina a jerky nod, and she nodded back. All the activity was apparently making him nervous, because his hands moved constantly, scratching and tapping. The toothpick in his mouth twitched.

The sheriff glared at Mitchell. "You can leave."

Mitchell crossed his arms. "I'm Regina's attorney on this matter. I think I'll stay."

The sheriff glanced at her for confirmation and she nodded uneasily.

"Okay, Cooke, but keep your mouth shut." Sheriff Shadowen regarded each of the girls with blatant disapproval. "You girls made a big mistake by not coming to me with your story—then and now. We're all in a heap of dog shit. Now you're saying that the murder weapon was a piece of junk I won in a damn poker game. How do you think that looks?"

Not good, she conceded, but since he obviously knew as much, she remained silent.

He brought his meaty fist down on the table. "These stinking lawyers are going to keep everything stirred up until they get that murdering sonofabitch off. We put the right man behind bars twenty years ago. By raising questions, you're only hurting yourselves, your uncle, this department, and the memory of your dear aunt."

"Our dear aunt was a slut," Justine said.

"Justine," Regina chided.

"It's the truth," Justine said. "Everyone in town talked about her; even some of the guys in high school had laid her, right, Pete?"

Pete blushed and leaned over to scratch his ankle. "There was some talk, I guess."

Justine arched a red eyebrow. "I heard you were the one talking, Pete."

Regina felt her eyes go wide—she hadn't heard that gossip, but she and Justine had run in different crowds in high school.

Pete's blush drained. "You mean Dean, don't you, Justine? They were supposedly quite the item."

Her eyes went wider—Dean and Lyla?

"Hush, boy," the sheriff scolded. "What does that have to do with the price of tea in China? I'm saying we worked our asses off around here to get Bracken convicted and now, because of you girls, he might go free."

"Hold on," Mitchell said. "The hearing is to determine only if circumstances warrant a new trial, not whether Elmore Bracken goes free. If your investigative work on the Gilbert murder was thorough, Sheriff, you have nothing to worry about."

The sheriff pointed his finger. "I thought I told you to keep your mouth shut."

"I take orders from my client, not from you."

Before the older man could blow a gasket, Regina interceded. "Sheriff, we still don't know who called in that tip, but—"

"I think it was Dean," Mica said.

All eyes went to her.

"What?" they chorused.

She covered her face with her hands, then sighed. "A few weeks ago, I told him about us witnessing the murder. It was stupid, I know, but I thought enough time had passed that it didn't matter."

"Idiot," Justine breathed; then she looked at Regina. "That pact didn't mean much to you two, did it?"

A pact on their sisterhood. Regina bit down on the tip of her tongue. Everything was unraveling.

"So," the sheriff said, "you believe that Dean called from a pay phone when he got to town."

"But why?" Regina asked.

"To flush us all down the damn drain," Justine said. "Why did Dean do anything? The asshole probably thought he could collect a reward."

Regina gave Mitchell an apologetic look across the table for blaming him. He returned a wry expression. She sighed. "Okay, well, what's done is done; we have to move forward. Sheriff, have you heard anything back from the Internet auction site?"

"No. They said it might take up to thirty days to respond."

"The hearing will be over by then."

"Nope," the sheriff said, whipping out a fax. "The

hearing has been delayed to allow those bloodsucking attorneys to pull even more fairy tales out of their butts. Congratulations, ladies; you are now involved in, count 'em, *two* murders."

# twenty-two

DO have the courage to cut harmful people out of your life.

Justine lay in the bed, smoking in the dark. Her tear ducts were completely tapped. It was mind-boggling how much the world could change in twenty-four hours. The love of her life was dead, and the only other man she'd ever loved, her father, was presumably on the lam. And it was her fault for luring Dean back so she could exorcise her demons.

She tapped ash into the dish sitting on her chest. She should have never come back. Monroeville was like some kind of bad karma vortex that seemed determined to suck her inside whenever she breached the city limits. Only last night Dean had been with her, warm and alive, and on the verge of making love to her. Now all her good memories would be overshadowed by the sight of his beautiful mouth slack, his unbelievable black eyes vacant, and his stylish clothes bloody. She closed her eyes, but the image of him remained.

The smell of fresh blood, the deadweight of his body, the uncooperative stiffness of his limbs.

Her cell phone rang, and she glanced at the screen.

Lando. Her spirits lifted curiously, and she pressed the talk button. "Hello."

"It's Lando."

"I could sure use a little good news."

"The Pirates won on the road tonight."

"You're going to have to do better than that."

"Sorry. No news."

God, if only one piece of this nightmare would end. "I'm starting to lose faith in a police department that can't find a gun-wielding housewife."

He made a rueful noise. "The consensus is she's holed up somewhere and—never mind."

She closed her eyes. "And that she's taken her life?"

"No," he said unconvincingly. "Don't jump to conclusions. How are things in Mayberry?"

She took a drag and exhaled. "Not as quiet as you might think."

"Oh?"

"I'm in trouble, Lando."

"How can I help?"

*Tell me how to fool a polygraph.* "Tell me everything's going to be okay."

"Everything's going to be okay."

That made her smile. "So why are you calling?"

"I wondered if you needed for me to do anything around your house while you're gone, like water your plants."

"All my plants are plastic."

"Oh. Guess you don't have pets, either."

"Nope."

"Hm. You have something against live things?"

"Just live things that expect something from me."

"Ah. It's not so bad. You should start off slow, maybe an aloe vera plant. Those are hard to kill." A beep sounded in the background. "Listen, I have to get that. Take care of yourself."

"I'll try."

She disconnected the phone and for some stupid reason, the tears were back. And the anger. Her glance strayed to the chest where her nutmeg was stashed. She longed to be transported from this misery for a few hours, but she resisted on principle alone—Mica had made her out to be some kind of addict, which was ridiculous. She looked at the bathroom door and gritted her teeth. Correction: this mess wasn't her fault, by God; it was Mica's.

*Mica.* How ironic that she'd been so thrilled when Cissy and John had brought that wriggly little baby home from the hospital. At five years old, she hadn't imagined that the black-headed infant would wreak so much havoc upon her heart and her life. No matter who had actually pulled the trigger that killed Dean, Mica shared the blame for the events she'd set into motion years ago. And during their interrogation, the little witch had done everything to point the finger at *her*.

She snubbed out the cigarette, passed the ashtray to the nightstand, and sat up. Mica, as usual, was coming out on top. She'd taken Dean when she wanted him, had allowed him to help launch her career; then she'd gotten rid of him when he became a nuisance. Now she'd simply return to LA and to her agent-lover, then go on with her charmed life. She'd probably never even miss Dean.

*"A person can't just go through life destroying relationships and get away with it!"*

Rage boiled in her stomach. Mica had been getting away with things her entire life. It was high time that she pay.

Justine walked to the bathroom door and opened it noiselessly. By the dim glow of a night-light she found her toiletry bag and rummaged until her fingers found the item she was looking for. She held them up to the light and smiled.

Long, strong, sharp . . . scissors.

She put her hand on the knob of the door leading to Mica's room and turned it quietly.

# twenty-three

After a breakup, DO try a new hairstyle.

Mica's eyes flew open, and she was relieved to see daylight streaming into her bedroom. But on the heels of her relief to be free of the general torments of the dark hours came the profound sadness of remembering: Dean was dead.

Her eyes filled instantly and stung around the raw edges. She couldn't bear it, knowing he would soon be sitting in a little urn at Williams's Funeral Home. She didn't know what else to do—Dean didn't have any family, and she couldn't afford a funeral. They didn't have a stitch of insurance. Cremation was the most economical choice, although she let Tate Williams believe it was Dean's preference—a "Hollywood" thing. No one in Monroeville had been cremated to Tate's knowledge, and since he didn't have a crematorium, he'd have to ship Dean to Boonton after the autopsy, then have his ashes carted back, but they'd be ready for "viewing" tomorrow evening. Too late she found out that ashes couldn't be buried in an inexpensive cemetery plot, as she'd hoped, and since she didn't have money to buy a tiny crypt, she told Tate she'd take the ashes with her.

She rolled over on her side and toyed with the end of her black braid. Tears curled over her cheeks and onto the pillow. Dean was dead, and her father was missing, presumably running from the law. She was conflicted—grieving for Dean, yet she couldn't bear the thought of John wasting away in prison for killing him. They wouldn't lock up an old man, would they? Not if he'd committed a crime trying to protect his daughters? Couldn't everyone see that Dean had it coming, that he plowed through other people's lives, burning through relationships and discarding them when they were no longer useful?

Mica closed her eyes and thought of all the issues plucking at her. She needed to call Everett and break the news of Dean's death and to brace him for a potential scandal. And see how quickly he could get her back to work, even if her health wasn't yet stellar. Before she returned to LA, though, she'd have to take a polygraph regarding Dean's murder. Luckily, she'd seen a movie where the person put a tack in the toe of their shoe and pressed down when they wanted to distort the readings of the machine. She'd be fine if she didn't bleed to death.

Then there was the Bracken case hanging over her head, which would be yet more bad publicity for her and for Uncle Lawrence. Rising starlet, love triangle, sensational murder, political relative, family skeletons, missing father, jealous sister, disoriented mother. All the makings of a celebrity scandal show.

She wondered how Justine was holding up—it was obvious that she was still in love with Dean. Seeing her sister in her wedding gown the other night, wearing rings that had never been exchanged, had shaken Mica to the core. Over the years she'd imagined Justine immersed in her successful corporate career, dating powerful men and commanding respect from everyone around her, with no time to dwell on the past. And although she'd expected Justine to harbor hurt feelings toward her for leaving with Dean, she hadn't expected that Justine would still harbor such deep feelings for him.

Before Dean arrived on Tuesday, she and Justine had been making progress toward healing their relationship. Today she would make an extra effort to reach out to her. After all, they could at least attend the memorial service together, grieve together. And they would need collective strength to help John and Cissy through whatever lay ahead. Maybe something good could come from all this sadness—maybe their sisterhood would be restored.

She sat up with a sigh, her limbs gloomy from the painkiller she'd taken last night. The medication had worked better than usual, though, she thought as she rolled her head from shoulder to shoulder, stretching the muscles. Her neck hadn't felt this good in a long while. Maybe it was the extra sleep she'd been getting. Or the extra calories she'd been forcing herself to consume. Or perhaps the infection had affected other areas of her body and was now leaving.

She reached for her purse and pulled out her cell phone. It was still early on the West Coast, but she wanted to get the call over with. And Everett had told her to call him anytime, day or night. As the phone rang, she cleared her throat and reminded herself to sound strong and in control—she wanted to come across as healthy and billable.

"Hello?"

His voice gave her such comfort, she wished she'd called him sooner. "Everett, it's Mica."

"Mica, how are you? Where are you?"

"I'm fine. I'm at my parents' house in North Carolina. But I'm afraid I have some bad news." Out of habit, she reached up to rub her neck, marveling once again at how good it felt. And how . . . *breezy*?

"Mica?"

Panic and confusion gripped her as she groped thin air where her hair used to be. She twisted and froze at the horrific sight in her bed. A long severed black braid, vivid against the white pillow.

"Mica?"

She screamed.

# twenty-four

**DON'T underestimate the therapeutic value of placing blame.**

Regina stood in the kitchen, drinking mostly cream laced with a little coffee, waiting for bread to toast so she could take a tray up to Cissy, who was bedridden and desolate over John's disappearance. Regina knew how her mother felt—as if things would never be good again.

She heard a noise on the side porch, and her heart jumped. John? She walked to the door and was a little disappointed to see Justine sitting in a glider with her feet tucked under her. She opened the door and Justine started.

"You're up early."

Justine lifted a half-smoked cigarette to her mouth. "Couldn't sleep."

"That makes two of us. I made coffee—want some?"

"Sure."

She set the toast aside for the time being, then poured another cup of sludge. She carried hers out, too, and sat across from Justine in a chair. Two birds trilled to each other from separate trees.

*Come over here.*

*No, come over here.*

*No, come over here.*

Typical male and female.

A breeze stirred, prodding a new day to life. Nature had already forgotten yesterday. If only humans could be so lucky.

After a few silent sips, she sighed. "Justine, I never slept with Dean."

"As if I care." Her voice was flat.

"I care, and I want you to know the truth. It happened two years before you were to be married, and it was only a kiss."

Justine's cheeks went concave as she drew on the cigarette. "But he *wanted* to sleep with you."

She was silent, then added, "I'm sorry, Justine, for not telling you, for not warning you. I was ashamed, and I didn't want to hurt you."

"Forget it, Regina. I know that it was Dean's doing—you don't have it in you to be bad."

Why didn't that sound more like a compliment?

"Have you seen this?" Justine picked up a copy of the Asheville daily newspaper—Monroeville's weekly paper wouldn't come out until Monday—and extended it. "It's the Metcalf family special edition."

The front page featured Dean's death and what must have been the only picture of Dean the reporter had been able to get his hands on, a high-school-annual shot taken before Dean had dropped out of school. He couldn't have been more than fifteen. Handsome and cool-looking, with challenging black eyes. Mean eyes, she decided. There was also a picture of the back of the antiques shop cordoned off with police tape, a graphic quote from the hefty dump truck driver, and a paragraph about local businessman John Metcalf, who had been missing since the incident and was considered the prime suspect.

A sidebar mentioned that in a "bizarre coincidence," John Metcalf's three adult daughters, one of whom was Mica Metcalf of Tara Hair Girl fame, had confessed to witnessing the twenty-year-old murder of Representative Lawrence Gilbert's wife. This just as the man convicted of the crime was appealing for a new trial in Charlotte. In lieu of the girls' high school pictures, thank God, they had used a press photo of Uncle Lawrence.

She refolded the paper and cast about for a cheerful angle. "Our names weren't mentioned."

"With Magnificent Mica in the mix? Of course not."

Regina frowned over the top of her cup. "I'm worried about you, Justine."

"Me?"

"Yes, you. What's up with getting high on nutmeg? I didn't even know that was possible."

Justine scoffed. "It's nothing. If you're going to worry, worry about Dad."

"I am—so much I can hardly talk about it."

Justine flicked her ash into a flowerpot. "So you think John killed the bastard?"

Regina drank deeply. "I can't imagine it, but I'm terrified. With everything that Dad's been through lately, he might not be in his right mind. And if he didn't do it, where the heck is he?"

"I don't know."

"And if John didn't kill Dean, then who did?"

Justine exhaled a plume of smoke. "Mica."

"Be serious."

"I am." She leaned back against the glider and pointed her cigarette. "Her career was on the line, he'd given her VD, plus she found him in my bed."

She scoffed. "I know you and Mica have your differences—but she's our *sister*. You surely can't believe that she would commit murder."

"Regina, Mica's been gone for twelve years—we don't know what she's capable of. People change."

"So where's Dad?"

"He's taking the rap."

*"What?"*

"You know Mica has always been his favorite—do you think he'd let her go to prison?"

She hadn't realized that her sisters' competition for John's attention ran so deep. "I think you're letting your animosity for Mica get in the way of your common sense. If there's a God, Dean shot himself, then crawled into that wardrobe to die."

Justine shook her head. "Regina, only you could think of such a perfect ending, where no one else gets hurt."

"I think there's been enough hurt in this family, don't you?"

"Don't look at me—I didn't start it."

"But you could end it."

Justine smiled the strangest little smile. "I'm actually feeling much better about the state of things between me and Mica."

Regina pursed her mouth and nodded, wondering what had changed since last night when her sisters could barely look at each other, much less be civil.

Then from inside the house, she heard what sounded like an animal caught in a trap. "What on earth?"

Justine seemed much less concerned, and before Regina could stand, the screen door was flung back. Mica appeared in a silky nightshirt, her face contorted, carrying a black something or other.

"What's wrong?" Regina asked.

"What's *wrong*?" Mica bawled. "What's wrong is this!" She held up a long black braid, and Regina gasped in horror.

"Oh, my God, is that your *hair*?"

Justine flicked more ash. "Eww."

"I'm going to kill you!" Mica screamed, and launched herself at Justine.

It took Regina a few seconds to figure out that Justine was behind the severed braid. An awfulness settled into her stomach, and she might have let them fight to the death if there weren't so many other more dire issues at hand. She put down her coffee and levered herself between them. "Stop it. Stop it!"

They pulled her down with them, arms and legs flailing. This couldn't be happening. She was a respected senior editor at a prestigious publishing firm.

They all went rolling to the edge of the porch and off the three-foot drop into the giant dew-laden ivy. She landed with a *whoof* and heard their grunts, too. She turned her head sideways and looked into the face of a blue concrete bunny. Another couple of inches to the right, and she might have wound up drooling for the rest of her life.

"Are you okay?"

She looked up to find Mitchell staring down at her. She nodded miserably. Then a big wet tongue licked her forehead.

"Hi, Sam."

Mitchell reached down to pull her up. "Looks like I came at a bad time."

"No," she assured him. "This is how we start every day around here." She assessed the carnage. Justine was sitting up in the ivy, finishing her cigarette. Mica sat up a few feet away, crying and ruffling her shorn hair. The disheveled braid lay nearby, looking like a dead animal. Sam went over for a sniff.

Mitchell made a clicking noise with his cheek. "Let me guess—they tried your coffee."

"Hardee-har. No, Justine whacked off Mica's hair."

He flinched.

"I know. Listen, could you give us a minute?"

"Sure, I'll . . . go make some coffee."

"Great."

"Come on, Sam."

She straightened her damp, disheveled clothing and took a few seconds to catch her breath. Justine and Mica sat in steeped silence, as if waiting for a lecture. She put her hands on her hips and studied them for a long time. Stubborn, spoiled girls who'd grown up to be stubborn, spoiled women. And she was through being a referee. Finished. The end. She turned her back and waded through the ivy toward the porch.

"Aren't you going to say something?" Justine called after her.

She kept walking and climbed the short set of stairs in silence.

"We know you want to," Mica said.

She crossed the porch, walked into the kitchen, and closed the door behind her. Sam had found a quiet corner to occupy. Mitchell leaned against the counter, baby-sitting the coffeepot. "Regina, we don't have to work today."

She sighed. "No, it's fine." Since the shop was now considered a crime scene, they'd decided to move on to the house to begin tagging the antiques there that would have to go.

"You don't have to help me, you know."

"It's the only productive thing I can do right now."

"No word from your father?"

"None."

"I passed Deputy Pete parked at the end of your driveway."

"In case Daddy returns, I suppose."

He made a noncommittal sound. "How's your mother holding up?"

"Not well. I was getting ready to take her breakfast when all sister hell broke loose."

He poured new coffee for both of them. "Women are scary."

She lifted an eyebrow. "How so?"

He handed her a cup. "Men fight fair. They tell each other what they think. Get pissed off. Pound each other into the ground. Then, usually, they go on being friends." He drank from his cup and swallowed with a shake of his head. "But with women, it's like guerrilla warfare—you never know what direction they're going to come from. And *vicious,* man, oh man."

She sipped from her cup. "You don't really expect me to agree with you, do you?"

"No." He bit into cold toast and nodded toward the door. "Doesn't your sister make a living with her hair?"

"She used to." She pushed aside thoughts of her sisters and busied herself making a tray for Cissy.

Mitchell walked the perimeter of the kitchen. She didn't have to look to know that he was studying the crush of bric-a-brac on the walls. Decorative statehood plates, chalk fruit plaques, metal signs advertising food products, antique calendars, and so much more. All hung against a busy floral-patterned wallpaper.

"Blinding, isn't it?"

He laughed. "Lots of tchotchkes. But it seems homey."

"There are some wonderful pieces in the house; it's just a matter of finding them. I thought we'd work from the attic down to tag items for the auction."

"Won't this be hard for you?"

She carefully cut an orange into wedges. "Before I came home, I thought it would be. But I've come to terms with the fact that this house will never be a gathering place for a cozy family." She turned to look at him. "Despite appearances, it isn't 'homey.' There are no family heirlooms here, just an accumulation of *other* people's family heirlooms. And at the moment, I have bigger things to worry about than hanging onto my childhood canopy bed." She hadn't meant to sound so grim, but there it was.

He studied her for a moment, then angled his head and wagged his eyebrows. "Canopy bed, huh?"

She smirked, grateful for the levity. "Is that all you ever think about?"

"Pretty much. Especially lately." He moved to stand next to her and put his hand on her waist. "Look, Regina—"

She pulled back. "Don't, okay?"

He assumed a hands-off position. "I was only going to say that I'm sorry you're going through such a rough time. It's obvious how much your family relies on you, and it doesn't seem fair for you to shoulder all this alone."

She remained silent.

He sighed. "I'm offering you a shoulder, that's all."

She lifted a disbelieving eyebrow. "That's all?"

A mischievous grin crept over his face. "Well, the shoulder bone's connected to the backbone, and the backbone's connected to the hipbone—"

"Stop." But she smiled, exasperated. "I'm taking this upstairs. How about if I meet you on the landing in fifteen minutes and we'll get started?"

"I'll get my laptop."

The doorbell rang as they were walking through the entryway.

"Maybe Dad's turned up," she said, her heart pounding. *Please be alive; this family can't take that kind of a hit.* She set down the tray and steeled herself as she rounded the corner, but her shoulders fell in relief at the sight of the man on the other side of the screen door, dressed, as always, in a suit. "Uncle Lawrence."

He smiled back. "Hello, my dear. I came to check on your mother and you girls."

She lifted the latch, then opened the door. "I thought you'd left town."

"When the hearing in Charlotte was postponed, I decided to get in a few days of R and R. Might be my last chance before the election."

She sobered. "Uncle Lawrence, I'm so sorry about the hearing. We didn't mean for any of this to happen."

"Cissy told me how you girls were dragged into this mess. I'm sorry you had to see such a terrible thing all those years ago." He gave her a sad smile. "Don't worry your pretty head; I'm a survivor. And now I'm glad I stayed in town. Dreadful business about the Haviland boy."

"Yes."

"Any news from John?"

She shook her head. "I'm worried, Uncle Lawrence."

"Do you have any idea where he might have gone?"

"No—you know yourself that Dad hasn't left the county in years." He and Cissy used to take vacations all the time, but after the wedding debacle, John seemed to have packed it all in. In hindsight, she realized it had been a big blow for him, losing Mica and Dean. And eventually Justine. "Dad's family is gone, but can you think of anyone he might have known in Virginia from school? An old friend, maybe?"

He thought and shook his head. "That's too many years ago. But he'll turn up." He patted her hand; then he looked Mitchell up and down.

"Uncle Lawrence, meet Mitchell Cooke, the appraiser I told you about. Mitchell, this is Lawrence Gilbert."

The men shook hands, but Lawrence seemed wary. "I understand you're also an attorney, Mr. Cooke."

"That's correct."

"With ties to another Cooke in Charlotte."

Mitchell inclined his head. "Also correct."

Her uncle looked back to her. "I guess now I know why his name seemed so familiar to me that day you first mentioned it." From his expression, he wanted to take back his flirting recommendation.

She spoke to smooth over the awkward moment. "I was just on my way up to see Mom, Uncle Lawrence, if you'd like to come with me."

"You go on up, dear. I'd like a moment with Mr. Cooke."

"Oh." She looked at Mitchell, and he looked back. "I'll meet you upstairs."

"Okay," she said, retrieving the tray and trying not to feel left out.

The men's voices were a solemn murmur as she climbed the steps and walked down the hall to Cissy's room. She knew her mother was awake because she'd seen a light under her door when she passed by earlier. She rapped. "Mom? It's Regina." She heard her mother's voice, so she opened the door and stuck her head inside. "I have breakfast."

Cissy was sitting up in bed, surrounded by a mountain of pillows and a box of Kleenex. "I'm not hungry, but juice sounds good."

"I brought coffee."

She wrinkled her petite nose. "Did you make it?"

"No, Mitchell did."

Cissy sniffed. "He's here early—did he stay last night?"

*"No."* Sometimes she wished her mother weren't so liberal-minded. "We moved the appraisal to the house." No need to mention that the shop was sealed tight with yellow crime scene tape. "We're starting in the attic."

"Forget the attic," Cissy said with a wave. "Your

father cleared everything out of that oven long ago. Nothing up there but bats."

Regina smiled wryly to herself—Justine's favorite threat had been to put bats in their beds if they didn't do something she wanted them to. Worked every time.

Cissy fell back against the pillows. "Sell it all—it's just a bunch of *stuff*." She burst into tears. "I've made so many mistakes, Regina."

Her mother couldn't have said anything that would have shaken her more. Her parents weren't perfect, but hearing it come out of Cissy's mouth . . . no child wanted to listen to that kind of admission. She set the tray on a nightstand and sat down on the side of the bed.

"Mom, everyone makes mistakes."

"But these were whoppers. I misjudged your father. Not only has he betrayed and bankrupted me, but now he goes and shoots our son-in-law."

"We don't know that he sh-shot Dean," Regina soothed. "And Dean wasn't your son-in-law."

Cissy blew her nose. "Dean was as close as we were going to get. And now your father will go to prison—"

"Mom, don't say that." Regina stood and walked over to raise the window shades. "Dad could be somewhere sleeping off a hangover."

"Regina, I know you love your father, but I think this time even you need to face facts."

She turned back. "Even me?"

Cissy sighed and reached for her cup of coffee. "I know you've always held out hope for a happily-ever-after for me and your father."

"And what's so bad about that?"

"It's unrealistic, dear. Especially in light of . . . everything."

Her gaze landed on the broken leg of a chest of drawers. Holding it level was a dusty copy of *Your*

*Emotional Checklist,* the book she'd dedicated to her mother. Nice.

Regina looked up and crossed her arms. "I'm not giving up on Daddy."

"Your father isn't the man you think he is."

"Mom, I know you're hurting and confused—"

"He had an affair with your Aunt Lyla."

Regina literally took a step back. "I . . . don't believe it."

"I didn't either, at first. But I came to believe it."

"When . . . when did you find out?"

"I suspected it when she was alive, but I found out for certain last week."

Regina closed her eyes briefly. "So that's why you and Dad are splitting up."

Cissy nodded.

"I'm not trying to make excuses for him, Mom, but that *was* twenty years ago."

"I don't care. When John and I committed to each other without a marriage license, it was a symbol of the faith and trust that we had in each other. Your father violated that trust, and I can never forgive him." She shook her finger. "I told you this because I thought you should know, but you can't tell *any*one."

Regina swallowed the lump of emotion in her throat. No wonder her family was crumbling—it was built on a foundation of lies and fantasies. "I won't."

Cissy patted the spot next to her on the bed, and Regina sat. "Prepare yourself, sweetheart, for further disappointment in the people around you. I wish, for your sake especially, that we could have been a more normal family. Mica and Justine didn't need normal, but you did."

Her mother made it sound like such a shortcoming.

Cissy sighed. "This is a double tragedy for Mica and Justine, losing Dean and their father. How are they?"

"They're, um, each dealing with their grief in their own way. Why don't you get dressed and come downstairs? Uncle Lawrence is here."

Her mother smiled sadly. "Lawrence is taking a big risk being with us during a time like this—his political reputation could suffer by association."

"He cares about you."

Cissy nodded and smiled with genuine fondness. A light knock sounded at the door.

"And there he is, I'll bet." Saved. "See you later?" She gave her mother a kiss, then went to the door. It was Lawrence, all smiles as he greeted his sister. Regina left them and closed the door, reeling over the news that her own father had slept with Lyla.

She remembered Lyla flirting with John, touching him when they talked, winking. But her father had never shown Lyla any special attention, except maybe the time she and Justine had argued over that broken vase and he'd taken Lyla's side.

That had happened a few weeks before she was murdered, because Justine had still been paying off that vase when it happened. Which might mean that their father had been fooling around with Lyla during the time she was murdered. A cold hand of fear clamped down on her heart.

Or fooling around with Lyla during the exact *moment* she was murdered.

# twenty-five

For a great aerobic workout, DO jump to conclusions.

Regina's knees weakened. Was it possible that her father had killed Lyla all those years ago and had killed Dean too? Now she understood why Cissy didn't want her to tell anyone about the affair—if Bracken's attorney got wind of the fact that the father of the girls who had witnessed the murder not only was sleeping with the victim but also had access to the murder weapon . . .

"Are you okay?" Mitchell asked.

She whirled around and resisted the overwhelming urge to confide in him. "Yes."

He seemed dubious but indicated his laptop. "I'm ready whenever you are."

She nodded and led the way down the hall. "The attic is empty, so we'll start in one of the bedrooms. There's a great Chippendale chest-on-chest in the rear guest room."

"Can't wait to see it," he murmured, but she could tell he was preoccupied.

"So," she said, trying to sound casual. "What did Uncle Lawrence want to talk to you about?"

"He just wanted to reiterate his belief that the right

man was behind bars and how he didn't want to see you girls dragged through the mud."

Was Uncle Lawrence, too, protecting John for Cissy's sake? Assuming he knew about the affair. She tried to put aside her worries as they set about tagging the items in the rarely used guest room. Mitchell was intrigued with the chest-on-chest and with an art glass lamp. After they finished, they moved down the hall to the next bedroom.

He made a humming sound. "White canopy bed—this must be your room."

She nodded. "For eighteen years." She pivoted, looking at the furnishings through his eyes. White, feminine furniture with pastel linens. Lazy ceiling fan. Two sets of tall bookshelves and a step stool.

"Looks girly," he observed. "I assumed you were more of a tomboy."

She laughed. "I was, but Cissy was determined to make me into a lady."

He walked over to her bookshelves. "Nancy Drew. Complete set?"

"For that particular edition, except for number twenty-one, *The Secret in the Old Attic*." She smiled, fingering the spines. "I'd like to buy them back from the estate, if that would be possible."

He frowned. "They're your books—take them."

"Is that allowed?"

"Sure. The bank isn't interested in auctioning off every last matchstick. Besides, I'd venture you've more than earned back your own books with all the hours you've put in."

She lifted her hands. "As you can see, there's nothing much of real value in here, except perhaps the desk. From the hand-painted scenes, I believe it's Edwardian."

He ran his hand over the wood and nodded. "You're

right," he said. "Nice piece." Then he looked down at the papers spread across the surface of the desk.

Too late, she realized the manuscript she'd been reading in her spare time lay there.

He picked up a sheet and read the page heading: " 'I THINK I LOVE YOU: Relationship DOs and DON'Ts for Grown Women.' "

He looked at her, and even though she fixed a nonchalant expression on her face, she felt her neck grow hot. "It's a manuscript I'm considering."

One side of his mouth pulled back and he continued to read from the page he was holding. " 'Don't be too available, especially after you sleep with him.' " He looked up briefly, then resumed. " 'You should ration intimacy because when it comes to sex, men are like cattle, which, if led into a field of green clover, will eat until they founder themselves and die. In short, men and cattle must be domesticated for their own survival.' " He looked over the top of the page. "You're not really going to print this, are you?"

She bit back a smile. "It's supposed to be funny."

"Well, it's not."

She laughed. "I think it is."

He flipped his finger against the page. "It's this kind of propaganda that keeps men and women at odds."

"No, I think that's plain old biology."

He smirked and returned the piece of paper to her desk, then walked the perimeter of the room. "This room smells like you."

"Is that good?"

"Yeah. Unless you're trying not to notice."

She watched his back, trying not to notice a few things herself.

He stopped at the closet door. "Any goodies in here?"

"A few old linens—Mom got on that kick in the

early eighties and we suddenly had tablecloths coming out of our ears."

He opened the door and hanging on a hook was her "How to Sleep Alone" nightshirt. Great.

"What is this, your armor?"

She bristled. "No. It's . . . none of your business."

He rummaged through the tablecloths. "Tell me—do you ever get the idea that people don't want to be happy?"

"I don't know what you mean."

"I think sometimes that people are afraid to be happy—afraid that it'll feel good, but it won't last, and then they'll feel worse than they did before."

She squirmed. "I don't think that's a conscious decision to not be happy; I think that's self-preservation."

He rummaged. "Doesn't sound like much fun."

She studied his profile, alarmed at how appealing it had become in such a short time. "Not everyone's top priority is fun." And to her abject horror, she teared up.

"True," he said mournfully, then closed the door. "We can bundle the linens—" He stopped when he saw her face. "Hey, I didn't mean to upset you. I was talking off the top of my head."

She turned her back and wiped her eyes. "It's not you—it's . . . everything. God, what a train wreck."

He came up behind her and more tears squeezed out. "Let's take a drive," he said. "I think we could both use some fresh air, and I have something to show you."

She relented, mildly curious, and happy for a change of scenery. Outside, Mitchell slid back the side door of the van and whistled for Sam, who happily jumped in. Regina climbed into the bucket seat on the passenger side and rolled down the window. Mitchell dropped into his seat and started the engine with practiced ease.

She hadn't told anyone that she was leaving, but she was pretty sure they'd never miss her.

At the end of the driveway sat Pete Shadowen in his cruiser. He got out and put on his hat, then waited for them to drive up. Today the bottom half of his uniform was short pants, undoubtedly in deference to the temperature. Indeed, he seemed to have some kind of heat rash between his knees and the tops of his white tube-top socks.

"Cute," Mitchell mumbled.

"Be nice," she said, then smiled at Pete when he walked up to the driver's side. "Hey, Pete."

"Hey, Regina. Cooke."

Sam bared his teeth and snarled. Mitchell snapped his fingers and apologized. "It's the uniform," he explained.

Pete frowned slightly. "No word from your dad, Regina?" The toothpick bobbed and he scratched heartily below her line of vision.

"No."

"Where are you two headed?" He sounded a tad accusatory, as if they were on their way to a torrid tryst. Or maybe she was simply projecting.

"Running errands," she said. "There's going to be a memorial service for Dean tomorrow night at Williams's if you'd like to come. I don't suspect there'll be much of a crowd."

"Nah," he agreed. "Even the regulars won't come just to look at an urn. You know how the folks around here prefer a good open-casket viewing."

Mitchell looked over. "His body is being cremated?"

She nodded. "Mica said it's what he wanted."

"Would never have thought that of Dean," Pete said.

"How well did you know him?" Mitchell asked.

Pete shrugged. "He was a dropout, older, kind of wild. We didn't run in the same circles. I knew him when I saw him, or when Dad talked about him."

"He was in trouble with the law?"

Another shrug. "Carousing, breaking city limits curfew, stuff like that." He scrunched up his face. "And then there was Rebecca Calvin—I'd forgotten all about her."

Regina's ears perked. "The daughter of the man who sells old books?"

"Sounds like the same man—sells cars on the side, too. Drives a flatbed truck?"

"Yes. What about his daughter?"

"Committed suicide when she was fifteen."

"I don't remember that."

"She was older than us, older than Justine, I think. Lived up Macken Hollow, just her and her dad."

"What happened?" Mitchell asked.

"Hung herself. Turns out she was pregnant, and rumor was the baby was Dean's. I think he was only fifteen at the time, too."

Regina swallowed hard. When Mr. Calvin had said his daughter had been gone a long time, he'd meant dead.

"Guess there was bad blood between the old man and Haviland?" Mitchell asked.

"Yeah. The old man was pretty torn up about it, wanted my dad to lock Dean up, but there wasn't anything he could charge Dean with."

"Has anyone questioned Mr. Calvin to see where he was the night Dean was shot?"

Pete shifted foot to foot. "I don't mean to sound crass, but it seems pretty clear that John is the guy we're looking for here."

"Right, the *obvious* theory," Mitchell said.

Pete leaned in. "Sorry, Regina. You know we'll go as easy on John as we can when he shows up."

She bit her tongue and nodded. "Thanks, Pete."

"Monroeville doesn't seem like a hotbed of crime," Mitchell said. "How many murders in the last twenty-five years?"

Pete thought hard. "There was Lyla Gilbert, then, about five years ago, Fitz Howard—"

"Who's he?"

"Local plumber. Was plumbing George Farrell's wife, and George ran him over with an Oldsmobile. That was a closed-casket funeral."

"Any others?"

He shook his head. "Not until Dean. We're more of a farm-accident kind of community." From the car, his radio screeched. He pointed. "I'd better get that. I'll see you tomorrow night at the memorial, Regina."

She said good-bye, and they pulled out onto the two-lane highway that led back to town. She slumped comfortably and leaned close enough to the window to catch the breeze.

"I can turn on the air conditioner."

"I'd rather have the fresh air."

He sped up and she closed her eyes, relishing the coolness on her lashes. The tension drained away as they put more distance between them and the house. After a few minutes of joyous silence, she sighed and looked over. "Thank you."

"You're welcome."

"I didn't realize how tightly I was wound."

"Understandable. Frankly, I'm surprised you haven't burst into flames."

She managed a laugh. "I've built up immunity over the years."

"No wonder you gravitated toward self-help books."

She frowned. "I didn't . . . *gravitate*. The opportunity at Green Label became available, and it sounded . . . challenging."

He nodded.

"And . . . *interesting.*"

He nodded again.

Gravitate, ha. She tried to recapture her calm of a minute ago. "Weren't you going to show me something?"

"It's back there," he said, motioning behind their seats.

She glanced in the back of the van past Sam and saw, among other things, a cot. She pursed her mouth. "I'm *not* in the mood."

"Huh?" Then he grinned. "Oh, that's not what I had in mind. I mean, that's always close to the surface, but . . . there's a blue file folder in the box directly behind my seat. Will you get it?"

She leaned over and retrieved the file with much licking assistance from Sam. "This one? What is it?"

"The investigative notes surrounding your aunt's murder. I got them from David."

She sighed. "Look, I realize your brother is hung up on the Bracken hearing, but I'm preoccupied with this situation involving my dad."

"I believe the cases could be connected."

"What? How?"

"Three murders in this town in the last twenty-five years and two of the victims knew each other intimately. That's an uncanny coincidence, don't you think?"

She shifted in her seat. "You're saying the same person committed both murders?"

"I don't know, but it's worth looking into."

She turned to look out the window and pressed her finger under her nose to stem the urge to cry.

"What is it?"

She swallowed hard.

"Regina, you're not telling me something. What is it?"

He slowed and eased off onto the grassy shoulder of the road. After putting the van into park, he turned sideways. "Look at me."

She did.

"I can't help you if you don't tell me everything."

"I . . . can't."

"I'm your attorney."

"You're also a witness—you're too involved already."

"Do you have a dollar?"

"What?"

"A dollar—do you have one?"

"I didn't bring my purse."

He pulled a wallet from his back pocket and peeled off a one-dollar bill. "Here."

She took it. "What's this for?"

"I'm loaning you a dollar for my retainer," he said, hand extended. "Give it back."

She gave it back, exasperated.

"Now, even if I'm subpoenaed as a witness, I can only testify to what I personally observe, not anything that you divulge to me."

She puffed out her cheeks, tapping her foot in indecision. She wanted to trust him, but could she?

"Regina?"

She exhaled with much embellishment. "Mom told me this morning that Dad had an affair with my Aunt Lyla."

He hummed. "Not good."

"My thought exactly."

"Do you believe he could have killed her?"

"Absolutely not. Could he have killed Dean? Maybe in self-defense or to protect one of us. But Dad would never have stabbed a woman in cold blood."

"Not even if she'd threatened to go public with the affair?"

"Not even."

"Not even if her husband was his brother-in-law?"

"Especially if her husband was his brother-in-law."

He smiled. "That's good enough for me. And I don't believe he killed Dean."

She looked at him in surprise. "Why not?"

"Well, for one thing, the day we went fishing, he could barely walk on that arthritic foot of his. When the three of us walked from the shop to the house through the woods, he was having a terrible time just putting his foot down."

"I noticed."

"So he's supposed to have knocked off Dean, stuffed him in a wardrobe, ditched Dean's car a mile away, then walked back to get his own car, and left."

"You're right," she murmured. "He would've had to have help."

"Could he be covering for one of your sisters?"

She pressed her lips together. "This morning Justine suggested he was taking the rap for Mica."

"What do you think?"

"I think Mica had plenty of motivation to get rid of Dean, and as Justine pointed out, we don't know Mica as well as we used to."

"What about Justine? She had plenty of reason to want him dead, too. Would John have covered for her?"

"Of course. Justine has this thing about Daddy preferring Mica, but like you said when you came back from fishing, he adores all of us."

"When do you-all take your polygraph tests?"

"Tomorrow morning. There's someone coming in from Asheville to administer them."

"Don't be nervous; it's not nearly as dramatic as they make it seem on television."

"I'm only nervous about the fact that I have to take one at all."

He smiled. "Chalk it up as a life experience."

"One I could happily die without."

He tapped his thumb on the steering wheel. "Let's assume that your sisters aren't involved. My brother told me the tip was called into his office around eight A.M., but Dean didn't show up here until three in the afternoon. Where was he in Monroeville during the hours between?"

She perked up. "Good question. You think he met up with an old friend?"

"Or an old enemy. Did you know any of his buddies?"

"Not really. And Mica said he didn't have any family left."

"Did he have a best man at the wedding?"

She nodded but struggled to remember the man's name. Short, ferretlike. "Stanley something. Kirby—his last name was Kirby."

"Do you know where we'd find him?"

"Dean grew up several miles from town, a wide spot in the road called Macken. Stanley lived there, too, and he seemed like the kind of guy who wouldn't venture too far."

"Near the place where the Calvins lived, Macken Hollow?"

"Yeah. That's probably how Dean knew Rebecca Calvin."

"Why don't we see if we can round up Stanley, then drop in on Mr. Calvin and ask a few questions?"

"Okay. You'll need to turn left at the next intersection."

He nodded toward the folder in her hands. "Meanwhile, why don't you take a look through those notes and see if anything jogs a new memory?"

She rolled up the window halfway, then opened the folder with trembling hands. On top was a heavily photocopied typed police report. Description of crime: Homicide. Victim: Lyla A. Gilbert. Location: 1 mi. south of railroad tracks on Bradley Road, near Armadillo Creek.

> Victim found in '78 Cadillac convertible, partially nude, with stablike wound in chest. No visible weapon. Apparent sexual activity. Body found by two hunters, Roger Bradley and Hilton Mann, at 4:30 P.M.

At least she'd lain there for only an hour or so. Regina closed her eyes briefly, then lifted her head to get her bearings.

"What?" he asked.

"Take the next right."

He did. She had to love a man who followed driving directions.

Well . . . not literally, of course.

"Where will this take us?" he asked.

"It's a roundabout way but eventually to Lovers' Lane."

She hadn't been back, not in all those years. After that awful day, any time that she and her sisters walked to the Dilly swimming hole, they had scrupulously avoided the overlook.

It took them a few minutes of driving up and down Bradley Road, a one-lane asphalt disaster, before she spotted the opening in the trees. "There."

He pulled in gingerly, keeping an eye out for low branches overhead. After a few feet into the trees, however, the green space opened up. The ground was crisscrossed with tire impressions in dried mud. Lovers' Lane, it seemed, remained a thriving local attraction.

Some conscientious soul had even contributed a fifty-gallon metal drum for a trash can.

"I hope no one's here," he murmured.

She laughed. "On a Thursday morning?"

"You got something against making whoopee on a Thursday morning?"

"N-not in general."

"Good."

Regina frowned. "Stop here and we'll walk the rest of the way."

Because the trees and foliage had matured so much, she didn't recognize the spot where Lyla's car had been parked until she looked up to see the rock ledge where they'd hovered prostrate and gotten more than an eyeful. The ledge was visible because the tree she'd shinnied down lay on its side, rotting. She waited for the terror of that day to take hold, but in truth, the dead-end grassy lane and the surrounding wall of rock and trees created a peaceful and, yes, romantic enclosure.

Mitchell followed her line of vision. "Is that where you were when it happened?"

"Yes."

"Where was the car?"

She panned the area, then paced over a few yards. "Here, I think. Facing that direction."

"Which way did the man run?"

"The way we came in."

"So he might have lived close by?"

*Her father?* "Maybe. Or maybe his car was parked nearby, or maybe he walked awhile and hitched a ride, or maybe he walked to town and called a friend."

He nodded, conceding that one theory didn't outweigh another; then he extended his hand.

She took it, confused. "What?"

He pulled her close, held her loosely. "I was thinking that maybe you'd like to have one good memory of this place."

She smiled up at him. "What did you have in mind?"

"A kiss, if you'll lose the glasses so I can do it properly."

She removed her glasses and leaned into the kiss he offered. Sweet and thorough and familiar, but not nearly long enough.

"How's that?" he asked.

"Memorable," she admitted, running a finger over her lips.

He looked pleased with himself.

She angled her head. "I was thinking . . ."

He grinned. "Yes?"

"I'd like to talk to the men who found Lyla's body."

His grin faded. "Oh. We can do that, I guess. Think they're still around here?"

"Maybe." She stabbed her glasses back in place, strode to the van, and scanned the papers in the blue file. "Here are their addresses. And we're not too far from the Bradley home."

He offered a surrendering smile. "What are we waiting for?"

# twenty-six

DO question everything he says. And does. And might do.

The Bradley residence was an ancient gray clapboard house that sat off a gravel road on a level piece of land that might have been picturesque except there was not a single blade of grass around the cement-block foundation. The reason slid into view as they parked next to a mud-spattered Jeep Wrangler—at least twenty dogs, all shapes and sizes, raising a nerve-jangling brouhaha with their hoarse barking. Sam went nuts.

"Easy, boy," Mitchell soothed, then looked at Regina for guidance.

"Toot your horn. Loud."

He did, and the dogs were shocked into silence. He honked again and they began to slink off, barking with much less menace. The front door opened and an elderly woman came out carrying a dish towel.

"Let me talk," Regina said, then climbed out and walked slowly toward the house. She was instantly surrounded by curious dogs, sniffing and whining at her heels. "Mrs. Bradley?"

"Yeah."

"My name is Regina Metcalf. I grew up around here; my parents are John Metcalf and Cissy Gilbert."

"They run that antique store."

"Right. And this is a friend of mine, Mitchell Cooke."

He nodded. "Hello."

The woman didn't reply.

"Is Mr. Bradley home?" Regina asked.

"Taking a nap."

"Would it be possible to talk to him? I'd like to ask him a few questions."

"What about?"

"Lyla Gilbert was my aunt, and I understand that he found her body when she was murdered."

"That was nigh on twenty years ago, and suddenly everyone's asking questions again."

Apparently Bracken's team had been retracing the steps of the initial investigation. "Yes, ma'am, I know. It's important."

"I'll see if he wants to talk to you."

As they waited in the yard, the dogs grew bored and disappeared. At last, the door opened and the Bradleys appeared. Roger Bradley was sleep-ruffled but invited them to come up on the porch. They introduced themselves and sat on dusty black wrought-iron chairs.

Mr. Bradley coughed a couple of times, then wheezed in a big breath. "There was some trouble over at your parents' place this week, wasn't there?"

She hesitated. "Unfortunately, yes." She cleared her throat. "Mr. Bradley, I was hoping you could answer some questions about my Aunt Lyla's death."

"Does this have anything to do with Elmore Bracken trying to get a new trial?"

"Yes, indirectly." She explained that she and her sisters had witnessed the murder from a distance and why they hadn't come forward. "When Elmore Bracken was arrested, we thought everything would be fine. But now, with all the new questions, we just want to make sure the right man is serving time. I actually saw the car and the murder scene up close, and I wanted to compare what I saw with what you saw."

He inclined his head. "Okay."

"How did you find the car?"

He clasped his big wrinkled fingers in front of him. "Walked up onto it, really. I was hunting with Hilton Mann—weren't after much, just training a new dog. It was hot as blazes. The dog ran off-scent, and we were looking for him. Found him next to the car, going berserk. Then we saw the Gilbert woman lying on the seat, dead as could be. Real still. Everything was so quiet."

The abiding stillness had embedded in her memory as well. She swallowed. "Did you see the murder weapon?"

He shook his head.

"Mr. Bradley," she said, wetting her lips. "This is very important. Are you certain there wasn't something that resembled a knife lying on the passenger seat?"

"Yep. Hilton and me, we thought she'd been shot because we didn't see anything that could've killed her."

She believed him—he didn't seem like the kind of man who would lift a souvenir from a murder scene. "Does Mr. Mann still live around here?"

He made a rueful noise. "Nah, Hilton's dead. Cancer took him a couple of years ago."

"I'm sorry. Thank you, Mr. Bradley, for your time." They stood and he shook their hands. She was halfway across the barren yard when something the man said clicked. She turned back.

"Mr. Bradley, you said that everything was quiet when you walked up to the car."

"Yeah."

"The radio wasn't playing?"

He thought a minute, then shook his head. "No. It

was dead quiet, except for our dog barking. I remember thinking it was spooky."

"Thank you."

As they settled back into the van, Mitchell looked over. "The radio was playing when you left the scene?"

"Not just playing—blaring. The guy kicked the volume as he jumped over the side of the car. I'm thinking whoever took the murder weapon also turned off the radio."

"The battery might have run down."

"In an hour's time?"

He backed out of the Bradley driveway and pulled onto the road. "Does the report say anything about the running condition of the car?"

She checked. "It says the car was towed to the jail parking lot, but that could have been because they didn't want to disturb fingerprints."

"I remember reading, though, that the car was wiped clean of fingerprints. They only picked up a couple of partials that matched Bracken's, but he admitted to having been in the car on other occasions, so that didn't prove anything."

Excitement flowered in her chest. "That's why the murderer came back, to wipe away his fingerprints!"

He stared at her. "Uh-huh."

"But don't you see? That means if we find the letter opener, we find the killer."

"Or at least a trail to the killer."

"Right." She sobered. "Do you think the fact that Dean's car was also wiped clean of fingerprints means anything?"

"You mean like a similar MO? Maybe, but not necessarily." He pointed to a tiny roadside grocery store. "How about something to drink before we continue our sleuthing?"

*Sleuthing?* She *was* sleuthing, wasn't she?

"Did I say something funny?"

"No. Something to drink sounds good." They let Sam out to run around while they purchased water and juice from the sweet-faced clerk inside. The girl blushed and stammered under Mitchell's smile, and Regina was struck by how winsome he was, how helpful he'd been despite her resistance, how easy it would be to . . .

No. She would not fall for him, not when her life was already on full tilt.

Of course, being on full tilt would explain why inappropriate emotions were flitting through her mind in the first place.

"You okay?" he asked, oblivious to the revelations exploding in her head.

"Yeah, let's go."

So they hit the road again, this time in the direction of Macken. Mowers had recently cut the grass alongside the narrow paved road. It lay long and seedy in random sheaths on the shoulders of the road, emitting the most perfect, sweet scent imaginable. On either side, fields of hay and tobacco and cattle spoke of the scenic but laborious way of life for dozens of small-farm families.

"This is God's country," he observed.

She nodded, wondering how her life would have been different if she'd grown up elsewhere. Better? Worse? Did a person's innate character develop along a preset pattern regardless of the surroundings? Possibly. Even if they'd grown up in a city, she would still have been the middle child, caught between the strong personalities of her sisters. And if not Dean Haviland, Justine and Mica would have found someone or something else to compete for.

"How do you like Boston?" he asked.

"Very much. I like the energy level, the excitement, of the city."

"Which part of the city do you live in?"

"Near Roxbury, and my office overlooks the Charles River. You're familiar with Boston?"

"In my previous life."

"Your life as an attorney?"

"Yeah. I went to law school at Boston College."

She blinked. "No kidding?"

"No kidding. I still follow the Red Sox."

"Why did you leave?"

He shrugged. "After I passed the bar exam, I got a job offer from the DA's office in Raleigh. It was close to family and seemed as good a place as any to practice criminal law."

"You were a prosecutor."

"Yes, ma'am."

"Don't you miss it?"

He pursed his mouth. "Some days. Some days not." He pointed. "Which way do I turn here?"

He didn't want to talk about it. "Left, and the pool hall is about a mile up on the right, next to the gas station. It's as good a place as any to ask about Stanley Kirby."

Tick's Pool Hall was a greasy little dive where underage kids could get free beer as long as they played pool all evening at three bucks each a game and where adults could purchase pot out back by the Dumpster. Predictably, the regulars weren't the cream of the small-town crop, but as long as Tick kept a lid on serious trouble, the sheriff turned a blind eye.

When they walked in, every eye in the place turned their way. "Act natural," she murmured.

"We stick out just a tad," he returned.

Indeed, she'd never seen so many tight jeans, tall boots, and ponytails—and that was just the men. The women clinging to the men looked like they'd been ridden hard and put up wet. Tattoos abounded, as did snuff, cigarettes, and perspiration. Tim McGraw boomed over the speakers.

Regina nodded and smiled at people they passed, then bellied up to the bar. "Hello," she said to the barrel-chested bartender, who was wolfing down a cheeseburger. "That looks good—I'll have one of those."

"Make that three," Mitchell said, sliding onto the stool next to her. Sam settled at their feet. "With two beers and a bowl of water. Is my dog okay in here?"

"I won't tell the health department if you won't." The man served up two glasses of draught and filled a leftover butter bowl with water. "Gimme three cheeseburgers!" he bellowed through the sliding glass window behind him, then took another bite out of his own.

Mitchell set the water down for Sam and dived into his beer. She waited for the head to dissolve a bit before taking a sip of hers. Cold, wet, good.

"Can I buy a pack of cigarettes?" Mitchell asked the bartender.

She lifted an eyebrow, but he ignored her.

The man reached under the bar and tossed a half-empty pack on the counter. "On the house."

Mitchell nodded his thanks, then lit a smoke with a match torn from a book with the pool hall's name on it.

"Don't get many tourists in here," the bartender said with a cheek full of burger.

"I grew up around here," she said, nodding casually. "Regina Metcalf."

He frowned. "Metcalf . . . John's daughter?"

"Yes."

"I only know about the hot one—the one who does commercials."

"My sister Mica," she said, still nodding.

"Yeah. And wasn't there a redhead?"

"My sister Justine."

"Yeah. Which one are you?"

She pushed up her glasses. "The other one."

"Ah. Hey—" He shook his fat finger. "Dean Haviland was found shot the other night at your place."

"Uh, yeah. Unfortunately."

"Your old man do it?"

"We don't believe so," Mitchell cut in. "Did you know Dean?"

"Yeah, sure. He hung out in here when he lived here—maybe ten, twelve years ago. Came in here Tuesday. I probably served him his last meal—ain't that some shit?"

She opened her mouth to ask a dozen questions, but Mitchell squeezed her knee under the bar and left his hand there. Then he took a drag from the cigarette and turned his head to exhale. "About what time was that?"

The bartender squinted. "You some kind of cop?"

"Nope. I have some unfinished business with Dean, and I need to know who he talked to that day."

The bartender rolled his tongue around his teeth with some impressive sucking sounds. "I don't rightly remember."

Mitchell pulled out his wallet, removed a hundred, and palmed it to Hefty. "What time did you say?"

The money disappeared. "About eleven."

"Did he come in alone?"

"Yeah, but he met Stan Kirby and Gary Covey in a booth over there."

"Why?"

He shrugged. "I don't know."

Mitchell palmed him another hundred. "Guess."

The bartender looked all around, then leaned in close and pretended to wipe the bar. "I heard Dean tell them that he'd hit the jackpot, but he needed help to pull off a job."

"What kind of help?"

"Stan's a small-time drug dealer—pot, Valium, Viagra."

"Viagra?"

"Housewives around here slip it in their old man's coffee. Anyway, Stan gave Dean a bottle of pills; I don't know what it was."

The pills that Dean had tried to get Justine to take? Regina had to force herself not to look at Mitchell. His hand snaked down and he squeezed her knee again. She couldn't tell if he was signaling her to be quiet or simply trying to cop a feel.

"Who's the other guy—Covey?"

The bartender scoffed. "Petty thief, all-around thug. Real lowlife. I didn't hear nothin' he said."

"How long were they here?"

"About an hour, long enough to have a burger and a couple of beers."

"Have you seen the other two men since Tuesday?"

"Nah."

A knot of customers came in and claimed the vacant bar stools around them, effectively ending the conversation.

"Burgers up!" someone yelled, and three plates appeared in the window.

The bartender passed the food-laden plates to them, and Mitchell passed one down to Sam. Steamy burgers and salty fries and a limp dill pickle spear. Her stomach howled with gratitude.

They ate their burgers and watched the sports news channel over the bar to avoid the temptation of discussing their new information.

"Your Red Sox aren't doing so well this year," he observed.

. "At least my city *has* a baseball team," she observed back, still feeling the impression of his hand on her knee.

They left, heavy with comfort food. Sam dropped to the carpet and was asleep before Regina buckled in. "What do you think Dean meant by 'hitting the jackpot'?"

"I don't know, but it must have something to do with those pills. Maybe he was going to drug Mica to take her back with him, and maybe Justine's room was the only way he could get into the house."

"But what did that have to do with a jackpot? Mica said that she's broke. Dean had no life insurance."

"On himself. Wonder if he had any on Mica?"

A horrific thought, but the fact that she could process the information at all spoke volumes about the current state of affairs.

"If he were going to blackmail the three of you with the information that Mica gave him, he wouldn't have called in the tip."

"Unless, like Justine said, he thought he'd be able to collect money." She looked at him carefully. "Could he have collected for providing information to support Bracken's hearing?"

"No, there was no kind of reward being offered. Plus the fact that he left an anonymous tip seems to negate that motivation." He pulled on his chin. "No, my guess is that he made that call either to make the three of you look bad, maybe to set up Mica's murder and try to pass it off as suicide and collect on life insurance, or to scare someone who might be connected to your aunt's murder."

"Blackmail?"

"Maybe. Maybe he told the person that you-all could identify them, but he would handle the situation for a fee."

"You mean kill us?" She swallowed. "But if Dean knew the person was connected to Lyla's murder, he wouldn't need us for blackmail."

"Maybe he suspected but didn't put it all together until Mica told him what you saw. Or maybe he couldn't have come forward before without implicating himself."

Her head was starting to pound.

"At least we have a couple of new leads to pass to the sheriff," he said. "Dean might have been onto something else, something illegal—a big drug sale, for instance—that he needed his buddies' help with. The deal could have gone wrong and he was shot. Or maybe his buddies got greedy and decided they could handle the deal without Dean."

"But how would that explain Justine's missing gun?"

"Maybe Dean came back and took it. Mica had *his* gun. The front door was unlocked, and we were pre-occupied—he could've easily come back and stolen it from the table."

"Do you remember if the gun was there when you and Dad left?"

He shook his head. "I didn't notice."

Regina didn't like the look of the sudden pinch between his eyebrows. "What?"

"Well, if your aunt's murderer is still out there, you and your sisters could be in danger."

She hadn't thought of that.

He turned in his seat to face her. "Tell me more about that day you all were shot at in the woods."

She waved off his concern. "That was just a lost hunter, happens all the time to people who live near the creek. Pete said—"

"Pete was there?"

"He got a report about a trespasser and thought it

might be Justine's stalker. He saw the guy, but he didn't chase him, so he could check on us."

"Did you see Pete before or after the shot?"

She frowned. "After. And it was two shots, actually. We hit the dirt because our first thought, too, was of the Crane woman. Justine yelled that she had a gun; then Pete called to us that it was just a hunter."

His eyes narrowed. "Did you see the hunter?"

"No. What are you implying?"

"That Pete might be involved somehow. He *was* involved with your aunt."

She shook her head. "Pete might have slept with her, but he didn't kill her. He and his girlfriend were parked at Lovers' Lane and left about twenty minutes before Lyla got there. We saw them."

"So maybe Pete was covering for someone else, didn't want his father's reputation called into question."

She gave a little laugh. "There's no way Pete would try to kill us."

"Maybe he was just trying to scare you."

"But that was before our story even came out."

"So Dean called ahead."

She considered his theory for a few seconds, then smiled and fanned herself, suddenly aware of their surroundings again. "I think we're getting carried away."

Mitchell frowned as he started the engine. "Still, it wouldn't hurt for you and your sisters to be on your guard."

He was overreacting, she knew, but the fact that he was making a fuss put a warm little wiggle in her stomach.

Macken Hollow was only a couple of miles away. A farmhand walking along the road with a hoe over his shoulder gave them directions to Mr. Calvin's place. It was a meager little house but neat, with a pretty yard. The garage sitting adjacent to the house was twice as nice and twice as large. She remembered that Pete had mentioned that Mr. Calvin also sold cars on the side.

They parked in front of the garage and left the van doors open so Sam would have plenty of air, then walked to the front door. There was no porch, just a concrete stoop jutting out and a clump of leggy yellow mums on either side.

"Looks like he's not home," Mitchell said.

"Maybe he's around back."

They followed brick stepping-stones along the side of the house, past a couple of apple trees, to the backyard. A molded plastic table and one matching chair sat on a little concrete pad next to a gas grill. Her heart went out to the old man who had lived by himself for so many years.

"Nice view," Mitchell remarked.

Indeed, Mr. Calvin's view was a study in depth—rolling hill behind rolling hill, crisscrossed with barbed-wire fences and countless rows of deep green tobacco plants. She inhaled and exhaled with pure appreciation.

"Look," he said, pointing to the right.

In the distance a big oak tree kept watch over two headstones.

She was drawn to the makeshift family graveyard, and Mitchell followed her down a well-worn path in the tough field grass. The shade of the sprawling tree offered a few degrees of coolness, but a chill had settled over her anyway. Flanking the neat plots and shining gray headstones was a little limestone bench. She could imagine Mr. Calvin sitting on the bench, communing with his dead daughter and wife. Catherine E. Calvin, age thirty-seven when she died, and Rebecca E. Calvin, age fifteen. Their likenesses had been cap-

tured in stone ovals that graced the fronts of the headstones, both red-haired and fair, both smiling.

Fresh-cut flowers lay on each grave, but Rebecca's
grave had one additional adornment—a picture of
Dean Haviland cut out of the newspaper, impaled with
a knife driven into the earth.

# twenty-seven

*If you cry after he's gone, DO wear waterproof mascara.*

Regina glanced up and down the row of folding chairs at the pitiful collection of mourners for Dean Haviland.

On her right sat Justine, impassive and dressed in go-to-hell red, muttering about no-smoking laws in funeral homes. On her left, Mica, teary and shrouded in black, her shorn hair covered with a dramatic hat—she'd sworn them all to secrecy until she and her agent could figure out what to do. Next to Justine was Pete Shadowen, scratching and sporting full deputy regalia. Next to Mica sat a local news reporter in a jumper who now looked as if she desperately wished she hadn't come, especially since they had all declined to speak to her. And on the other side of Jumper sat an elderly woman wearing huge spectacles and a silvery suit who, she'd told Regina, had come on the wrong night for a distant relative and decided that sitting in on a memorial for a cremated person was better than going home to watch *The Price Is Right*.

Speaking of home, Cissy was still bedridden, now with a summer cold; real or manufactured, Regina wasn't sure. Uncle Lawrence was doing double duty by reading to his sister and posting his bodyguard in front of the house to thwart the throng of reporters that had descended upon the Metcalf home after their juicy story leaked and no other regional news had developed that was more titillating.

She and her sisters had endured the humiliation of taking a polygraph test at the sheriff's office this morning. Even though she had nothing to hide, her nervousness had bordered on hysteria for fear she would somehow incriminate her father when they asked her, "Do you know who killed Dean Haviland?" by hesitating a second too long. Less critical but nerve-racking nonetheless were her unreasonable fears that they were going to ask her trick questions like if she'd ever seen a porn flick or eaten an entire Pepperidge Farm cake in one sitting. They hadn't, but the results wouldn't be interpreted for several hours. By tomorrow, the girls would know if they were liars.

Mitchell had passed some of the day at the sheriff's office as well, trying to convince someone to follow up on the leads they'd uncovered. But since John was still missing, their jumbled theories seemed thin at best, even to her, now that she had a day's distance from the conversations. Only the questions about the pills Dean tried to give Justine seemed legit, and those had already been sent to a lab in Asheville.

Meanwhile, she hadn't slept at all last night, imagining her father ill or injured or . . . worse. Uncle Lawrence was worried sick, too, and had spent hours on the phone calling people and hospitals and hotels, pulling in favors from police departments all over the state.

Mitchell had offered to come with her to the service, but she'd assured him there was no need, mostly because she was shaken by her desire to have him there. The last thing she needed was to start depending on him for emotional support when at this point she suspected he was only sticking around to satisfy a resurrected sense of judicial obligation.

She had hoped this memorial ceremony would provide them all a small measure of closure on the horrible events of the past few days, although she conceded that the service might have proved more therapeutic if they were actually viewing a body. It was almost impossible to believe that the incorrigible Dean Haviland was now contained in what resembled an oversized martini shaker.

The stainless-steel burial urn was presented atop a marble plant stand, surrounded by silk fern fronds, and backlit with a pinkish bulb meant to flatter flesh. It was, at best, tacky and, at worst, anticlimactic.

The cremation had been another point of contention between her sisters, but when the topic arose, she had simply left the room before the fur started flying. How it ended she wasn't sure, but they had all come to the service in the same car, so that was something.

Tate Williams, the shiny-suited owner and director of the funeral home, walked to the front of the room and coughed politely as a sign that the service was about to begin, in case anyone needed to hit the rest room. Since Mica had opted for a nonreligious ceremony—probably for fear that they'd all be struck by lightning—Tate had agreed to deliver the eulogy. He was an odd-looking man with waxy skin and lacquered hair that made a person wonder if over the years he had absorbed too much formaldehyde through his hands.

"Welcome, friends," he began. "We're here today to celebrate the life of Dean Matthew Haviland, a life that was cut tragically short."

Mica started crying quietly, and Regina squeezed her hand. On her other side, Justine stared stonily ahead.

In solemn tones, Tate delivered a generic send-off speech suitable for a murder victim who had no family, no friends, and no real accomplishments. Tate compared life to a candle flame, an hourglass, and a marathon. He spoke of trials and tribulation and troubled waters. And when at last he'd run out of uplifting song lyrics from the seventies, he said the two words that everyone had been waiting to hear.

*"And finally,"* he said, his voice ponderous, his expression wistful, "death is a lesson for the living." He left them to draw their own conclusions, but to Regina the moral of the story was that if you live your life as a cheating, conniving, manipulative parasite, you might get shot.

"Would anyone like to say a few words about Dean?" Tate asked.

At Justine's first muscle movement, Regina gave her sister's hand a bruising crush along with a warning shake of her head. Mica was still crying and in no shape to say anything, so in the wake of an awkward silence, Regina stood. Her mind raced for something soothing to say, but at the looks on her sisters' faces, all she could think was how this man had trampled on all of them, had pecked at their vulnerabilities until they were laid open, then laughed in their faces.

"Dean was a complex man," she began, hoping that one word might lead to another. She shifted from foot to foot. "But . . . he was a liver of life." More like a bowel, actually. "And he left an impression on everyone he met." So far, so good. Her sisters were rapt, and hungry for comfort. Oh, God. But in their profoundly sad expressions, she found her next words.

"Yet regardless of his human frailties," she said with a little smile, "Dean enjoyed an abundance of what every one of us hopes to have at some point in our lives. He was loved." She reclaimed her seat and was surprised when she received a hand squeeze from each side.

Tate Williams seemed enormously relieved for the unexpected assistance and, apparently recognizing the advantage of ending on a positive note, abruptly thanked everyone for coming and explained that coffee and pop and sausage balls were available in the lounge. He stepped forward to shake Mica's hand, then Justine's, then her own, and must have figured what the heck, because he shook Pete's, Jumper's, and Spectacles's hands, too.

Then he picked up the urn and held it out to Mica. "May he rest in peace."

Mica stared at the urn. "Do I just carry him out of here?"

Tate nodded encouragement and pressed the urn into her hands. "Are you going to scatter his ashes here or when you get back to LA?"

"I hadn't thought about where would be the best place."

Justine scoffed. "That's easy. Just think of the place where he'd get under our skin the most, and that's where he'd be the happiest."

"Mica?"

They all turned at the sound of a man's voice. He was a stranger. Fortyish, attractive, well-dressed.

Mica's face lit up. "Everett?" She handed the urn to Justine and ran to embrace him. "What are you doing here?"

Regina and Justine exchanged surprised looks; then Justine frowned down at the urn.

Mica pulled the man over and introduced him as her agent, Everett Collier.

He eyed Justine suspiciously, obviously aware that because of her, his million-dollar product was at home in a shoe box. "I apologize for being late," he said. "I had a little trouble finding the funeral home." He looked at Mica with sad eyes. "I wanted to be here for my favorite client."

"I'll just bet you did," Justine muttered. Regina nudged her, but she wondered if Mica was involved with the man or if he was simply concerned about the viability of her career.

Deputy Pete walked over, holding his hat in his hands. "I'm sorry, Mica, Justine, for . . ." He gestured toward the urn Justine held. "You know."

Justine seemed surprised to be lumped in with Mica but nodded her thanks.

He turned to Regina. "Can I talk to you for a minute?"

She followed him to the end of the empty row of chairs. At his expression, her heart skipped a couple of beats. "Do you have news of Dad?"

He shook his head. "But *my* dad is pretty upset about you and that Cooke fellow poking around asking questions."

"Pete, we're all on the same side—we just want to get to the truth."

He frowned, looked away, then back. "I just can't figure out why you trust that Cooke clown more than you trust me. How much do you really know about him, other than what he's told you?"

She blinked. "Mitchell has been a good friend."

"Seems to me he's managed to involve himself in your family's problems mighty quick."

Anger sparked in her stomach at his implication that she was a needy little thing who would fall for a stranger's pickup line. She was *not* little.

He used the heel of his boot to scratch the shin of his other leg. "And then turns out he's mixed up with the Bracken hearing, too."

"Mitchell believes that Lyla's murder and Dean's are related."

He sighed, then wiped his hand over his mouth. "Regina, I know you don't want to believe your dad did what he did, but you're allowing Cooke to lead you on a wild-goose chase. All he's trying to do is build reasonable doubt on the Gilbert case so that when his brother wins a new trial, they'll get Bracken off. You're playing right into his hands."

She tried to calm her breathing and fight the tiny voice in her head that whispered, *He's right. You had reservations, too, but you threw them out the window because Mitchell flattered and flirted and did that squiggle maneuver.*

His frown was rueful. "Guys like Haviland and Cooke go through life using people, and I don't want to see you get hurt."

The anxiety in his blue eyes doused her previous anger. She hadn't given him a chance, choosing Mitchell's smooth-talking charm over Pete's good-hearted attentions.

*"Women can't get enough of that kind of thing. Take it from a former bad boy."*

A new sense of self-awareness settled over her, and not comfortably. Regina wet her lips and touched Pete's arm. "I really appreciate your concern, and I'm grateful for your advice. Thanks for coming tonight—I know you did it for us."

"I did it for *you*," he corrected, and picked up her hand.

"Regina?"

She looked up to see Mitchell walking toward them, wearing slacks and a sport coat.

Pete frowned and released her hand. "Speak of the devil," he murmured. "I guess I'll be going."

"Pete."

He turned back.

"Maybe when all this mess is over, we can have dinner. For real, next time."

He smiled. "I'd like that." He ignored Mitchell as the men passed.

Mitchell walked up and watched Pete walk away. "What's his problem?"

"You," she said, and couldn't keep the indictment out of her voice.

His eyebrows went up. "Let me guess—he said that we should stay out of police business."

She turned to walk toward the entrance where Justine, Mica, and her agent were heading. "Something like that."

"Who's the new guy?"

"Mica's agent. I think he came to assess the damage."

"What's she going to do—have her hair woven back on?"

"I really don't know."

"Have your sisters patched things up?"

She gave him a bright smile. "I really don't know."

"So you're finally letting them fight their own battles."

She set her jaw at his ease in evaluating her interaction with her sisters. "I could do without the analysis," she said over her shoulder.

"Sorry. How did the service go?"

"Fine. I'm glad it's over."

"I thought maybe we could have dinner," he said. "And talk about some things I found out today."

"I was planning to spend the evening at home with my family."

He caught up to her. "Hey, what's wrong?"

She took in his handsome face, his crinkly eyes that made her heart jerk sideways. Pete was right—Mitchell had smiled and smirked his way into the corners of her life, and she'd put up very little resistance. What a sucker she was to think that he'd actually been attracted to her on some kind of connective level. "Wrong?" she managed to say. "Nothing new."

"At least let me give you a ride home."

She stopped beside Justine at the door. "I'm riding with Justine."

Justine looked back and forth between them with pursed mouth, then turned to Mica. "Are you riding with us?"

Mica looked at Everett.

"Absolutely. Go with your sisters," he said.

"Follow us home," Mica said. "And we can talk there."

Mitchell looked at her as if he, too, was waiting for an invitation, but Regina stubbornly refused. "Maybe we can talk tomorrow," she said, then followed Mica and Justine outside and across the parking lot to Justine's car. Williams's was deserted tonight—only the hearse, Mitchell's van, and Everett's expensive rental car sat in the lot opposite Justine's Mercedes. She frowned, remembering the lady who had crashed the service. The woman must have been dropped off by one of the blue-hair regulars who considered the funeral home a social haunt.

Justine stopped a few feet in front of her car and fished out her keys. She looked at Mica, then pointed to the urn. "Do you want Dean back? Or do you want me to take him, now that your boyfriend's here?"

Regina rolled her eyes—whatever truce her sisters had called hadn't lasted long.

Mica glared at Justine and wrapped her hands around the urn. "Everett is not my boyfriend."

Justine refused to relinquish the urn. "Then why was his coat hanging in your bathroom?"

Mica tugged. "That's none of your business, impersonating snoop. If you hadn't hacked off my hair, Everett wouldn't have had to come."

Justine tugged. "I should've used an ax like I did on that wardrobe."

Regina looked longingly in the direction of Mitchell's van—maybe it wasn't too late to catch a ride after all. He was looking back. She made a mental note not to be so predictable, then plucked Justine's keys from her hand. "Whenever you two grow up, get in."

She opened the door and slid behind the steering wheel, shaking her head as the urn went back and forth, back and forth. She inserted the key and turned, tempted to leave them altogether. A loud boom shattered the air and shook the car, and for a moment she thought someone had fired a gun. But when she saw the spiderwebbed windshield and the buckled hood spewing smoke, she registered some type of explosion. More frightening still, she could see through the smoke that her sisters were no longer standing in front of the car.

Regina hurtled herself out the door. She heard rather than saw Mitchell and Everett run toward them. Justine and Mica lay on the pavement several feet in front of the car, moving, thank God, but covered with pale smoky ash.

Then she saw the topless urn next to a tire and realized the ash wasn't just any old ash.

"What happened?" Justine asked, unwittingly spitting Dean off her tongue. She looked as if she'd been powdered with a giant puff—only her eyes stood out in relief.

"Car engine fire," she said, giving Justine and Mica both a hand to their feet, dreading the moment they realized the true extent of the disaster. She relinquished Mica to Everett and pulled Justine away as Mitchell lifted the hood. A small fire licked at the engine block. He shrugged out of his sport coat and used it to smother the flames.

"Are you okay?" she asked her sisters. "Any broken bones?"

They shook their heads and peered down at their ash-covered fronts, arms extended. Justine suddenly went still. "Oh, God—is this what I think it is?"

Regina pressed a fist to her mouth to quell a wholly inappropriate urge to laugh. She nodded.

"What?" Mica asked, shaking her arms. "What is this?"

Justine released a muffled scream. "It's Dean, you idiot!"

# twenty-eight

**DO wash that man right outta your hair.**

Justine stood under the hottest shower she could withstand and scoured her body with soap and a stiff brush. She tried not to think about Dean's remains swirling around her feet, washing down the drain. She'd eaten her words about putting him somewhere to get under their skin, and she'd eaten a good bit of him to boot. Tate Williams had assured her that ingesting a little human ash wouldn't harm her, but she was sure if anyone could reach back from the dead and ruin her life just a tad more, it would be Dean Freaking Haviland.

The door opened.

"Justine!" Regina called into the bathroom.

"Yes?"

"The sheriff is here and he needs to talk to you." The door closed.

She said every curse word she could think of, and made up a few. After a final rinse, she wrapped her hair in a towel and pulled a yellow terry-cloth robe from the back of the door. Another one of the non-cosmetic items she'd added to the Cocoon line a year ago. And now it seemed likely she would never return to that penthouse corner office.

God, what she wouldn't give for a cup of nutmeg tea right now. Instead, she dressed quickly in jeans and casual pullover and slipped on sandals. She finger-combed her hair and walked downstairs, half-hoping and half-dreading that the sheriff had word of her father. But wouldn't Regina have told her if they'd found him? She'd never forgive herself if he got into trouble . . . all because of her.

Everyone had gathered in the TV room, including Cissy and Uncle Lawrence. Mica looked pink and fresh-scrubbed, and her agent, perplexed. Regina stood in front of the bookcase, next to Deputy Pete and across the room from Mitchell—curious. And Sheriff Hank Shadowen dominated the room in the center. He gestured to an empty wing chair. "Sit down, Justine. I need to talk to you girls about a few things."

"Did you find Daddy?" she asked. "Tell me now."

"No, we didn't find your daddy."

She sat. "What, then?"

"Someone tampered with your car."

She frowned. "What?"

"Old trick," Pete said. "Pull a plug wire, cut the fuel line, lay the wire in the fuel, and when you crank the engine—*pow.*"

"Your gas tank was almost empty," the sheriff said. "Else all you girls would probably be dead."

She swallowed, then murmured, "I always ride on empty." She looked vaguely around the room. "Does anyone have a cigarette?"

Mitchell handed her a smoke and a light, and she nodded her thanks. "Somebody rigged it while we were in the funeral home?"

"Looks that way."

"Was it Lisa Crane?"

"We're not sure, but she seems a likely suspect. Regina and Mica tell me there was a woman at the memorial service that they didn't recognize."

She squinted. "Yeah . . . big glasses."

Regina nodded. "Could it have been her, disguised?"

Justine drew deeply on the cigarette that was jerking in her hand. "I don't know—maybe. I only remember the glasses."

The sheriff grunted. "Tate Williams had never seen her before, and she disappeared right after the service and before the explosion."

She exhaled a plume of smoke. "So, Sheriff, you're telling me I'm being stalked by a maniac."

"Maybe, but I'm afraid I have more bad news." He handed her a piece of paper that looked like some sort of lab results.

"Those pills that Dean was trying to get you to take were ecstasy, laced with something called PMA, parametho-something or other. The chemist said it's a stimulant that raises your body temperature to the point where your nervous system fries. Two would've probably killed you."

And Dean had wanted her to take three. Her blood ran cold. "Are you saying he meant to kill me?"

"I don't know. Do *you* think he meant to kill you?"

"Sheriff, we could go in circles all night—I can't pretend to know what Dean Haviland was thinking."

He stared at her long and hard. "Fair enough," he said finally. "But you've got some explaining to do about your own state of mind that night." He made a sorrowful noise and looked across the room to Mica. "You, too, Mica. We got back the results of the polygraph tests, and both of you girls failed. Now maybe you didn't kill Dean, but you're lying about a whole bunch of details."

Justine closed her eyes.

"You got two choices," he said. "I can arrest you both right now and you can call a lawyer, or you can tell me what the hell happened that night."

She opened her eyes and stared across at Mica, who stared back, big-eyed. Christ, were they to be forever embroiled in each other's lives? She gave Mica a challenging look. "I don't need a lawyer."

Mica's chin went up and she ignored her agent's pleas. "Neither do I."

Regina looked ready to come out of her skin. Cissy started crying.

"The rest of us should leave," Mitchell suggested.

"No, I want everyone to hear," Mica said.

Justine splayed her hand. "I just want to get it off my chest."

The sheriff signaled Pete, who pulled a notebook out of his pocket. "Who wants to go first?"

"I will," Mica said, and stood up to escape her agent's protests. "I lied about Justine's gun on the table downstairs. The truth is, I picked it up, and I was going to go after Dean. I wanted to hurt him back for everything he'd done." She teared up and the end of her tongue appeared between her teeth. "But I got as far as the front porch before I realized the gun wasn't loaded. I left it there and went back inside to get a shell from my gun. I ran into Regina and she asked me to help her sweep up the plaster in Justine's room."

The sheriff looked at Regina, and she nodded confirmation.

"By the time I removed the round from the gun in my suitcase and went back outside, the revolver was gone."

"Then what?" Sheriff Shadowen asked.

"Then nothing. That missing gun was a wake-up call. I sat there and shook like a leaf for ten minutes; then I went upstairs and put the shell back into the gun in my suitcase."

Justine narrowed her eyes. "You were going to shoot him with my gun?"

"I wasn't trying to frame you—I just didn't think I'd be able to get my gun downstairs without someone seeing me." Mica looked at the sheriff. "I wanted to kill him, but I didn't; I swear. And I don't know what happened to the revolver."

"Was your daddy around when you left that gun on the porch?"

"He was in the house."

"Was he still here when it went missing?"

She hesitated, then shook her head. She looked at Cissy. "I'm sorry, Mom. I didn't want to make things worse for Daddy."

Justine studied them morosely—they hadn't seen worse yet.

All eyes swung in her direction, and she tasted filter on her next drag. She stubbed it out and exhaled. "I wanted to go after Dean, too, but I was more worried about Daddy. Around midnight, I took a flashlight and climbed down the trellis, then walked through the woods to the shop. Daddy's car wasn't there, but Dean's was, and he was sitting in it. I assumed he was waiting for Mica. I was so angry for what he'd done, I was going to hit him, kick him—something. I thought he was sleeping." Her vision blurred as her eyes filled with tears.

"I opened the door, and he fell out, dead. Shot. And my gun fell out on the ground, too." She wiped her eyes. "I panicked—I thought Daddy or Mica had killed him, and I didn't know what to do. All that trash was sitting out for the dump, and I saw the wardrobe. It seemed perfect—I could get rid of the body and maybe no one would be the wiser." She laughed, hysterically. "I know it was a crazy scheme, but I wasn't about to let Dean take any more of my family away." She sniffed mightily, then exhaled. "I had an awful time getting him in that damn wardrobe. His arms and legs—" She choked. "But I did it. Then I drove down by Dilly Creek and tossed the gun. I drove back and pulled off the side of the road and left the keys, hoping someone would steal the car. I wiped it down thinking I'd get rid of my fingerprints and Daddy's or Mica's, too; then I walked back and climbed the trellis to my bedroom."

She breathed into steepled hands. "Would've worked, too, if Regina and Mitchell hadn't found the body." She gave them a tight smile. Regina's face was wet with tears. "What I did was wrong, Sheriff, but I did *not* kill Dean, and I know the polygraph bears me out on that account."

The look on his face said it did.

She stood. "So, are you going to arrest me?"

"I could," he said. "Messing with a corpse. Tampering with evidence."

Cissy was bawling like a calf.

Lawrence stood. "Can't you do something, Hank? She wasn't thinking straight—she was trying to protect John."

The sheriff sighed. "The point is, Justine, taking you into protective custody might be the safest thing for everyone until we can find that Crane woman."

She put her hand to an ache in her temple and nodded. "Okay. Can I pack a bag?"

"Look at her, Hank," Lawrence said. "She's been to a funeral, was nearly blown sky-high, and now all this. She needs to eat and get a good night's sleep in her own bed. Why don't I drive her down myself first thing in the morning? My security guard will keep an eye on things around here tonight."

"And I'll stay," Pete offered.

The sheriff worked his mouth back and forth, then nodded. "Okay. First thing in the morning."

Justine rose and gave her uncle a grateful smile and her mother a comforting hug. "I'm sorry, Mom. I know this looks bad for John."

Cissy hugged her back. "John is responsible for his own actions. You have to think of your own safety, your own future."

She blinked back tears. What future? "I think I'll call it a night." She looked around the room—Cissy had Uncle Lawrence, Regina had Pete *and* Mitchell, Mica had Everett, and once again, the cheese stood alone.

Regina stood. "Justine—"

"Not now, Regina. I'd like to be alone."

She escaped and climbed the stairs to her room. She closed the window and pressed her nose to the glass, comforted by the sight of Lawrence's security guard patrolling. Then Pete appeared and shook hands with the man. She was safe.

Once the tears started falling, she couldn't stop them. Dean had wanted to *kill* her. She had squandered the prime of her life loving a man who not only didn't love her but also was willing to kill her for . . . what? Regina and Mitchell seemed to think he was onto some kind of big moneymaking deal, blackmail or insurance or something. She couldn't care less what his motivations might have been. She accepted the fact that he was a liar and a cheat, but the boy she'd fallen in love with when she was seventeen was no murderer. She would have thought herself capable of murder before she would have attributed it to Dean.

Her head felt light and fuzzy with sensory overload.

A week ago she'd been on top of the world. Now she was scraping bottom. She glanced toward the chest where the nutmeg was stashed. If ever there was a time for a dreamless night's sleep, it was tonight.

# twenty-nine

**DON'T** overdose on love.

Mica handed Everett a cup of coffee. "I still can't believe you're here."

His smile put a kink in her chest. "I couldn't bear the thought of you being alone. And now that I realize everything you've been going through, I wish I'd come sooner."

"My family is one big mess, isn't it? I'm worried sick about my dad—I'm just so afraid he might've . . . I can't even say it. I could see how he would be angry enough to kill Dean, but if John did something like that, he's the kind of man who would drive to the jail and turn himself in. That's why I'm so afraid—I'm sorry; I don't mean to drag you into this."

He sipped the coffee and set down the cup. "I'm sad about your father, Mica, and it's tragic that Dean died so young, but I was never a fan of Dean's, and I won't miss him." He clasped her fingers. "But I know you will. How are you feeling physically?"

"Much better. Stronger. I have more energy." Then she ruffled her hair ruefully. "The back and neck pain are gone." She sighed and lifted the lid of the shoe box where she had stored the disheveled braid. "I've always heard rumors that my hair is insured—is that true?"

He fingered the end of the braid. "Yes and no. The insurance is actually a life-insurance policy that the client has in case something happens to you."

"In case I die?"

He nodded. "Or are disfigured or disabled in some way. It's standard when a company sinks all its advertising dollars into one face."

Her heart sank. "So what will happen to my career?"

Everett sighed and squeezed her hand. "Well, we could always go with extensions using your real hair, but it wouldn't be the same. To be honest, Mica, the marketing director for Tara was already on the fence over the missed shoots. This could be the excuse she needs to cancel the contract altogether."

She was tempted to lash out at Justine for jeopardizing her career, but deep down she knew that her own cruel behavior years ago had triggered her sister's retaliation. In truth, the loss of her hair, even the loss of her livelihood, was superficial compared to what she'd taken from Justine.

"You're still a lovely woman," he said. "Even without the hair."

She patted his hand gratefully. "My face is too old to compete with fifteen-year-old skin."

"Maybe we can find a company that skews to a slightly older customer." Then he angled his head. "I'll think of something. I have over five years invested in you."

The oven timer went off, and she reached for an insulated mitt. "Would you mind if I run one of these croissants up to Justine? She hasn't eaten, and I'd like to check on her."

When she turned around, he was staring at her with the strangest expression.

"Everett?"

He stood. "Do whatever you need to do. I'm going back to my hotel room. I'll call you tomorrow before I leave." He tucked the shoe box under his arm. "I'll take your hair back with me."

She bit down on the inside of her cheek. "Okay, if you think that would be best."

"I do."

Mica put two croissants on a saucer and walked Everett to the door. Pete Shadowen's form was silhouetted in the yard, distinguished by his hat. "I'll call you," Everett said, then dropped a kiss to her temple.

Surprised, she could only nod. Then she closed the door and fairly floated upstairs to Justine's room carrying the tray. She knocked. "Justine, open up; it's Mica. I have warm buttered croissants."

When there was no answer, she turned the knob, but it was locked. "Justine, I'm not going away; you need to eat something."

Thinking maybe she was in the bathroom, Mica went through her own bedroom, but Justine wasn't in the bathroom. She tried the knob and frowned when she found it was also locked. "Justine?" She pressed her ear to the door and heard nothing, so she felt along top of the doorsill until her fingers closed over an ancient skeleton key. She'd just stick her head in—if Justine was sleeping, she'd leave her alone. But if Justine was simply shutting them out, she had something to tell her, something long overdue.

The door unlocked with a faint click. Mica opened it a few inches. "Justine?"

It was only then that she heard a persistent clicking noise. Something wasn't right. Mica flipped on the light and horror washed over her. The clicking noise was Justine's teeth coming together as her body wracked with convulsions.

# thirty

**DO hide things in plain view.**

"I can't believe this is happening," Regina said for the hundredth time, pacing their little corner of the emergency waiting room. Other people in the waiting room kept their distance, probably because she was still wearing her smoky funeral garb. She was out of tears. Everything that wasn't numb throbbed.

"You're going to wear yourself out," Mitchell said. "Why don't you sit down?"

Because she was afraid she'd collapse onto that shoulder bone he'd offered her the other day. "Who would've thought a person could *overdose* on nutmeg? Why don't I know these things?"

"Because you don't want to know these things."

She stopped pacing. "What's that supposed to mean?"

He spread his hands. "You don't search out deviant ways to entertain yourself, and I suspect you don't have friends who do, either."

"And what's wrong with that?"

"Absolutely nothing. But in return for living a squeaky clean life, you give up a certain amount of street smarts."

"*I'm* street-smart. I live in the city, remember? I've seen prostitutes. I carry pepper spray. I know the pressure points that will take a man down."

A smile curved his mouth. "Yes, you do."

She indulged in a stab of pleasure at his intimate reference but refused to publicly acknowledge the thrill. "Just because I'm the only one in the family who doesn't pack heat, doesn't mean I'm not street-smart."

"Pack heat? No more coffee for you. At least until the doctor comes out."

"Where's Mica?"

"I saw her head toward the ladies' room. While we have a few minutes alone, I need to talk to you about a couple of things."

"Okay, talk."

"Will you please sit down? Or at least stand still."

She sat.

He angled his head. "Do you believe Justine's story about finding Dean already dead?"

"I know what you're thinking. You're thinking that she killed him and tried to kill herself tonight." From his expression, she knew she'd hit the nail on the head. "But if she were planning to commit suicide, then why would she lie?"

"Perhaps she wasn't contemplating suicide when she talked to the sheriff."

"If Justine killed Dean, she would never allow John to take the blame."

"Do you believe Mica?"

She hesitated. "Yes."

"Are you certain?"

"I . . . yes. Could we change the subject, please?"

He steepled his hands under his chin. "That car explosion today took ten years off my life. I'm glad you're okay."

She was glad he was glad. "Thank you for putting

out the fire. Sorry about your jacket." She shook her head. "I can't believe that lunatic Lisa Crane was so close and we didn't even know it."

He cleared his throat. "What if wasn't Lisa Crane?"

"What do you mean?"

"Everyone could be naively thinking that Justine is in danger from a crazy person when all three of you could be in danger from a different, albeit just as crazy, person."

*"All he's trying to do is build reasonable doubt on the Gilbert case ... You're playing right into his hands."* "Mitchell, please—"

"The E-mail account was traced to a computer at the Monroeville public library."

She went still. "No kidding?"

"David called me this morning to let me know."

*"... so that when his brother wins a new trial, they'll get Bracken off."*

"But the address can't be tied to a specific person," he said. "Three-thousand-plus library cards issued, and all of them have access to the computers. Any user can reserve an address for the duration of a session." He leaned forward and rested his elbows on his knees. "So it appears that the letter opener you saw at the murder scene and the one you saw on-line could be one and the same."

Her body was becoming acclimated to the constant adrenaline rush. "The person I E-mailed knows I can link them to the murder."

"If they read the papers and connect the 'ReginaM' who sent the E-mail message with the Regina Metcalf who's set to give new testimony about the murder."

"The library must have logs to tell *when* the address was used—maybe the librarians could remember who was on the computers at those times."

"David checked. The electronic logs are maintained

for only three days before they're overwritten." He pursed his mouth. "What do you think the chances are that Mr. Calvin the book man has a library card?"

"Probably pretty high, but what connection would he have with my Aunt Lyla?"

He shrugged. "Lonely widower, small town, he and your aunt both frequented the antiques shop—maybe their paths crossed."

She winced. "Maybe. *Someone* in Monroeville has that letter opener."

"Probably not anymore."

True, by now the guilty party would've gotten rid of it—that letter opener was probably lying on the bottom of Armadillo Creek with Justine's gun. "Did you give this information to the sheriff?"

He nodded. "At least I tried. He got a little huffy, though, when I asked to see his library card."

"That wasn't the smartest move."

"Regina," he said quietly. "You're the only link to that piece of evidence. I believe you're the one who's in danger, not Justine."

She liked the way her name rolled off his tongue . . . too bad he was talking about murder. She took in his rumpled hair and tired eyes and shadowed jaw— all her family's doing—and thoroughly agreed with him. She was very much in danger . . . of falling in love with this man. Fortunately, he was oblivious to the inner workings of her mind. Like most men, he assumed silence meant acceptance of whatever he was talking about.

He stood. "First there was the so-called hunting accident, now the car fire. Someone doesn't want you to testify."

What was it the sheriff had said about lawyers twisting things around? If she squinted, Mitchell's words almost made sense. She lifted her hands. "So I'll sign an affidavit, and then there won't be any point in getting rid of me."

His mouth hardened. "This isn't funny."

She sighed. "I'm sorry. Did you have someone particular in mind who would want me dead?"

"Well, if your Mr. Calvin sells cars on the side, he probably knows how to rig a gas line."

"I just can't imagine Mr. Calvin hurting innocent people like that."

"No one likes to think that a person who blends into the community could be a killer. In fact—" He pulled on his chin. "Pete Shadowen was nearby when both incidents occurred, and even though he doesn't strike me as much of a reader, I'd like to find out if *he* has a library card."

Regina crossed her arms. "Okay, now *that* is funny. Because Pete seems to think that these strange events coincide with *your* appearance in town."

His face darkened. "Is that what he was filling your head with at the funeral home?"

She stood to face him. "Filling my head?"

Someone cleared her throat and Regina looked over. Mica had returned, looking young and thin in baggy clothes and a hat. "Has the doctor come out?"

"Not yet."

"What could be taking so long?"

"Let's ask." She threw Mitchell a look that said, didn't she have enough to deal with without him making things worse? and approached the nurses' station. They talked to a woman in pink scrubs who disappeared, then returned with a lady doctor in tow.

"Family of Justine Metcalf?"

"We're her sisters," Regina said, heart pounding.

"Sorry for the delay—I just finished processing the paperwork for her treatment."

"How is she?"

"The next couple of days will be rough, but she'll be fine."

Regina's shoulders fell in relief.

"There were no traces of other drugs in her system, but do you know if she uses other substances?"

Regina shook her head ruefully—in the past few days she'd learned she didn't know much about her sisters' intimate lives. Mica, too, shook her head.

"Has she ever overdosed on nutmeg before?"

Again, they didn't know.

"This is only the second case of nutmeg poisoning I've ever treated, but judging from the amount of myristicin in her bloodstream, I'd say that she's a moderate user and the overdose was accidental."

Another huge relief. "Can we see her?"

"She's being admitted, so you can see her when she gets settled into a room. She won't be responsive, though, until sometime tomorrow. I gave her a sedative and an anticonvulsant. She's dehydrated, so we'll put her on an IV. And she'll be on a liquid diet for a few days." She frowned. "The deputy indicated that she's being stalked; is that correct?"

They nodded. Regina said a prayer of thanks for Pete, who had driven Justine to the county hospital in the backseat of his cruiser. Mica had ridden along, frantic. She and Mitchell had followed. He was another one who always seemed to be in the right place at the right time.

But was that by chance or by design?

"Justine has been under an enormous amount of stress lately," Regina said.

The doctor folded her arms over a clipboard. "The hallucinogenic ingredient in nutmeg isn't addictive, but the behavior in taking it is. It's a dangerous habit because it seems harmless, but there's no standard dosage or delivery, just trial and error. If a person takes too much, she not only experiences a bad trip but potentially can have severe cramping, convulsions, or renal complications."

"Could Justine have died?"

"Not likely, but the body expels the poison quite violently. She'll feel like hell for forty-eight hours, and it's possible that she'll have temporary psychosis." Her mouth went flat. "This is not a pretty way for a person to get her kicks. After this experience, she might not use nutmeg again, but if she doesn't get help, she might look for other outlets."

They thanked the doctor, and Regina and Mica threw their arms around each other in abject relief, rocking back and forth. They didn't touch, her family. Not often enough, based on how good it felt.

When they released each other, Mica said, "Go home, Regina. I'll stay with Justine."

"I'll stay, too."

"Let me," Mica said. "I need to talk to her alone. To . . . set things right." She suddenly smiled. "This might be my only chance to speak to her without being interrupted."

Regina wanted to stay, but she saw how much it meant to Mica, and if leaving meant that her sisters could be sisters again, it would be a small price. Mica promised she'd call as soon as Justine was settled into a room. Regina said she'd bring Cissy to visit the next day.

She was silent the first few minutes of the ride home in Mitchell's van. It was only ten-thirty of what just might go down as the longest day of her life. The acrid smell of their clothes filled the cab. "Think Sam's okay?" she asked. They'd left him with Cissy and Lawrence.

"Oh, sure. Sam and I, we fit in wherever we go."
He found a blues station on the radio.

Nothing special about this situation, he was telling
her. He and Sam would move on shortly. She shouldn't
get attached to that crotch-nudging thing—from either
one of them.

She'd called Cissy from the hospital to let her know
that Justine was all right. Her mother had been relieved,
of course, and even though Regina had thought it was
better under the circumstances for Cissy to stay behind,
she was beginning to wonder about her mother's pre-
occupation with staying near the house . . . as if she
were protecting something . . . or hiding something . . .

She straightened. Or hiding some*one*.

*"Forget the attic. . . . Your father cleared everything
out of that oven long ago. Nothing up there but bats."*

"Hurry," she said, sitting up.

"What's wrong?"

"I have an idea where my father is hiding."

He broke a few posted speeding recommendations
on the way but got them back to the Doll in record
time. Uncle Lawrence's security guard stood near the
base of the steps and nodded when they passed him.

They entered the house and Sam jumped up from
his resting place in the hall, his tongue lolling happily.
Man and dog followed her up the stairs to the second
floor. The light shone under Cissy's door, and the murmur of her uncle's voice reached her. Regina strode
past to the tapered stairs leading to the attic and flipped
on a harsh overhead light.

The door to Cissy's room opened, and Lawrence
emerged. "Regina, you're home." Then he frowned at
her position—one foot on the bottom step to the attic.
"What's wrong, dear?"

Cissy appeared behind him in her dressing gown and

peered out into the hallway. "Regina, what are you doing?"

"I'm going to check the attic."

"For what? I told you it was empty." Was it her imagination, or did her mother sound strident?

She ignored Cissy and grasped the handrail. Her heart thumped like a drum as she climbed to the tiny landing. She turned the glass knob and pushed on the narrow door, swollen shut from the heat. She put her shoulder into it, and the door scraped open. A haze of stifling air rolled out, along with sleeping dust motes.

"Dad? Dad, are you in here?" She reached around the corner and groped for the chain. A high, bare bulb flooded light over the space, revealing sheets of plywood flooring, plastic-covered pink insulation, and yes, a handful of fluttering bats in the eaves.

But no John.

Disappointment rolled over her. Behind her, Mitchell placed a hand on her arm. She backed out and pulled the door closed behind her. She stared down at her mother's anxious face, and descended slowly. "I thought that Dad . . . It was crazy, I guess."

"Regina," her uncle said gently. "I've made phone calls all day, but no one has seen your father. You need to accept that you might never see him again."

She nodded numbly.

"Some issues have sprung up in my Washington office since I left that I need to address."

"You're leaving town?"

"No. I set up a temporary office at my cabin; I can handle things from there. But I'll leave my security man—will you and your mother be okay for the night?"

"I'll stay," Mitchell offered.

Her uncle perused Mitchell with suspicious eyes.

"It's okay, Uncle Lawrence," she heard herself say, and walked him to the door. "Thank you for everything."

"You're welcome." He looked over her shoulder, then leaned in close. "I don't trust that man, Regina. Be careful."

"I will," she promised, mostly to humor him.

"Call me if you need me."

"I will."

"Is Hank's boy guarding Justine?"

"Yes."

"And she's going to be okay?"

"Yes. The doctor said that she accidentally overdosed and she'd be fine in a couple of days."

"Good." He sighed. "I don't know how much more stress your mother can withstand."

"I'm going up to check on her right now." She closed the door and inhaled deeply before climbing back up to Cissy's room.

Her mother had returned to her bed. Regina sat on the edge and held her mother's hand. Cissy's eyes were so bleak. "I miss John, Regina. And I'm worried. Where could he be?"

She shook her head. "I don't know."

"And your sisters seem determined to kill themselves or each other."

"I have a feeling that a cease-fire is in the works."

Cissy laid her head back on a mound of pillows. "I hope so."

Regina smoothed the fold of a sheet unnecessarily. "Mom, I need to ask you some questions about Aunt Lyla."

Cissy went rigid. "What kind of questions?"

"The personal kind. Do you know if she was involved with other men around town?"

"Like who?"

"Like Mr. Calvin, for instance?"

"Tom Calvin? Yes, there was some talk about him and Lyla, before and after his wife died. Catherine and Lyla were sisters, you know."

She hadn't known. "How did his wife die?"

"She and Tom were fishing in Dilly Creek in a john-boat. It capsized, she couldn't swim, and he couldn't save her. Very sad affair."

And very incriminating. Regina swallowed. "What about the sheriff?"

Cissy nodded. "There was always talk about Lyla and Hank Shadowen."

"Isn't Pete's mother wheelchair-bound?"

"Yes, and has been most of her adult life. She always looked the other way when Hank stepped out."

"Anyone else?"

"The only other name that comes to mind is Tate Williams. Once Sarah Williams confronted Lyla in the Grab 'N Go—threw a Slurpee on her and said if Lyla didn't leave Tate alone, she was going to fix her wagon."

Monroeville was quite the Peyton Place.

The phone rang, and Regina picked up the receiver from the nightstand. "Hello?"

"It's Mica. Justine is settled into a room, and sleeping."

"Good. Do you want me to come and get you?"

"No. The nurses were kind enough to move in a cot for me. I'm going to stay."

"If you're sure."

"I am. I'll see you tomorrow."

She hung up the phone and gave the news to Cissy, whose eyelids were already fluttering. Regina kissed her mother's cheek and dimmed the lights, then retreated to the hall. Mitchell was fastening the deadbolt on the front door.

"I checked all the windows and doors."

"Thanks." She sat down on the top step and told him about her mother's revelations. When he heard about Sheriff Shadowen's alleged liaison with Lyla, his jaw hardened. "I guess I'll be talking with the sheriff again tomorrow."

She studied his wide-legged stance and marveled at the sense of security his presence gave her. Was she grasping at emotional straws? "You don't have to do all this, you know."

He shrugged. "I have this hang-up about justice."

She looked at him and conceded calmly that she wouldn't mind being Mitchell Cooke's hang-up. "Are you finished with the appraisals?"

"Except for a few items in the shop, maybe a half-day's work. I'll ask the sheriff tomorrow how soon I can get back inside."

The silence stretched between them, and her nerves sang at the intimacy of the atmosphere.

Mitchell felt it, too. He rubbed his neck, then jerked his thumb in the direction of the family room. "I thought I'd bunk down on the couch. It'll be easier to keep an eye on things."

She nodded, glad he hadn't asked to sleep in her bed because she wasn't sure what she would've said. "Where's Sam?"

He smiled. "Already zonked out."

"I'll get you some sheets."

"No need," he assured her. "Try to get some rest."

She nodded and pushed to her feet, contemplating the world's longest hot shower. Maybe things would be better tomorrow.

And then again, maybe not.

# thirty-one

DO forgive and forget, but keep a list just in case.

Justine moaned. Someone had turned her body inside out and set it on fire.

"Justine, can you hear me?"

Mica. She creaked open one eye. Her sister was sitting in a chair, wearing a floppy hat, leaning toward her.

"You're in the hospital," she said. "We brought you in last night—you have nutmeg poisoning."

Which would explain the unspeakable taste in her mouth and the inferno in her stomach.

"You gave me quite a scare when I found you."

Mica had found her and actually called for help?

"But the doctor says you'll be fine in a couple of days."

She moved her head a millimeter and twin bombs detonated in her temples. "Ohhhhhh."

"Easy. Want some ice chips?"

She managed to nod. She was in a tidy private room of mauves and taupes, with a rumpled cot pushed against the wall. Mica held a little plastic container to her mouth and put ice chips on her lips. Justine flicked out her tongue to take them and studied her sister's face—pale, sleep-smudged, and exquisite.

She tried out her voice. "Did . . . you . . . sleep here?"

Mica nodded and kept feeding her ice. "It gave me plenty of time to really soak you in, and to think." Her eyes filled with tears. "I've treated you so abominably, Justine. I don't blame you for hating me, but do you think you could ever forgive me?"

She kept taking the chips and letting them dissolve on her parched tongue. One part of her wanted to scream that now that Dean was gone, apologies were cheap. But Regina's words still weighed heavily on her heart.

*"There's been enough hurt in this family . . . you could end it."*

And hadn't she taken her revenge tenfold when she'd destroyed her sister's identity and career with one slice of the shears?

Justine's own eyes teared over, and twelve years of emotion came spilling out. "I . . . was angry when you left with Dean . . . but Dean was the one I hated." She choked. "For taking my sister away from me. I knew things would never be the same between you and me."

Mica was a beautiful crier, dammit. She buried her face in Justine's neck and sobbed until Justine felt her sister's tears pool to the back of her nape and soak into the pillow. "There now," she murmured, and instinctively moved to stroke her sister's hair. When she didn't encounter the silky mass of black waves, the enormity of her own cruelty slammed into her. Her throat ached with unshed tears. "Can you forgive me for cutting your gorgeous hair?"

Mica nodded against her neck, and they both dissolved into ridiculous tears. Ridiculous that they had allowed their relationship to languish for so long. So many missed moments, so much to make up for.

A knock on the door sounded, and Mica sat up, wiping her eyes with the backs of her hands. "I'll get it. It's probably Pete—he guarded your door all night in case that crazy Crane woman showed up."

Justine tried to mop up her own tears, but her arms felt like lead planks. Mica opened the door and held a whispered conversation with a man, then slipped outside. When the door opened, a burly guy in a blue uniform filled the doorway. She frowned in disbelief. "Lando?"

"In the flesh," he said with a big smile. He walked over and set a plant on the windowsill.

She pulled at the sheet self-consciously to cover the paper-thin, split-up-the-back rag that hospitals make a person wear. "What are you doing here?"

"Sheriff Shadowen called last night to tell me about the car explosion and that you . . . were ill. I thought I'd better come down myself and see if Lisa Crane might be hanging around."

"Did you find her?"

"No."

"What's that?" she asked, pointing to the spiky plant.

"Aloe vera. I don't think even you could kill it. Plus it's great for burns and skin abrasions, which I figured might come in handy since you're so prone to trouble."

She wet her lips—she knew she looked like hell. "Do you think the Crane woman was behind the car explosion?"

"I just don't know. The sheriff tells me you're in the middle of all kinds of interesting situations."

She swallowed past her raw throat—her family was in shambles and she hadn't helped matters by pulling this stunt. To her horror, she burst into tears.

Lando's eyes widened; then he sat next to the bed. He awkwardly patted her foot through the sheet and made comforting noises in his throat. "Everything's going to be okay; you just wait and see." He handed her a tissue, but her arms refused to cooperate. Undaunted, he wiped her eyes, the picture of calm.

"My father," she croaked. "We can't find him."

"Yes, I heard. You care a lot about your family, don't you?"

She nodded against the pillow and swallowed more tears.

"I suspected there was a heart somewhere under that crust."

She smiled, confounded by his attention, and confused by her own feelings when she looked at this ordinary man who seemed to have such extraordinary insight. His features were mediocre at best, but his eyes were kind and his smile ready.

"I'd better go and let you rest," he said. "But I'll stop in again before I leave town."

She nodded.

"Take care of yourself better this time."

She nodded.

He left and she stared at the aloe vera plant for a very long time. It was grocery store variety, the plastic pot covered with green foil, and tied with a plastic yellow ribbon. Tacky beyond belief, yet remarkably beautiful. For the first time in a long time, a sliver of optimism made its way into her heart.

The door opened and she turned her head carefully, expecting Mica and a boatload of questions. Instead, her heart surged in her chest.

It was Mica, all right, but on her arm was their father, looking remarkably clean-shaven and alert. She lifted her hand to him and the blasted tears came back again. "Daddy."

"Justine," he murmured, and hugged her gently. "Are you okay, sweetheart?"

"I'll be fine. *Where* have you been?"

He pulled back but clasped her limp hand to his cheek. "Doing what I should've done years ago—drying out. Seems like I picked a pretty lousy time to check myself into a clinic, though."

"You've been in a rehab clinic?"

He nodded.

She closed her eyes in sweet relief. That explained a lot of things.

"Dean was right," he said. "I've been a drunk most of my life, standing on the periphery of my family. I knew I had to get sober and make it up to you girls. Especially to you, Justine. I wasn't there for you when you needed me."

She bit into her lip. "You know about Dean?"

"Yeah. This morning was the first time the clinic would allow me to make a phone call. I called Cissy to let her know where I was, and she told me the entire story. I had to come and see you first. What you all must have gone through."

"We were worried about you."

The door opened and Deputy Pete walked in with a rueful expression. "Gotta take you in now, John."

"Thanks, Pete, for letting me see my girl first." He gave her a sad smile. "See you soon."

"They're arresting you?"

"Just taking him into custody," Pete said, clasping John by the arm. "At least until we can verify his alibi."

"Everything will be fine," John assured her with unnatural calm as Pete clicked on the handcuffs and led him toward the door.

"Is Officer Lando still here?" she asked Pete.

"No, he left." He gave her a little smile. "But don't worry about the Crane woman—hospital security has been alerted, and I'll be right back."

She lay back on the pillow, feeling utterly vulnerable.

# thirty-two

**DO be concerned when he wants to talk.**

Mica smiled up at Everett. "This is a nice surprise."

He shrugged. "After you called, I thought maybe you could use a ride home before I left to catch my plane."

She looked back to the closed door to Justine's hospital room and wavered. "I just spoke to Regina, and I told her I'd wait for her and Mom to come by." She sighed. "But Justine is sleeping so soundly. And I wouldn't mind a shower."

"Let me take you home; then you can freshen up and ride back with them."

"Good idea." She rummaged in her purse. "Let me call Regina."

"Oh, I'll practically have you home in the time it would take to call."

"Okay." She shouldered her purse. "This will give us a chance to brainstorm about my career. Have you thought of a way to get me—*us*—out of this jam?"

"I believe so."

His voice was cautious, his expression unreadable.

He didn't want to get her hopes up, but her hopes climbed anyway. "What's your idea?"

He gave her a tight smile and swept his arm in front of her. "Why don't we talk about it in the car?"

# thirty-three

DO recognize that some men are snakes.

Regina hugged Cissy. "See? I told you not to give up on Daddy."

Cissy puffed out her cheeks in joyous relief. Regina was heartened not only by the color in Cissy's cheeks but also by the love she saw shining in her eyes—love for John. Maybe there was hope for their relationship after all.

Then Cissy sobered. "Mica said that Pete took John into custody."

"But when they check out his alibi, they'll have to let him go." She looked to Mitchell for confirmation, but he glanced down at the coffee cup he held. "What?" she asked. "What are you thinking?"

He took a slow drink. "I'm thinking that if the sheriff and his son were involved in Lyla's or Dean's death, they're not all of a sudden going to start playing by the rules." He took another drink. "Your father needs an attorney, and I'd feel a lot better if he was moved to another holding facility."

Regina felt heavy with dread that they weren't out of the woods just yet. Mitchell was right.

"Lawrence can help," Cissy said. "I'll call him."

"Why don't I drive out to his place?" Regina offered. "Then we can ride down to the sheriff's office together. Mitchell, would you mind taking Mom by the hospital first, then meeting us at the sheriff's?"

"Fine," he said, but he was preoccupied, his mind spinning a thousand miles a minute, she knew.

She gave him a grateful smile. "I'll take Sam with me so you won't have to leave him in the car."

Sam was glad to get out of the house and acclimated rather quickly to the compact passenger seat of her rental car. He poked his nose out the six-inch gap she'd allowed in the window and let his tongue flap in the wind. He was good, quiet company. She turned the radio on low and allowed her mind to run rampant. When the details of Lyla's murder and Dean's murder began to intermingle and muddy her thoughts, she reminded herself that at least her father was alive and well, and all else paled in comparison.

Something the radio announcer said caught her attention, so she turned up the volume.

"Kirby, age forty-one, was a lifetime resident of Monroeville. His remains were discovered Saturday in a wooded area two miles from Tipton Road, near Macken, but the coroner said Kirby probably died Wednesday or Thursday. His death has been ruled a hunting accident."

A chill went through her—Stan Kirby was dead. It seemed too coincidental that he had been associating with Dean and they had died only hours apart. Had the third man—Covey—offed both of the men to claim the "jackpot" for himself? And Kirby's body had been found only miles from Mr. Calvin's place. Things only got curiouser and curiouser, but surely this new wrinkle would bode well for proving John's innocence.

When Lyla had been alive, she and Uncle Lawrence had lived in a home within the city limits to maintain his eligibility to hold city office. They also had owned a hobby farm outside the city to satisfy Lawrence's passion for outdoor sports. After Lyla's death and after Lawrence was elected a U.S. representative, he'd sold the house in town and built a log cabin on his piece of wild land. But since he spent most of his time in D.C., Regina hadn't had many occasions to visit his home, although she fondly remembered a picnic and a hayride he'd given for the entire town to celebrate some political milestone.

The gravel road leading to the farm was winding and bumpy but passable. She drove slowly and rolled down the windows so she and Sam could enjoy the scenery—thick green hay sticking through the split-rail fences lining either side of the road, patches of goldenrod, apples trees heavy with yellow fruit. Sam barked at something, probably a rabbit or other varmint. She laughed and patted his head. After a couple of more curves, Lawrence's log home came into view. It had been built from a kit in a matter of weeks, she remembered her father saying. Two stories with a two-sided porch, and a sunroom off the back. The driveway went up to the house but petered out into wild grass, which flanked either side of the sidewalk. The ungroomed yard seemed to fit the picturesque backdrop of towering pines and kingly oaks. She pulled in next to Lawrence's Lincoln and stepped out. Sam promptly jumped out and ran in the direction they'd come, toward a twitching bush. She turned in appreciative circles as she made her way up to Lawrence's front door. It was a beautiful spot.

She knocked on the door loudly in case he was in his office. After a few minutes, she knocked again, and this time the door opened. She wasn't accustomed to seeing him in casual clothes—jeans and a short-sleeve plaid shirt.

"Hi, Uncle Lawrence."

He peered at her over his reading glasses. "Regina—what brings you out this way? Not bad news, I hope."

"Just the opposite—John's home."

Her uncle seemed truly shocked. "When?"

"This morning. He's been in a rehab clinic all this time—he didn't even know that Dean was dead. Isn't that wonderful?"

Her uncle was still scratching his head. "A clinic, huh? Yeah, that's great."

"He said he wasn't allowed to make phone calls for the first few days, and since his treatment was confidential, even if someone on the staff saw his picture on the news, they couldn't have turned him in."

"Right. Well, come in, come in."

She glanced back but didn't see Sam.

"Are you alone?"

"Yes." She stepped inside. "I came to ask yet another favor, Uncle Lawrence."

"Anything in my power, dear."

She followed him through the house to the screened-in sunroom that he'd turned into his office. "Mitchell is convinced that the sheriff isn't on the up-and-up."

"I know—he informed me the other day that he suspected the sheriff might have had something to do with Lyla's death."

His voice was so sad, she felt chagrined. "I'm sorry that all this is being rehashed—I can't imagine how painful it must be for you."

"I'm a survivor," he said, as he'd said many times before. Now she wondered how many times his stoic philosophy masked a deeper pain.

"Well, the point is, Mitchell thinks it would be a good idea to have Dad moved to another holding facility until his alibi can be confirmed."

Lawrence motioned for her to sit in a rocking chair.

"Good breeze coming in through the screen door."

She claimed the chair and nudged the rocker into motion.

He leaned on the front of his desk and pulled up his leg for a good scratch above his western boots. "Damn chiggers." He rummaged around for his pipe and tobacco. "This Cooke fellow is mighty free with his opinions."

His scratch gave her a sense of déjà vu, but she shook it off. "Yes, he's opinionated, but he's been very helpful. Like you," she added hastily.

He smiled as he tamped the tobacco into the bowl of the pipe. Her nostrils flared as the scent of the rum-flavored leaf traveled on the light breeze. "Yes, I've tried to be helpful to Cissy. Helpful to all the women in my life." He reached for a matchbook to light his pipe.

Pete, she remembered suddenly. He'd been scratching himself all during their dinner date and since. The day he'd been parked at the end of their driveway, she'd noticed a rash on his legs—but it wasn't a rash; it was chiggers.

"Have you been hunting?" she asked.

"Nah, no time this trip," he said.

"But you've been in the woods," she said, pointing to his legs.

He looked down, then shrugged. "Probably picked them up in the yard or something." He struck the match and held it over the bowl, drawing on the stem to light the tobacco.

That's when she noticed the matchbook—Tick's Pool Hall. Icy fingers clenched her heart as she tried to reconcile the bits of information. Pete had gotten chiggers the day they'd been shot at, so it wasn't far-fetched to assume the lost hunter had gotten them as well. And when she returned from the walk, Uncle

Lawrence had been sitting on the porch with Cissy.

Too late, she realized she was staring at the match-book. And that telltale face of hers got her in trouble every time. She knew from the flash of desperation on his face that *he* knew she knew.

She pushed to her feet abruptly. "I really should be going, I barged right in on you." She turned to walk back toward the front door. Out of the corner of her eye, she saw him reach for a chunk of pink quartz on his desk—a paperweight, no doubt. But heavy enough for her to see stars when he clunked her on the back of the head.

She cried out, but even in her disoriented state, she knew the situation was hopeless. She was alone, with no neighbors for miles around.

"Dammit, Regina," Lawrence said, dragging her across the floor. "You always were a persnickety little thing—you never could leave well enough alone. I didn't want it to come to this; I really didn't. Now I'm going to have to figure out a way for this to look like an accident. Like you fell or something. Dammit!"

Darkness threatened to overcome her, but when she heard the screen door open and close she tried to rouse herself. She managed to flop over onto her belly before he returned, but the effort put spots behind her eyes.

"Sorry to have to do this to you, sweetheart," he said. "I know how you feel about snakes."

She managed to open one eye and shrank in horror. Tangled in the tines of a pitchfork were at least a dozen small snakes. Copperheads, no doubt. Poisonous, absolutely.

# thirty-four

DON'T go down without a fight. Or a least a good cry.

"Was getting ready to burn out the nest," he said. "Never figured on 'em coming in handy."

"Why?" she whispered, and laid her bleeding head on the floor.

"Because you wouldn't keep your mouth shut about that stupid letter opener. God, how that thing has haunted me."

*Keep him talking. Buy time to regain your strength.*
"You killed Aunt Lyla?"

"Yes, I killed that whore. Sleeping with anything that had a zipper, including that sonofabitch Haviland." He laughed bitterly. "They were in cahoots to bilk your parents, did you know that? Dean was pulling robberies, and she was selling stuff to your folks as 'treasures she'd found during her travels.' She even had the nerve to steal from the store. Bragged about the letter opener she'd taken right out of the case. A whore I could live with, but not a whore who would steal from my own family."

She breathed as deeply as she could to get oxygen to her brain, although her heart practically stopped at the thud of something slithery hitting the floor. One of the baby snakes skittered by, close enough for Regina to catch a whiff of a copperhead's unique scent—similar to the smell of cucumbers.

Regina shuddered. "But . . . Bracken."

"That convict belonged in jail anyway—no loss. Lyla had just screwed the guy, so his body fluid and stink was all over her. I talked her into going to Lovers' Lane, told her I wanted to make things right. And I did." He grunted. "Everything was fine until you girls started talking. That idiot Dean had been calling me for weeks, saying he had information about a witness to Lyla's murder, and seeing as how a new trial would damage my career, he thought I'd pay big to get rid of the witnesses. He was too goddamn stupid to realize he was talking to the person who'd killed her."

She gasped. "You . . . killed Dean . . . too?"

He sighed. "Had to. Told him I'd meet him at the antiques shop and give him a down payment. When I got there, he wasn't in his car. Figured he was at your house, so I parked down the road and walked back. I heard a shot, so I hid. That Cooke guy tossed Dean out of the house, and Dean drove off. I had to stay put, and next thing I know, Mica is sitting on the porch holding a gun. When she put it down, I decided that killing Dean with one of your daddy's guns would be the smart thing to do—I didn't realize it was Justine's. I had shells with me, so I loaded it, walked back through the woods, and when Dean drove up again to meet me, I shot the little peckerwood. Did everyone a big favor."

Another snake fell to the floor and slithered close before veering off.

"You shot at us . . . the car."

"I was just trying to scare you all into going home that day in the woods. That imbecile Kirby rigged your car. Had to take care of him, too. What a goddamn mess. Would make a hell of a biography, though. Shame you're going to miss out on that."

She was losing consciousness again. "I need help, Uncle Lawrence. Please help me."

"Did you know that baby copperheads are more venomous than adults? Adults conserve their venom when they strike, but a baby doesn't know any better and shoots the full load on the first bite."

He was rambling, had gone over the edge. Her jaw locked in terror. Anything but snakes, please God. She gulped a deep breath and screamed as loud and long as she could.

He tsk-tsked. "You're just getting them riled up."

Another noise invaded her senses. Barking . . . *Sam*.

"Sam!" she yelled. "Help me, Sam!" Gathering all her energy, she rolled. Once, twice, and again, then hit an obstacle. It was all the power she had anyway. Noises converged, then faded. She struggled to stay conscious. Sam's frantic barking mingled with her uncle's bellowing. A crash, a howl of pain—human or animal, she couldn't tell.

She gave in to the blackness and floated for a while. Her family had just started to heal, and she wanted to stick around. And then there was Mitchell, with his grin and his squiggle maneuver. She conjured up his voice.

"Regina?"

"Uhm."

"I'm here."

"Uhm."

# thirty-five

**DO know when to bury the hatchet.**

Regina had never attended such a large funeral. Lawrence Gilbert had known everyone in the state and practically everyone in the tristate. Throw in the horde of reporters, the contingency of D.C. politicians, plus the curiosity seekers, and Williams's Funeral Home was bursting at the beams.

Against her doctor's wishes, she attended the service out of respect for her mother. Her glasses had been broken beyond repair during her fall. The bandaged gash on her head was hidden under a hat. She still had woozy moments from the concussion but in general was just darn glad to be alive.

From her seat in the front row, she caught Mitchell's eye across the room. He was standing against the wall with Deputy Pete, Sheriff Shadowen, and assorted other men who had given up their seats. Mitchell's eyebrows rose slightly, as if to ask if she was okay, and she nodded. Since he'd rescued her from Lawrence, they'd maintained an arm's length distance, fraught with tension and an awkward bond. She was grateful beyond belief but concerned that he might think she expected something long-term to materialize out of

their frenetic few days together. But even with the concussion she was coherent enough to realize that this . . .
*connection* she sensed was born of proximity, adrenaline, and indebtedness.

After all, the man had almost lost his dog because
of her. She couldn't remember the details—only
snatches of sounds and sensations—but apparently
Sam had pawed through the screen and either attacked
Lawrence or disoriented him to the point of causing
him to fall on the pitchfork. The pitchfork hadn't killed
him, but the angry baby copperheads had been less
charitable. When Mitchell and Cissy arrived, Sam was
guarding her still figure, weakened from his own venomous encounter.

Mitchell, too, had heard about the Kirby death on
the radio. Another hunting "incident" seemed too coincidental to him, too. He'd asked Cissy if she remembered seeing anyone around the day the girls had been
shot at in the woods. Cissy wasn't aware of the accident but recalled that Lawrence had visited that day.
Mitchell's suspicions about Lawrence's involvement
and Regina's impending danger grew when neither she
nor Lawrence answered their cell phones.

Rather than waiting for an ambulance, Mitchell had
bundled her and Sam into the van and torn a new path
to the county hospital. She remembered some of the
ride—or thought she did. Cissy had ridden in the back
sobbing that everything was her fault.

Regina glanced sideways at her mother now, flanked
by John and a pale but recovered Justine. Cissy was
dry-eyed and rigid, devastated by her brother's betrayal. But at a time when she might have succumbed
to depression, she had instead exhibited her old spunk
and had been Regina's rock in the aftermath of the
attack. Cissy declared she would attend Lawrence's funeral to honor the brother who had raised her, not the

man who had committed such heinous acts. When Regina gave her statement to the sheriff, she reported that Lawrence had lost his grip on reality at the end. It was the only solace to her soul—that even he hadn't been able to rationally comprehend what he was about to do. She wished that she'd been able to ask him more questions, to fill in more blanks.

The organist began to play and everyone zoned in on the closed rosewood casket surrounded by a fortune in flowers. Uncle Lawrence was going out in style. The singing was lovely and mournful, and the service was conducted by a long-winded Baptist minister who seemed to realize he might never again have such a large captive audience and was determined to capitalize. He thumped and jumped until people began to shift in their seats. When the air-conditioning conked out, Tate Williams cued the singers for a farewell verse and everyone filed outside into the one hundred–plus temperature that had descended upon Monroeville.

Regina rode to the graveyard in the limousine with her sisters and Cissy and John. The caravan of vehicles behind them stretched for miles. She wondered if Mitchell was somewhere in the soup and if she should have ridden with him instead. On the other hand, there was no reason to implicate him even further into her family's misery—maybe he'd escaped to go fishing. Or to put a stick in his eye.

They all crept along at a respectable fifteen miles an hour—she supposed it couldn't appear as if they were in too big of a hurry to get Lawrence into the ground. At the graveside, the family and a few whoop-de-do politicians were seated in wobbly chairs on uneven ground covered with a turf tarp. She hovered somewhere just above awareness, anesthetized by her uncle's profound treachery.

*"Things don't always turn out the way you want,*

*but things generally turn out for the best."*

Only because Mitchell had interceded. Otherwise, Lawrence would have gotten away with yet another murder.

The preacher, perhaps threatened by Tate Williams, sent Uncle Lawrence on his way with a mercifully short prayer. In deference to his military service, a bugler played taps. As mourners dropped away and returned to their cars, Regina was gripped with a powerful sense of loneliness, despite the fact that her sisters and parents stood steps away. She turned and scanned the retreating crowd, telling herself she wasn't looking for Mitchell but conceding a rush of gladness when she spotted him leaning against a tree down the hill.

He lifted his hand.

*Busted.* As he approached, she attributed her lightheadedness to her head wound and the temperature.

He gestured to the tent. "I didn't want to intrude on your grief, but I thought I'd stick around and offer you a ride back to your parents' house."

Self-preservation kicked in. "I should stay with my family, but you're welcome to come by the house for platefuls of potato salad and inane small talk with strangers."

He smiled. "Do you mind if I pick up Sam? I left him sleeping at the hotel, but I'm sure he's bored by now."

"I'll be glad to see him up and around."

She watched Mitchell walk away, thinking she might as well get used to the image—she suspected his hours in Monroeville were numbered. They both had very different lives to get back to.

True to local custom, friends and acquaintances congregated at the Doll for tables of coleslaw and deviled eggs and honey-baked ham. There was no tragedy in the South that could not be survived with enormous quantities of food. Regina accepted a plate of potluck and remained standing to discourage pointed questions. When people did get nosy, she simply made a vague comment and moved away. One hour passed, then two, and the crowd thinned considerably. Her neck hurt from turning her head every time footsteps sounded, and still Mitchell hadn't arrived. She was starting to worry that Sam might have had a relapse and was headed inside to phone the hotel when Pete found her, armed with two glasses of lemonade. She smiled her appreciation and suggested they sit in the shade of an oak tree in the side yard.

"Regina, I'm really sorry for the way things turned out," he said when they settled into chairs. "My dad feels terrible, too. He's decided to retire."

She touched his arm. "Pete, I don't blame you or your father. No one imagined that Uncle Lawrence was capable of . . . those things."

He seemed grateful for her words and drank from his glass. He looked around. "I thought Cooke would be here to keep you company."

She opened her mouth to refute his company-keeping perceptions; then Sam's bark sounded from around the corner. The black dog loped into view, followed by his long-legged master.

Her heart lifted absurdly. To cover, she patted Sam's head and made soothing noises in his ear. "My hero," she murmured. He licked her hand and the bandage on his front leg.

"Sorry we're late," Mitchell said, and lowered himself to the grass next to her chair. He nodded to Pete. Pete nodded back.

"There's still plenty of food," she said.

"Good." Mitchell leaned back on his hands. "I've been talking to my brother David. You'll both be glad to know that Elmore Bracken will be released from prison tomorrow."

Pete grunted, and she shook her head. Twenty years of the man's life were gone. How could one human being do that to another?

"Regina?"

She looked up to see Mica approaching.

"Mom wants to talk to all of us upstairs. She said you, too, Mitchell, if you were here. And Pete."

Regina frowned. "What about?"

"She wouldn't say, just that I should come and get you."

She exchanged a curious glance with Mitchell, then shrugged. She pushed to her feet slowly, but still experienced a head rush. Pete and Mitchell both reached for her arm. She leaned into one man, then the other, until she regained her balance.

"I'm fine," she said, and glanced back and forth until they both released her. She walked through the maze of concrete animals, up the front steps, and into the house. At the top of the landing, Cissy, John, Justine, Mica, and Sheriff Shadowen made up a confused-looking crowd. When she, Mitchell, and Pete arrived, her mother seemed satisfied, if anxious. Regina expected some kind of speech or toast or something.

Cissy wrung her hands and inhaled. "Our lives have been turned upside down these past few days, and the time has come for me to own up to my part in the events of twenty years ago."

Alarm seeped through Regina's chest. She reached for the stair railing to steady herself and found Mitchell's arm instead. It would have to do.

"Cissy—" John began.

But she held up her hand. "Don't, John. I need to do this."

Her mother walked to the base of the attic stairs and

climbed them slowly. No one made a sound as her shoes scraped the old runners. With a determined push, she opened the swollen door and disappeared inside. She emerged a few seconds later with a small object bound in a cloth. She carried it downstairs and carefully unwrapped it.

The Russian gold-and-sterling letter opener.

Regina gasped, taking no pleasure in the confirmation of her suspicions that Cissy had been hiding something.

Sheriff Shadowen wiped his hand down his face. "What's the meaning of this, Cissy?"

Her mother stood ramrod-straight but made a remorseful noise. "Twenty years ago, I suspected that John and Lyla Gilbert were seeing each other."

"But we weren't," John insisted. His hands shook.

"I know you weren't," she said. "Now. But Lyla flirted with you so outrageously, and she was sleeping with half the county." She shrugged. "We weren't married, and I just thought that you had fallen under her spell. I'd heard that she frequented Lovers' Lane, and one day I saw her car go past our shop. She had a man with her, and I knew where she was going. You had left earlier that morning, and I got it into my head that you were with her. So I followed. She was dead when I found her, and when I saw the letter opener, I thought you had taken it from the store and . . . had done something terrible. I was afraid for you, and for me and the girls, so I took it."

"You thought I killed her?" John asked.

"I didn't want to, but you were drinking, and business wasn't so good—I panicked. I couldn't let you go to prison."

She gave the sheriff an apologetic look. "Then when Elmore Bracken was convicted, I was so relieved. I kept the letter opener, though, out of guilt, I suppose."

Regina stepped forward. "So *you* put it up for auction?"

Her mother nodded. "I heard that Bracken was trying to get a new trial—I was spooked. And we needed the money. I'd heard it was easy to sell things privately on-line." She gave Regina a watery smile. "I couldn't believe it when my own daughter E-mailed back asking for details." She handed the letter opener to the sheriff. "I'm sorry, Hank. If I had come forward all those years ago, Elmore Bracken might not have been convicted."

"Maybe," he admitted. "Maybe not."

"But Lawrence's fingerprints might have been on the weapon."

"Uncle Lawrence said he set up Bracken," Regina said. "He probably made sure Bracken's fingerprints were on it."

"Still," Cissy said with a sigh. "What I did was wrong, and I'm ready to face the consequences."

"No, Sheriff," John said. "Cissy did what she did to protect me—I should be the one to take the blame."

"Hold on, both of you," the sheriff said with a chopping motion. "Give me some time to sort all this out." Then he looked at Mitchell. "If Cissy agreed to take a polygraph, do you think the DA's office in Charlotte might ignore a tampering-with-evidence charge? In light of what this family has gone through and the fact that the Metcalfs' testimony was crucial to breaking the case?"

Mitchell hesitated, then nodded. "DAs have been known to make deals that are beneficial to everyone. I'll see if my brother can pull in a favor."

On the heels of Regina's relief was the knowledge that she owed Mitchell yet again. As her family talked among themselves, she quietly descended the stairs and escaped to the kitchen. To her chagrin, he followed her.

"I need to talk to you," he said to her back.

"Thank you for helping my mother." She looked down at the counter. "Seems like I'm always saying thank you."

"Don't mention it."

She turned. "I mean it, Mitchell. I'll never be able to repay you for everything you've done."

"Sure you will." He angled his head. "How about one of those smiles?"

It was involuntary, but it seemed to suffice.

"There. Listen, Regina . . . I'm leaving tomorrow."

She blinked but fought to retain her smile. "Tomorrow?"

"Yeah, after I finish tagging everything in the shop in the morning, I'll be heading to a job in Orlando." He shrugged—no big deal.

And why shouldn't he leave? Hadn't he gone above and beyond the call of duty here? How else was it supposed to end? He probably couldn't wait to get away from her and all the noise in her life. Quite a style-cramper for a former bad-boy drifter.

"I'll help you finish up in the morning," she said.

"That's not necessary."

"I'll see you at eight."

"I'll bring doughnuts."

# thirty-six

**DO look for hidden treasure in a dance.**

Mitchell's van was already at the shop when Regina arrived ten minutes early. She cringed at the slivers of yellow crime scene tape that clung to the back door. Shaking off the willies, she entered and allowed the chime to sound. John was once again staying at the house, so she didn't have to worry about waking him upstairs. Her parents would still have to liquidate their business and personal assets, but at least they would have each other.

Sam came loping up to meet her, favoring his bandaged leg. He said good morning with a familiar nudge, but she didn't mind—he had, after all, saved her life. She patted his head and scratched his ears in gratitude.

Mitchell sat with his legs propped up on the metal desk, reviewing the inventory list and tapping his foot to B. B. King. He looked up. "Good morning."

"Good morning," she said, heading toward the coffeepot. "I'm going to miss your coffee."

"Is that all?" he asked.

She wasn't about to fall for that "love 'em and leave 'em" trick. She turned around and sipped. "Was there something else?"

"Yeah," he said quietly.

Her heart skipped a beat.

He pointed. "My doughnuts."

She manufactured a little laugh. "Oh, of course. Jelly-filled." She plucked one from the box and assumed a nonchalant position. "I'm going to have to hit the gym double-time when I get back."

"Everything looks okay from this angle," he murmured; then his gaze flicked upward. "You lost your bandage."

"It was in the way, more of a hassle than help." At least her French twist covered the bald spot where they'd given her stitches.

"How are you feeling?"

"Like my entire life has passed before my eyes."

"How about physically?"

"Fine. Reading isn't the easiest task at the moment, so I'm taking off the rest of the week to spend with my family."

"Good." He nodded.

"Uh-huh." She nodded.

"So," he said, clapping his hands. "Ready to get started?"

"Sure."

She followed him down the hall to the main showroom, telling herself she was not going to miss his blues music or his bizarre T-shirt wardrobe or the way he put his feet down.

"This shouldn't take too long," he said over his shoulder. "Couple of hours, max. Then I'll review all the reports with your parents and get them to sign off."

"Will you come back for the auction?" She stopped—had that sounded as if she wanted him to?

He shook his head. "No. It'll be handed off to an auction house. They'll come in and merchandise everything, advertise the sale, all that. But I'll alert collectors on my list." He laughed ruefully. "With all the publicity lately, the sale should draw quite a crowd."

*In every black cloud,* she mused.

The items left, she realized, were the white elephants of the business—the offbeat, one-of-a-kind items that would be difficult to price and even harder to sell—the eight-foot stuffed giraffe and the six-foot neon sign blazing DANCES FOR 10 CENTS, for example.

"Who would manufacture a two-foot lightbulb?" she asked, wiping down the novelty item.

He shrugged. "Maybe it was for a World's Fair or some kind of exhibition. Believe me, someone out there is looking for a two-foot lightbulb—we just have to make sure they know it's here waiting for them."

"What do you think is the story behind the sign?"

"A dance hall from the twenties, maybe?" He grinned, reached for her hand, and spun her close. "Do you dance?"

"Not well," she mumbled, suddenly tongue-tied at being up against him. Her body remembered this posture. Fondly.

"That's okay, because I'll lead."

He moved into a light-hearted waltz, with impromptu turns and fancy hand-offs that required very little skill and movement on her part. But soon she was laughing so hard, she could barely catch her breath. "I'm getting light-headed."

He stopped, concerned. "Do you need to sit down?"

Their faces were inches apart, and they were both short of breath. Longing pooled in her stomach.

He kissed her—a good-bye kiss, she realized. Firm and warm and flavored with powdered sugar. Bittersweet and fun and thanks-for-the-memories. She moved her mouth against his, memorizing the taste and feel of him. Suddenly Sam was at their knees, barking frantically.

They parted and Mitchell frowned down. "What's wrong, boy?"

Sam barked again, looking back and forth between them.

Mitchell grinned. "He's getting protective—he thinks I'm hurting you."

She manufactured a smile, too, then squatted. "See, Sam? I'm perfectly intact." She lifted her gaze to Mitchell to let him know, too, that he hadn't broken any hearts in the vicinity.

His expression was unreadable. A few seconds later, it was as if the kiss had never happened—at least for him. He walked over to wipe a layer of dust from the huge sign. "How long has it been since this thing was moved?"

She straightened. "It's been leaning against that wall for as long as I can remember. Want some help?"

"No, I got it. Just want to take a look at the back to see if it has any identification marks." With a low grunt, he scooted the massive sign out from the wall a few inches and peeked behind. "Hm."

"Hm, what?"

"There are a few canvases back here, dusty as hell." He pulled them out, seven in all, ranging from small to medium in size, all unframed. "Good shape, considering." He blew the dust off one and uncovered a section of a still life. "Probably hobby stuff, but it looks like the kind of thing that people want to hang on their walls. Would you hand me that brush?"

She did, and stood back as he gently removed over thirty years of dust from the stiff canvases. Sam sneezed a half-dozen times, then retreated for fresher air.

Regina reached for Mitchell's laptop and clicked on the fine arts category in the appraisal software, then tabbed down to the area where they'd listed the canvases they'd already processed.

"Anything interesting?" she asked. When he didn't answer, she looked up. His face was dirt-smudged. And set in a peculiar expression. "Mitchell?"

He turned his head. "Remember when you asked me what was the most remarkable find I've ever come across?"

Her pulse picked up, and she nodded.

"Well," he said. "Don't get your hopes up, but this either is a Frieseke or a very good copy."

She frowned and came to stand behind him. "Is that good? Fine art isn't my forte." The painting was small, about sixteen inches by twenty inches. A gardenscape. Very pretty but, to her untrained eye, unexceptional.

"Frieseke is one of the few American impressionist painters to gain notability."

She tried to stay calm. "What year?"

"He died in 1939. This is dated—" He pulled the canvas closer. "Nineteen twenty-nine."

"Okay," she said calmly. "Let's just say it is a Frieseke. How much are we talking, ballpark?"

"Ballpark, half a mil."

She nodded. "Would that be 'mil' as in 'million'?"

"It would be."

*So,* she thought later that evening as he let Sam in the back of the van before hitting the road to Orlando, *at least his last day in Monroeville ended on a high note.*

"The guy from Sotheby's should be here tomorrow," he said, then smiled. "But I'll bet his coffee isn't nearly as good."

She laughed just as if he'd made the most hilarious joke. "Bye, Sam." She reached inside and scratched his head, then looked at Mitchell. "And bye . . . you."

He studied her for a moment, then smiled wide. "Bye, you, too. It's been fun."

"Yes," she agreed as he climbed in and shut the door. "Fun."

He hesitated, then started the engine. "Stay in touch."

"Sure thing," she said, just as if she had his phone or PO box number or any way at all to get in touch with him.

He smiled and waved a cheerful good-bye, and she smiled and waved a cheerful good-bye, just as if she meant it. And she kept meaning it until his van was out of sight.

# thirty-seven

DON'T swim in your troubles.

"Watch out!"

Regina and Justine looked up in time to each receive a faceful of water. They sputtered, and Mica came up laughing. Regina and Justine immediately dunked her under the cool creek water in retaliation, which descended into a full-fledged squealing splash fest. Exhausted, they swam to the shallow end of the Dilly swimming hole, waded to the bank, and flopped down on their backs in the grass.

"God, I'm so winded," Regina said.

"That's because you're old," Justine said.

"You're older than I am."

"I'm old, too."

"I'm not old," Mica said, which earned her groans and hisses.

They lay under a sycamore tree, shaded from the blazing sun. They were healthy and together. Life was good.

"I can't believe that Mom and Dad are going to be millionaires," Justine said.

"Well, not quite millionaires," Regina said, "after they deduct the commissions and pay off their debts."

"Still," Mica said. "Imagine that painting sitting in the shop all those years and no one knew it was worth a fortune."

Regina smiled—it was sort of like the massive slush pile of manuscripts back at her office.

"Well, I think it's hysterical," Justine said, propping herself up on her elbow, "that the painting was under Dean's nose all those years."

They laughed, and Regina was relieved that they could.

"So, Justine," Mica said slyly. "Have you talked to your Officer Lando since he went back to Shively?"

"He calls me occasionally," she said in a noncommittal voice. "Just to keep me updated on Lisa Crane."

"He'll have to come up with a different excuse when they find her," Regina said.

Justine frowned and picked a blade of grass. "Don't be ridiculous."

"He's crazy about you. And he's *cute*."

She placed the blade between her thumbs and blew, to no avail. "I don't date men who are cute."

"You might have to start," Mica said, picking a blade of grass. She blew through her folded hands and produced a low whistle.

Justine eyed her. "Speaking of cute, how is Everett surviving in LA without you?"

Mica held her hands up to show Justine her technique. "He wants me to stay here while he lays a few plans to jump-start my career. Everett and I aren't involved; we never were."

"He'd like to be," Justine said, then blew. A squeak emerged.

Mica ran her fingers through her short locks. "Everett is wonderful, and I think the world of him. But I'm going to enjoy being by myself for a long while."

"That's all right," Regina said. "He's not going anywhere." Unlike Mitchell. She closed her eyes briefly and willed the image of him from her mind. She had hoped that after four days, she would've at least forgotten the color of his eyes. Godiva brown.

"Have you heard from Mitchell?" Justine asked.

Dear God, had she spoken aloud? "No. And I don't expect to."

"Why not?" Justine coaxed another squeak through her hands. "I thought you two sort of hit it off, seeing as how he saved your ass and all."

"And I'm sure he can find plenty of girls in Florida who are a lot less trouble."

"Florida? Yeah, that's for sure."

She frowned.

"You like him, don't you?" Mica asked.

"I'm grateful for everything he did."

"*We're* grateful," Justine said. "I think you're something else entirely."

She sat up. "My head is hurting. I think I'll walk home."

"Liar," Justine said, pushing to her feet. "But I'm ready to go, too."

"Me, too," Mica said.

They picked their way down the bank to where they'd left their clothes. She pulled her loose clothing on over her wet suit and pushed her feet into her tennis shoes. Her sisters did the same, and they set off for the walk home, a path they'd traveled hundreds of times.

"You know," Justine said, "you could always call him."

Regina looked over. "You mean me call Mitchell?"

"Yes."

She shook her head. "No, it's not like that between us. He's a bona fide bachelor."

Mica grinned. "You are so in love with him."

"No, I'm not."

"Oh, yeah," Justine said. "You're in love."

She squinted. "How did we get from 'he's a bona fide bachelor' to 'you're in love'?"

"You have that look," Justine said. "Whenever we mention his name—as if you're trying hard not to care."

"It's awful, isn't it?" Mica asked.

"What?" Regina asked.

"Being in love," they said in unison.

"I don't feel that way about Mitchell Cooke," she insisted carefully. Then she pressed her lips together. "But . . . for future reference . . . how do you know if you're in love?" She felt both of them looking at her, so she shrugged. "I might use it in a book."

She got a shove and a laugh from both sides.

"I'm serious—what made each of you think you were in love?"

Justine and Mica exchanged glances, and she was afraid she'd broken the spell of easy camaraderie they had enjoyed over the past several days. But Justine hugged herself and got a dreamy look on her face. "I thought I was in love with Dean because he talked to me in the dark. Isn't that crazy? But I thought it was so romantic. I didn't realize that it was because he couldn't communicate in the light of day."

Mica emitted a thoughtful sound. "I think I fell in love with Dean because he was the first man who treated me as if I mattered. And now I realize that he only treated me well at his convenience and when he thought it would result in more money in his pocket."

"But we were young," Justine added. "I have a feeling the next time I fall in love, it won't be the same."

"Right," Mica said, her expression feathery. "I mean, I'll probably still think of the person all the time."

"Uh-huh," Justine said, equally preoccupied. "And

everything will seem just a little . . . *better* when that person's around."

"But not in a needy way."

"Exactly. Because you'll have the impression that the person feels the same about you."

"That you offer something to complete that person's life."

"And that you don't have to talk all the time to know what the other person is thinking."

"And even though that person hasn't touched you, you somehow just know the sex is going to be incredible."

Justine nodded. "Uh-hmm."

Mica nodded. "Uh-hmm."

Regina looked back and forth between them and refrained from snapping her fingers to bring them back from their reverie. Justine seemed to come around first.

"That is . . . if I ever fall in love again."

"Right," Mica said, nodding.

Regina smiled and hooked her arms in theirs. "Well, if either of you ever fall in love again, I hope you'll keep me posted."

"You'll be the first to know," Justine said.

"Absolutely," Mica said.

They walked home leisurely, enjoying the lush scenery. When they reached the Doll, John and Cissy were sitting on the front porch, holding hands. Their mother fairly glowed. "We have news," she said.

Justine and Mica claimed chairs. Regina lowered herself to the front step. "What?"

"Well—" Cissy glanced at John, then back. "Your father and I are getting married."

Her sisters exclaimed and jumped to their feet to embrace their parents, but Regina simply smiled and propped her chin in her hand to take in the flurry of activity, marveling at her new-and-improved family.

Warmth swelled her chest. The people she belonged to did care about her and one another. She leaned back against the column to release thirty-four years of yearning into the air with a sigh.

# thirty-eight

DO revisit the scene of the crime.

Justine gripped the back of the chair in front of her as she glanced around the meeting room. "I'd like to thank Terri Birch for putting together this meeting, and I'd like to thank each of you for taking time out of your busy day to attend on such short notice."

Pensive faces stared back at her. Everyone in the room was remembering two weeks ago when Lisa Crane had stormed the meeting and started firing. The image was vivid in Justine's mind, too, and they all kept looking toward the door, as if the gunwoman, who was still at large, might reappear.

Justine gestured toward the young woman seated on her right. "I would especially like to publicly thank Bobbie Donetti for her heroics on the last day we were together, and for very likely saving my life."

Bobbie, sporting a sling, nodded demurely.

Justine cleared her throat. "I realize that I haven't been the easiest person to work with over the years. I thought to be successful and to have the things that I wanted, I had to grab onto power and guard it. Over the past couple of weeks . . ." She gave them a wry smile. "Let's just say that my priorities have changed."

She took a deep breath into the silence. "I don't know what my future holds here at Cocoon, but I hope I have the chance to work with each of you again to repair any damage I've caused. Thank you for hearing me out." She gathered her purse and left the room, shoulders straight, chin high. She said hello to the secretary outside the door, who seemed surprised that she was acknowledged.

Justine was halfway down the hall when she heard a voice behind her.

"Justine."

She turned to see Terri Birch striding toward her. "Thanks again, Terri, for setting up the meeting."

"You're welcome. The oversight committee will be meeting tomorrow morning." She extended a small smile. "Based on what I've just seen, I think it would be safe to say we'll find a place for you here. At a level that will keep you close to your current salary range."

Justine nodded. "You're very generous, Terri."

"Despite some of your tactics, you've done some wonderful things for the company. We need you here."

"Thank you. You won't be disappointed."

"I'll call you tomorrow afternoon."

Justine left the building with a curious sense of detachment. If she'd learned anything over the past few days, she'd learned that in the scheme of her life, relationships mattered most. Even if she was fired, she'd find her way. She'd put her mistakes behind her and move on.

Her next stop was at the city hall building to meet with her probation officer—according to Lando, a year's probation for mucking up Dean's murder scene was fair. The woman she would be reporting to over the next twelve months seemed nice enough but harried and overworked. Justine offered to give her a makeover on her next visit and left humming an old song. *Humming,* for God's sake.

She walked back down to the first floor, which housed the police department, and asked for Officer Lando. The man at the front desk covered the phone with his hand and gave her directions. She wound her way through hallways and bullpens to the general area, then asked someone else for Lando's whereabouts. He pointed to a far corner. Lando sat hunched over a tiny typewriter and, from the scowl on his face, was not hitting the keys he'd intended.

"Hello," she said.

He turned around and the scowl dropped from his face. "Hello. You're back."

She nodded. "And my plant is still alive."

He stood and smiled. "That's a good sign."

"I came to talk to you about Lisa Crane."

His expression turned stoic. "Oh. Okay. Do you want to sit?"

She shook her head. "I have an idea where she might be."

"Where?"

"I'll ride with you."

"I can't let you go on a police call."

She turned to go. "Then I'll go by myself."

Behind her, he sighed. "Wait up. I'll drive."

A few minutes later, she sat in the passenger seat of his cruiser and gave directions.

He looked up at the building she indicated before pulling into the parking lot. "The Rosewood Hotel?"

She shrugged. "Just a hunch." If Lisa Crane had found her husband's hotel receipts, then it was possible that, just as she had wanted to relive her wedding day, Mrs. Crane might also have felt compelled to visit "the scene of the crime."

They walked into the lobby and she smiled at the

male desk clerk. "Can you tell me if Room 410 is occupied?" Lando backed her up with a badge flash.

The man checked a computer screen. "That room is unavailable. A homeless person broke in the week before last and set a fire. The damage was nominal, but we're waiting to have the room professionally cleaned before we reopen it to guests."

She exchanged glances with Lando. He looked back to the clerk. "We'll need to evacuate the fourth-floor rooms and shut down the elevators."

The man burst into action and twenty minutes later Lando stood in front of the door to Room 410. Justine had insisted on staying and stood next to him, her heart thumping.

He rapped and said, "Housekeeping."

There was no answer, no sound from within.

He slipped the key into the door and turned the lock. "Housekeeping," he repeated loudly; then the door caught on a six-inch chain—someone was definitely inside the room.

He drew his gun and gestured for Justine to go to the end of the hall—unnecessary since she was already moving in that direction.

He stepped back and kicked the door open with a *blam*, then disappeared inside. A few seconds later, a muffled noise sounded, then a shot. Justine screamed and ran toward the room. Along the way she yanked a tall lamp off a table and hefted it, fringed shade and all, like a weapon. Not exactly lethal, but it might distract the Crane woman with laughter.

"Lando!" she yelled, then rushed into the room, poised to strike.

"All's clear," he said from the rumpled bed where he straddled a face-down Lisa Crane and handcuffed her hands behind her back. The minibar stood open, ransacked of food and drink.

"Who fired?"

He pointed to a small black hole in the wall. "She did." He radioed to the lobby to send up the EMTs he'd requested.

The woman didn't fight him but focused on Justine as he placed her under arrest and recited her rights. "This is where you did it with my husband." She sounded like a child.

Justine bit down on the tip of her tongue. "Mrs. Crane, I'm very sorry for all the pain I've caused you. I know it doesn't change things, but I am very, very sorry. I'll help you; I'll speak to the DA on your behalf."

Lisa Crane closed her eyes and seemed to lose consciousness. Indeed, she was as limp as a rag doll when the EMTs transferred her to a gurney. They checked her vitals. "She passed out," one of them said. "But her pulse is strong."

They wheeled her out, and Justine collapsed into a chair, floppy with relief and despair. She stared at the bed where she and Randall had humped away their lunch hours, and her stomach rolled. "I destroyed that woman's life."

Lando exhaled noisily. "You were the one who said the woman's husband took the vows, not you."

"I seduced Randall," she said. "He wouldn't have come on to me if I hadn't initiated an affair. I'm not exonerating him, but I've learned a big lesson about myself." She shook her head. "No more married men." And no more empty affairs, even if it meant being alone.

"Glad to hear that," he said. He dropped the woman's gun into an evidence bag and scanned the scene, taking notes. She sat in silence, watching the big man move around the room. What he must think of her.

He relieved her of the lamp. "What were you going to do with this?"

"I hadn't thought it through exactly."

He smiled. "Seems as though you do a lot of that."

She squinted. "Do you think a person can change, Lando?"

"Sure," he said. "If they get tired enough of their old self."

"I'm tired."

He nodded toward the door. "I'll take you home."

She pushed herself to her feet.

Lando scratched his temple. "By the way . . . my name is Kevin."

She smiled.

# thirty-nine

DO have a Plan B.

Mica pasted on a smile for the imposing group of reporters, executives, gossip columnists, and philanthropists that Everett had brought together for a combined breakfast/press conference. Only a handful of people in the room knew the details of the "exciting charity challenge" that was about to be announced. She sat holding a gold foil box, her head and shoulders swathed in a long scarf. She focused on Everett, who had claimed the microphone. His presence had become so dear.

"Ladies and gentlemen, consumers all over the world identify Mica Metcalf's face and long gorgeous hair with Tara Hair products. Today I'd like to announce that Mica and the wonderful folks at Tara have come up with a way to pool their resources to support the efforts of a precious children's charity. "Mica?"

She joined Everett at the podium and began to unwind the scarf. Since she'd returned to LA, she'd kept a low profile that involved hats and head wraps. When her cropped hair was revealed, the audience gasped. Cameras flashed.

Everett spoke into the microphone. "Mica has generously donated her beautiful hair to Care About Kids, an organization that makes wigs for child victims of diseases who lose their own hair during medical treatments."

The room erupted into applause, and Mica beamed. While Everett had been agonizing over how to break the news of her shorn locks to Tara, she had shared an observation she'd made while walking the halls of the hospital during Justine's recovery. The patients in the children's wing had broken her heart—some of them had little or no hair, and she had plenty at home in a box. It hadn't seemed fair. So she'd asked Everett if, regardless of the future of her career, he could look into the possibility of her severed braid being put to good use?

To put it mildly, he had run with the idea. She wasn't accustomed to her suggestions being taken seriously—Dean had always dismissed her out of hand. She still marveled at the way the idea had gained momentum.

Before the applause died, Mica removed her long braid from the gold box and presented it to a representative with the organization. The room sparkled with camera flashes. Mica's braid, the woman announced, would provide wigs for several children who simply wanted to look as normal as possible as they recovered from their illnesses and returned to school. The marketing director from Tara Hair followed up with words of support and confidence in Mica—they'd just re-upped her contract to kick off a new ad campaign. The executive also extended a charity challenge to any models or other celebrities willing to crop their hair and donate it to the organization. Top stylists all over LA had volunteered their services to make "The Big Cut." Industry buzz was high. The charity drive had all the makings of a phenomenon.

"Mica, you are a good-hearted genius," Everett said

later over dinner, his eyes sparkling. "Not only is your career back on track, but this event will help hundreds of kids."

She smiled, pleased, and pleased that he was pleased. But despite the exciting whirlwind of returning to LA, she was plagued with homesickness for her sisters. And now that her schedule had ballooned, she was afraid she wouldn't have time to visit them as often as she'd hoped.

Everett set down his glass. "I received an offer today that I think you'll find interesting."

She sipped from her water glass. "Oh?"

"Cocoon Cosmetics is looking for a new model for their print ads."

A few seconds passed before she comprehended his meaning. She grinned. "Me?"

His dimples appeared. "The job is yours if you want it. The offer is lucrative, although I suspect you'll be able to negotiate regular visits to their headquarters."

Her chest swelled, and on impulse, she reached across the table to clasp his warm fingers. "No woman should be this happy."

Everett's gray eyes reflected humble surprise at her touch. He squeezed her hand. "Or man."

# forty

Regina blinked when a knock sounded at her office door. She glanced at the clock on her desk, dismayed to see that an hour had passed and she had nothing to show for it. She'd been blaming her inability to concentrate on the concussion she'd sustained, but after six weeks, that argument was growing a bit thin.

Shaking herself mentally, she called, "Yes?"

The door opened, and Jill walked in, holding up a piece of paper. "I thought you'd like to see this."

"What is it?"

"One of the best cover quotes we'll get this year."

She took the paper and scanned the text. It was a glowing review of the hairstylist's book from Mica. She smiled. "This is good."

"Good? You mean *great.* I saw your sister on a celebrity news show again last night—two supermodels and a rock diva had their hair cut off to donate to charity. I believe Mica has single-handedly made short hair politically correct."

A secret smile curved her mouth. Leave it to Mica to turn a thorny situation into a positive experience for so many people.

"Hey," Jill said, picking up a picture frame. "This is new."

"My parents' wedding photo," she said, warming at the memories of the simple ceremony. Cissy and John stood center, with her and Justine and Mica next to them, wearing matching sundresses and hats. The hats had been Justine's idea to protect Mica's secret until she could return to LA.

"You look terrific without your glasses."

After they'd been broken during the incident at the cabin, it had seemed silly to replace them. "Thanks."

"Everyone looks so happy."

"We were," she said, then added, "We are." She was. Her family had recovered. She and Justine and Mica had stayed in touch in the weeks since they'd left Monroeville. All was well.

Yes. All . . . was . . . well.

Jill returned the photo to the desk, then pointed to another new frame. "Who are those little girls?"

Regina ran her finger over the faces of the sepia-toned, chubby-cheeked, banana-curled girls. "They're . . . sisters."

Jill nodded, waiting for an explanation. Regina experienced a pang of guilt—she knew she'd been behaving strangely since her return. Quiet, preoccupied. And Jill was a gem not to point it out.

"Have you heard from your fellow?"

She played dumb. "My fellow?"

"Mr. Brad Pitt meets Harrison Ford."

"Oh, him. No, he's . . . moved on, I'm sure." She manufactured a smile. "It was nothing serious."

"What was his name?"

She squinted, as if she had to dredge his name from the recesses of her memory. "Mitchell. Mitchell Cooke."

"Nice name."

She nodded, determined to keep mum on the subject, no matter how much her assistant hinted for details.

Jill pursed her mouth. "Do you think you might be seeing Alan Garvo again?"

"No," she said, a little too quickly. She didn't want Jill or anyone else to think that Mitchell had ruined her for all other men or something ludicrous like that. "I mean, Alan is a great guy, but we'll never be anything more than friends."

"Oh." Jill wet her lips. "Does that mean it would be okay if I called Alan to go to lunch?"

Realization dawned, and she wondered why she hadn't picked up on Jill's interest in Alan sooner. She smiled wide. "Of course it would be okay. In fact, you two would make a great couple."

Jill grinned. "You think?"

Regina nodded.

"And you wouldn't mind?"

"Not at all."

"Thanks, Boss." Jill walked back to the door with a little bounce in her step. At the door, she turned. "Oh, by the way, good pickup on that *I Think I Love You* manuscript—it's going to be a fun project."

She smiled in agreement.

Jill looked down, then frowned. "I didn't say anything earlier, but you do realize that you're wearing two different shoes, don't you?"

Regina's gaze dropped to the floor and she discovered, to her horror, that she was indeed sporting one brown pump and one navy pump. She glanced back up and tried to smile. "I guess I was in a hurry this morning."

Jill's eyebrows climbed curiously, but she exited with no questions.

When the door closed, Regina leaned back in her

chair with a frustrated sigh. "Get a grip," she murmured. "Life is good. You're happy, remember? Happy."

But Jill's questions had unleashed a flood of memories of Mitchell, and as she had discovered over the weeks, if he crept into her mind early in the day, he typically stuck around until she managed to fall asleep in her "How to Sleep Alone" nightshirt.

She pushed to her feet and circled around to the front of her desk with the cup of bad coffee that had gone stone cold while she'd zoned out. It was silly, she knew, this lingering infatuation. Wherever Mitchell was, he certainly wasn't pining away for her.

When she rotated the African violet to give it a drink of creamless coffee, she smiled at the sight of a tiny pink bloom emerging from the depths of the dark fuzzy leaves. "I knew you'd come around," she said, absurdly cheered. She made a mental note to drop Mr. Calvin a card to say she was thinking of him and to thank him for the age-old plant-watering tip.

Her phone buzzed, and she reached across the desk to pick it up. "Yes?"

"There's a man here with a book who says he needs to see you."

"Is he an agent?"

"No."

"Who, then?"

"A walk-in," Jill said.

She sighed. Some authors thought the best way to sell their manuscript was to barrel their way through the front door. "Take down his information and have him leave his book."

Jill hesitated. "He's pretty insistent."

She frowned. "He gets five minutes." She returned the receiver and lamented the empty cup of coffee. She could sure use a pick-me-up.

The door opened and when she turned, she was nearly knocked down by a firm nudge to her crotch. Sam's tail wagged furiously.

Disbelief and happiness welled in her chest. "Hello, Sam." She leaned over to scratch his ears, then lifted her gaze as his master walked in. Faded Red Sox T-shirt, newish jeans. If she'd had any doubts that she'd fallen in love with Mitchell, those doubts were erased as soon as she saw his lopsided grin. She recalled a piece of advice from the manuscript she'd read. *"Be calm. Don't act like a lovesick idiot."*

"Hi," she said. To her amazement, her voice sounded normal.

"Hi, yourself."

"This is a surprise."

"A good one, I hope."

She nodded. "Do you have a job up this way?"

He shook his head. "No, I just got homesick for Boston."

Her heart lifted a little. "Really?"

"Yeah, you know, Fenway Park and all."

"Oh. Right."

"I brought you something."

He handed her a brown-paper package that looked like a book. She unwrapped it, and a smile claimed her as the yellow cover was revealed. *The Secret in the Old Attic*—her missing Nancy Drew book. She turned it over, stalling for time to regain her composure, then looked up. "Thank you, Mitchell."

He shrugged. "No problem."

No problem—don't read anything into it. She pulled a teasing smile from thin air. "I have to admit, though, I was hoping for doughnuts."

He stepped forward and picked up her hand. "I thought we could have those for breakfast."

Her heart stalled out.

He entwined his fingers with hers. "That is—if you have a real hankering for . . . doughnuts."

She swallowed hard. "I do."

He pulled her close and nuzzled her chin. "Good, because I can't seem to get you out of my mind."

He kissed her, and she fairly groaned under his familiar touch. How she'd get through the rest of the afternoon, she had no idea.

Sam barked loudly, nudging their knees. They pulled apart, and Mitchell laughed. "Over time, I hope he'll realize that I'm not hurting you when I do this."

She smiled and looped her arms around his neck. "Over time?"

"Well, I was thinking I might stick around, if that's okay with you."

"Hm. Through baseball season?"

He pursed his mouth. "Yeah, but then the Celtics season begins, and I wouldn't want to miss that."

"Of course not."

"And then there are the Bruins—how do you feel about hockey?"

"I'm in favor of it."

He smiled and kissed her until Sam started up again. When Mitchell lifted his head, he looked over her shoulder to her slush pile. "Did you buy that manuscript you were reading in North Carolina?"

"As a matter of fact, I did."

"Catchy title."

"Yes."

He squinted. "What was it again?"

"*Relationship DOs and DON'Ts for Grown Women.*"

"No, the other one."

"*I Think I Love You?*"

"Really?" He grinned and leaned his forehead against hers. "I think I love you, too."

She closed her eyes and sighed.

"Do you know you're wearing two different shoes?"

Meet the driving divas of relationship
DOs and DON'Ts.

Four carpooling queens of Atlanta find themselves thrust
into a titillating murder mystery as a result of
ignoring their own good advice on men.

# Breaking All the Rules

## by STEPHANIE BOND

COMING FROM ST. MARTIN'S PRESS IN 2003

# Our Husband

ACCLAIMED AWARD-WINNING AUTHOR

## STEPHANIE BOND

"Compelling, absorbing and rich."
—*Publishers Weekly*

Fate has just thrown a curve ball at the women in Ray Carmichael's life—all three of them. When they meet at his hospital bed, they discover they're all married to the same man. And when Ray suddenly dies, the police suspect that one of these spunky ladies has committed murder. Now they're three women left with a man's betrayal—and worse, each other. But one thing they each insist—they didn't kill Ray. What can they do? Something outrageous and probably impossible: stick together to catch a murderer . . .

"Treat yourself to an evening of memorable characters." —Susan Andersen, author of *Baby, Don't Go*

"A rollicking first novel that's got everything—humor, romance, suspense, and not one but THREE memorable heroines! Great fun!" —Jane Heller

AVAILABLE WHEREVER BOOKS ARE SOLD
FROM ST. MARTIN'S PAPERBACKS

OH 5/01

# GOT YOUR NUMBER

A Novel by
## STEPHANIE BOND
author of *Our Husband*

Roxann Beadleman just received an ominous message that resurrects old secrets, and her debutante cousin Angora Ryder was just jilted at the altar. A roadtrip to accomplish things on a life list they made in college leads them back to their alma mater for Homecoming, and to the professor they were both in love with…But Angora doesn't know that Roxann is wanted for questioning in a police matter, or that a dangerous criminal could be following them. Detective Joe Capistrano is on their heels, too, determined to charm information out of Roxann and to protect her, whether she wants it or not…Roxann and Angora soon find themselves thrust into a chilling lesson of murder, and if either of them gets out of this mess alive, could true love be at the end of their chase?

"An enjoyable read…Bond's fun and frothy story keeps the plot twists coming…[a] talented new author."

—PUBLISHERS WEEKLY on *Our Husband*

"An entertaining contemporary tale…well-written…an enjoyable novel that successfully combines elements from romance, suspense, and mystery."

—THE MIDWEST BOOK REVIEW on *Our Husband*

AVAILABLE WHEREVER BOOKS ARE SOLD
FROM ST. MARTIN'S PAPERBACKS

GYN 10/01